A Dangerous Trade

Mara came to St. Aubyn's bed with cold-blooded calculation. She was trading her body for her birthright—her virginity for her family honor.

But with St. Aubyn's first kiss, she sensed she was getting more than she bargained for. Now he lowered his head to her again. This time his mouth was even more demanding, making every nerve ending alive and on fire.

With speed and skill he unfastened the tiny pearl buttons that lined the front of her nightdress. Mara tensed. She dared not move. Her chest rose and fell as his hands moved upward, brushing the soft fabric away from her breasts.

Mara closed her eyes. No man had ever seen her this way, and when he took her with his mouth, she gasped aloud as excitement rocked through her, tremor after tremor.

Mara had been braced to withstand the pain of St. Aubyn's passion. But could she steel her flesh against the pleasure that had only just begun . . . ?

TEMPTING FATE

by

Jaclyn Reding

O! What a tangled web we weave,
when first we practice to deceive.
—SIR WALTER SCOTT

A TOPAZ BOOK

TOPAZ
Published by the Penguin Group
Penguin Books USA Inc., 375 Hudson Street,
New York, New York 10014, U.S.A.
Penguin Books Ltd, 27 Wrights Lane,
London W8 5TZ, England
Penguin Books Australia Ltd, Ringwood,
Victoria, Australia
Penguin Books Canada Ltd, 10 Alcorn Avenue,
Toronto, Ontario, Canada M4V 3B2
Penguin Books (N.Z.) Ltd, 182-190 Wairau Road,
Auckland 10, New Zealand

Penguin Books Ltd, Registered Offices:
Harmondsworth, Middlesex, England

First published by Topaz, an imprint of Dutton Signet,
a division of Penguin Books USA Inc.

First Printing, January, 1995
10 9 8 7 6 5 4 3 2 1

Printed in the United States of America

To my husband, Steve,
for his constant faith in my abilities,
for his support in urging me to pursue my dreams,
and for making me believe in fairy tales again,
by living one with me these past ten years.

Chapter One

Dublin

It was the thirtieth of July, 1658, the summer of her twenty-third year, and she couldn't have asked for a better day on which to start the Plan.

The day had dawned with a brilliant sunrise, scattering the heavy rainclouds that had long plagued the city and filling the sky, the very air around them, with a burst of renewing warmth. Five years. Five long and difficult years she had been waiting for this day. This fated day. And, now it was upon them. She wanted to leap with joy and sing with the knowledge of it. The air smelled crisp. The rhododendrons lining the park walkways along St. Stephen's Green flourished in bright and brilliant bloom as if celebrating the fact that soon she would have her revenge on that wretched bastard.

It was market day and the area around Merchants' Quay was, as usual, a scene of chaos and confusion. Everyone, it seemed, had emerged from beneath their rooftops to revel in the unusual late-summer clemency. Dockworkers called out to young ladies as they strolled between the shop stalls surveying the goods. Hucksters pushing crude wooden carts filled with every sort of notion cried out their wares. Mothers sang to napping babies through open windows. Merchants argued the price of wool. Through it all one could hear the faint cry of an osprey soaring high above the slanted rooftops, plunging beneath the water's surface to rise seconds later, clutching its codling supper.

Yes, it was a perfect day, a most fitting day for revenge.

Bracing herself against a stack of wooden crates, Mara Despencer stood on her slippered toes atop an empty ale cask behind the raucous Bull's Head Tavern, oblivious of the goings-on around her. Her attention was fixed on the narrow opening of Dublin Harbor at the wide mouth of the River Liffey.

And she waited.

No one paid her any mind. Just one of the many, she was partially hidden behind a short wall of casks similar to the ones on which she stood. Her face was hidden beneath the hood of her brown woolen cloak and a black velvet face mask, the sort of mask that had openings for the eyes, nose, and mouth and was worn by ladies to protect their fair skin from inclement weather.

Today, with the sun shining down and the unseasonable warmth, the mask was making it quite difficult to breathe. But Mara didn't care. It did not matter. Nothing mattered, except that she would have her revenge, just as soon as her long-awaited guests arrived in Dublin.

They had to be arriving today, she thought, shifting her position to ease the growing numbness in her toes. For the past four days, she had been standing on the dock, at this very spot, watching and waiting until her entire body ached and not a speck of daylight remained. The back of her neck pinched from craning to look beyond the wharf area. Her vision was blurred from squinting against the bright sunlight. Yet, still she stood, refusing to quit her vigil, waiting for that expected sight on the horizon.

And then, almost as if the heavens above had heard her begging and had answered her plea, she saw it. A tiny speck had appeared far off in the distance floating on the murky black waters beyond what used to be the old Buttevant's Tower, renamed Newman's Tower some fifty years ago. She blinked to assure herself she hadn't imagined it, that she hadn't been standing and staring too long, making her mind see things that weren't truly there.

The speck obligingly remained.

Her heart started beating faster. *It had to be them, it just had to be.*

Mara watched with building anticipation as the speck drew nearer, growing larger and larger still. Each second brought it closer and, after a long quarter hour, the shape of a small oar-driven craft bobbed sluggishly on the waves before the Dublin Customs House.

"Is that it, Cyma? Can you see? Is that the ship *Wayfarer*'s longboat?"

Her maid neglected to reply.

"It is low tide," Mara went on. "They must not have been able to navigate their way past the sandbank between North and South Bull, so they would have had to anchor at Clantarfe Poole just below Ringsend near Dalkey to come up the river by longboat, don't you think? With the recent rain we've had, the road by coach would have been a veritable impasse."

This time, she received a decisive snort for a response.

Ignoring her maid's sidewise glance, Mara leaned forward against the stack of crates, mindful not to topple them, as the object she'd been watching for at the mouth of the harbor over the past days 6 glided to the landing at Wood Quay further down along the Strand. It was a small skiff, dwarfed by the larger craft moored at the quay's edge, yet even at its distance away, she could see two slight-looking figures among three larger ones seated upon the planked seats inside, all but confirming her suspicions.

"Yes, that must be them," she said with conviction. "Do you see her, Cyma? The one wearing the mustard-colored daygown? Do you think that could be her?"

When, again, her maid did not respond, Mara turned to see if she had gone deaf of a sudden. "Cyma? I was speaking to you. Did you not hear me?"

The grim look darkening Cyma's eyes told her she had heard and purposely hadn't answered. Cyma did not agree with this plan, nay, she'd protested against it every day since its conception, but having known Mara since she'd been in leading strings, she realized her protestations were beyond futile. Mara had decided long ago on this course of action. She'd been given the means and with it she'd plotted and perfected the Plan over the past five years.

And, once decided, the maid knew there was nothing on this earth that would deter her young charge.

Mara had turned back to the harbor and was now shading her eyes against the midday light. A small smile lifted one corner of her mouth at knowing the waiting would finally be over, the years spent planning this fated day at an end. Soon, she would have what was rightfully hers. She would have her vengeance. She would have her due. She would be back at Kulhaven where she belonged.

And *he* would have to pay.

She squinted an eye through the tarnished brass perspective glass that hung from a leathern cord at her waist, watching while the skiff was secured with mooring ropes to the dock. She couldn't have chosen a better time for them to have arrived. With the warm and pleasant weather, every fishmonger and breadseller from here to Limerick was out to peddle their goods, and, being midday, the docks were at their busiest, which was in her favor.

Everything, it seemed, was going as planned.

The girl in the mustard daygown had disembarked and was taking a waiting dockhand's hand as she stepped gingerly onto land. The second figure, taller, thinner, and covered from neck to toe in somber brown woolen followed directly behind while giving the grinning dockhand a quelling stare.

The time had come to put things to action.

As Mara turned to step down from her ale cask perch, she hesitated to admit it, but a niggling sense of fear at what lay ahead began to descend upon her. Stubbornly she pushed that feeling aside. She'd come too far, had gone through too much to quit this plan now.

"Yes, Cyma, that must be her and with her vigilant mother hovering not a step behind. Come. We must go. It is time to hurl the seeds of fortune to the wind and let them fall and sprout where they may."

Cyma snorted. "Seeds nothing. 'Tis tempting fate you

are with this fool scheme of yours. And fate has a way of handing you a troublesome package when you least expect it. You never should have listened to your *bráthair,* what with his telling you all about the earl having Kulhaven and all. There's naught but darkness on the horizon. You'll see."

Mara shook her off and started for the dock. "You sound like the *Bean Sídhe,* always portending death and gloom. This plan is sound. If we give it a fighting chance, I just know it will work, but not if we continue to stand here all day and argue about it like two haggling Galway fishwives. Come, Cyma, we must hurry."

She sprang forward without giving the maid a chance to respond, skirts flying, her eyes fixed to the girl and her mother through the pandemonium that surrounded them. Chickens squawked and scurried in every direction, surrounding a fat sow who was basking in the sun near a foul-smelling slop pile. Doxies just waking from their night's employ called out lurid invitations from their chamber windows to the dockhands working below. Closer to the water, the smell of fish and stagnant water was strong, but even that was nearly overpowered by the stench from the garbage left by the vendors piling up along the walkways.

Mara had to dodge two sailors who were scuffling over the result of a game of chance and momentarily lost sight of the girl and her mother in the confusion. She rounded the corner and spotted them again a moment later supervising the unloading of their trunks from the skiff. She settled her gaze on the younger woman, who was quietly looking about. She assessed every inch of the girl from head to shoe.

Her hair was black as sloe, arranged simply and

pulled back beneath a white linen cap to avoid attention. Dark eyes peeked out from behind a perfectly porcelain complexion, a complexion needless of any cosmetic addition. She wore a gown fastened to her chin and made of modest colors so as to allow her to blend into her surroundings. In her hand she clutched a small book that Mara would have wagered her life was the Bible.

Yes, it was her. It must be her. A proper Puritan miss, fresh from the schoolroom, and making her emergence directly into the marriage bed. Miss Arabella Wentworth, godchild of the Lord Protector, Oliver Cromwell, and, most importantly, the future bride of the Bastard Earl of St. Aubyn.

Until now.

The rumble of coach wheels on the cobbles behind them pulled Mara from her inspection. She turned. A black carriage, conspicuous among the crude carts and wagons that littered the dock area, rolled quickly along the main thoroughfare, pulled by a magnificent pair of matched bays.

"Cyma, that must be the earl's coach coming to fetch them now. We must hurry."

"Aye."

As she watched the maid turn, Mara thought to herself that she could not think of a day in her life when this woman, this faithful and ever-constant friend, had not been at her side. With a smack on her bottom, she'd brought Mara into this world, squalling like a drowned cat, she liked to say.

Her exact age was a mystery, even to Mara, and one she refused to reveal. She kept her plain brown hair caught up beneath a white lawn cap that tied under her small chin. Her skin was as smooth as that of a younger woman, a result of the many secret face lotions she applied. Only her hands, which had seen a lifetime of work, gave proof of her advanced age, the knuckles on her fingers gnarled beneath veined and spotted skin.

Without saying a word, Cyma looked out over the churning dock area. Her eyes settled on a young dockhand sitting atop a rainwater barrel. He looked to her as if she had shouted his name, and she nodded, giving the signal. The young man leapt from the barrel and ran across the dock, weaving his way through the crowd to disappear behind a tall stack of crates.

Moments later, a two-wheeled wagon laden with coal and drawn by a swaybacked nag emerged from the shadow of a nearby pub.

Mara chewed on her lower lip as the wagon rolled sluggishly forward, a habit she'd had ever since the day her mother had made her sit on the hard wooden bench outside her father's study, waiting to be punished for filling her brother Colin's boots full of mud when he'd refused to take her out with him to practice shooting his new musket. What would Father say if he were here now?

The coal wagon seemed to move so slowly, too slowly perhaps. What if it did not reach the earl's coach in time? Mara closed her eyes and said a silent prayer of thanks as the wagon halted sidewise at the narrow opening of Lowestock Lane.

The driver stood and kicked at the rear wheel, then leapt to the ground, disappearing around a dark corner. The wagon creaked beneath its uneven weight and lurched over with a resounding crash. The load it carried spilled across the dock in a huge onyx pile.

It wasn't seconds before a bystander took notice.

"Coal!"

Since the outbreak of the war, coal had become a scarce and valued commodity. Most Dubliners had resorted to burning whatever sort of scrap they could gather to keep their hearth fires warm at night. At the dockhand's shout, footsteps pounded on the weathered wooden decking and near-every soul within earshot ran to gather what he could of the precious rock. Fishermen's wives deserted their stands and started filling their aprons, stuffing smaller pieces of the stuff down their bodices and into dress pockets. Dockhands tossed rigging to the side to scramble among the others in search of the shiny blackened chunks. Within moments, the wagon became indiscernible behind the wall of frenzied bodies, the coach beyond unable to come and retrieve its waiting passengers.

"Come, Cyma. You're always to bragging about the acting ability you inherited from your dear mother. It is time to put your stage talents to the test."

Mara started down the rise to where the mustard-gowned girl and her mother were now standing and surveying the area around them in search, no doubt, of the coach detained behind the toppled coal cart. The mother, tall and reedy with thin brownish hair that was pulled tightly back and a backbone stiff as a whalebone stay, was looking for someone to ask direction. No one, it seemed, would assist them for they were too occupied with finding the cause of the mass of confusion by the toppled-over coal cart.

Mara checked that her black velvet mask was in

place, urged Cyma to do the same, then together they approached the waiting women.

"Be you the Mistress Arabella?" Cyma asked the younger one, her voice slightly muffled beneath her mask.

"Yes," the girl said, turning toward them, "yes, I am."

"Arabella," her mother said, pulling at the starched white cuff of her sleeve, "I've told you before you should never tell strangers your true name. Ireland isn't a safe place for members of our family. You know how the Irish feel about your godfather, Oliver. You've no idea who these"—she turned, her nostrils flaring—"these people are."

"But, Mama, they could have news of our coach. Hadrian wrote and said he'd have someone awaiting us at the dock, did he not?"

Hadrian. Mara stiffened at the sound of that name.

"Aye," Cyma broke in, assuming her best Londonderry accent, "we've been sent by my Lord St. Aubyn to ye, we have."

"See, Mama, Hadrian did send them." Arabella turned wide and hopeful eyes to the still-masked Cyma. "Where is Lord St. Aubyn? They say he is powerfully handsome. They say he's the most handsome man in all Ireland. Is his coach waiting far? I cannot wait to see him. We're to be married, you know."

Mara checked the urge to yell. How could anyone be so besotted with such a beast?

Cyma stepped closer, her voice dropping. "I'm afraid his lordship has not come, Mistress Arabella. He wishes me to tell you that if you decided to return to England, he'd understand."

"Return to England?" The mother's pinpoint eyes

went wide. "But we've only just arrived, my good woman. Lord St. Aubyn was told we would be arriving weeks ago. Why would he wish us to leave now?"

"'Tis the *bolgach Dé.*"

Arabella's mother looked at her in obvious bewilderment. "I beg your pardon?"

"I guess I must needs show you."

Cyma reached up and slowly untied the ribbons that held her black velvet mask in place.

"Oh, my Lord!"

Arabella's perfectly porcelain complexion paled. "Mama, what is wrong with her face?"

Arabella's mother was silent as stone, her mouth gaping, her hand pressed at her bosom in horror. She looked on the verge of apoplexy.

Everyone around them stopped to stare. Mara had to bite her lip to keep from laughing out loud beneath her mask. The marks on Cyma's face had been prepared to just the right consistency. She'd attained a perfect mixture of the cochineal and face clay to create its tincture of inflamed red. Her hours of preparing had certainly been well worth it, for no one could ever guess the hideous pustules that dotted the woman's skin were not real, nor would one dare get close enough to inspect the horror that was her face.

"'Tis all right," Cyma said, stepping forward to reassure them.

The two ladies took a retreating step.

"I din't mean to frighten ye. 'Tis no need to worry. The pox has finally passed me, sparing me life, but leaving me with this scarred face. And I were one of the luckier ones. At last count, we'd lost twenty-eight, includin' my dear Harry." She paused and took an obligatory sniff, wiping an imaginary tear from her eye. "Din't you receive his lordship's letter?"

Arabella and her mother were still so stunned by the gruesome apparition before them they couldn't speak.

"His lordship wrote tellin' ye of the outbreak of the pox at Kulhaven. Tried to tell ye not to come, but he feared his letter would 'ave missed ye. Sent us to meet yer ship since we're the only ones who's survived it so far. Seen as 'ow yer here now, ye may as well come to Kulhaven and marry 'im anyways, that is if the pox 'asn't gotten him bad yet. Come along. Ye can follow me. The coach is waitin' not far from 'ere."

Cyma reached out to take the mother's valise. Before she could grasp it, the mother swept a protective arm outward, urging her daughter back.

"Just a moment, if you please." She swallowed with some difficulty before continuing. "Do you mean to tell me that Lord St. Aubyn has contracted the smallpox?"

Cyma shrugged. "Can't say for certain. 'Aven't been able to tell if the marks on 'is face are from the pox or if they're just a rash of some sort. Only time will tell. And we've been gone fer near a week now." She looked to Arabella and shook her head dolefully. "I'm afraid ye could already be a widow, young miss, e'en before yer wedding day."

"Mama . . ." Arabella's voice began to falter.

The mother patted her hand. "'Twill be all right, Arabella."

With their attentions still riveted on Cyma's face, Mara stole a glance over her shoulder. The coal was nearly gone. The crowd had already begun to disperse. In moments the coach would be free to continue on its errand, free to come and fetch its waiting guests.

Time was quickly running out. They had to hurry.

She turned to Arabella.

"Now, if ye'll follow us," she broke in, her own face still hidden beneath her mask, "we'll get ye on the coach to Kulhaven right away so ye can see his lordship before 'tis too late altogether."

She reached for the other valise.

"Wait just a moment."

Mara froze, her hand still clutching the leather handles of the valise as Arabella's mother peered narrowly at her masked head.

Chapter Two

"Why does the girl not remove her mask?" Arabella's mother asked, her eyes narrowing with suspicion.

Cyma stepped between them, pushing Mara back behind her. "Oh, no, ma'am, you'd not be wantin' her to do that. Me poor daughter's face weren't spared nearly as well as me own. Pox near ate away 'alf her cheek, it did, enough to make a strong man weep just looking at 'er. Her own intended, that cowardly James Martin, he turned tail and ran at the sight of her. Still nursing a broken heart, she is."

She patted Mara's arm. "'Tis all right, my dear. Ye can't be hiding yer face behind that mask forever, ye know. Ye've got to come out sometime. Come, be brace, my dearling, show'm your face now."

Mara hesitated a long moment as if trying to summon the courage before reaching up toward the mask with the one hand that had been covered with the hideous clay mixture. Her heart pounded against her chest, knowing that her own face had not been disguised, wondering what she would do, hoping Arabella's mother would stop her before—

"Wait!"

Mara quickly dropped her hand to her side.

Arabella's mother stepped back, shaking her head, her expression one of revulsion. "Please, miss, keep your mask in place. It will not be necessary for you to uncover your face. I completely understand your hesitation and I do extend my deepest sympathies for your affliction. You may thank the good Lord you've still your life. You were mercifully spared when others have not fared nearly so well." She stepped back and crossed herself even as she continued her sermon. "It is just as well that you came to meet us. You may return to the earl's coach without us. I thank you for coming all the way here."

"What do you mean, ma'am?" Cyma asked, affecting surprise.

"I said you may leave us here."

"Ye mean ye're not goin' to Kulhaven?"

"No. We are not going to Kulhaven nor anywhere else on this godforsaken heathen rock island. We are not going anywhere except right back from where we came. I am taking my daughter and we are returning home. You may tell Lord St. Aubyn that we took sick and had to turn back. Tell him our ship went down in the Irish Sea if you wish, but there will be no wedding. Not now. Not ever!"

She turned on Arabella then, grabbing her by the forearm. "Ireland is a changed place, he said. A new and safe place in which to prosper. I always knew coming here would portend horrible things but your godfather, Oliver, refused to listen. He said you'd be safe here. He said he'd have the entire New Model Army to protect you. Well, a thousand armies could not stop the smallpox. He arranged this marriage to an absolute stranger, a man whose family caused no less than one of the biggest scandals in London society, a man known across England as the Bastard Earl of St. Aubyn, and without even consulting me. Did you know that his mother was an adulteress?"

"Mama . . ."

"Really, Arabella, his own father tried to have him disinherited because he did not believe that St. Aubyn was his son and then the poor man was forced to accept him anyway. This"—she flung her hand outward—"this is the man your father agreed for you to marry, the man we crossed an ocean to meet. And we come here to find what?" She threw her other hand outward then. "Disease and filth and now the smallpox. It is an omen, I tell you. I tried to tell your father, I warned him something like this would happen, but he refused to listen to me. The Lord has released his wrath on the Irish for refusing to give up that pagan Catholic religion."

She turned on Mara and Cyma then, who were staring at the ranting woman. "I will not allow my daughter to suffer for your sins. 'Tis the judgment of God, it is. You may mark my words. You have brought Armageddon upon yourselves and I do not plan to be one of the fallen. Thank the Lord the vows had not yet been said. Come along, Arabella, I will see about getting us on the next ship back to England. Then we will see about finding you a new husband, a good husband who is free from scandal and disease."

"But, Mama, what of our trunks? My wedding trousseau? We cannot leave it . . ."

"We will buy new clothing when we reach England, Arabella. For all we could know everything has already been touched by the pox. Do you want your face to end up looking like that? Come along. Hurry now. Do not breathe deeply and cover your nose and mouth with your kerchief before we, too, catch the deadly sickness. Oh, dear, I believe my skin is already starting to itch. They say in the early stages, the disease can cause quiverings of the heart and I am beginning to feel a bit faint. Perhaps I have already begun to contract the sickness. Hurry now, Arabella, step quickly."

They were gone before Mara could blink an eye. She and Cyma stood in silence and watched them go. Mara thought to herself that she was surely doing St. Aubyn a favor, and not a disservice, by sending that mouse of a girl and her shrewish mother away.

"Imagine that," Cyma said. "It seems the young bride has had second thoughts about wedding his lordship. Even left you her trunks. Quite thoughtful of the girl, don't you think?"

"And with but a moment to spare." Mara looked to the coal cart. It was empty, every last crumb of coal snatched away. The fallen wheel had already been replaced. The driver of the cart, the true driver, still clutching his mug of frothy ale, had been roused from his pub chair and was loudly lamenting the loss of his load. He clamored up to his driving seat, waved a fist, and returned the curse shouted at him from the coachman driving the Kulhaven carriage.

"Hurry, Cyma, cover your face with your mask. We haven't the time for you to wash off the clay. The earl's coach is coming now to fetch his long-awaited betrothed and we mustn't disappoint him."

Mara removed her own mask and smoothed a hand over the folds of her gown, a dove gray silk bought with the last of the precious groats she'd been able to save in the bottom of her stocking from her meager wages working at the bread baker's the past months. She assumed an expression much like Arabella's mother as the coach pulled to a halt directly before them. She tapped her toe as an added touch.

"Be you the Mistress Arabella?" the coachman said, peering down at her from beneath the brim of his wide black hat. He was a squat man with a belly that strained at the fastenings of his homespun breeches, his dingy gray shirt stained with a dribbling of his luncheon gravy.

Mara lifted her chin. "Yes, yes, I am. 'Tis past time you arrived. I was beginning to believe I'd been left to rot on this wretched dock."

"His lordship said you'd have hair blacker than midnight and a face to rival the angels. He certainly was right on that account."

His flowery oration, Mara decided, was more likely meant to cool her anger at having to wait than to compliment her. He hopped to the ground, which Mara found quite an accomplishment for one so corpulent, doffed his hat, and bowed, affording her a view of his very round and balding head.

"George Danvers, Miss Arabella, but you can call me Pudge like everyone else. My apologies for the delay. Got stuck behind that blasted coal cart there. Couldn't get by for the life of me. But I gave the bloody buggers—" He stopped short. "Excuse me, Miss Arabella, I gave the man a piece of business for keeping me from fetching you on time. We best be going as soon as possible. The streets are crowded, some of them even blocked off completely by the crush of carts and carriages, what with it being market day and all.

It'll take a bit of time to find our way through. We'll have to hurry if we want to make it out of the city by nightfall. These your trunks here?"

He pointed to the abandoned trunks which stood beside the space that had moments earlier been occupied by Arabella and her mother. Mara nodded. She stood back and waited while Pudge loaded them onto the coach.

"We'll be off then," he said, after securing the last one with straps to the back of the coach. "Want to get far away from the city as I can. Country roads are a bit muddy from the recent rain and the highways are crawling with robbers and the like. But you've nothing to worry about." He patted his pocket. "His lordship gave me a pistol for protecting you ladies with."

Mara nodded, rather doubting the man could shoot the side of a barn much less a thief as nervous as he was, but said anyway, "That is reassuring, Mr. Danvers."

"Pudge, Miss Arabella." He looked over at Cyma then, his gaze lingering on her masked face. "Would your mother be wantin' me to take her cloak? 'Tis a late summer we're havin' and the coach might get stuffy on the journey to Kulhaven."

"She is not my mother. This is my maid, Cyma. The crossing did not agree with her, seasickness and all. She has a tendency to take to a chill, so she will keep her cloak and will ride with me inside."

Pudge narrowed his eyes behind his rounded cheeks, resulting in an expression that reminded Mara of a wallowing pig. "I thought his lordship said your mother would be traveling with you."

"She was to but took ill moments before we were to leave. I'm afraid she was not fit to travel. We could not hold the ship for her, so Cyma came in her stead. Mother will join us at Kulhaven as soon as she is fit to travel."

This explanation seemed to satisfy Pudge, for he nodded and started for the driving seat, shoving his hat back onto his head. "We'll be off to Kulhaven then."

When Mara did not move, he stopped, remembering his coachman's duty, turned, and doffed his hat once again. "My apologies, Miss Arabella. Not used to driving fine ladies like yourselves. Allow me."

He opened the coach door and lowered the wooden steps for her to climb inside. Mara stared at him. She did not move.

Pudge smiled sheepishly and offered her his hand. "May I, Miss Arabella?"

Mara extended her right hand for him to assist her inside. Pudge took her fingers and his eyes went wide at the reddened clay marks that covered her pale skin. "Sweet Lord above. What's the matter with yer hand?"

Mara pulled away, hiding her hand in the folds of her gown. "'Tis nothing. Just a rash from the sea air. I did not heed my dear maid's advice to wear my gloves one day and look what became of it. She wears the mask for much the same reason, fair skin and all. It is nothing to cause alarm, though, I assure you. Cyma has promised me it will have gone by the time we reach Kulhaven."

Giving Pudge little opportunity to reflect further, she grasped the boarding bar and climbed unassisted into the coach. Cyma quickly followed, closing the door firmly in Pudge's astonished face.

"That certainly was close," Mara said, pulling the oiled linen covering down over the window opening.

She fell back in the cracked leather seat and let out a heavy breath. "Thought his eyes were going to pop right out of his head when he saw the marks on my hand." She peered out the flap as the coach started rolling forward. "He'd probably have dropped in a fit had he seen your pockmarked face. All right, Cyma, we're away from the quay. You may pull off your mask now."

Cyma's pustulated face emerged from beneath the black velvet covering. "You had to choose today, the hottest day in Irish history no doubt, to have me hidden beneath a cloak and mask. Thought I'd suffocate beneath all that fabric." She shrugged off the cloak and tossed it on the seat across, putting her feet atop it, then unfastened the top two buttons at the neck of her gown.

"First the pox, then seasickness," she said fanning herself with her hand. "Soon you'll be pronouncing me dead with this crazed scheme of yours." She looked to Mara, who was fighting hard to keep from laughing. "What is it you find so funny, missy?"

"Oh, Cyma, it's your face. It looks absolutely dreadful. You could frighten even a brave man into an early grave with it. It is no wonder the two of them fled as they did. They couldn't get away from us fast enough. I thought for certain Arabella's mother was going to swoon just looking at you. Did you see the expression on her face? Actually she underwent many expressions, each more horrified than the last."

Cyma smiled, an action that only resulted in making the marks grow even more pronounced. She reached up and plucked a single fleshy pustule from her nose, rolling it between her fingers till it formed a tiny pink-red clay ball. "Aye, guess my mum's taking to the stage did have some benefit after all. Taught me all about altering one's appearance. I did a fine job on you as well." She reached out and tugged on a lock of dark hair that had come loose and was falling over Mara's shoulder. "Can't even tell it's really red under all that black coloring. Thank the good Lord that Arabella weren't no blonde. I'd have had a devil of a time bleaching your fiery hair that color. And that would have been permanent. Least this way you can always wash it out if you decide to quit this foolishness."

"Well, I won't, so just get that thought out of your head. We've made it this far successfully, haven't we?"

Cyma sat back, her expression turning grim. "Posing as that devil Cromwell's goddaughter is bad enough, but marrying an Englishman as well? Your dear *máthair* would turn in her grave if she knew of this."

"My dear mother also married an Englishman, in case you have forgotten."

"Your *daid* was different. He never acted like any Englishman I ever saw. He was a Gael if I ever saw one."

"Da's family was as blue blood English as they come."

"Well, I still don't agree with this plan of yours. I don't know what your brother Owen could have been thinking when he planted the seed of this scheme into that stubborn head of yours. Going to get us both a ticket to Tyburn gallows, if you ask me." She glanced at Mara out of the corner of her eye, adding in a voice that sounded much like Arabella's mother, "Or Armageddon."

Mara refused to be daunted, especially when things were progressing so well. "Owen merely supplied the information I needed. This was *my* idea. And I certainly do not see anyone forcing you to come along. You do not owe me any service. You are free to leave anytime you wish. In fact"—she smiled teasingly—"would you like me to ask the driver to stop so we can let you off now before we are away from the city gates?"

Cyma did not answer. Knowing she would never abandon her charge, she busied herself with looking at the passing scenery afforded through the slit in the covering over the coach window. They had just passed through St. Nicholas's Gate by the River Poddle and were now rolling toward the tall spire of St. Patrick's Cathedral. "Just don't be getting yourself caught in any downpours or all that dye will run blacker than the waters of the River Liffey."

Mara reached inside her reticule and pulled a small cloth from inside. She tossed it to Cyma. "Here. You had better wipe your face clean of that clay else his lordship, Hadrian Augustus Ross, the Earl of St. Aubyn, will refuse us entrance to my castle."

Cyma took the cloth and started removing her disguise. "I wish you would abandon this scheme. It just doesn't bode well with me. What if Lord St. Aubyn finds out you are not the true Arabella? I hear it said he's got the beast of a temper and the strength to match it. I hear he caught a poacher taking a rabbit off Kulhaven land and clubbed him so hard, it knocked his nose clear into his face."

A shudder settled on Mara at the image that presented itself, but she quickly pushed the thought away. "Nonsense. He and his kind are the ones who are the thieves. Kulhaven had belonged to my family for over one hundred years before that wretched Cromwell stole it from us. And for what? Because my *English* father married my *Irish* mother, that is all. They had no proof that my father was a supporter of O'Neill and those like him. He wasn't even Catholic. He had no part in what happened at Ulster. But he married an Irish woman which, in their eyes, caused him to forfeit any right to his own land. He starved in a Dublin prison trying to obtain a dispensation against having Kulhaven taken. My mother was killed trying to defend our home against Cromwell's murderous soldiers."

"I know that as well as you, but that doesn't matter to the Protectorate."

"The Protectorate be damned to perdition."

"Your tongue, missy!"

"I'm sorry, Cyma, but I believe I am justified in trying to get back what was unlawfully taken from me. Besides, how could Lord St. Aubyn ever learn I'm not the true Arabella? He's never even seen her. Their entire courtship was done by post and that only during the past six months. Owen had all their letters intercepted. I know everything I need to know about him. And you heard what her mother said. Their marriage was arranged by Arabella's father and Lord Protector Cromwell. They did not even know the earl and all he knows of this Arabella person is that she was coming to Dublin to marry him.

"He's been told she has black hair, which, thanks to your recipe, my hair now is. He's no possible idea she is now booking passage back across the Channel to England rather than face marriage to a pox-infested man she's never set eyes upon. He obviously does not have that much of a tendresse for his intended bride, else he'd have come to fetch her to Kulhaven himself."

"Aye, but what if the mother writes to the earl after they return to England?"

Mara shrugged. "What care I? By the time they sail across the Irish Sea and ride back to their little country manor, explain the disaster to Arabella's father, post a letter and have it sent back here, assuming it would even arrive safely, I will have gotten everything I wanted. I will be married to St. Aubyn, will hopefully be carrying his child, and will finally have my revenge on him for destroying my family."

Chapter Three

Mara lifted the corner of the hatch that covered the coach window and looked out at the bright morning sunrise. It was dawning on what promised to be another glorious day, the skies above clear and blue for as far as the eye could see. At Mara's urging Pudge had driven through the night, stopping only twice to water the horses and allow Mara and Cyma to eat the dinner of cold meat pie and tasty cheese wedges he had brought along.

The food and the jostling of the coach ride had only served to make her already nervous stomach a churning upset. She'd led Pudge to believe the reason for her haste was that she was an overanxious bride-to-be eager to see her bridegroom. Inwardly she was anxious to get home to Kulhaven again and growing more so with each passing mile.

That, coupled with the nagging fear of finally facing Lord St. Aubyn posing as his intended bride had made the confines of the coach seem even more confining.

Mara took in a deep breath of the morning air, hoping to release some of the tension that filled her. She hadn't slept a wink all night, her mind too busy racing with what lay ahead. Cyma, on the other hand, seemed not to have a worry in the world, for she had snored like a drunken sailor through every bump and pothole of the ride along the way. She'd not so much as stirred when Pudge had driven them off the road and directly into a smelly bog marsh, leaving Mara to wonder just where St. Aubyn had found his coachman, a coachman who couldn't drive.

During the long and sleepless night, Mara had contented herself with staring out the coach window, counting the stars in the night sky, and reminiscing about her childhood. She'd nearly forgotten just how much she loved this wild and beautiful land, for it had been so many years since she'd last seen it.

Since daybreak, the countryside had taken on a more familiar appearance and she began to recognize several of the more prominent landmarks. Late yesterday, just as the sun had begun its nocturnal descent, they'd passed by the great oak of Almu near County Kildare where it was said the head of the mythical hero Fergal Mac Máile Dúin had been placed after he was slain in battle. They'd rolled by Ogre Rock at dawn which, in the shadows of the late afternoon sun, looked much like a giant troll waiting to snatch an unwary passerby. She remembered the oldest of her brothers, Niall, telling her when she'd been a wee thing that the rock had once been a giant who had been turned to stone by the great Gaelic god Dagda for eating the townspeople of the village nearby. How she used to stare at that rock whenever they would happen to pass by, frightened that it would somehow come back to life to eat her, too. Little had she known then that a true demon would one day come to devour Ireland—a demon called Cromwell.

Away from the city, the woodland had grown denser, sometimes blocking out the sunlight completely when they made a pass through a particularly thick patch of trees. At these times, Pudge would usually urge the horses on faster, obviously hoping to outrun any robbers who might be lurking about in the tree shadows.

But with the familiarity of the land where she had been born and had grown also came the shock of seeing the desecration and the destruction wrought by the vicious hands of Cromwell.

Tens of miles would pass without seeing another living being, animal or human. Tall and mighty castles which had stood for centuries, fortresses she'd thought would remain till the end of time, had been reduced to crumbling blackened shells, burned and destroyed by the Cromwellian army on their pillage across the country. Fields once filled with miles of golden wheat and corn and lush green pastures that had nourished Irish sheep had been burned and then salted so as never to give life from the soil again.

This was the Protectorate's retaliation for the English lives lost at Ulster in the Irish uprising headed by Sir Phelim O'Neill in what had come to be known as "The Great Massacre." Cromwell called it his "Judgment of God," exacting his punishment mercilessly on the women and children left occupying the estates while the men were off fighting in the war, or for their lives in a prison cell in Dublin, like her father.

Mile after mile Mara witnessed the result of Cromwell's wrath; the living left to starve on what was left of the land, the dead, so many dead, lying in ditches or hanging in chains from every available tree limb, their flesh picked from their bodies by wolves and scavenger birds, a warning to any who dared oppose Cromwell's law. And the smell, that awful odor of death that seemed to cling to everything it touched. Mara wondered if she'd ever be able to wash it from her skin.

With each mile that brought them closer, and with each estate they passed that had been destroyed, Mara began to fear what lay ahead for her. What, if any, was left of Kulhaven for her to fight for? She knew that Lord St. Aubyn owned and occupied the land. He'd been given it by his uncle, James Ross, an adventurer who'd received the estate for his monetary support of Cromwell's cause. Yet what if the castle, her home, had been razed like so many others, leaving her with naught but the crumbling remains and the memories of what had been? What would she do if she had embarked on this dangerous mission, posing as someone she was not, only to find there was nothing of Kulhaven left for her to have?

It mattered not, she told herself firmly. Cromwell himself could never take away the true Kulhaven, the Kulhaven that had withstood fiercer armies only to rise again, each time victorious, each time greater than before. Just then, as if to tell her that her fears were for nothing, the coach rounded a slow curve in the road and ahead, beyond a deep ravine that rose on the rocky cliffs hundreds of feet above the River Nore, Castle Kulhaven suddenly came into view.

Mara's breath caught in her throat at the sight of her beloved home. It had been built nearly two centuries earlier by a medieval knight named Rupert de Kaleven. It consisted of two wards with walls six feet thick, the outer walls weathered and ivy-covered. A small creek ran beside its walls on the southern side, leading to a small lough hidden deep in the wood. A single tall tower rose majestically through the hovering morning mist, the second tower having been crumbled by the continual pounding from the Cromwellian's great mortar.

No, Kulhaven had not changed. Despite the war and the killing its beautiful gray walls had seen, despite the invasion of the enemy within it, it still remained the fairy-tale castle she'd always known it to be.

But it had changed, she realized as the coach came around to its facade. A newer structure adjoined it on its western side, a more modern structure made of red brick and white lime with tall glazed windows and wide sweeping front stairs leading to a double-doored entrance so different from the portcullis and heavy wooden draw she'd known before. Caryatids of the goddesses Aphrodite and Athena stood at each side of the door, two stone lions poised and ready to pounce guarded the stairs leading up to it.

Mara didn't know why but after seeing Kulhaven still standing from the coach window, she'd expected it to have remained the same. Seeing it now, in its altered, unfamiliar state momentarily made her falter.

It only took her a moment to regain her resolve.

At the sight of a pack of barking, grizzled wolfhounds bounding down the carriage drive toward them, Mara knew in an instant what she was about. This was Kulhaven, despite its additions, and Kulhaven was rightfully and undeniably hers. Her family. Her history. And no one, not even Oliver Cromwell himself, had the right to take it away from her.

"Looks different," Cyma said as if reading her thoughts like a well-worn book.

Mara hadn't even realized the maid had awakened. "Yes, it is, but at least they did not tear it down completely like at Castle Clunnis. They left it intact, even the remains of the fallen tower. Even so, the new structure seems more to compliment the true Kulhaven than to overshadow it, do you not think?"

Once again, as had become her custom these past two days, Cyma responded with silence as if to tell Mara she wasn't fooling anyone. Mara hated that her maid was right, but she refused to let this small change deter her from her purpose. How could she have expected Kulhaven not to be the slightest bit different? They'd been under siege for nearly ten months, keeping the Cromwellian soldiers at bay by dropping stones or hot embers from the hearths on their heads when they'd tried to come over the walls with their scaling ladders. But, despite their valiant fight, the Cromwellians had finally gained entrance, battering their way through, one stormy night. In the years since she'd been away, much had happened to change her home. Many had tried to destroy it, but despite its altered appearance, it would still and ever live on in her heart.

Mara closed her eyes, envisioning the Kulhaven she remembered, the Kulhaven she loved more than anything else in life. She took a deep breath, breathing in the sweet perfume of the cherry and lime blossoms in the trees that lined the narrow roadway. She was home, finally home, that gloriously regal stone castle, in whose chambers she had been born and had run with Cyma chasing behind as she hid in every nook and scaled the hundred steps leading to the top of the "Bloody Tower."

The tower.

Mara's throat tightened at the memory of the tower's

lifelong name. No one really knew for certain when the tower had first acquired its gruesome distinction. For centuries, it seemed, this place alone at Kulhaven had been associated with misfortune and tragedy. For generations, stories had been handed down of the untimely death that had befallen the unfortunate, each somehow mysteriously occurring at that very place.

But as a child, the tower had never frightened her, for its evil reputation had not touched her. *Yet.* Her brother, Owen, used to tease her with stories of evil spirits, but she had merely laughed at him, not believing his tall tales. Not until her last day at Kulhaven, when the soldiers had finally breached the protective walls, did the prophecy of the tower become true for her.

She could still see her mother, the beautiful Edana, named for the sixth century Irish saint, her red hair flying out behind her like a cape made of brilliant burnished fire, defying the soldier's orders to come down and surrender Kulhaven. With the guns of the enemy aimed at every doorway, Edana had taken Mara and Owen, the youngest of her three older brothers, and the only one remaining, aside.

"My children," she had said, clutching them tightly to her breast, "if this castle should fall to the enemy this night, you must promise me you will return one day to reclaim it and exact revenge on those who have taken it. You must promise to restore the Despencer heirs to this land. For if you do not, Kulhaven will perish."

Edana had received a summons from the English commander ordering her to give over. Her response was swift: She would rather die still holding Kulhaven than to live seeing it given to the bloody Cromwellians. The commanding officer informed her she and her children would be given no quarter. She'd had to endure every sordid insult shouted at her from the soldiers outside hoping to frighten her into surrender. Yet her mother was made of sterner stuff. Even when the soldiers had breached the outside walls and were fairly breathing in their faces, her mother had bravely raised her husband's ancient culverin, readying herself to pull the hammer on the first who dared step foot on Kulhaven's sacred stone.

And in the barest of seconds, she'd jerked back, the musket clattering to the floor as she crumbled lifelessly to the ground.

Mara had watched her mother die that night, sure as her father had been killed before her, at the hands of the Cromwellian Roundheads. Driven by greed, the soldiers had quickly stormed the castle. They'd been given spirits to make them "pot valiant," and the incentive of free booty by their commanders. They looted the castle of all its valuables and Mara and Cyma had fled for their lives, down through the hidden passageways beneath Kulhaven's great stone walls to hide in the homes of the villagers at the foot of the great rise Kulhaven stood upon.

It was that night that Kulhaven became, in the eyes of the world, the property of the Protectorate, to be doled out like some sugared sweetmeat to one of Cromwell's more trusted colleagues.

It was that same night Mara had vowed to return and live up to the promise she'd made to her mother.

"Look, my lady Mara," Cyma said, pointing outward

as the coach circled toward the front of the newer structure. "'Tis your mother's garden."

Mara couldn't help the smile that came to her at the sight of the flourishing roses and rhododendron bushes that lined the drive leading toward the front of the structure. The last time she'd seen it, the garden in whose fertile blackened soil her mother's fair hands had dug and planted, it had been trampled to destruction beneath the bootheels of the Roundhead soldiers, its fragile blossoms set afire for sport. Seeing it now, its blooms full and alive with color, its sweet perfume filling the air, it could almost seem as if none of the past had happened, almost, if only her mother could be standing atop the front stair instead of cold and buried in an unmarked grave somewhere beneath the castle walls.

The coach rolled to a slow halt then and Mara's pulsebeat began to hammer as she heard the coachman, Pudge, climb down from his seat. It felt so truly *right* to be back. She knew she was doing what her mother would have wanted.

Even Cyma, despite her protestations, seemed happy to have finally returned, for her eyes were lit with a warm shimmer. "We're here, my lady Mara. We're finally home."

Home. "Yes, I know. I can hardly believe it true. Cyma. It has been so long, I almost began to think we'd never see this day. It is time to begin the Plan now and remember, from here on out, you must call me Arabella."

The coach door swung open with a flourish. A gloved hand pushed forward to assist her down. Mara took it, steeling herself for the certain reaction of revulsion at meeting the man she was to marry.

But the man who held her hand so lightly was not Lord St. Aubyn, it seemed. This man was dressed in fine-looking livery of gold and black; a footman, or perhaps the butler of the household.

"Welcome, Miss Arabella, welcome to Kulhaven. I am Peter Shipley, Lord St. Aubyn's steward." He was an older man who spoke like a gentleman, lean and bowing before her despite his great height. His brown hair was graying at the temples and his eyes reminded her of a curious sparrow. "His lordship sends his regrets that he could not be here to welcome you himself, but his presence was required on the northern skirts of the estate. Some of those bothersome Irish Tories have been pilfering the sheep, I fear. Nothing to be alarmed about though. You are perfectly safe here at Kulhaven."

Mara held herself silent at his choice of words. If only he realized the hand he held was one of those *bothersome Irish*. "Will Lord St. Aubyn be gone long?"

Her practiced English passed easily.

"No, Miss Arabella. His lordship expects to return by nightfall. He thought that you might be tired from your journey so he asked that we show you to your chamber so that you might take a respite before his return at supper this evening. I trust your journey wasn't too tiresome." He walked her up the front stairs to where an older maid awaited. "This is Mrs. Danbury, our housekeeper. She will take you to your chamber. The footmen will follow directly with your baggage. Your mother's chamber has been prepared directly across from your own."

Mara turned. "Oh, my mother did not travel with

me. She took ill before we were to leave. This is my maid, Cyma. I would that she will stay in my chamber."

"We'll have a truckle bed brought into the withdrawing chamber for her," Mrs. Danbury, a stout woman with salt-and-pepper hair whose cheeks were as round and fat as new spring apples, said, taking charge of the situation as they left Peter Shipley standing in the entrance hall. "Pleased to finally have you here, Miss Arabella. What with all this recent trouble so near, we worried you'd not be able to make the trip from Dublin."

"Trouble?"

"Aye. As Mr. Shipley was saying, there's a band of Irish Tories living in the woodland nearby. They've been stealing sheep and cattle off Kulhaven and the neighboring estates, even robbed the wife of Lord Lakewood on the other side of the river as she traveled in her carriage. Took all her jewels they did, even her wedding ring. Poor thing has locked herself away in her chamber and won't come out for fear of being robbed again."

Mara instantly thought of her brother Owen. "But the thieves did not harm her?"

"Gave her quite a fright, but, no, they did not cause her any other harm. Don't you worry, now, Miss Arabella. His lordship guaranteed your safe delivery. Of course, with your fine godfather's position, he'd have had the whole Cromwellian Army escorting you through if need be."

Mara just nodded in response. She'd not heard from Owen in nearly six weeks, not since he'd given her the last bit of information to aid her in her plan. He had been the one who'd learned of St. Aubyn's ownership of Kulhaven and he'd been supplying her with the necessary information to make her disguise as Arabella a success. He did not even know if she'd really gone through with it.

When last she'd heard, he'd taken up with a band of Tories much like the ones Mrs. Danbury described, and she feared he had been captured and could now very well be on his way to the South Seas to live out his life in bondage, or worse, hanging from the gibbet along some deserted country road.

All during the ride from Dublin, every time the coach had passed one of those macabre iron cages bearing the remains of some unfortunate fellow, she'd tried to tell herself it couldn't be Owen. But she would never be sure. The bodies had all been badly decomposed, long since picked over by the birds, so there was no way she could honestly say if any of them had been her brother. But, seeing the growing number of corpses and knowing how he had taken to the road, every one they passed made it even more likely one of them could have been him.

"This way, Miss Arabella."

As the doors to Kulhaven closed behind her, Mara was suddenly overwhelmed by a sense of uneasiness. What if they discovered she was not the true Arabella after all? Would they have her arrested and thrown into the Dublin Castle prison to rot? She had heard of women being hanged for so much as harboring Irish patriots in their cellars. What would they do to her for disguising herself as the goddaughter of their Lord Protector himself?

Mrs. Danbury's next words were drowned out by the excited barking of several wolfhounds who had come bounding forward to greet her. One of them, a pup, jumped up on hind legs against her, its dark eyes dancing eagerly.

"Why, hello," Mara laughed, patting the pup's grizzled head.

"Ach, get down there, mongrel." Mrs. Danbury quickly shooed the beast away with a snap of her dusting cloth. "My apologies, Miss Arabella, these animals don't realize their size sometimes. They feel it their duty to leap upon every visitor the moment they come through the door. They are nothing to fear, though. Quite harmless. His lordship keeps them around more for company and to keep his feet warm on cold nights than for protection."

"It is all right. I think they are wonderful." Mara had nearly said they reminded her of her own hound she'd had as a child, a great brindle-colored beast whose name, Toirneach, in Gaelic meant "thunder," but quickly kept her tongue. She remembered how he'd sit at the bottom of the stairs waiting for her each morning to come down from her chamber, for her mother would not allow him upstairs. She wondered what had happened to the gentle giant after the castle had been stormed. Had he been thrown out like all the other former inhabitants of the castle, discarded and left to starve while watching the new English lord eat like a king, getting fat off their years of hard labor?

Mara followed Mrs. Danbury through a central hall that smelled of beeswax and lemon oil and whose furnishings gleamed with a thorough polishing to a great oaken staircase leading to the second floor. The walls around them were paneled from floor to ceiling in the same dark oak, glowing golden in the candlelight, the wood carved in a linen fold design. The high ceiling was plastered and decorated with an elaborate scroll-work pattern, images of frolicking cherubs and birds painted throughout.

As they turned to ascend the second riser on the stairwell, Mara stopped to stare at a large portrait hanging on the landing directly above. Its subject was a man of vast size and presence astride a great and mighty black stallion. His rich chestnut hair gleamed in the sunlight that seemed to beam down from the very heavens above him. Fierce golden brown eyes glared down at her from the canvas as if piercing straight through her, his mouth curving slightly upward as if already detecting her ruse.

Without being told, Mara knew it to be *him.*

The Bastard Earl of St. Aubyn, Hadrian Augustus Ross, and close advisor to the Lord Protector. Even his image appeared so large, so menacing, as if he could smash her with his mighty gloved fist. Staring up at him now, Mara found herself shivering against a sudden chill.

"Ah, yes, that is our Lord St. Aubyn," Mrs. Danbury said. "I'd forgotten you have never seen him before. Is he not the most handsome man? Commands respect, he does. He's had to, what with *the scandal* and all, but he's risen above his unfortunate past. Pay you no mind to that nasty expression. He's not nearly so frightening in person and is really quite agreeable when one gets to know him well, and being his wife, you'll surely do that. Pray continue to follow me, Miss Arabella. We've prepared a bedchamber in the western wing for you. Quite light and airy now that we've changed it to a more feminine decor what with your coming and all. I do hope you'll like it."

Mara barely heard Mrs. Danbury's words. She was still caught by the portrait, St. Aubyn's portrait, unable to look away from those oddly colored golden brown eyes. They held her somehow, setting her heartbeat to nervous pounding, the palms of her hands dampening as she clenched them into fists. She recalled some of Mrs. Danbury's words. Nasty expression. Nay, more downright terrifying. His expression alone could turn most men's legs to jelly. It was no wonder he'd risen through Cromwell's ranks so quickly.

Dear Heaven, what had she done?

She'd thought this would be so easy, fooling some coddled English lord who'd turned his back on his king for his own advantage. She'd thought he'd be spending most of his time in England at his estates there, that Kulhaven was just another of his holdings, but from the looks of this hall, he'd taken up residency. And he looked the sort of man who would tolerate no argument. He looked the type whose word was law. Without question. Without doubt. Still what could she have expected, she told herself. He was named for two Roman emperors, wasn't he? And this was the man she was to marry?

Mara forced her gaze away from his forbidding image. She could not allow him, this man she had yet to meet, to have this effect on her even before coming to face him. It was a portrait, sakes alive, not a flesh and blood man towering before her. The artist had most probably embellished to make him appear so large and frightening.

Of course, that must be it. No man could be so fierce in real life. It was a case of nerves, that was all, at being back in her home after all the years, at facing the memories of that horrible night, at playing the dangerous game she was playing. There would be no turning back, she told herself. Not now that she was so very close to having her reprisal, the reprisal she'd dreamt of and planned for since that horrible autumn night when she'd watched her mother fall brokenly on the stone floor of the Bloody Tower.

Chapter Four

Hadrian reined in his stallion at the crest of the grassy hill, steadying himself as the great horse danced sidewise beneath him. Patting the beast's muscled neck, he sat back, the saddle leather creaking beneath his weight and surveyed the wide-stretching area below.

God, this land was beautiful. In winter, the hills would be sparsely dusted with white powder, the trees bare beneath an endless and brilliant blue sky. Now, in summer, his first summer at Kulhaven, the trees were thick and full and green, lush fields filled with a colorful myriad of wildflowers stretching for as far as the eye could see and beyond. High above him, a lone kestrel soared effortlessly overhead, its blue-gray body hovering against a strong eastern wind. In the distance, the tall tower at Kulhaven rose like a great gray sentinel through the treetops to keep watch on the surrounding lands.

Aye, there was something about this place, this untamed, untouched place, something that drew him as none other had. He didn't know what, but since his arrival nearly seven months earlier, it seemed as if he'd never lived, never truly belonged anywhere else before.

And it was his.

How he wished that paragon of righteousness, Orestes Ross, former Earl of St. Aubyn, and the man who most would have called his father, could be there now to see him. He, his *bastard* son, who controlled over one thousand acres of the finest and most arable land in all Ireland. The estate of Kulhaven rivaled the St. Aubyn ancestral seat, Rossingham, nestled in the hills of Dorset, in both size and beauty. He hoped the pious earl rotted in hell, knowing the son he refused to acknowledge, the son he had tried to label a bastard before all humanity, had risen above the status he'd given him.

It hadn't been an easy task. His father, Orestes, had seen to it that he would forever be touched by the scandal of his dubious parentage, leaving him to live out his life being known throughout England as the Bastard Earl of St. Aubyn. And even after that humiliation, his father had taken away the only true person whom Hadrian knew he belonged to, his mother, Elizabeth, by shooting her dead while she slept. The only favorable thing Orestes had ever done in his life was to turn the gun on himself right after, ending his wretched existence.

Hadrian touched his heels to the horse's sides and started down the hill, allowing the horse to pick its way along the narrow, overgrown trail. Thoughts of his father had turned his mood foul and he let out a deep breath, hoping to release some of his inner anger. He reined back at the sound of a rustle beside him, reached for his pistol, and watched as a white-tailed doe leapt from the tall reeds, bounding out of sight through a break in the thicket.

He let the deer run, replacing his pistol. He wasn't hunting deer this day. Instead he was hunting for the bloody poachers who had been plaguing Kulhaven for the past three weeks.

He skirted the wood's edge at a leisurely pace, his mount taking an occasional nibble of the tall sweet grass which grew along the crooked pathway. And then he heard it, the sound that broke the natural rhythm of this peaceful picture.

"Whoa, Hugin," he said lowly to the huge black stallion he'd named for the mythical Norse raven on whom the great chief of the gods, Odin, relied for his knowledge. Slowly, he gathered the slack in the rein and turned his ear to listen.

The sound of water splashing, not the customary sound such as a river running, but of something, or someone moving through it came to him then. He looked to the trees from where the sound had come. He'd not been aware of any water near here. He listened again.

Silence.

He swung his leg over the saddle, dropping the reins to allow Hugin to graze, and pulled his pistol from the saddle holster. The poachers would get far more than they'd planned on this day. He started for the trees, his booted feet making nary a sound.

The sounds of the water lapping grew louder as he delved deeper into the brush. He wanted to catch the poachers unawares. Years of military training assured him that even at his size he'd not be heard. He stepped lightly and slowly to keep from alerting the poachers so that he might catch them in the act of setting one of their infernal traps. He'd lost eleven sheep and a mare in foal in the past two weeks alone, and just yesterday, one of his best hunting hounds had been crippled when its leg had been mangled in the locking iron jaws.

Hadrian halted near the edge of the thicket and pushed a leafy branch aside with his gloved hand. A distance away, he spotted a small lough, its water sparkling in the sunlight that shimmered down through a break in the tall trees. It was a beautiful spot and he wondered why he'd not found it before. Two ancient-looking boulders were set at the far end of the lough, moss-covered and shaded by the branches of a massive oak. A curiously colored object was lying atop them, looking oddly out of place and catching his attention.

Was it some sort of camouflage for one of their traps?

Hadrian started forward and spotted something moving just beneath the water's surface. He froze.

Rising from the water like the goddess Aphrodite springing from the foaming sea near Cythera came a fiery-haired woman. He shook his head to clear the image, but the woman—surely this was a figment, a vision, nothing more—did not vanish. First her shoulders, her shapely hips, and rounded buttocks, then her legs rose above the surface, long legs that tapered to trim ankles. Her hair slapped wet and clinging to her white back, trailing down to a point at her waist.

Hadrian stared, dumbfounded, stunned, as she then took the colored object lying upon the rock and dried her hair, rubbing hard until the dark red curls sprang free and thick.

God, she was so beautiful it hurt just to look at her. He stepped back behind the cover of the trees, taking in every inch of her white-skinned body. Her breasts were rounded and rose-peaked, not over-big, but just the shape to fit a man's hands. Her hips were rounded nicely from a narrow waist. Shapely and long legs, the kind that seemed to go on forever, were settled beneath the dark red triangle of curls nestled at the joining of her thighs.

The woman turned then, as if sensing his presence and Hadrian suddenly realized that his heart was drumming. Nay, not drumming, but pounding fiercely. The sight of her standing there like a wood fairy in all her naked splendor brought an instant and nearly painful tightening to his groin. His throat had gone dry and he was staring at her like some sort of Tom Peep ogling the fair Lady Godiva. He pictured himself standing before her, pulling her atop him as they fell back into the crystalline waters. He pictured her breasts—somehow he knew they would feel like silk—filling his hands as he suckled them. He thought of burying himself in her softness, feeling her hot flesh surrounding him, drawing him in. He imagined the taste of that white skin as he ran his tongue over her belly.

He nearly groaned aloud.

The girl, this lovely creature who surely had to be a woodland fairy, bent down then and Hadrian nearly expected her to take flight, so graceful were her movements. She lifted her arms and pulled the colored object that had been lying on the rock, a simple blue frock, over her head, covering her completely. *Be damned.* Tousling her hair, she combed her fingers through the springy curls as they began to dry in the sunlight. Each winding tress glistened like brilliant red fire. He wondered if it would burn at the touch. He wondered . . .

"My lord!"

Hadrian started from his thoughts.

"Are you there, my lord?"

He turned quickly enough to see only a flash of blue as the girl bolted for the cover of the woods. She was gone in seconds, disappearing through a slight break in the trees. She did not make a sound. Everything was still. It was as if he had just woken from a dream. One instant she'd been standing there, filling his senses, his mind, his very being, and next she was gone, leaving nothing but a deep and urgent burning in her place.

Hadrian cursed.

"My lord, oh, there you are. Thank the Lord, my lord. We saw your mount free and riderless and worried that you might have been beset by the poachers."

"Damnation, Davey," Hadrian said, wanting to cuff the lad. "If there had been poachers anywhere within a square mile of here, they'd no doubt be long gone now for all your infernal shouting. The objective of catching a poacher is not to alert him to your presence."

Davey, a boy of about sixteen whose father, Pudge, was Kulhaven's gamekeeper, and of late, coachman as well, lowered his head at the master's fury, his eyes disappearing beneath the brim of his coarse brown hat. "My apologies, my lord. I was worried when I saw your mount grazing in the field unattended."

"Yes, you already said that." Hadrian removed the hat and ruffled Davey's sandy-colored hair. "It is all right, Davey. As you can see I'm quite well. I thought I heard someone in the water and came on foot to investigate."

"Did you catch the bloody buggers?"

Hadrian raised a brow.

"Pardon, my lord."

He chuckled. "It is all right, Davey. Your sentiments echo mine when it comes to poachers." He turned to gaze at the spot where the girl had appeared, praying, he supposed, that somehow magically she'd returned.

She had not.

"But, I am afraid I did not find any poachers, Davey. Not this time, at least." *But, I did find something of infinitely more interest.*

Hadrian turned to leave then, giving one last glance to the spot where his lovely vision had first surfaced. The water was calm and still now, as if having never been disturbed. Perhaps it had been a dream of sorts, he told himself, somehow conjured up by his mind. Aye, that was it, a delusional result of having been too long without a woman in his bed.

Still he was reluctant to leave, but knew he very well could not stand there with Davey waiting for his wood fairy to reappear to him.

"Well, we'd best be getting back to Kulhaven. The sun will soon be setting for the night. The new moon is upon us and we've no need to be caught out here without a light to guide us home."

Davey smiled, obviously relieved his master's temper had improved. "Aye, and your bride should have arrived today. My father was rightfully honored to fetch her home to Kulhaven for you. My mother says its romantic you and Miss Arabella getting betrothed without even seeing each other first. But, from what I hear, you've naught to worry, my lord. I hear it said she's prettier than the angels. 'Tis no wonder you're wanting to get back to Kulhaven. You probably can't wait to see her."

Hadrian's smile faded. His bride. He'd completely

forgotten Arabella was to arrive, forgotten, or more likely, had chosen not to think about it at all, as if ignoring the fact that she was coming would keep her arrival from happening at all.

Arabella. Her name alone was like a dousing of cold water. Any thought he'd entertained of taking a woman to his bed vanished at the mere mention of her name. He could imagine the effect she would have on him once he came to face her. His manhood would most probably shrivel and die at the sight of her.

It had taken months to arrange this meeting, months of careful planning and meticulous attention to the finest of detail. He knew he should be there at Kulhaven standing atop the front stair to welcome her, to make the best impression in order to convince her and her mother he would make her a proper husband. He'd done things far more distasteful in the past years to achieve the place he now held. With this one and final task to complete, he would be assured of his position.

Aye, he should be eager to see her, if only to know that he would finally be reaching his objective. It mattered naught if she were an angel or had the face of a horse long left to pasture. All that mattered was what this marriage would bring to him.

If only the thought of wedding this woman did not make the blood in his veins run ice cold.

Chapter Five

Mara had been given a roomy chamber along the western side of the house that gave a commanding view of the bend in the river and the colorful sunrise on the mountains beyond. The rosewood poster bed stood across the room on a dias and was decorated in shades of gold and light blue. The other furnishings throughout were made of mahogany and were carved in a decidedly feminine fashion.

Sitting at the dressing table, her chin set on her hand, Mara looked to the brass lantern clock on the wall shelf beside her. She frowned. It was late, very late, and still no damned bridegroom.

"After seven o'clock and not a sign of him," she said aloud to the empty room. "It is nearly nightfall. Fine welcome it is for a bride-to-be. He must be a prince in his manners. A veritable gallant. But what to expect from an Englishman, and a bastard Englishman at that?"

Cyma appeared from behind the floral embroidered dressing screen, carrying a tray full of mixtures in several small bowls. "Were I you, I'd curb your frequent use of that word before his lordship returns. Last one who made the mistake of calling him a bastard ended up swallowing his own teeth. And 'tis better he's not here yet, missy. It'll take me a full hour to get your hair redyed. What were you thinking by jumping in that lough? You've washed every last bit of the black out of your hair. And what if you'd been seen out there, leaping about naked as a shorn sheep? Someone could have come upon you and your little charade would be exposed. Then what would you do?"

Mara did not have the chance to open her mouth to respond for at that moment there were loud shouts from outside her chamber window, dogs barking, a distant hunting horn blowing, and swift hoofbeats pounding over the moist ground. "Cyma, cease your prattle and look to see what everyone is up in the boughs about out there."

Cyma poked her head out the open casement window. "Arrah! Speak of the devil and you'll see his horns. 'Tis him, missy. He's finally arrived. And what an arrival. I vow I haven't seen the likes since Owen Roe O'Neill returned from Spanish shores to lead our men to victory at Benburb."

She turned then, crossing herself in silent prayer before moving across the chamber to Mara. "Best prepare yourself, missy. Your future bridegroom has come home to meet you."

Mara's heart instantly started pounding as an image of the portrait on the stairwell came to mind. She leapt from the chair, completely forgetting that only moments before she had been lamenting her bridegroom's seeming indifference to her arrival. "He's here? Already? Blast and damn! We've got to hurry! Quickly, Cyma, is that dye ready yet?"

Cyma moved to the hearth and stirred the concoction brewing in a small iron kettle there. "Aye, just about. If you hadn't gone off like a fool and washed all the other coloring from your hair, I wouldn't be having to hurry like this now." She took up a small mortar and began grinding some nasty-looking substance with a pestle, pouring the contents into the simmering kettle.

"You are right, Cyma. I'm sorry. The lough just looked so inviting. I had meant only to walk along its edge, but when I saw it through the trees, it was as if I were a child again. You know how I always loved swimming there and it had been so long. I couldn't help myself. I just had to dive in."

Cyma tipped Mara's head back over the porcelain washbasin, smiling. "Always knew where you were when your *máthair* couldn't find you. Instead of doing your needlework sampler or practicing at the virginal, you'd be off wearing naught but your lily-skinned hide, leaping off those mossy rocks like a bloody pond frog."

She poured a small amount of the mixture from the kettle over Mara's head. "'Tis the fault of your *bráthair* Owen. With your ages being so close and all, you always were tagging along after him, proving you could do whatever he could. Should have been twins the two of you. I wonder what dear Owen is doing nowadays."

Mara frowned at the mention of the youngest of her brothers, and the most bullheaded of the lot. "He's most probably hanging from a gibbet along some country road with the birds feeding off his eyes for robbing an Englishman's coach. I haven't heard from him in nearly two months now. Not since he gave me the information on when Arabella would be arriving. I should have known he wouldn't stay near to see this plan through to fruition."

She wrinkled her nose at the stench of Cyma's potion. "Cyma, what is in that witch's brew? It smells positively hideous, more horrible than the last one."

Cyma began to rub the thick mixture through Mara's red hair. "Some walnut peelings, myrtle leaves, sage, and other things. 'Tis better you do not know. It would make you retch to your toes."

Mara did not question further as to what the "other things" were, knowing Cyma's insistence on protecting her secret potions. "Does it have to smell so terrible? His lordship won't want to come near me if he gets a whiff of that."

"It must be this strong in order to darken your hair as black as Arabella's. Cease your fussing now. The smell will lessen as it dries."

She emptied the remainder of the kettle's contents over Mara's head.

"That's hot!"

"Just hold still a moment longer. It will cool in a second's time."

Cyma squeezed the excess of the black concoction from Mara's hair and twisted the now-darkened tresses atop her head. "Here, put this cloth about your shoulders so you won't stain your gown with the dye and sit you by the fire so we can get your hair dry."

Mara did as she was told, watching as Cyma dumped the leftover dye from the washbasin into the corner chamber pot. For certain the chambermaids would think Lord St. Aubyn was wedding a guttersnipe with a rotten gullet when they caught a sniff of that offal.

"Did you have time to alter one of Arabella's gowns

for me to wear this evening?" she asked, taking a seat on the small stool before the fire.

"Aye, and it was no small task either. That girl needs to keep clear of the sweet cakes else she'll be big as a house and will catch no husband at all." Cyma began pulling a tortoise shell comb through Mara's wet and tangled curls. "Mayhaps she thinks the sweets will grow her a more ample bosom. Takes after the mother in that respect."

"Will the gown fit?"

"Aye. No one looking would think it wasn't made for you. Just be glad I'm here with you. What with your sewing abilities, had you gotten your hands on that frock, you'd have ended up looking like a down-on-her-luck orange peddler."

"Sewing never was one of my better accomplishments."

"Aye. The gown is being pressed by one of the laundry maids this minute. I wish there were some other way of doing this. I see only a bad end to this charade of yours. Are you certain you will be able to convince his lordship you are this Arabella? He could know something of her that you do not. What if he catches on to your scheme? He certainly doesn't look the type to carry any coals. No, he looks more the type that would beat you blue and black if he ever learned the truth."

"But I must convince him, Cyma. Don't you see? This is the only way I'll ever get Kulhaven back, even if it's not truly all mine. At least Despencer children will run through these corridors again. I promised my mother I would see her grandchildren restored to Kulhaven. I must see that promise through, even at the risk of being caught, or Kulhaven will perish. And it is the only way I will be able to have my revenge on St. Aubyn for taking Kulhaven from us. He mustn't learn the truth, at least not until I am well with child. Then he will be faced with the decision of dissolving the marriage and in doing so, naming his son as the second Bastard Earl of St. Aubyn as his father did him."

"And what will you be doing with a bastard child, and an Englishman's bastard child at that, if he does disclaim your union? Your mother would turn in her grave if she knew her grandchildren carried English blood."

Mara looked up at her. "You seem to keep forgetting that I carry the blood of an Englishman as well."

"Your father was different, God rest his soul." Cyma shook her head dolefully. "Your brother Owen never should have told you about Lord St. Aubyn now owning Kulhaven. 'Tis too risky. 'Twill be the devil himself to pay the day Lord St. Aubyn ever learns you're not the true Arabella."

Mara smiled teasingly. "Ah, but he will have fallen hopelessly in love with me by then. That I'm not the true Arabella will matter naught."

"For your sake, I hope so, missy. I truly hope so."

Mara's smile faded as Cyma moved behind her and continued combing out her hair. She stared out the window, settling her gaze on a distant cragged mountaintop, and said a silent prayer that Hadrian Augustus Ross, the Earl of St. Aubyn, was not a violent man.

Nearly two hours and another kettleful of black dye later, Mara followed the footman who'd been sent to fetch her along the corridor to supper. The castle was curiously dark and she'd seen nary another servant since the maid had brought her gown back from the pressing. She had to slow her stride to keep pace with the aging footman's unsteady gait. She didn't speak, having learned any attempt at conversation fruitless when she'd remarked on a fine painting depicting the skyline of some unknown city only to receive a low grunt for a response.

Actually she was grateful for the silence. Her nerves were taut as a corset string at knowing she was about to meet *him.* St. Aubyn. She'd conjured up such a picture in her mind since seeing his portrait earlier that day that now he was gargantuan and a heathen as well. She wondered if he would take pleasure in torturing the lady who impersonated his betrothed. She wondered if he'd see right through her facade and hang her from the nearest tree. She wondered if she should run as far and as quickly away as she could.

Her skirts rustled along the carpeted floor as they turned down another dark corridor. Cyma had done an excellent job of altering Arabella's gown of burgundy silk. Anyone looking would think it made for Mara now, except that in style it was far too modest for her taste. The color was not at all to her liking, though with her hair blackened, she had to admit, it was at the least a complimenting shade.

Any neckline the garment might have had was completely hidden by the white laced falling band that fastened beneath her neck and covered her shoulders. The same fashion stood for the full puffed sleeves that ended at her wrist with a wide starched white cuff.

Catching a glimpse of herself in the mirror near the stairs, Mara wondered how she would ever manage to capture his lordship's attention covered head to toe as she was and looking like a bloody nun. She would have to do something, she told herself, what she did not know, all in all feeling very much unlike Mara and more and more like Miss Arabella Wentworth.

"This way, Miss Arabella."

Mara nearly missed the first step down the stairwell. She was wearing a pair of spectacles she'd found stashed in Arabella's trunk, hoping to better improve her disguise, but also making her vision slightly blurred in the process. The branch of candles the footman held gave off only a minimal amount of light and she had to grip the carved banister to keep from tumbling to the bottom stair.

When they reached the first floor, she saw candlelight burning through an open doorway to the right. The rest of the castle was dark, the doors closed on the other chambers.

Mara stiffened as they turned toward the door. *He* was waiting for her on the other side of that doorway, her future bridegroom.

No sound came from within the lighted chamber. The footman stood at the door, holding his branch of candles aloft, and motioned wordlessly for her to enter.

Mara moved past him into the room and noticed she was alone. St. Aubyn was not there. She released the breath she had been holding, removed the spectacles, and began to look around.

The room was a gentleman's study, though it was so very different from her father's study in the older part of Kulhaven. It was strange, she thought, being new to the house where she'd spent her entire childhood.

But this wasn't the same Kulhaven. Dark walnut paneling covered the walls where the bookshelves crammed with aging volumes did not. The ceiling was low and decoratively plastered, giving the room a more cramped appearance. Sconces were set at intervals around the room and she recognized several of the paintings hanging on the walls, having once been in the long carpeted gallery where the Despencer family portraits had hung. They looked out of place, she thought, in their new surroundings.

An inviting fire crackled in the hearth beside the huge mahogany desk across the room. She walked over to it. Despite the warmth of the fire she felt a sudden chill but put it down to nerves and wrapped her arms about herself, rubbing her upper arms. Her edginess began to ebb as the minutes ticked by on the carved case clock with no sign of St. Aubyn.

Perhaps he'd decided not to come down to supper after all, she thought as she inventoried several of the titles on the shelves. She was impressed to find such a diversified collection. She took an aged bound volume of Spenser's poetry and leafed through several of the pages before setting it back in its place again. A copy of Woodhouse's *A Guide for Strangers in the Kingdom of Ireland* stood half in and half out of its place. She smiled to herself, thinking it rather appropriate.

As she crossed the room to peer out the tall draped windows at the night sky, she spotted a portrait hanging high above the black marble mantelpiece, half hidden in the shadows. She didn't know why, but for some reason she was drawn to it.

Slowly she walked toward it. A strange feeling of recognition came over her at the sight of her mother's face staring down at her.

It had been painted long before Cromwell's troops

had come to Kulhaven, back when the worst of Mara's troubles had been how to avoid her dancing instruction with Mrs. Peebles, her governess. The beautiful Edana, everyone in the region had called her mother. In the painting she was standing at the battlements of one of the castle towers, the Bloody Tower, the same tower where she'd been shot down by the Roundhead soldiers. Her hair hung loose in brilliant red curls, lifted by the wind as she stared off at the bright summer sky.

Mara recalled the day the portrait had been painted, the quarrel her mother and father had had over the gown she was to wear. He wished for the sky blue satin; she wanted the deep emerald. Her father had won in the end, but at the expense of her mother's fiery temper shining clear and true in the artist's depiction. Even now Mara could see the stubborn lift of her chin, the strength lighting her bright blue eyes.

Mara closed her eyes. *Oh, Mother, I do miss you.*

If only she could go back to that carefree time. If only the soldiers hadn't come through that ill-fated day. If only her mother had not refused to give Kulhaven over. If only . . .

"Good evening, Miss Wentworth."

Chapter Six

Mara whirled around at the sound of a man's deep voice behind her.

Her breath stuck in her throat. It was him, the earl, standing in the doorway and looking even larger than she had expected. The portrait on the stairwell hadn't embellished. In fact, he appeared even more menacing in person. She quickly placed Arabella's spectacles back on her nose, throwing his features into a blur. She swallowed before attempting to speak and hated herself for the fear.

"Good evening, my lord. I was just admiring this unusual portrait."

He walked forward and leaned against a tall bookcase, crossing his arms over his chest. "It is a beautiful likeness, isn't it? It was left behind by the former owners of Kulhaven and oddly it survived after the castle was stormed. It used to hang in the gallery with countless other portraits, but its subject intrigued me so that I had it moved here where I could view it more often."

Left behind by the former owners . . . His choice of words relieved Mara of her initial trepidation at being face-to-face with him—the enemy. She longed to inform him that the portrait had not been left behind, but rather had been stolen along with everything else that had been confiscated from her family by the Roundhead troops, but held the words in check. She must think, act, and respond as Arabella would. Arabella would never dare gainsay him or speak out of turn. She would never even think of doing so.

Instead she lowered her eyes, affecting a soft-spoken voice and said simply, "It is a lovely portrait, my lord. But do you not think the woman appears too bold, too certain of herself?"

St. Aubyn paused for a moment, staring at her with an odd sort of expression on his face, then turned to move across the room. "Would you care for a cordial, Miss Wentworth?"

Mara wondered why he hadn't responded to her question, but decided not to pursue it. "Yes, my lord, that would be most pleasant."

With her head lowered, Mara could see Hadrian clearly over the top of the spectacles as he moved to the sideboard to pour. He was dressed quite simply in black breeches and white shirt, polished black boots reaching above his knees. A neck cloth hung loosely around his collar, his cuffs rolled back to his elbows over sun-bronzed hands, hands that looked like to squeeze the life from a bear.

Everything about this man exuded power and strength. Even the fashion in which his great hands grasped the bottle to pour. She found herself staring at the smooth and rigid line of his jaw, the way his rich brown hair shone in the firelight, giving it burnished highlights that matched his golden brown eyes.

He looked at her then from the corner of his eye and Mara quickly looked away.

"I hope you are not offended by the casualness of my attire, Miss Wentworth. I prefer comfort over society's strictures here at Kulhaven."

"Oh, no, my lord. I do not mind."

In fact, she thought to herself, she would dearly love to remove these stupid spectacles and the blasted choking collar from Arabella's gown this minute. She started to turn, but he handed her a glass.

"We may sit here by the fire, if you would like."

Mara took a seat on one of the twin cushioned armchairs he'd motioned to. She looked for a place on which to set her glass and finding none in the blur that was her vision, held it with both hands in her lap.

"It will be a few moments before dinner will be served," he said, staring at the liquid in his glass in the firelight. "I thought we might use the time to get better acquainted."

Mara didn't know why but she was getting a feeling that St. Aubyn wasn't particularly pleased with her being there. Odd, she thought, especially when they were supposed to marry. She took a small sip of her cordial to ease her throat's sudden dryness. It was a tasty mixture made with currants and cherries that warmed her belly instantly.

"You appear nervous, Miss Wentworth. Do I make you uncomfortable?"

What did he expect, damn his eyes? "No, it is just the unfamiliarity with my surroundings, my lord. I feel quite foreign and alone among all your people. It is not that they have been inhospitable to me. Quite the contrary. Everyone has been more than welcoming. It is just a little frightening being in a new place such as this. I am certain in time I will adjust."

He nodded. "I was sorry to hear your mother was unable to accompany you on the crossing. Her presence, I'm sure, would have made it easier for you to adjust to being here. Huntington, my valet, said she had fallen ill before your departure from England. I trust her illness is nothing too serious?"

Past the initial excitement of their first meeting, Mara began to assume the roll of Arabella. "It came upon her at the last minute." She paused, attempting to sound sincere. "Although my father assured me it wasn't anything to fret over. I'm hopeful she will recover and will be able to join us very soon. It is just difficult, my lord. Do forgive me if I seem to go on overmuch about it. It is just that everything is so very different here. I have never been away from my home like this, let alone in a totally different country. While it would seem an exciting adventure, it is also quite overwhelming." She lowered her eyes, adding modestly, "You are correct in saying that it would be easier if my mother were here."

Hadrian sipped his brandy. "I'm hopeful your mother will come soon as well so we'll not have to delay the wedding very long."

Be damned! She'd gone too far in her attempt to convince him of her false identity. Delay the wedding? Not if she had anything to do with it. She would have to appeal to his male instincts. Make him unwilling to wait for the mother's arrival. But how was she to do that looking for all the world like a bespectacled nun?

Hadrian broke in. "That is, of course, entirely dependent on your acceptance of my offer of marriage."

This statement took Mara aback. She had thought

the terms of their engagement quite settled upon. "But, is that not the purpose of my coming here?"

Hadrian raised one brow. "Not entirely. You had never seen me before. For example, you could find my appearance repulsive and cry off. You could discover that my teeth are rotten and that I have breath that smells fouler than the wind coming from the privy."

He smiled and Mara eased at his gentle teasing.

"I have already seen your teeth, my lord, and they are quite clean and white." She leaned close to him to where their faces were but inches apart. "And as for your breath"—she took in a breath—"I assure you that is not at all the case."

When she looked up at him, he was staring at her directly. She pulled back then, looking at him through her lashes. "But who is to say you would not wish to cry off after finally seeing me?"

The corner of his mouth quirked slightly. "I assure you, Miss Wentworth, your appearance does not at all repulse me either. But there is still the fact of my past."

"Your past, my lord?"

"Yes, you have, no doubt, heard of the scandal involving my family?"

Mara hesitated. She had heard somewhat of the blemish on his social standing, of how he had come to be known of as the *Bastard Earl*, but wondered how much she should reveal. "I was told something about your father being responsible for your mother's death. It must have been truly tragic for you."

Hadrian's jaw grew rigid. "To put it more directly, Miss Wentworth, my father *murdered* my mother. In cold blood. But before either of us commit ourselves to this union, I would like to put everything out on the table, if you will. I will attempt to be brief.

"When my mother was carrying me in the womb, my father learned through means unknown to anyone that my mother had been having a clandestine love affair with another man almost from the day they were married. That other man was my father's brother, my uncle, James Ross."

Mara had not known that much. "Your uncle, James? The man who left you this castle?"

"Yes, one and the same. You see, because my mother was"—he hesitated—"intimate with both men, I will never know for certain who my true father was, though I feel in my heart that it was my uncle and not my father. I believe my uncle felt the same, which is why he left me this castle, but to claim me as his son would have made me illegitimate in the eyes of society. It also would have kept me from inheriting my birthright in his eyes, the St. Aubyn title from my father.

"But this did not deter my father—while my uncle kept silent, he was quite vocal. He made a public proclamation stating that it had been some months since he had last visited my mother's bed and if I was not born by the tenth of September, I would not be deemed his. Unfortunately for him, I was born on the exact day of his target date, the tenth of September." He smiled, adding, "At precisely five minutes before the stroke of midnight."

Hadrian paused then as if expecting some response from her.

Mara said simply, "That should have satisfied everyone of his paternity."

"One would think, but my father was still not convinced and it didn't prevent him from attempting to disclaim me besides. He brought a petition before the King, a very public petition, discounting my mother as an adulteress and me as a bastard not of his creation. But since he was within the four seas and not a great distance away from my mother at the approximate time of conception, and since I had been born by his self-imposed birth date, the King refused to declare me illegitimate."

"Your father must have been very displeased."

"That, Miss Wentworth, is putting it lightly. After his failure with the King, he decided he could not live with my mother any longer. He attempted to gain a divorce from her through an Act of Parliament, but in this he failed as well. It had taken over a decade, and having come to the end of his possibilities, he decided to take matters into his own hands. He took a very old and very valuable dueling pistol that had been passed down through the earls of St. Aubyn for generations, drank two full bottles of brandy, and while my mother was sleeping in her bed, he shot her. Dead. Then, in his usual cowardly fashion, he turned the pistol on himself, sparing me the task of killing him myself."

Mara's eyes were filling by the time he reached the end of his diatribe. "I am so sorry, my lord."

"I was fifteen at the time. These matters do not move swiftly. It had taken my father all that time to bring his petitions before the King, Parliament, and society. It was the most talked about scandal for nearly two decades. Songs were sung about it and it made for quite a many supper conversations in London for many years. In the end, I inherited the title, much, I'm sure, to my father's chagrin. But from that day forward I was to be known as the Bastard Earl of St. Aubyn, despite the fact that I was legally declared legitimate."

Although she had known about the scandal surrounding his upbringing, Mara could never have dreamed he would have had such a tortured childhood. Without thought, she reached out and touched him on the shoulder. "It was not your fault. You should not blame yourself."

"I do not blame myself. I was merely the end result to all this treachery and deceit. Please remember that, Miss Wentworth, should you decide you still wish to wed me."

He looked at her levelly then, his eyes darkening. "I will tolerate no treachery from my wife."

Mara swallowed hard against the lump his words brought to her throat, knowing he meant it. "You need not concern yourself with me in that respect, my lord. I can assure you I am not hiding any clandestine assignations from you. I believe in trust between married couples."

"That pleases me, Miss Wentworth. Please see to it that you always adhere to that standard. I will honor that promise as well. So, with knowing all about my past, you would still be willing to wed the Bastard Earl of St. Aubyn?"

Mara frowned. "You are not a bastard, and yes, I would still like to wed with you."

"Except, there is one more thing," he added.

"My lord?"

"You have heard of the Curse, have you not?"

Mara feigned ignorance. "The curse, my lord?"

"The Curse of Kulhaven. You see," he went on, motioning toward her mother's portrait, "it is said that the woman in that portrait placed a curse on Kulhaven when the soldiers were coming to confiscate this estate."

"So she was very bold then. I am not one usually given to superstition, but, I am curious. What sort of curse was it, my lord?"

"Legend has it she deemed there would be no living issue beget to the master of Kulhaven until the blood it carried was the blood of her own. My uncle who lived here before me seems a testament to that prediction. His wife delivered him three stillborn sons before succumbing to death on the fourth. He wrote in a diary that the spirit of this woman, this Flaming Lady, haunted him in sleep. Rumor among the villagers still here from that time is that this ghostly apparition even pushed him to his death from the tower."

"How very odd. Have you ever seen this Flaming Lady, my lord?"

Hadrian hesitated, remembering the vision he'd seen at the lough. Could it have been . . . ? He shook his head, refusing to so much as consider that as a possible explanation for what he had seen. "No, I have not, still the Curse of Kulhaven lives on in the hearts and minds of many who live here, as does the legend of the Flaming Lady. As there are no survivors of this spirit woman's family remaining, it would seem that the Curse may never be lifted."

"How can you be so certain there were no survivors, my lord?"

"From what I have been told, the lady's husband, an earl, I believe, was apprehended early on in the war and put in prison at Dublin Castle. He contracted gaol fever and died there."

Gaol fever? Is that what they called starvation these days? Mara wondered how much more St. Aubyn knew. "Why was the earl imprisoned?"

"Apparently being a major stronghold, Kulhaven was one of the estates designated for confiscation by the Protectorate. Like many of the landholders, the earl had gone to Dublin to seek a dispensation against having it taken. He was apprehended there on suspicion of being a Catholic Confederate."

"He was Irish?"

"No, he was English, but he'd taken an Irish to wife."

"And this constituted his support of the Catholic Confederacy?"

Mara did not realize the rising of her own voice until Hadrian looked at her oddly.

"Excuse me, my lord. I do not know much about the war, only little bits I hear then and now. My father does not believe a woman's mind can comprehend such things. He says all a woman's mind can understand is needlepoint patterns and sweetmeat recipes, but I find the aspects of war quite fascinating."

Hadrian chuckled. "Perhaps you should be working for your godfather." His smile faded just as quickly as it came. "However, I am not of the same opinion as your father. I believe a woman's mind can understand such things quite well." He paused, adding under his breath, "As well as a great many other things."

"What was that, my lord?"

"Nothing. As I was saying, apparently the old earl had four children; three sons and a daughter. The two older sons joined the Irish Army early on in the war and they were responsible for a great many lost English lives before they were killed in the battle of Drogheda."

"And the other son?"

"He was nineteen at the time, I believe. He hadn't left to join the Irish cause like his brothers. From all accounts, it seems, he left shortly after the estate was seized and joined a band of Tories marauding through the Irish countryside robbing only English landowners. It is my understanding that he was apprehended and hanged not three weeks ago in Galway."

A chill came to Mara at these words. So Owen was dead. She tried to subdue her natural reaction at hearing of her brother's tragic demise. "And the daughter, my lord?"

"She was the youngest of the children; eighteen at the time, I believe. Like many others, the women were left alone at the Irish estates and when the soldiers came, the mother shown in the portrait there refused to give Kulhaven over. She held them off for nearly a year, fighting valiantly and, I am told, strategic as any general, but in the end, the struggle was won by the New Model soldiers."

"And . . ."

Hadrian looked at her levelly. "I think I'd better not continue, Miss Wentworth."

"Why? Did she escape? What of her daughter? Please, my lord, if I am to be mistress of Kulhaven, I really should like to know everything that has happened here."

"I will only say that the soldiers did not take kindly to a woman standing up to them so well. They were a crude lot, the worst of the rabble, hungry for revenge against the Irish. Any Irish. They punished her for her defiance as only men of that sort know how. It is said she was gunned down before they got to her. One can only mercifully hope she died from the gunshot rather than from what they all did to her afterward."

Mara closed her eyes against the horror of his words.

"I apologize if I have offended you." Hadrian's voice had softened.

"No, it is all right. And the daughter, my lord? What became of the daughter?"

Hadrian twirled the brandy snifter between his fingers, not looking at her. "Her fate remains a mystery. No one can say for certain what became of her for she has since never been seen. As she has not surfaced, I can only assume the same misfortune befell her as did her mother."

Mara looked over to him. He was now staring at her mother's portrait and his eyes had taken on a distant look, the sort of faraway look that told her he was somewhere else in his thoughts. His mouth was turned down in a frown. What could he be thinking? If she didn't know better, she might actually believe he was troubled by the events of the past. But how could he be troubled when he was one of the people responsible himself?

"But that is to be expected with war," he said, looking away from the portrait of her mother. "Unfortunately some of the innocent are caught in the cross fire and lost as well. It is a consequence that is unavoidable, I'm afraid."

"Now," he said, setting his brandy aside. He stood and held his hand out to her. "Since I have turned the mood of the evening entirely to the morose, might I suggest we adjourn to the dining room for our meal?"

Mara looked up at him. After meeting him and seeing firsthand the type of man he was, she suddenly wondered if she had bitten off more than she could chew with this venture. This man would not be so easily fooled. What would he do when he did learn the truth?

No turning back. The words echoed in her mind, renewing her courage. She must see this through.

Taking a deep breath, Mara took his offered arm and went off with him to supper.

The clock had just struck eleven times when Mara opened the door to her chamber later that night. While Cyma brushed out her hair and braided it into a single plait for the night, Mara told her all she had learned in the past several hours, starting with the details of the scandal of Hadrian's past and ending finally an hour later with the report of Owen's death.

"It is the chance young Owen took in taking to the roads with those outlaw Tories like he did," Cyma said. "Now will you see that you should quit this foolishness and leave this place while you still can?"

"No. I have already told you, Cyma, I will not quit now, not after making it this far. If ever I doubted what I was doing here, I can assure you I am even more determined to succeed in getting Kulhaven back now. Hearing of Owen's death only makes me that much more determined. I am the only one left, Cyma. I am the last of the Despencer clan. If I do not at least try, there will be no hope for Kulhaven."

"I will never understand this connection you have with this pile of rocks."

"Kulhaven is more than a pile of rocks, Cyma. Don't you understand? It is all I have to live for. I promised my mother as she lay dying that I would return. It was all she asked of me. I must do this thing for her."

"And have you found the tapestry yet?" Cyma asked.

Mara hadn't even given thought to that part of her mother's last words. "No, I haven't yet had the opportunity to search for it. I've been too busy just trying to get past actually being here again. I have not seen the tapestry hanging anywhere. I thought to wait until St. Aubyn was away to look further so as to avoid arousing any suspicion. I've a feeling, if the tapestry was found, he has it somewhere in this part of the castle. Everything else he kept that belonged to my family seems to be here. As soon as I can slip away, I'll go to the place where Mother said it would be. If it is gone, I'll start searching from there."

"I would hope it wasn't destroyed or sold."

"I do not think St. Aubyn would have sold it. He seems to know what items have more value and he doesn't seem like a man who would have parted with something so dear."

Cyma clucked her tongue. "What could you possibly know of this man? You've only just met him. He's nothing but a bloody *sasanach* murderer, just as you expected."

Mara shook her head. "He's not at all what I expected, Cyma. Actually just the contrary. I expected him to be older, much older than his two-and-thirty years, and I expected him to be a much harder man."

"What do you mean?"

"Being one of Cromwell's most trusted men, I guess I expected a man like the soldiers who killed my mother. His people did behead their own king. I expected him to be cold, unfeeling, hateful of the Irish, but he does not seem to be. Sometimes, when he would speak of the war, it would almost seem as if he regretted it. He spoke little of his involvement in the fighting, saying only that he had been posted in Dublin before coming to Kulhaven. He did not tell me why he left his post there."

Mara's words drifted off as she remembered something she had seen in Hadrian's eyes when he'd spoken of his time in Dublin, a glimmer of pain so real it had touched her to her heart, but so fleeting, she'd nearly forgotten it. She wondered what had happened to him there.

"Just you don't be forgetting who he truly is, missy." Cyma came around to face her, her eyes dark with warning. "All you've told me is how good this man seems to be, not that he is in alliance with the same man who is responsible for the deaths of your parents and brothers. Yes, you are the only Despencer left. And it is because of him that you are. He thinks he's to marry Cromwell's goddaughter, child. He is a *brúid,* a filthy, lying Englishman just like the lot of them and don't you be forgetting that."

Mara lowered her eyes then, feeling guilty for defending Hadrian against her. Cyma was right. She mustn't let herself forget why she was here. "You needn't worry that I will ever feel anything for this man but loathing."

Cyma said nothing more, just clucked her tongue and gave her a look as she turned away as if to say her words had been less than believable. And who could fault her? Even Mara was not convinced by her own words.

She thought back to earlier that night when Hadrian

had taken her hand in his and had pressed his lips to it. Though simply an innocent and chivalrous gesture, her own reaction had taken her by surprise. Even now, just thinking of the warmth of his mouth on her wrist set her pulsebeat to racing.

"The problem now is how to make him wed you immediately and without waiting for Arabella's mother to arrive. If that were to happen, you would be ruined," Cyma said, breaking into her thoughts.

"Looking like this, he'd have to be stupid as well as blind to want to marry me."

Cyma put her fingers to her chin, staring off in the distance. "The only solution I can see is for his lordship to compromise your innocence in some way, before witnesses, so he'll have no other choice but to do what any other gentleman would do."

"Precisely what I was thinking, but the question is—how?"

Cyma finished braiding Mara's hair, tying it off with a white ribbon and flinging the heavy tail over her shoulder. "That, miss, you may leave to me."

Chapter Seven

Hadrian stood at the window of his bedchamber, wearing his dressing robe cinched at the waist, nothing else, and staring out at the night sky. It was late, the clock hanging on the wall beside him just striking the three o'clock hour, but he found the prospect of sleep eluded him. Not that it mattered now. In two hours he would be rising for the day, his faithful valet Huntington waking him at dawn with a gentle nudge and a basin of hot water to wash and shave his face with. He should be asleep. He should be nestled in that warm and comfortable bed, his mind filled with nothing but pleasant thoughts of red-haired wood fairies swimming naked before him. But, as it was, he wasn't. He was awake, wide awake, and there wasn't a damned thing he could do about it.

For the past three hours, he'd been sitting in the cushioned armchair that sat before the hearth, reading a completely boring text about the mating habits of the fallow deer which had been first brought to Ireland by the Normans for food in the twelfth century. Even that had not been able to coax him into a slumber. He'd tried Mrs. Danbury's chamomile and mint tea, but two pots later he was still standing here, wide awake, his mind racing with a jumble of confused thoughts.

He'd had these bouts of insomnia before, through various stages of his life, sometimes lasting for months on end, and always for a reason. The last time had been after his time in Dublin, after what had happened there. Not since he'd come to Kulhaven had he had this trouble with sleeping. Being a man of habit he always retired at midnight, rising precisely at five without interruption in between. Still, here he stood, wide awake. He wondered at the cause of it, not wanting to admit it was due to his new visitor.

Arabella was, it seemed from first impressions, everything he'd thought she would be. She might have been pretty, passing fair, if one could get past the severe hairstyle and those irritatingly ridiculous spectacles.

And those somber clothes. They were truly unbecoming. He'd always thought women preferred to dress in bright colors with feminine lace and ribbons and bows, but not Arabella, it seemed. Not that any of it mattered. Had she been big as a house with a hairy upper lip, he still would have asked her to wed him.

He had no other choice.

With her chin-high gowns, she would, most probably, shudder at the sight of a man's naked body. His naked body. None of the women he'd been with in his life had ever shown him any sign of distaste. The thought of spending the rest of his days with a wife who suffered his presence in her bed, submitting because all good wives do, made the prospect of his wedding night less than desirable. He wondered if she would wear that silly little white linen cap to bed. He could picture her so very clearly in his mind sitting on the bed, the covers clutched to her quivering chin as he, the beast, the naked beast, came to claim his husbandly rights.

Oh, what a way to kill a man's desire. If ever there was an anaphrodisiac he was obviously about to wed it.

He should earn a knighthood for what he was about to do. He'd heard of men sacrificing their lives for the good of their king and country and wondered if his marriage to Miss Arabella Wentworth would qualify. He heard a noise then and turned just as his valet came shuffling into the room, rubbing his eyes.

"My lord, you are awake."

"Yes, it would seem so, Huntington."

This man who had the look and demeanor of an owl, wise beyond his forty-six years, had been with Hadrian since the day he'd inherited the earldom at fifteen. He'd traveled with him to every post and Hadrian had come to be dependent on him both for his incomparable service and his unfailing advice, which he would now ask for again.

"Shall I fetch you some brandy, my lord?"

Hadrian smiled. "No, Huntington, I think I will stay up for the duration of the day now, and it probably wouldn't do any good anyway."

"The insomnia again, my lord?"

"Yes. I thought it passed me this time, Huntington. It's been nearly a year now since . . ."

"Wedding jitters, is it, my lord?"

Huntington always had a most eloquent way of putting things, and of changing the subject at precisely the right moment. "You've seen Miss Wentworth, I presume?"

"Yes, my lord."

"And, what is your opinion of her?"

Huntington took a moment before responding. "It appears as if she will do quite well at managing the household affairs, my lord. She seems well suited to it."

If ever there was someone who could find something of value in everyone, it was Huntington as well. "Is that your judicious way of saying that I need not worry Miss Wentworth will take a lover like my mother did?"

Huntington nodded. "Quite right, my lord."

"I always said if I ever married, I'd take a wife who would not draw attention with her beauty like my mother did. Beauty breeds trouble, is that not right, Huntington?"

"Quite right, my lord."

"The homelier, the better."

"Aye, my lord. You have made a good choice."

Hadrian turned, looking out the window again, wondering how he ever could have believed such an utterly foolish thing.

Mara woke late the following morning after a long night filled with tossing about on a huge and strange bed. Despite the feathered mattress and lilac-perfumed pillows, her head pounded and she tried to forget that what little sleep she'd stolen had been plagued by images of a man with golden brown eyes that seemed to see straight through her.

Cyma had finally left her the night before after two full hours spent trying to convince her that Mara still believed St. Aubyn was the worst sort of beast alive. After she'd gone, Mara had spent the remainder of the night chastising herself for ever thinking differently. St. Aubyn was a beast whose unfortunate upbringing was no excuse for his support of the Protectorate, or the fact that he now dwelt in a stolen house. He was her enemy, and she could never allow herself to forget that.

As she made her way down the stairs to breakfast, she was greeted at the bottom floor by the steward, Peter Shipley, who informed her that Lord St. Aubyn had left for the day before dawn to ride about the grounds of the estate. He'd asked Shipley to extend his apologies, leaving his permission for "Arabella" to walk freely about the castle and the surrounding area nearby in order to acquaint herself with her new home.

Permission. Mara's ill mood took a decided turn for the worst at his eloquent choice of words. She ripped at the piece of toasted bread she'd just spread with a liberal amount of Mrs. Danbury's strawberry conserve, wishing she could tell his high and mighty lordship exactly what she thought of his generosity. She had spent the majority of her life exploring every nook of this ancient castle, every tree that grew in the forest surrounding it, and never with the requirement of anyone's permission.

Especially that of the very person who had stolen it from her family.

The realization that she no longer had the freedoms of her childhood only renewed her determination to see her plan through. She didn't know why she'd even begun to think that St. Aubyn might regret what had been done to the Irish people and to her family. She must have been a fool. A consummate idiot. Here he sat, living on stolen land, admiring stolen paintings that had been in her family for generations, while the people who had worked the soil and made Kulhaven the grand estate it was were left to lying in ditches and drowning in their own blood.

She took a bite of her breakfast toast, chewing reflectively and not even tasting the delicious conserve Mrs. Danbury had pressed upon her so earnestly. This was her home. Her mother and her father should be sitting at breakfast this moment, drinking elder flower tea and debating whether Kulhaven wool would fetch a fair price at market that year. They should be discussing the weaving of that wool and the harvesting of the crops that filled the Kulhaven fields to come later that fall. They should not be buried in separate and unmarked graves with a hundred miles standing between them.

And her brothers, Colin, and Niall, and even Owen should be the ones riding about the estate and visiting with the villagers. Certainly not some Englishman who'd profited from the work of others—and the stolen work of others at that.

She would see this plan through. She would have Kulhaven back and she would walk about the grounds however and whenever she pleased. Even if it was the last thing she ever did.

Mara tossed the crisp white napkin atop her breakfast plate, a fine china decorated with the St. Aubyn seal, a lion and a dove facing each other on opposite sides of a shield with branches from an olive tree intertwined beneath them. She rose, smoothing down the folds of yet another of Arabella's somber gowns, a charcoal brown with a maroon quilted underskirt, its only ornamentation the white lace that decorated the prim and plain white falling band around her shoulders.

How she longed for a gown of emerald green satin with lace of gold and an underskirt of the softest, sky blue silk. She wanted her hair free and loose and hanging about her shoulders and *red*, the fiery red of her Irish heritage, not this dreadful mourning black hidden beneath this prim little white cap, secured at her nape, and pulled back so severely it made her temples throb.

But until she no longer had to play the part of Arabella, until she no longer assumed the guise of the proper Puritan miss, she would dress and behave with the modesty and empty-brained obedience required—even if it killed her.

Her mood now completely at its worst, Mara was grateful for St. Aubyn's absence. Had he been there, standing before her in all his arrogant form, she'd have had a difficult time of it trying to suppress her churning emotions. She needed to get away, to get back to something she knew, something familiar. Not this alien version of Kulhaven with its very *English* styling and decor. She needed to see the real Kulhaven, drafty walls and all, the Kulhaven she'd come all this way to fight for.

She strode purposefully through the grand entrance hall with its polished oak paneled walls gleaming in the candlelight, aware of the eyes of the servants looking on. She took her time to pause at the carved walnut sideboard to inspect a gilt candlestick set there. Running a curious hand along the frazzled edge of an aging and dust-ridden hanging tapestry, one most probably stolen from some other unfortunate family, she made a quick turn down the darkened hallway leading toward the eastern wing and the older portion of Kulhaven.

The newer portion which had been added on after Kulhaven had been confiscated from the Despencers was the part of the castle which comprised the current living quarters. It was more a manor house than a castle with walls of red brick and white lime and countless chimneys dotting its double-pitched roof. There were larger chambers here with tall diamond-paned glass windows that allowed in the golden sunlight. At the time that the older portion had been built, centuries earlier when the great castles would often fall under attack, windows would have been a weakness to the enemy. The only windows Mara could recall in the Kulhaven of her youth were set high on the walls, reaching nearly to the ceiling, and they were small and too narrow to give off much light.

Mara stopped when she reached the thick oaken door leading to the older part of the castle, the true Kulhaven of her childhood. Above it, carved into the stone wall was the word "*salvete,*" the Latin word for welcome. Always known for his hospitality, the knight Rupert de Kaleven, who had built Kulhaven, had wanted everyone who came to know they were welcome, whatever their reason for being there. She smiled, knowing that on the other side of the door was the Latin word for farewell, "*valete.*"

Mara ran a hand over the door, tracing each line, each crevice along the rough wood. The door was scarred from ages past, the stone surrounding it so much darker and coarser than the smooth lime of the newer Kulhaven. She could still see the chinks left in the thick wood showing her brothers' heights on each of their birthdays.

She remembered asking her father when she was seven years old why her growth was not charted on the door as well. Her father had taken the great sword that had hung on the wall in his study and had cut a chink in the fine carved oak mantelpiece there, saying that she should have her own special place.

This door was the gateway to her childhood, she thought to herself, the door that had withstood centuries of gunfire and battering rams.

This was the door to her life.

Mara wrapped her hand slowly around the heavy iron latch even though she knew it would be locked. She was surprised when it lifted quite easily. She pushed at the door but it stuck from years of disuse and she had to lean her shoulder full upon it to push it inward. With some effort, it finally burst open, scraping along the jagged stone floor and echoing through the emptiness beyond.

A litter of forgotten autumn leaves swirled about the threshold inside the door. She knew the other side of that door contained memories, memories of happiness and a carefree childhood.

But it also held the memories of fear and helplessness and death.

She wondered if she could face them even as she took a hesitant step forward, pushing away a low-hanging cobweb as she walked through the doorway.

The sight on the other side did not bring back the horror of what had happened there before. Instead it gave her a feeling of belonging, a warm and pleasant sense of finally being home.

This vast and imposing room, the very core of the castle, had been the great chamber where meals had been taken and where the people had gathered for news or entertainment when a traveling troupe would happen by to perform. A bright shaft of sunlight streamed down through the louvered opening in the ceiling that rose two stories above, where smoke had escaped from the great fire that had burned in the huge center hearth back in the days of the knight Rupert de Kaleven. The great marble-framed fireplace that stood against the far wall had been added not fifty years earlier by her mother's people, throwing the central hearth of the olden days into obsolescence.

High above her head, strewn with cobwebs and dust, hung the huge iron chandelier, suspended from a thick rope on a pulley system that tied to a ring by the door and that had been in working order since the castle had been built. The gray stone walls were bare save the markings left by the Flemish arras and colored cloths that had once graced them to keep out the winter's draft. The only furnishing that remained in the oversized room was a small three-legged stool perched in the corner where the Kulhaven page had watched out a peephole for sign of anyone coming. A gilded mirror, shattered with but a shard left at its corner, clung drunkenly to the wall beside her.

As she looked about this great and empty room, a room that held so many memories, Mara was seized by a feeling of melancholy so fierce she began to shake with it. To turn back time, to regain the happy days of her youth before the war had come to Ireland, to be a part of a family again. If she closed her eyes, she could clearly see it as it had once been, so grand, so beautiful. The huge polished table standing at its place beside the fire. Music coming from the minstrels playing at their place on the dias in the far corner. Laughter echoing through the rafters. Flames cracking in the hearth. Richly colored tapestries hanging on the walls . . .

Tapestries.

Mara was suddenly reminded of her purpose in coming there, to see if the one Despencer heirloom that mattered above all else had survived.

She had seen the Kulhaven Tapestry only once as a child, when her mother had brought it to her while she sat in the parlor complaining about having to practice her embroidery on a cushion her mother was making. The tapestry was small, about the size of a pillow, but it was more beautiful than the finest painting hanging in the Palace of St. James before the Protectorate had stripped it bare. Her mother had told her that the tapestry had been woven hundreds of years earlier by a young and beautiful maiden named Gráinne who was the daughter of Rupert de Kaleven. She'd had hair red as fire, the legacy of the Kulhaven women, and the tapestry had been handed down through the generations to each succeeding Kulhaven lady since.

It was a magnificent creation, strung with the thinnest and finest spun threads of gold and silver, depicting the coming marriage of the maid and her warrior lover. The glorious castle of Kulhaven stood in the background with rays of golden light shooting out from behind its regal walls. When the firelight would hit the tapestry just right, the threads would sparkle and shine and one would swear the image had come to life.

Legend had it the warrior had been killed in battle days before the two lovers were to wed. Upon hearing of her knight's tragic demise, the maiden Gráinne had thrown herself from the top of the Bloody Tower, dashing her head on the rocks below. It was said a white flower spotted with red had sprouted from the rocks where she had landed, a flower known from then on as

Gráinne's Blood, and that grew in no other place in Ireland.

Mara could still remember as a child staring down from the top of the tower battlements at the craggy rocks below and feeling sadness at the beautiful maiden's fate. Of all the stories handed down of misfortune related to that tower, this maiden's was the only one that Mara truly believed. The tapestry that had been woven by her fair hands was all that was left of the maiden's short existence.

Mara now stood before the opening to the eastern hallway, the hallway that led to the family's bedchambers. Its great black mouth looked ready to swallow her whole. The sconces on the walls were bare, so she took the small candle stick she'd brought and holding it aloft at a slant to allow the tallow to drip off, took her skirts in hand and started forward.

Her footsteps echoed softly on the stone floor, her skirts rustling with each step she took. Somewhere in the darkness, she heard the sound of a small creature scampering away from her candle's light. The doors lining the corridor were closed and as she passed each one, the light from the great chamber behind her grew dimmer, the darkness around her starting to close in. But she wasn't afraid. How could she be? This was her home, where she belonged more than anywhere else on this earth.

Mara stopped at the end of the hallway and her heart began to beat faster. Before her stood another closed door, a door she had entered so many times before. She lifted the heavy and rusted latch. The door swung easily open.

Inside, the window above her head was broken, the

draperies, once a fine royal blue velvet were now tattered and faded to a grayish lilac. A songbird perched on the sill chirped happily to her, and outside she could see the leaves of the tall oaks fluttering softly in the summer breeze. Mara closed her eyes against the destruction that lay before her and tried to picture this once happy place as it had been.

"Cyma, get Mara to the passageway! Go to the village! I'll be following right behind!"

Her mother's voice was nearly drowned out by the thunderous pounding of the mortar on the great oaken doors of the lower ward and the voices raised in panic throughout every chamber within. Maids and footmen were running about trying to hide what they could of the Despencer plate and silver, tossing ornately carved candlesticks down the privy hole in hopes to keep them from falling into the marauding Roundheads' hands. Mara caught a glimpse of her mother's deep blue velvet skirts as Cyma pushed her through the door.

"Come, missy, you heard your máthair. *To the passageway with you to hide before those wretched Roundheads get inside!"*

"But, Cyma, we cannot leave Mother."

"You heard what she said. She'll be coming right behind us."

They were in the great chamber now, with the castle's inhabitants rushing about in a panic around them. No one noticed them in all the commotion. Cyma lifted the hidden lever beneath the hearth mantel and urged Mara forward into the darkness beyond the secret door hidden behind the fireplace. Just then there came a loud crashing sound followed by screams and shouts from outside.

"Bloody Roundheads must have broken through the

lower ward. We best hurry. It won't be long before they make it through to here and are tramping their muddy feet all over your máthair's *fine Turkey carpet." Cyma tugged on Mara's arm. "Come now, missy, we've got to close this door before they get here."*

"But, Mother—"

"Your máthair *will find a way. She always has."*

"No, I cannot leave her."

Mara tore away and raced to the stairs leading up to the top of the Bloody Tower. She lifted her skirts to her knees and took the steps two at a time. When she reached the top, she flung open the door and raced out onto the battlement. She spotted her mother standing with her father's musket aimed down below. She was shouting something, refusing to surrender to the soldiers. Suddenly she jerked back, dropping the musket as she fell to the floor.

"Mother!"

Mara started out of her thoughts then, just as she always did at that same point, when this memory invaded her dreams. She was still standing in her mother's chamber. She didn't know how long she'd been standing there, but her heart was pounding and tears were running down her face in thick streams.

She wiped her eyes, pushing the memory back into the far recesses of her mind and started back to her reason for coming there.

The chamber was barely a shadow of what it had once been. Across the room, one of the doors to the high ebony wardrobe stood ajar, hanging crookedly off its hinges. Its contents were gone except for a small forgotten hair riband trailing carelessly from the inside. Mara took the riband and smoothed back its frayed ends before absently tucking it inside her dress pocket.

She leaned against the high bedpost of the massive tester bed, wrapping her hand around the thick spirally twisted wood. Her mother's chamber had once smelled of lemon oil and roses, the furnishings gleaming from a thorough polishing. Now the room only smelled of mildew and decay. And death.

The floor, always so clean, was now littered at the corners with dirt and dried leaves. She looked over each wall, each stone, at the porcelain wash bowl lying shattered on the floor, at her mother's small leather-bound missal of prayers, its pages torn out and scattered. The charred remnants of the fire which had kept her mother warm that last night still lay in the blackened pile inside the huge stone hearth. Mara walked over to it and ran her hand along the cold stone mantelpiece, hearing her mother's words in her mind.

Start at the corner and move three stones right. . . .

Mara ran her fingers over the rough pitted surface. Her hand stopped on the third stone.

Two stones up and two across more . . .

She traced her fingers upward.

When you've reached the stone you seek . . .

She stopped on the second stone.

Turn it left to open the door.

She turned the stone, releasing it as the two stones beside it slid back to reveal a small shelf hidden inside the hearth stone.

Chapter Eight

Mara reached carefully inside the hidden vault, feeling about in the emptiness. Against the far wall, she felt something, something small and square with the surface of smooth, polished wood. Slowly she removed it.

Her heart was pounding as she took a seat on a small, crooked stool and set the carved box upon her lap. It was made of the wood from a tree that had supposedly been blessed by fairies, or so her mother had said, and was so dark, it looked nearly black. Mara ran her fingers across the smooth cover, wiping away the thick layer of dust that had settled atop it.

Hidden beneath its protective cover was an intricately carved inscription. Two letters. An "E" and a "C," intertwined and surrounded by a wreath of roses, meant to symbolize the joining of her parents, Edana and Charles, in marriage. Her father had said he'd bought the box from an old wise woman and he had given his wife this box on their wedding day. Only her mother's most prized possessions were kept inside of it. Letters filled with promises of undying love that her father had written to her mother long before they'd ever wed. A lock of baby-fine dark hair from her oldest brother Colin, tied off with a blue silk ribbon. A fragile rosebud, dried and brittle, its once brilliant red petals having long since turned black, given to her mother by her father the first time they'd danced.

And, the Kulhaven Tapestry.

All these things had been stowed in the treasure box, to be handed down to Mara for her to fill with her own mementos to give to her daughter one day. It was to be a tradition started by her mother, like the passing of the Kulhaven Tapestry, to each succeeding Kulhaven lady for the next two hundred years.

Mara carefully turned the tarnished brass closure on the box to release its lid. Inside would lay the only evidence remaining of her family, the last vestiges of proof of their existence. Inside she would find what Cromwell and his army could never take from her, small mementos, happy memories of what once had been.

Slowly she lifted the lid.

Her heart sank to the pit of her stomach.

The box was empty inside.

The memories, the final treasured keepsakes that were to be handed down to her from her mother were gone. The treasures most people would think inconsequential but to her were more valuable than any of the fine paintings or silver candlesticks, everything was gone.

As was the Kulhaven Tapestry.

Failure settled deep in Mara's soul as she stared at the empty insides of her mother's treasure box, knowing the tapestry, everything was gone. How had they found the box? Who had found it? The vault was completely undetectable. It had been fashioned that way over two hundred years earlier so no one would ever discover it. No one could have known about its existence, unless the soldiers had happened upon it by chance. But if they had, if, in their blood-thirsty looting spree, they'd found the secret stone which revealed the hidden vault, why then had the box been left behind? It just didn't make any sense.

Mara suddenly heard a sound behind her, like a footstep scraping along the stone floor in the corridor outside. She slammed the lid to the treasure box closed and shoved it back inside its hidden vault, twisting the secret stone to conceal it once again. She waited, standing very still, and listening for any sound beyond the door.

"Hello? Is someone there?"

Silence.

Mara ran to the door and looked out into the hallway. It was dark as a moonless night, the only sound a faint breeze whistling through an obscure crack somewhere in the blackness above her head. But someone had been there. She was certain of it. She had heard the footstep. Someone had been standing there and had watched her.

Fearing that St. Aubyn had perhaps returned early, Mara quickly left her mother's bedchamber and hurried down the corridor, pulling the great oaken door between the older and newer sections of Kulhaven tightly closed behind her. There was no one about as she continued on through the entrance hall and to the stairs and she kept on going, taking a glimpse behind her at every turn. She did not stop until she had reached her chamber door.

"*Och,* missy," Cyma said when she'd shut the door

behind herself, "you've been gone for hours and no one knew to where. With St. Aubyn gone as well, I feared he may have learned the truth and had taken you away. I've been worried near to sickness about you."

It took Mara a moment to catch her breath. "It is all right, Cyma. I was not with St. Aubyn. He left early this morning and plans to be gone all day. I went to my mother's bedchamber in the older part of Kulhaven to see if the tapestry was still there."

"Did you find it? Was the tapestry still where your *máthair* said 'twould be?"

"No. It is gone, Cyma. I don't understand how someone could have discovered it, but obviously someone did. It's just gone."

Cyma's mouth fell open. "Gone? No, it cannot be. How could the soldiers have ever found it hidden away like it was?"

Mara strode across the room, rubbing her hands together. "I don't know. I cannot believe the soldiers did find it. The box my mother said it would be in, her treasure box, was still there, empty, but there. All her mementos were gone as well. But the box remained. It is quite odd. If the soldiers had indeed taken the tapestry from it, and the other items, why then would they have left the box? It just doesn't make any sense." Before Cyma could answer, Mara went on. "No, the soldiers did not find the tapestry. It had to be someone else. Someone who knew about the secret vault. But who could it have been?"

"Do you think it was Lord St. Aubyn?"

Mara stopped pacing, staring at the floor, her brow creased. "I do not know. He could have, I suppose, but it doesn't seem likely. If he did find the tapestry, he must have it here somewhere. He has kept the most valuable things from my family. He never would have sold that. He couldn't have. It is more precious than one thousand gold pieces. Mother told me she had folded it carefully and had placed it in a velvet pouch of sorts inside the treasure box. No, it must be here at Kulhaven somewhere. St. Aubyn must have hidden it. But where?"

She paused a moment to think. "Perhaps it is time I took his lordship up on his kind offer to explore the castle at my leisure. If he has the tapestry, it will be here somewhere, and if it is, I will find it."

Mara spent the remainder of the day combing through the rooms in the western wing in search of the Kulhaven Tapestry, but to no avail. All day, though, while she had searched through every drawer and under every bed, she'd had the niggling sense of being watched, much like she'd had when she'd been in her mother's bedchamber. It felt as if someone or something was following her as she went through every room, but each time she turned to look behind her, there would be nothing there but emptiness and air. In the end, she tried to put it off as a case of nerves, thinking she must have been mistaken.

Mara was relieved to learn later that evening, as she started getting herself ready to go down to supper, that the footstep she'd heard in the corridor outside her mother's chamber had not been St. Aubyn's after all. He did not return from his outing until well after dusk, having spent the entire day riding about the grounds and visiting with the landowner at a neighboring estate.

This thought, while easing her anxiety, also gave her cause to wonder. Why, after months of planning and waiting to meet his future bride, would this man avoid spending any more than the least amount of time with her? She had heard it reported that it had been St. Aubyn who had sought the engagement, St. Aubyn who had pursued it with a purpose. Owen had St. Aubyn's letters to Arabella intercepted and sent to Mara so she would know everything she needed when she came to Kulhaven.

Filled with flowery prose about his eagerness to see her lovely face, he'd professed to ache to hold Arabella in his arms, to have his dreams filled with visions of her beauty, to spend the rest of his days in her sweet company.

And now that "Arabella" was at Kulhaven, now that the months of waiting were over, he seemed as receptive to her as he would be to the plague.

Like the disappearance of the tapestry, it didn't make any sense. Did he find her that unsightly that he could not even bear to be in her presence? And if that was true, how would she ever entice him to compromise her innocence, thereby necessitating their immediate marriage?

More importantly, she wondered, if it hadn't been St. Aubyn in that corridor, then who had it been?

Mara's head ached from the score of unanswered questions running rampant through her puzzled mind. As she made her way down to join St. Aubyn for supper, she decided the easiest thing to do would be to tackle one problem at a time.

The first and most immediate was the compromising of her own virtue and their marriage soon after. She had to secure her place at Kulhaven and they certainly couldn't wait for Arabella's mother to arrive. She had to act quickly.

Mara started for the dining room, determined to succeed in her endeavor and ready for their second encounter in as many days. She hesitated just outside at the sound of voices coming from the other side of the doorway.

"A red-haired fairy swimming in your lough? Next you'll be telling me all about a visit you received from the 'little people.' Come, Hadrian, surely you've been in the country too long. Is this what happens to a man's mind once he passses the age of thirty-two? At least I've relatively six years of logic left to me. I think you are finally beginning to lose your mind. Perhaps it is time you left this remote monstrosity of a castle and returned to civilization in London."

Deep and rich in timbre, the man's voice was unknown to Mara. Silently she listened on.

"Civilization? London? Where I am known as the Bastard Earl of St. Aubyn? I think I'd be better off staying here at Kulhaven, fairies and all. I know it sounds as if I am completely off the hooks, but I tell you, Rolfe, I saw her. Plain as a pikestaff and in clear daylight, swimming gloriously naked in that lough. She was beautiful. My uncle wrote of her, you know, and the people of this castle and the village truly believe in her existence. This Flaming Lady is a legend here at Kulhaven."

"And, now you, too, are being haunted by this spirit woman. Well, if you see any other naked spirit women floating about, send one to my chamber tonight. I've long been in need of a good toss and one ghost is as good as another."

Hadrian's voice grew quieter. "I tell you, Rolfe, it was more than passing strange. One moment, she appears from the water in all her naked splendor, and the next she's gone. Vanished. Without a trace. No one here at the castle or in the village comes close to her description. Believe me, I spent all day looking for this lovely creature. She truly was the most striking woman I've ever beheld."

Mara could not believe what she was hearing. He had seen her! He'd seen her swimming in the lough, completely naked and now, here she was, trying to find a way to have him compromise her innocence. The irony of the situation could nearly be amusing, if only for the fact that she'd almost been found out.

What would St. Aubyn have done had she not run off when she had? All the planning and arranging would have been for nothing and she'd most probably be rotting in a prison cell this moment. Cyma would surely split her seams if she knew of this.

After the initial shock had subsided, Mara remembered something St. Aubyn had said. It was not her he believed he had seen in the lough. He was convinced he had seen a ghost, a red-haired spirit called The Flaming Lady, her mother's spirit come to haunt him from beyond the grave. He had spent all day searching for her, or at least someone who looked like her. His uncle, James, had even claimed to have seen her.

As long as St. Aubyn continued to believe in the Flaming Lady's existence, her secret would be safe. He knew of her mother's fate. There was no way she could have survived the soldier's onslaught. And his own uncle had written of her, claiming she haunted him. Having found no one who could be her, Hadrian truly believed he'd seen a vision and Mara planned to do everything within her power to keep him thinking that way.

"Good evening, gentlemen," she said, stepping on through into the room.

Having now perfected the talent of looking over the rim of her spectacles, Mara could see the other man quite clearly. He was tall, younger, quite handsome, though not as handsome as St. Aubyn, and rather gallant-looking, standing with St. Aubyn at the hearth, and holding a glass of wine in his hand.

"Good evening, Arabella, you are looking lovely this evening. May I present Rolfe Brodigan, Viscount Blackwood. Rolfe, this is my betrothed, Miss Arabella Wentworth."

Rolfe stepped forward and took her hand, brushing it with his lips. He smiled as he looked up into her bespectacled eyes. "A pleasure, Miss Wentworth. Hadrian," he said, turning to St. Aubyn, "you certainly weren't embellishing when you said she was lovely. She truly is quite a striking creature."

Mara bowed her head as she thought Arabella would do and moved to her place at St. Aubyn's side. The man was obviously blind as well as a liar. How could any sane man find her striking? Her gown was plain and brown and utterly drab, her hair was braided tightly and stuck beneath a hideous white cap, and he was calling her lovely? Perhaps he was the one in need of the spectacles.

While Mara was thankful for not having to be alone with St. Aubyn, this man's presence would present somewhat of an obstacle to the evening's objective of getting him to compromise her innocence.

But Cyma had assured her that she had the situation in hand. Mara would just have to rely on that promise.

Supper was a pleasant affair, prepared by the castle's cook, a very large and very robust woman named Mrs. Philpot who'd welcomed "Arabella" to Kulhaven with a tight hug to her rather large breast, squeezing the very breath from her. The roast pheasant was delicious, the baby potatoes in a pungent herb sauce tender, and through it all, there was ceaseless conversation from Lord Blackwood.

He was the type of man, Mara thought as she watched him over the top of her lenses, most mothers would warn their daughters about, with hair blacker than sin and an easy, winning smile that most certainly must have turned quite a few female heads in the past.

Like St. Aubyn, his face was dark, swarthy one might call it, from many hours spent in the sun, but he lacked something when compared to his host, what exactly Mara could not quite pinpoint. Still, his manner was light and carefree and he filled the conversation with anecdotes of his travels and had circumstances been different, had they not been on opposite sides of the war, Mara believed she would have really liked him.

Lord Blackwood had been to the new Colonies, across the vast ocean, to a place he called Virginia. He spoke of the settlers forging a new life there, describing in vivid detail the untamed wildness of the place and the savage beauty of a river called the James. Through it all, Mara ate quietly, sipping her wine as she watched the two friends together. It was obvious theirs was a close and long-time relationship, for they were completely at ease with one another, the dialogue flowing easily between them.

She noticed that while Rolfe's grin came easily, St. Aubyn rarely smiled, almost as if he feared it some sort of weakness. But there was nothing weak about this man, Mara thought as she stared at his fingers resting lightly on his wineglass. She wondered if those fingers would inflict great pain when he found out who she truly was.

Somehow between the witty remarks and stories of boyhood adventures, Rolfe ate enough to feed a grown stallion, finishing off the half glass of wine remaining in his glass with one solid gulp.

"Enough of boring stories," he said, wiping his mouth with his napkin and sitting back in his chair. He leveled his gaze on Mara. "I hear they offered Cromwell the Crown of England and he turned them down. So tell me, Miss Wentworth, just what does your godfather plan as his next course of action?"

"Rolfe," St. Aubyn interrupted before Mara could respond, for which she was vastly grateful, since she knew not what to say, "Arabella knows nothing of her godfather's plans. Military or otherwise."

St. Aubyn's voice had deepened, revealing to Mara something else hidden behind the words, something she wasn't privy to.

"Forgive me, Miss Wentworth," Rolfe stated after staring at St. Aubyn a silent moment. He bowed his head contritely. "It seems I have overstepped my bounds. Of course, being a genteel young lady, you would know nothing of your godfather's military strategies. I apologize for the indiscretion."

Mara took a small sip of her claret, swallowing slowly before responding. "It is all right, Lord Blackwood. Please, let us just forget it."

He smiled, showing white and even teeth. "Agreed, if you will please quit with the formalities. I would that you would call me Rolfe. You are going to be the wife of my closest friend."

"Rolfe it is, and, please, feel free to call me Arabella." She looked up as the tall double doors of the dining room opened and Cyma slipped inside, motioning to her. Mara stood. "Now, if you gentlemen would excuse me, it seems my maid requires my attention."

Hadrian stood from his chair. "Of course, Arabella. Rolfe and I will finish our conversation over port while you see to your maid. If you would, I would like for you to favor us with your company in the parlor afterward for a game of l'ombre. If you play, that is."

Mara met his eyes. She was a bit surprised at his request, knowing the Puritan disapproval of gaming and cards. She wondered if this was some sort of test on his part. Obviously, if he played, he did not disapprove of it himself, so she smiled and said simply, "As you wish, my lord."

Cyma followed Mara from the room, closing the doors behind them. "I've prepared the potion for you."

"Potion?" Mara glanced quickly about, praying there were no servants around to hear them. "What are you talking about?" she asked in a hushed voice.

"The potion you must give his lordship St. Aubyn in order for him to compromise your innocence."

"You want me to give him a potion? We cannot do that tonight, Cyma. Rolfe"—she hesitated—"Lord Blackwood is here."

"But, you must give it to him tonight. The potion will lose its potency after twenty-four hours. I will not be able to prepare another for a while. The vervain is a very difficult herb to come by and it could take days, even weeks to locate another plant. You've nothing to worry over with St. Aubyn's friend. I've prepared a potion for him as well and I sprinkled his pillows with fresh buds from the hop plant so he'll sleep like a babe at his mother's breast till sunrise."

"What about the servants? What if someone notices something is strange?"

"His lordship's already dismissed the staff for the evening. Even his valet, that nosy Huntington. Tonight is the perfect opportunity. We haven't the time to waste. We must act quickly to get you married to his lordship before he begins to wonder why Arabella's mother is not coming. This may be the only night we can accomplish the task, however distasteful as I know it must be for you."

She handed Mara a tray bearing two glasses. "Gentlemen always take brandy after supping. The glass on the right is for St. Aubyn. The other is for Lord Blackwood. Do not confuse them for if you do, the results will be disastrous. Go now and when you are certain they've drunk it all down, return to your chamber. We've much work to do with very little time if we are to succeed with this tonight."

She patted Mara's hand, adding, "If all goes well, your wedding vows will be said by week's end."

Chapter Nine

Mara stopped before the closed door and slowly twisted the handle to St. Aubyn's bedchamber. It clicked once, seeming overloud in the still silence of the western wing. The single flame atop the candle she held flickered as she pushed the door inward with painstaking slowness. There was no movement, no sound from within, the only light coming from a slow burning fire in the hearth across the room. Its dying flames cast a strange sort of orange glow about the darkly paneled walls, sending shadows moving across the richly woven Flanders carpet and polished floorboards underneath.

Mara took a single step inside and pulled the door quietly behind her. Her hands were shaking. She snuffed out the candle before setting it upon a table beside her and moved further into the room.

The furnishings, quite different from the delicate rosewood and mahogany that filled her chamber, were made of thick carved walnut, dark, large, and solidly proportioned to their master. Everything about the room seemed fashioned on a grander scale, from the marble-framed hearth that could easily fit seven men standing, to the cushioned armchair standing before it whose arms were carved in the shape of lions' heads.

As she moved carefully across the room, she noticed St. Aubyn's boots lying beneath a bench, his shirt and breeches in a pile beside them. A glass of brandy sat on a small table by the washstand, half filled. Across the room, in a shadowed corner on a raised dias stood the high tester bed where he lay sleeping. Mara moved toward it, her bare feet making no sound.

The bed's thick posters were carved with the same lion's head design that decorated the hearth chair, the clawed feet fashioned to appear as the beast's great paws. Royal blue-and-gold draperies hung open about it, their brocade design shimmering richly in the glowing firelight. She could hear his heavy breathing coming from the bed, slow and even in sleep. She stopped when she reached the foot of the bed and looked down at him.

He was lying on his back, one arm flung outward across the pillow beside him. He was deeply asleep, and it seemed his dreams were unpleasant for his face looked quiet angry in the low firelight. His chest was bare with thick, dark hair patterned across the well-defined muscles, trailing downward to a line at his flat belly and disappearing beneath the cover of the sheet. The sheet was tangled about his long legs and she could clearly see the bare outline of his muscled hip, his skin dark against the whiteness of the sheet.

He was naked.

That thought alone sent Mara's heart to pounding. The time had come, she thought to herself. She knew what she had to do. She stepped closer, hesitating at the side of the bed and stared down at his face in the firelight.

His angry scowl had relaxed, giving him a gentler and

peaceful appearance. His hair looked darker out of the sunlight and she spotted a slight dimple in his chin and wondered why she'd never noticed it before. Before she even realized what she was doing, she reached out to brush back a stray lock of hair that had fallen across his forehead.

She nearly gasped when he opened his eyes and his fingers closed around her wrist.

Mara didn't move, she couldn't move, and her heart was pounding fiercely. She didn't know what to do. She stood still as the stone statues of the lions that guarded the entrance to Kulhaven, afraid to so much as blink an eye. St. Aubyn did not speak to her, but simply stared up at her, his grip on her wrist tightening. His hand looked like it could easily snap her bones in half. He was supposed to be drugged. Cyma had told her the potion would have dulled his senses, all, except the ones which ruled his desire. But here he was, eyes wide, staring up at her as if he was completely aware of her being there.

Still she didn't struggle or try to pull away. Something in his eyes, a distant, faraway look, told her he was not truly seeing her. He was seeing someone else, someone in his dreams, perhaps. Slowly she lifted her other hand and finished with pushing back the hair on his forehead. His other arm came around her from behind then and circled her waist, drawing her closer to him. He pulled her down to lie across his bare chest, the braid in her hair falling over his shoulder.

Her breasts were crushed against him and she could feel the heat of him through the filmy fabric of her nightdress. The closeness was oddly exciting to her. Mara splayed her hands against his shoulders to better brace herself. She could feel the steady beating of his heart, his skin hot against her palm. His hand was cupping her buttocks, gently kneading her there and sending a rush of awareness thundering through her.

She was at once frightened and curious, having never been held in such an intimate fashion. How could she be feeling this way, she asked herself. This man was the enemy. He and all those like him had been responsible for the deaths of her family, for the end to the life she had known. He was just as responsible for the destruction and robbery of her home. How could she be lying here atop him, allowing him to touch her like this?

No, she told herself, she was not lying in his bed. It was Arabella. She was Arabella. And if she managed to make it through this night, she was going to be his wife.

But somehow she could not see Arabella, the prim little Puritan miss, lying across a naked man's chest and with naught but a flimsy nightdress to cover her.

Mara pulled at her inner resolve. She could do this thing, she told herself with increasing mental volume. She had to do this if she ever thought to realize the dream of having Kulhaven back.

Hesitantly she lowered her head and touched her lips to his. She'd never kissed a man before and she found his mouth warm and soft, not at all unpleasant. She closed her eyes and attempted to relax against him. She did not notice at first when his mouth began to move against hers. Not until his tongue was running against her lower lip did she realize he wanted her.

Mara shifted her position, slightly parting her lips and his tongue entered her mouth as his hand came up behind her to cradle her neck. This unknown invasion caused Mara to instinctively pull away, but she forced herself to relax, fearing what would happen if she did anything unsettling. She could taste the brandy on his breath and the intimate meeting of his mouth on hers, though foreign, was not at all repulsive to her. When his tongue touched hers, flicking softly across it, it sent a strange sort of tingle running through her. Her breath was coming in quick gasps and she hesitantly kissed him back.

St. Aubyn's hands moved downward to her waist now, slowly caressing, and he lifted her slightly as he rolled atop her. Pinned beneath him now, her head buried in his pillow, Mara knew there would be no turning back. He was so large, so strong, even had she wanted, she'd never be able to escape. Their joining was inevitable. She tried to relax her tense body but her heart was pounding against her chest. She looked up at him and wondered at the strange golden fire she saw glowing in his eyes there, realizing it was desire.

St. Aubyn towered over her, resting on his elbows, his fingers running lightly over her temple. He lowered his head to her again and Mara prepared herself for his kiss. This time his mouth was firm, demanding, and when he pulled away, it left her breathless. Every part of her screamed at her to get away, still every nerve ending was alive and on fire in her body.

He lifted his head and stared down at her in the firelight. He did not say a word. He looked down and his fingers followed his line of vision, stopping at the row of tiny pearl buttons that lined the neck of her nightdress. Suddenly and with a speed that belied the size of his hands, he unfastened each button until he reached the final one at her belly. Mara tensed. She dared not move. Her chest rose and fell as his hands moved upward, brushing the soft fabric aside over her breasts.

Mara closed her eyes in fear and humiliation. No man had ever seen her this way and when he lowered his head and took one soft nipple with his mouth, she gasped aloud at the shock of it. A curious sort of excitement rocked through her even as she wanted to turn away. Never had she felt such total awareness of her body as if every nerve and sense were alive and singing. She suddenly wanted him to give her more and she arched her back against him as his hands slid beneath her. He held her tightly as he suckled at her breast, sending tremor after tremor coursing through her so that she was gasping for breath when he finally pulled away.

St. Aubyn sat back on his knees over her and the sheet fell away from his body. Mara could but stare at the sight of his sex standing hard and erect from the dark covering of hair below his belly. She knew what he would do to her, how he would come inside of her and break her maidenhead and how that would bring her pain. It frightened her but at the same time, she could not help but wonder at what it would be like.

He pushed the hem of her nightdress over her thighs, pooling it at her waist. His rough hands on her skin gave her a shiver and he moved atop her, positioning himself between her legs. He lifted her knees gently upward. Mara closed her eyes, preparing herself as he brought his mouth down on hers again. His hand moved between them, caressing her belly. She stiffened, waiting, wondering what he would do next, then gasped when she felt his finger slide slowly into her.

Her muscles tightened instinctively around him. He withdrew his finger, circling her woman's flesh, finding her moist and hot center. She cried out at the unexpected jolt of feeling the motion of his fingers brought to her. She'd never felt anything like it before. It was at once wondrous and frightening. She closed her eyes as the sensations came again, building this time, feeling the tautness in her body increase. She didn't understand what was happening to her, but she knew she didn't want it to end. The feelings were growing stronger, more urgent now, and she thought she'd surely die from what was building inside of her.

St. Aubyn removed his hand then and lowered his hips between her legs. She could feel his sex pushing against her there, hard and unrelenting. She tensed, the pain building as he pushed further inside of her, stretching her, filling her completely. He gathered her into his arms and rested his head against her shoulder. Mara tensed every muscle in her body, waiting for him to bury himself inside her, expecting the pain that she knew was to come. There was something inside of her that wanted him to take her, wanted him to fill her utterly and completely, and this above all else frightened her.

Then, suddenly, she felt his body slacken and his head fell to the side against her ear. His hands no longer touched her, his mouth no longer held hers. Every muscle in his body had loosened where moments before he had been tense and poised above her. In moments she heard his steady breathing and knew he was asleep.

Asleep. On the very verge of taking her virginity and he'd collapsed atop her into a drugged stupor. Cyma's potion had put him to sleep before he could complete the act. Unable to believe what was happening, Mara lay there for several long moments, her body throbbing, the sensations subsiding now, leaving her feeling sadly unfulfilled and staring up at the velvet curtains on the bed.

She wanted to curse out loud but was afraid to move or even breathe. She felt confused and frightened at what had occurred, at the way in which she had reacted to him. She hadn't wanted, hadn't planned to feel anything, but she had and that knowledge terrorized her. She had approached this as something of necessity, her duty, no matter how distasteful, in regaining Kulhaven. But, she realized now, when Hadrian's fingers had caressed her, when he'd covered her, ready to take her, all thought of Kulhaven had left her mind and for the briefest of moments, she'd wanted him.

"Missy?"

Cyma's voice whispered to her from across the room.

Mara turned toward the sound of her voice, but St. Aubyn's shoulder was in the way.

Cyma came closer, stopping at the side of the bed. Her eyes were filled with concern at the sight of St. Aubyn's naked body sprawled atop her young mistress. "Oh, my child, are you all right? Did the beast hurt you?"

"No, Cyma, he did not hurt me. He did not have the chance to. Your potion did more than its promise of good. He's oblivious of anything but his dreams now." She attempted to move, but it was of no use. "I feel as if a horse has fallen atop me. He must weigh twice as much in sleep. You must help me to get him off for I do not think I can do it myself."

With Cyma lifting and Mara pushing, they managed

to roll St. Aubyn onto the other side of the bed. He was so soundly asleep he did not even stir. Mara started to rise and Cyma's eyes darkened at the sight of her nightdress opened and her breasts bared beneath it. "Did he take you?"

Mara rose from the bed, pulling her nightdress closed. "No, in fact, he fell asleep before he could complete the act. Now, it seems our efforts this night have been wasted."

She thought she heard Cyma utter something that sounded like "Thank the heavens," but chose to ignore it. "What are we to do? We've no way to prove he has truly compromised Arabella's—my innocence. How will we get him to wed me now?"

Cyma peered out the door to be sure no one was about then motioned for Mara to follow her. "Perhaps we can still salvage something of this night. But we must hurry. We've much work to do and only a few hours before sunrise in which to do it."

Hadrian opened his eyes, wondering why his head felt like it was weighted down to the pillow. The bright sunlight pouring through the open windows sent a stab of pain shooting straight through his brain.

Where the hell was Huntington? And why hadn't he woken him before now? Hadrian closed his eyes and groaned. His mouth felt as if it were filled with sand, making any effort at swallowing a near impossibility. His head ached, his body ached, even his teeth ached whenever he made the slightest movement, and with one arm shielding his eyes from that blasted sunlight, he reached beside himself in search of another pillow.

His hand, however, found something else entirely.

A body. A body that lay stiff and tense beside him. Oh, God, he groaned inwardly, now I've got to face some frightened chambermaid I took to my bed last night feeling like I've just been run over by an entire herd of cattle. No wonder Huntington hadn't come to wake him.

The body beside him stirred.

With painstaking slowness, so as to keep the throbbing in his head at a minimum, Hadrian turned on his side and opened his eyes. He squinted to better see, then closed his eyes against the image that had presented itself.

No, it could not be.

Please tell me it isn't so.

He opened his eyes again, wishing it were all a bad dream.

"Arabella?" he managed with some effort.

She just stared at him through those ridiculous spectacles—did she sleep with the damned things on?—not speaking, or denying his assumption.

In an instant, Hadrian came fully awake. "Arabella, what the devil are you doing here in my bed? Where the hell is my valet?" He sat up and shook his head, then pressed his hand against the sharp pain rioting through his temples. "No, don't answer that. It's obvious what you're doing here. I only wish I could remember how the devil you got here."

He rested his head in his hands a moment, hoping to calm the throbbing within and trying to remember anything of the previous night's events. He could remember nothing. Not even how he had gotten into his own bed. He chanced a glance at Arabella, hoping somehow she had disappeared.

She was still there, staring at him as if he were the very Devil himself. She did not speak. Instead her eyes were wide and gaping at his very naked body. And she was wearing that stupid white linen cap, slightly askew but nonetheless she was wearing it.

"Don't be frightened," he said, reaching out to reassure her. She backed away, clutching the covers to her chin. "Damnation, Arabella, I'm not going to harm you. I just want to make certain you're not hurt."

Arabella sat very still as he reached out and took the sheet, pulling it back. She was stiff with fear, every inch of her tensed. His eyes traveled quickly downward and he found the reason why.

Bright blotches of blood stained her white nightdress. The sleeve was torn at her shoulder and the lace at the neckline was hanging by a thread. Dear God, no wonder she looked at him as if he'd grown three heads.

"Arabella, I do not know what to offer as an explanation for whatever transpired here last night. I don't know what came over me. I cannot even remember what happened, but I obviously have caused you injury and have compromised your innocence in the most heinous of ways. For that I am truly sorry."

Still she stared, looking like a frightened doe standing before the sights of the hunter.

"Don't look at me like that. Say something. Anything. Say you are all right. Say you will forgive me. Say you will marry me as soon as I can secure a special license."

Arabella blinked. "Marry you?"

So she could still speak. "Yes, I know that is most probably the last thing you wish for right now, but it is the only way in which to remedy this—this *thing* I did to you. I know you had hoped to wait for your family to come, to plan a grand and glorious affair. But I am afraid we will not be able to wait that long. You see, a child could very well have been planted from this last night and . . ."

"A child?"

"Yes, and I know after what I must have done to you, you would wish me to perdition and beyond, but understand this, Arabella, I was not in my right mind last night. I obviously drank far too much with Rolfe and lost all sense of propriety and manner. I don't even know how you came to be here last night. I wish I could remember."

"You brought me here."

That stopped Hadrian short. "I brought you here? What did I do? Break through your chamber door and spirit you here over my shoulder like some sort of barbarian?"

"No, that was not the way of it. I was in the corridor, in the eastern wing, on my way to the library to find something to read. It was late. You said I would be allowed access to your books and I couldn't sleep so I was looking for something to read. You came upon me on the stairs then and asked me to come to your chamber. You said you had something to show me," she paused, "something I would find more interesting than a book."

Hadrian winced at her words. He'd ravished her, an innocent, and had told her it would be interesting? God, he was a barbarian, the worst sort of animal on earth. He reached out to her, hoping to reassure her, but she shrank away from his reach. "Arabella, I cannot blame you for what you must be feeling. I know this is frightening and you have every right to hate me right now, but—"

The door to Hadrian's bedchamber suddenly flew open and Rolfe came charging in.

"Hadrian, get up. Arabella's gone and—" He stopped when he saw where Arabella had obviously gone to. "Oh, I guess you know where she—"

"Where is he? Has he been told my baby is gone? What does he plan to do about it?"

Cyma came in directly behind. She, too, halted the moment she saw her mistress in Hadrian's bed. Her hand flew to her mouth in an expression of shock. "Oh, the good Lord help us, my baby is ruined."

"No one is ruined," Hadrian said, growing irritated now. He stood. "Marital events merely happened in the reverse order is all and . . ."

Cyma was staring at him as if he were the gentleman of the cloven hoof himself, her eyes fixed on his obvious nudity.

Hadrian looked to his friend. "Rolfe, my robe, if you please."

Once covered, he turned again to the maid. "As I was saying, Arabella is not ruined."

Just then Arabella stood from the bed, the bloodstains more than apparent on her torn nightdress. Cyma let out a gasp.

"Take your mistress to her chamber and see that she has a bath. Some of Mrs. Danbury's cowslip tea would probably help as well. Should anyone ask, tell them Arabella is not feeling well. I will go immediately to see about procuring a special license for us to marry."

"But what of—"

Hadrian cut in before Cyma could finish. "No one,

save the four of us here, will know of the events which transpired here last night, whatever they were. We will simply say Arabella and I took such a fondness for one another that we could not wait to wed before her family arrived. Anyone who says differently will have to face me." He then turned to Arabella, who had remained silent through all his orders. He softened his voice. "I am afraid a grand wedding as you had planned will be impossible now."

"Impossible and rather inappropriate given the circumstances, my lord."

Her wounded tone sent a stab at Hadrian's pride. "I am truly sorry, Arabella. I have been issuing commands right and left without even asking for your agreement. You do not have to wed me. I know that the prospect of marriage to me must seem less than appealing to you now, but I promise you, I will never hurt you this way again. If you can find it in your heart to believe me, I assure you nothing of this nature has ever occurred before last night. And it never will happen again. I do not know what could have come over me. I have never before forced myself on a woman. I know it must be difficult for you to forgive me and it may be nigh impossible for you to consent to be my bride. But, I offer you this, Arabella. You will be mistress of Castle Kulhaven, my countess, and you will be given every courtesy and freedom you wish in running this estate, if you will have me."

Mara looked at him standing before her so penitent and shamefaced, offering her everything she had been seeking these past five years and more, and all she could think of was the guilt she felt over how she had achieved it. She had deceived him in the worst of all possible ways, making him think himself a ravisher, a blackguard, making him doubt his own decency, and somehow this thought made her victory seem all the more hollow.

For a brief moment, Mara thought to refuse, to leave Kulhaven and forget all her plans for revenge, but something deep inside held her back, she didn't know what, some hidden force that spurred her onward.

Instead she took a step forward and extended her hand to him. "I will wed with you, my lord."

Chapter Ten

Hadrian and Mara were wed three days later in a simple and quiet ceremony that took place in the quaint little chapel at Kulhaven. The minister had been as hastily procured as the license Hadrian had somehow obtained. Rolfe and Cyma stood as their witnesses and Mara walked down the aisle alone. There was no grand gown, no glorious ceremony, nor were the aisles strewn with flowers and ribbons as she had dreamed of as a child. Only a small posy of lily blossoms and the most colorful gown Arabella owned, a sky blue affair with puffed sleeves that lacked anything in the way of ornamentation.

Now, as Mara looked down at the plain gold band on her fourth finger marking her as St. Aubyn's bride, she found very little glory in her victory. The guilt she'd felt at duping St. Aubyn into thinking he'd attacked her that night had more than trebled since. No matter how many times she told herself he was the enemy. No matter how much she argued with herself that it was the only way. All she could think of was his warning to her the night she'd first met him in his study.

He would tolerate no treachery.

What would Hadrian do if he ever learned the truth?

That he had not ravished her as he believed he had. That she'd really drugged him and had feigned the taking of her virginity only so she could force him into marrying her. That he was not married to Arabella Wentworth, the woman he thought he had wed, but to someone whom he did not even believe existed any longer. What would he do?

As she had so many times before, Mara pushed her nagging conscience to the far reaches of her mind, concentrating instead on the fact that she was now mistress of Kulhaven, just as she had wanted. Her plan had worked brilliantly and St. Aubyn need not know better.

Putting a fresh smile on her face, Mara cast aside her guilty feelings and prepared herself for the introductions to the Kulhaven staff as their new mistress.

As each person came forward to greet her, from Horace Crow, the castle's man of ledgers, to the smallest page, whose sole assignment was the snuffing of the candles each evening at midnight, Mara found herself drawn more and more into the role of Arabella, the new Lady St. Aubyn. None of the people could know her from before, for the castle's staff had been completely replaced after Kulhaven had been stormed by the Roundheads.

Mara smiled and committed each face and name to memory. And when they'd finally reached the last one, a sweet, honey-blond scullery maid named Anna, she felt certain her head would never cease its spinning. After a flowery toast made by Rolfe to a long and happy union, she and St. Aubyn shared an obligatory dance, a reel accented by a small orchestra made up of the castle dwellers. Mrs. Danbury led the extemporary performance on the harpsichord, which Mara found surprising, knowing that dancing and any other sort of frolic had been forbidden by Arabella's own godfather. She did not question it, though, grateful for whatever small amusement she was to be granted this day.

Through it all St. Aubyn did not attempt to speak to her. In fact, he didn't even look at her, rather at the people around them, or at the floor, or anything inconsequential, it seemed, to avoid having any eye contact with her. Mara thought St. Aubyn must be thinking himself the lowest form of life on earth. In turn, she hated herself as well for making him feel that way.

Hadrian bowed when they were finished dancing, and he took Mara's hand, whispering softly in her ear, "Stay and enjoy yourself, madam. I must leave for a short while. I've an errand to attend to."

"But, my lord, it is our wedding day."

He was gone before she could finish her sentence, leaving with Rolfe through the front door of the castle where his horse awaited him, saddled and ready.

A cloud of dust was all he left in his wake as he galloped away.

Long after the celebrating had come to an end and the servants had all retired for the evening, Mara sat before the cozy hearth fire in her bedchamber, awaiting her new husband's return. Even before the ink had dried on their certificate of marriage, her belongings had been moved into her new bedchamber, the countess's bedchamber which adjoined his own. It was a much larger version of the one she'd had before that looked out over the front of the house onto the drive below. The walls were plastered and painted in a pale yellow, the bed decorated in shades of pale blue, giving it a light and cheerful atmosphere.

St. Aubyn had not returned all evening, nor had he sent any word, and after eating her nuptial feast alone, her anger at his neglect had grown by the moment. Mrs. Philpot, the cook, had quite outdone herself with a joint of beef roasted slowly before the fire on a spit, pigeon pie with a tender flaky crust, custards, puddings, various sweetmeats, and marzipan made from sugared almonds and formed, for the occasion, into the shape of small hearts.

And the bridegroom hadn't been there to enjoy it.

"He is a thoughtless beast," Mara said aloud to the shadows, rising from the soft, plush cushions of the armchair where she'd been reading by the fire. She began to pace the carpet once again. She caught a glimpse of herself in the looking glass and frowned. Who was that strange-looking woman in the glass? If she didn't know better, she would not have recognized herself, so steeped in the role of Arabella had she become. She'd even taken to carrying the small Bible she'd found among Arabella's things in her trunk, anything to add to the legitimacy of her persona.

Anything, too, to make her forget the means by which she'd reached her new station.

Mara crossed to the windows and pushed aside the heavy brocade drapery to look out at the carriage drive below. It was empty in the moonlight as it had been each time she'd looked before. The young page who waited to attend to his lordship's horse on his return had long since fallen asleep at his place on the step. Even the dogs were dozing beside him, their great grizzled bodies providing him with a warm pillow on which to rest.

Where the devil had St. Aubyn gone to? And what was so bloody important as to take him from his own wedding celebration? Was it his guilt for his supposed ravishment of her? Was that his reason for leaving? Even as Mara wondered about these things to herself, she glanced at the door adjoining her chamber to his.

Perhaps he had returned earlier and she hadn't heard him come in. But why would he have not come to her? Even if only to bid her good night. She was his wife now, after all.

Mara stood at the door, uncertain as to what she was doing. She should be merry as mice in malt that he'd chosen not to join her in her bed. Why should it bother her that he seemed more interested in his other business than in his nuptial bed? She was acting as Arabella would to this evening's events, she told herself, feeling hurt and rejected by St. Aubyn's neglect.

Even this was going on a bit too far.

She turned, ready to forget about marriage beds and absent husbands, and caught a glimpse of the carved mantel clock at the hearth. Three in the morning? Was it really that late? He had said he'd be gone only a short while. St. Aubyn had been gone nearly twelve hours. What sort of business took twelve hours to conduct?

Mara twisted the handle to the door and took a candle from the table beside her, holding it aloft as she stepped on through.

It was dark, the room was empty, and it didn't appear as if anyone had been there all night. St. Aubyn's bed was empty and still neatly made. He'd not returned at all.

Setting the candle on the table beside his bed, Mara took a moment to study the lion's den. A blue brocade dressing gown lay across the coverlet, its fleur-de-lis design shimmering on the rich fabric in the candlelight. She ran her hand across the sleek fabric as she moved about the foot of the bed, surveying the area around her.

A pair of boots, polished to a looking glass shine, stood beside the walnut wardrobe, tall and straight, looking as if a pair of invisible legs still filled them. A comb made of tortoise shell sat beside a porcelain washbowl on a chest near the bed. Everything was set in order, not a single item out of place.

Standing in her night rail, Mara was suddenly aware of the chill that filled the room. The hearth was dark and rather than return to her chamber for a wrap, she took St. Aubyn's dressing gown from the bed and slipped it over her shoulders.

His scent, to which she had become so quickly familiar, enveloped her instantly, a woodsy, masculine smell that Mara found quite pleasant. Had she not known better, she would have sworn he had entered the room behind her. The sleeves of the robe fell far below her fingers so that she had to roll the cuff back several times in order to make it serviceable.

When several minutes had passed and St. Aubyn had still not returned, she began to search through every drawer and cabinet, looking for the treasured Kulhaven Tapestry, but to no success. This failure only added to her growing irritation.

What she did find, though, was that her new husband was a man of meticulous habit. His shirts were all neatly folded in his wardrobe, his breeches arranged by order of color. Even his toiletries were kept in their proper order, which Mara passed off as a result of his military background.

A small brass clock that showed the phases of the moon stood by the bed on his night table. Its bell chimed softly, signaling that it was now half past the three o'clock hour. Mara narrowed her eyes at the still-vacant doorway. What sort of groom left his bride thusly, and on their wedding night? If he had no liking for her as his wife, why then had he been so anxious to wed her in the first place? Did he think that he could just abandon her as soon as the vows had been said?

Well, he would have these and many more questions to answer when he returned. If he returned. Even Arabella had the right to complain.

Resolutely Mara dropped into the worn and soft cushions of the chair beside the cold and empty hearth to wait St. Aubyn out. The minutes passed by at an infuriating slowness, accentuated by the infernal ticking of the clock across the room. Her eyes began to blur after staring at the doorway for such a long period of time.

Taking the book which lay open on the table beside her, she thought to read to pass the time. She curled her legs beneath her, tucking the soft brocade around her toes and started reading where St. Aubyn had last left off, ready to wait till winter if need be to face him when he returned.

Unfortunately St. Aubyn's taste in late-night reading did not so much as border on the exciting, rather an ancient tome on the intricacies of raising sheep that soon set her eyes to drooping. Before she realized it, her head was resting on her knees, the book having fallen from her fingers to rest on the richly woven carpet below.

It was thus that Hadrian found her when he entered his chamber not long after. At first he was not pleased at her intrusion. This was his chamber, his private domain, and he was not accustomed to sharing it with anyone. Even a wife.

But, after a moment, when he'd noticed his dressing gown wrapped around her slim body, her face soft in the glow of the candlelight, his displeasure quickly vanished.

Arabella had only done what any other new wife would have done. She'd waited for her husband to return, most probably wondering where the devil he'd been so long. He could not fault her that. She'd no idea of the purpose for his leaving and was most probably feeling rather neglected by now.

Hadrian removed his coat and tossed it on the bench at the foot of his bed. He loosened his neck cloth, rubbing the back of his neck, which ached from the past hours spent of riding. He was so bloody tired. The past few nights he'd spent unable to sleep had finally caught up to him, that, coupled with the fact that he'd just spent nearly twelve hours riding about the Irish countryside on a fool's errand. He wanted to collapse on his bed and sleep for three days as exhausted as he felt.

But first he had to deal with the sleeping wifely form curled up in his armchair.

Arabella was still lying wrapped in his dressing robe, her legs tucked beneath her, her spectacles slipping from her nose. Her hair was not pulled back to her nape as was her usual style, but was loosely braided and hanging over one shoulder, that silly white cap perched slightly askew atop it. A dark ebony curl twisted freely at her forehead, giving her a softer, gentler appearance.

His mood began to lighten as he stared at her. Arabella should have married a man who wanted to marry her for herself, not for what she could bring him. She certainly shouldn't have had an arranged marriage to a man she'd never met, and man who really didn't want her for his wife but who'd ravished her before her trunks were even unpacked.

Hadrian frowned to himself. Never had he taken a woman unwilling. The fact that he had did not sit well with him. It went against every instinct, every code of honor that had been drilled into his head from birth.

He remembered very little of that night, only sitting with Rolfe in the study, drinking brandy and exchanging old stories. What he did recall of that evening did not include Arabella. Even in his dreams, it had been the spirit woman, the Flaming Lady, that red-haired hallucination that he'd seen by the lough. She was the one who'd come to him that night, but obviously in some sort of dream, a dream that he'd acted out on an innocent.

When he'd first come to Kulhaven after the death of his uncle, Hadrian had read of the Flaming Lady in James's diary. Pages and pages filled with descriptions of her standing at the tower battlements or floating down a dark hallway moaning after him. He had thought the man mad, stark raving about this ghostly apparition that had haunted him. Hadrian had learned at a very early age that everything had a logical and reasonable explanation, if one took the time to look for it.

The stillborn sons delivered his uncle could be explained as a mischance of the belly, a wife with a miscarrying womb, and not some supposed witch's curse coming true. He'd discounted his uncle's untimely death as a drunken fall from the tower. James had always been one to imbibe, quite heavily after the death of his wife in childbed, it was said.

Never did Hadrian believe the rumors that *she* had pushed him from the tower.

Still, who could he have seen swimming in the lough that day if not the Flaming Lady?

At that moment, he was too tired to make a closer study of any logical explanations. And he hadn't seen her since, so he was more apt to put it off as his imagination. All he knew at that moment was that he wanted the bed beneath him, a fire in the hearth, and a glass of brandy to warm his gullet.

Hadrian knelt before the hearth and arranged a pile of kindling, striking a flint along the hearthstone. He couldn't see waking Huntington to light the fire when he was perfectly capable of doing it himself. And as soon as he had a fire going, he would take Arabella up and return her to her own bed.

"My lord?"

Arabella had awakened. He would not have to take her up and return her to her chamber after all. As the wood caught and the flame quickly consumed it, Hadrian turned and stood to face her.

"Good morning, Arabella."

She sat up in the chair, rubbing her sleepy eyes beneath her spectacles. "What hour is it?"

"Far too early for you to be rising. Why don't you take yourself off to your bed now. It was a thoughtful gesture for you to have waited up for me, but I am back, so you needn't remain here in my chamber any longer."

That she was puzzled by his curt dismissal was obvious by the look of sheer confusion on her face.

"What I am saying is that I do not require that you share my bed, Arabella."

"But I am your wife."

Hadrian sat upon the bed and began to remove his muddy boots. "Yes, you are, but as you well know, we have already done with the necessity of consummation. Many married couples sleep in separate chambers. It is quite a common practice. I have fitted you with a very large and comfortable chamber of your own. If the decor is not to your liking, you have my permission to change it as you see fit. Do whatever you like to make it your own. There is no reason for you to be waiting till the wee hours for me every night when you have your own bed and hearth to keep you warm."

Arabella stood from the chair. The hem of his dressing robe pooled at her feet. "Every night? Do you mean to say you will be out till this time often?"

"It is very possible. I have business to which I must attend. Estate business of which you have no concept. It often takes a great deal of my time."

"What sort of business would require your attention at this hour of the night?"

She was beginning to sound like a practiced shrew, he thought, anxious to have her take her leave from him now. He was tired and easily irritated. He knew it wasn't her fault, but he had no plan for her to become any more familiar with his doings than was absolutely necessary.

It would be best to put an end to her questions right now.

"Arabella, you are now my wife, but that does not entitle you to become involved with all my business in running this estate. Your attentions are better focused on the interior of Kulhaven, the running of the household, mending of the linen and such. You need not concern yourself with other business that takes place outside these walls. That is my responsibility. Now, if you wouldn't mind, I should like to retire. I'll be leaving around eight this morning to tour the grounds and visit with the people. I should like to get some rest before then."

He had moved to the door and was now standing before it, waiting for her to leave. Mara stared at him a moment, wanting to argue against his demands, but knowing she could not. Arabella would never think to refute her husband's word. No matter how pigheaded he might be. But perhaps there was a way around that.

Without another word, she marched through the door, thinking that while he may have won this round, he certainly had not even begun to win the entire tournament as yet.

Chapter Eleven

Mara waited until after she heard St. Aubyn's door close softly and his footsteps had faded down the length of the corridor. And then she waited a moment longer. She clutched her high-crowned riding hat with its stylish white ostrich plume in her hand and after she was certain he was indeed gone, she emerged from her bedchamber to follow.

Hadrian had already mounted his stallion, Hugin, and was donning his kidskin riding gloves before he noticed the second horse saddled and ready beside him.

"Who ordered this horse saddled?" he asked the freckle-faced young groom, Davey.

"I did, my lord," Mara said before the lad could answer, moving on through the door to stand atop the front steps of Kulhaven.

St. Aubyn crossed his gloved hands on the pommel of his saddle, slackening the reins. His riding crop dangled loosely from the cord wrapped round his wrist. He looked up at her squarely, but his expression gave little indication of the reaction she would receive to her announcement.

"I would, Arabella, that you take an escort with you at all times if you plan to ride about the estate. Even at the closest distances, some of our neighboring landholders have had their family members set upon by the Irish Tories who live among the more densely wooded areas."

"Yes, I am well aware of that, my lord. All too aware. Mrs. Danbury has already informed me of the perils hereabout. But, you see, I was planning on having an escort."

"You were? I see no other horse here. Who might that escort have been?"

Mara paused, smiling her sweetest smile. "You."

Before he could object, she continued. "You had said you planned to ride out among the people of Kulhaven this morning. I feel it my responsibility as lady of this household to accompany you and meet them as well. I am mistress of Kulhaven now, my lord, in case you had forgotten, and that includes my duty of being mistress of her people as well."

St. Aubyn did not readily respond. He was staring at her with that damnably oblique expression of his on his damnably handsome face and Mara somehow knew he wanted to refuse her, but he could broach no argument because what she had said was true. She was the new mistress of Kulhaven, and thus her request was a valid one.

He stared at her for a moment longer, as if waiting for her to back down. The birds chirped happily in the trees. Davey shuffled from one foot to the other. Somewhere in the distance behind them Mara heard the deep sustained lowing of a cow.

Well, he could stand there waiting till weeds grew at his feet and birds took up residence in his hair, Mara thought. She was not going to acquiesce like the good little Arabella this time.

Seeing that she was standing firm, Hadrian set his booted feet in the stirrups, gathered up the slack in the reins, and said simply, "Very well," before wheeling his mount around and cantering off in a cloud of gravel and dust.

With some assistance from Davey, Mara swiftly mounted her horse and kicked her heels to its sides to follow in Hadrian's wake, wondering once again why it was he didn't seem to wish to be in his new wife's company.

She had caught up to him by the time they reached the first rise in the grassy field that lay just to the east of the castle. The sheep were out and grazing, their woolly bodies dotting the entire hillside as they munched on the sweet green grass. They vaulted over the first of three rock line fences that enclosed the eastern fields, and Mara laughed out loud, reveling in the feel of the wind whipping at her face.

Hadrian glanced over at her once and did not say a word, but continued to stare straight ahead, a sullen expression on his face. They rode beside each other in silence for quite some time. Though she knew every path on Kulhaven land, Mara made certain to follow St. Aubyn's lead so as not to arouse suspicion. They crested a small hill at the edge of a thick copse of oak trees and below, spreading outward toward the main post road, lay the small wattle and daub cottages of the centuries old village of Kulhaven.

"Arabella," St. Aubyn said, drawing his horse up atop the hill, "please stop for a moment."

He waited until she had drawn up beside him. "I

hadn't planned on bringing you about to meet the villagers so soon. We have been wed not even two days. The villagers have only begun to accept me as the new landholder here and even that has not come without some effort. There are many who still resent having an Englishman lording over Kulhaven. I cannot say how they will react to my bringing them an English wife. I hope you will not become too upset if they do not welcome you readily."

Mara nodded. "It is most understandable, my lord, that they would not look kindly upon someone they consider the enemy as the source of their livelihood. I am sure they continue to hold a great loyalty to the former earl and his family. As I understand it, many of the new English landholders have shown little restraint in masking their contempt for the Irish people. But I am not like that. I will show the villagers I do not find them at all distasteful and will do my best to win them over."

St. Aubyn did not say a word. He just stared at her with a slight look of disbelief on his face as if to say her reaction had not been the one he'd expected.

He had meant well with his carefully worded warning, trying to prepare her for the icy reception he had obviously received when he'd first come to meet the villagers as their new lord. But what St. Aubyn could never realize was although the villagers did not know that she was truly the daughter of the former earl, these were her people, they had been her people all her life, and her reaction had been the only response she could have had at his statement.

Mara had no fear of recognition by the villagers for even without her dyed hair and the spectacles perched on her nose, these people believed, nay, they knew that she had perished with the other members of her family that night. It had been five years, and much had happened in that time to erase the memory of her from their minds.

"Shall we proceed then?" Hadrian asked.

Mara nodded and together they trotted down the grassy slope.

They directed the horses to the center of the small village where the communal well stood as it had for centuries. It was washing day and the women were out hanging their brightly colored garments across fence posts and tree limbs to dry in the early morning sun. A small girl sat beneath the wide-spreading branches of a huge oak playing with a doll fashioned out of rags. Beside her, a hen and her chicks pecked at the gravel in search of a wormy tidbit.

As Mara and Hadrian approached on their horses, several of the people began to leave their fields and emerge from within the small thatched cottages to see what the Kulhaven lord had come about.

St. Aubyn helped Mara down from her mount, taking her about the waist and setting her gently on the ground beside him before turning to the small crowd gathered there.

"Good morning," he said.

Not one of the people standing before them returned the greeting. An awkward silence followed where it seemed even the creatures in the woodland did not breathe, and finally St. Aubyn turned to a tall man standing at his right whom Mara did not recognize.

"John, how go the plans for the harvesting?"

As the man John began to tell St. Aubyn which

fields had been cleared and which remained, Mara took a moment to survey the many faces around her. She was pleased to see so many familiar ones, for many of the villagers on the other estates had been banished to Connaught with the former landowners, their cottages set fire to and their meager livestock taken.

This was the Protectorate's way of "persuading" the Irish peasants to follow their landlords into exile, leaving the villages open for new English settlers to take up. But, it seemed that was not the case here. These villagers had been spared. How Mara wished she could run to them, to tell them she had returned.

There was Brighid, once the fair beauty of the Kulhaven villagers. She was of the same age as Mara and they'd gathered whortleberries together as young girls, giggling at the young boys who'd attempted to impress them with their archery skills.

But, the Brighid who stood before her now looked many years older than she remembered. The once golden blond hair that had curled below her waist and had been the envy of all the village girls was now dull and thin with stray wisps hanging about her sunken cheeks. Several young children surrounded her skirts, skirts which were badly tattered at the hem. The youngest child sucked at a dirty thumb as she stared at the new Kulhaven mistress with a mixture of fear and curiosity.

Mara knelt down before the child. "Why, hello, pretty little girl. What is your name?"

The child looked to her mother as if asking how to respond.

"She's Caitrin," Brighid said, her voice barely masking her contempt for the new English mistress.

Mara fought back the tears at the hatred she saw glaring at her from her old friend's eyes.

"Caitrin," she said, standing to face Brighid, "what a lovely name. She is yours?"

"Aye, as are the others."

Brighid was staring closely at her, studying her face as if trying to find something there, and for a moment, Mara feared recognition, before Caitrin tugged at her mother's skirts, pulling her attentions elsewhere. "*Mamaí,* I'm hungry."

Brighid looked down and her expression softened as a mother's often would when looking at her child, and she lightly stroked the youngster's blond head. "I know, *leanbh,* I know. But, there is nothing for us to eat right now."

It was then Mara noticed just how very thin Caitrin was. She didn't know how she'd not noticed it earlier, for now it hit her like a slap in the face. In fact, everyone about them showed signs of malnourishment, their eyes sunken deep, their faces drawn. And, their clothing, or what there was of it, looked as if it had been worn and mended over for many years. The colors had long since faded, the hems were all ragged, and most of the children were left to running about barefoot or with cloths fashioned into a crude sort of shoe tied about the ankle with a bit of twine.

A fierce anger swept through Mara as she continued to look around them, seeing more and more signs of their misery. Their cottages were in sorry need of repair, the thatched roofs caving in at places, and the walls were beginning to crumble around them. What stock they did have, the meager number of sheep and oxen, looked as malnourished and pitiful as the people. This was an utter outrage. How could St. Aubyn have allowed the villagers to continue to live like this? Did he not see? Was he truly that blind to their standard of living?

The villagers were slowly wasting away. Or, perhaps that was the Protectorate's plan. Something must be done. This could not be allowed to continue. Had she no connection to these people, had she truly been Arabella fresh from the shores of England, she still could never have ignored the plight of these people.

Mara looked down at herself and suddenly felt ashamed for wearing the finery she wore. Even though the navy blue riding habit lacked much in the way of ornamentation, it was new and fresh, the cuffs and falling band embroidered with silk in the design of flowers and birds, and the looks of longing in the women's eyes around her told her they hadn't seen the like in their lifetimes.

No, something must be done. Immediately.

"My lord . . ."

St. Aubyn took her hand, readying himself to make his announcement. "My good people, I have brought your new mistress to meet you all. She is Lady Arabella Ross, Countess of St. Aubyn. She is most anxious to acquaint herself with all of you. I hope you will welcome her to Kulhaven as kindly as you have me."

There was no response from the people around them. They just continued to stare at her as if she were some sort of foreign object, and indeed, she was to them. Mara suddenly hated that she was disguised as Arabella. She wanted to run to the villagers, to discard her disguise and these fine clothes, and assure them she was one of them, that she was not the enemy as they believed. She'd thought she would be able to endure this. She'd thought just knowing her true identity in her own mind, regardless of their reaction, would be enough to keep her at ease. But, after seeing the looks in the people's eyes, the darkness and the disgust for what they believed she stood for, it was truly too much to bear.

Mara had to bite her lip to keep from showing the tears that were filling her eyes more with every minute that passed in that infernal silence. St. Aubyn must have seen her teetering on the brink of shedding those tears for he squeezed her hand to comfort her.

"Perhaps it would be better if we go."

He started to turn back toward the horses.

Suddenly a tiny voice called out from somewhere in the vicinity of the crowd.

"Wait!"

Everyone turned their heads toward the source of the voice and the crowd parted to allow the protestor a forward entrance.

Mara's heart was pounding and she could barely contain the feeling that came over her at the sight of one more familiar face, a face that did not look upon her with contempt.

But as quickly as she recognized that face, her elation turned to fear for she knew somehow that this person had recognized her.

Chapter Twelve

Her name was Sadbh, and she was more ancient, it was said, than the very ground they stood upon. Even as a child, when Mara would visit her in her tiny cottage at the edge of the village to hear her stories with the other children, she had seemed quite old. She was what the Irish referred to as a *pishogue,* a wise old village woman who would make potions and charms for keeping evil spirits at bay. She tended to the sick and the dying, speaking strange Gaelic incantations, and she could portend the future at times, just by looking at the pattern of tea leaves in a cup.

Edana, Mara's mother, had once told her that Sadbh's family had lived on Kulhaven land for centuries, long before the Despencer family or even the Knight Rupert de Kaleven, back to the time when Dagda, the great chief of the Gaelic gods, had ruled over the land. Some even claimed one of Sadbh's ancestors had been the bastard offspring of Dagda, thus explaining her longevity and the mysterious powers she was purported to possess.

Though there existed no proof of this allegation, Mara had grown up knowing of Sadbh's powers, never questioning, always respecting her strange and magical ways.

It was Sadbh who had taught Cyma of the secret and powerful medicinal properties of herbs, passing on her ancient wisdom to her. It was Sadbh who had even foretold the coming of Cromwell, refusing to be daunted when no one would believe that this monster would rise from the east to devour the very soul of Ireland.

And it was Sadbh who had recognized Mara.

She should have expected it. She had been a fool not to think that of all the villagers, Sadbh would still be there and would know her.

And, now, because of it, her plans could very well come tumbling to the ground.

It took Sadbh quite some time to reach them through the crowd now gathered by the well before Hadrian and Mara. She relied on a cane fashioned from a crooked tree limb, her hand shaking when she was forced to put her weight upon it. The eyes of the villagers were focused on Sadbh's slight form as she shuffled slowly forward. It was silent. No one dared speak even a whisper. Even the birds did not sing. Mara wondered if anyone else could hear the panicked beating of her heart.

What would she do? If Sadbh revealed her true identity, everything, Kulhaven, the tapestry, her life, would be lost. To have come this far and to be felled so easily. Mara wanted to curse at the misfortune of it.

Sadbh stopped directly before them, her eyes scanning the length of her. She barely reached to the height of Mara's chin, but her presence was awe-inspiring.

Mara looked down at her, silently beseeching the old

woman not to reveal her secret. She had always believed Sadbh to be magical. Who could forget the day when she had saved the life of Conor MacFerguson, who, after eating a handful of the poisonous berries that grew along the creek bed, was vomiting up his innards? With a few drops of some unknown potion and a strange Gaelic incantation, Sadbh had saved his surely fleeting life.

And if ever Mara wanted to believe in Sadbh's mysterious powers, it was now.

Sadbh had to shield her eyes against the bright morning sun to look up at her. She had aged in the years since Mara's departure, if that was possible. Her hair was now merely grizzled wisps that flew about from beneath the yellowed linen cap she wore. Her simple gown was faded to a dingy gray, the apron tied about her waist frazzled and worn. Her lips pulled inward from a lack of teeth and her skin was so pale that one could see the webwork of veins that ran beneath its surface.

But, her eyes, those black and bottomless eyes, had remained as clear and seeing as they'd always been.

"Do you know who I am?" Sadbh asked in a shaky voice, staring at Mara quite intently.

Mara looked to St. Aubyn before responding. "No, madam, I am sorry, I do not. You see I have only just arrived at Kulhaven and—"

Sadbh held up a quivering hand, silencing her. "I am Sadbh. Everyone at Kulhaven knows me for I have lived here all my life." She reached out and took Mara's hand in hers. She pressed something into it. Her fingers shook and her skin was cold despite the clement weather. "Kulhaven has seen much bloodshed, much killing. Too much killing. It is time for her renewal. Kulhaven must be healed." She smiled then, the corners of her eyes crinkling. "I believe you are the one who can heal her. If ever you have need of me, all you need do is come. I have assisted many a mistress of Kulhaven."

Mara looked down at her hand to see what Sadbh had given her. It was a sprig of a small, white-flowered plant that had a strong, peppery smell to it. She looked at Sadbh.

"It is the branch of the yarrow plant and it will keep evil spirits away from anyone who holds it."

Sadbh smiled at her again, the sunlight twinkling in her eyes.

At that moment, Mara knew her secret would be safe. She allowed herself a breath of relief. "Thank you, Sadbh. I am most grateful for your generosity." She opened the gold filigree pomander ball that hung from a chain around her waist and tucked the yarrow sprig inside. "I will keep this with me wherever I go."

Sadbh turned toward the assemblage then. "Come, everyone, and greet the new mistress of Kulhaven. You have nothing to fear from her. She is our *slánaitheoir*."

Slowly, reluctantly at first, one, and then two of the villagers stepped forward. Several more approached until they were soon surrounded by them, each stopping to greet the lord and lady, introducing themselves and each family member. Mara smiled and committed the ones she did not know to memory while reacquainting herself with those from her childhood. She wondered if any of the other villagers would recognize her, if they would keep her secret as Sadbh just had.

No one seemed to think that she was anything else

than what she was supposed to be; the lord's new English wife. Mara knew what Sadbh had told the people to bring them forward, that she was their savior, their redeemer. She also knew that St. Aubyn did not know enough Gaelic to know what had been said. But, what brought the people forward mattered naught. All that mattered was that they had accepted her, coming forward to greet her as if in awe of the old woman's words.

And Mara was determined to live up to that promise, to bring these people out of the wretchedness they'd been left to. If it was the last thing she did.

Arabella was in a decidedly lighter mood during the ride back to Kulhaven, brought on, Hadrian surmised, by the people's ready acceptance of her.

Acceptance. It was more of a miraculous welcome. Even he was amazed. Nay, he was stunned, for he'd never seen anything like it. He'd been at Kulhaven nearly a year and still had not received the reception his new wife had in a matter of minutes.

He'd spent months carefully trying to win the villagers over, trying to break down the walls of distrust that had been erected against the English after Cromwell's bloody rampage through Ireland. He'd been patient, realizing their reluctance, nurturing the slow process of winning them over to him. It was a difficult and arduous task, for while he saw the poor quality of the life they'd been forced to and hated it, he could do little in the way of helping them.

It wasn't that he lacked the coin to help them, but an English landowner giving freely to his tenants would quickly draw suspicion, suspicion he must avoid. Laws had been passed forbidding any acts of kindness to the

Irish. So, any acceptance he received from the villagers was come by with great difficulty.

Yet, in seconds, Arabella had breached the walls of distrust, only to be hoisted upon the shoulders of the people her own godfather had defeated. It boggled the mind. She certainly was not at all what Hadrian had looked for in his English-bred wife. He'd never expected her to take the slightest interest in the people of the estate, let alone putting herself in the tenuous position of facing their outright scorn. But, she had, and without treating them as the heathens she'd no doubt been told they were.

Even when they'd rejected her, she'd shown a brave front. Most women would have fled in a rain of sobs at the people's initial reaction to her. But, Arabella had stood strong and somehow had shown them her true and gentle nature, causing Hadrian to take a second look at his new wife.

Then, there was the old crone, Sadbh. If not for her, Arabella surely would not have been welcomed. He'd heard the tales of Sadbh's supposed powers. His uncle had written of her being a witch in his diaries, blaming her for the appearances of the famed Flaming Lady whom he believed had haunted his final days. Hadrian had also heard the stories whispered by the castle dwellers about her, stories of how the old woman's potions and mixtures had saved many lives at Kulhaven.

He'd never seen her before now. Actually he'd figured her long dead, so ancient did the stories of her seem to be. He'd never really given it much thought. But, now, he found it curious and somewhat interesting that the sudden appearance of this Flaming Lady had brought about the appearance likewise of her supposed conjurer.

When they arrived back at the stables, windblown and exhilarated from their ride, there was no one about to take the horses. Hadrian called for Davey, but he did not answer, and judging from the aroma of freshly baked apple tart that wafted from the area of Mrs. Philpot's kitchen, he had a good idea where the lad had taken off to.

"Seems we've been left to our own devices," Hadrian said as he helped Arabella down from her horse.

She turned to face him. "Yes, my lord, it would seem so."

Just then, Arabella's mount stepped sideways, pushing her against Hadrian's chest. His arms instinctively closed around her to steady her. He did not draw back when the animal stepped away.

"It would seem your mount doesn't have much of a good temperament. I'll have to see about getting you a more suitable horse."

Her breasts were pressed against him and her hands were holding on to his upper arms. Her scent, a pleasant mixture of the rain and some unknown flower, suddenly filled his senses. She looked up at him, their faces close, and he could feel her warm breath on his chin. Her hair had come loose from the rigid bun at her nape, the braid she kept it in frazzled and trailing over her shoulder, and for the first time, Hadrian noticed the eyes usually hidden behind those spectacles, a soft gray-green that reminded him of the moss that grew beside the pond's edge.

Her elevated mood at the result of the day had brought some bright color to her cheeks. He didn't know why, but he rubbed the back of his hand against her cheek. Her skin felt as soft as the petals of a rose.

She really was quite lovely, he realized, now seeing Arabella, truly seeing her for the first time. An image of her came to him, of her body soft and inviting beneath him. Taking it as a memory of their one night together, he brought his mouth down to hers then, touching his lips to hers. He'd almost expected her to pull away, but when she did not, and more, moved closer into his arms, he drew her against his chest and deepened the kiss.

Arabella responded with eagerness. He ran his tongue along her bottom lip and she opened her mouth for him.

He'd been most proud of her today, of her willingness to face the people of Kulhaven and her mettle when faced with those same people's rejection. At that moment he felt that together with her, he could surely conquer anything. He would never have expected such bravery from this English godchild of Cromwell. But, he thought as he pulled away from the kiss, would she be as willing to be his bride and embrace this new life if he were to reveal his true reason for wedding her?

Somehow he did not believe she would.

Hadrian set Arabella back from him. "We'd best be getting these horses unsaddled and back to their stalls."

"But, my lord . . ."

Her words dropped off. Hadrian had turned and was leading his horse away, leaving Mara to stare after him in bewilderment.

The heat of humiliation burned her face. How could he go from kissing her passionately one moment to near indifference seconds later? Her heart was still pounding from his kiss and now she was left standing in the courtyard to watch him disappear inside the stables. Had she done something wrong, something to anger him? Sometimes he could be quite puzzling and even, like right now, downright infuriating.

"Come along," she said sourly to her mount, tugging at the reins as she followed St. Aubyn to the stables. It was dark inside and smelled of fresh hay and it took her eyes a moment to adjust to the faint light. She walked slowly along the center aisle, looking for an empty stall. The opening to the last one was ajar and her horse stepped in without the slightest hesitation, affirming it must be his usual place. She loosened the bit and slid it from his mouth then pulled the sidesaddle from his back. She had turned and was making her way to the tack when a low, rumbling growl suddenly brought her up short.

Standing between herself and the door to the tack was a very large, very fierce-looking wolfhound. Its eyes gleamed yellow in the low light. White teeth showed from beneath its warning snarl. Its grizzled hair stood on end along its backbone.

St. Aubyn's voice came from somewhere beside her, from where she did not know, for she dared not even move her eyes to look. "Don't move, Arabella. He is dangerous. He came at me once when I first came to Kulhaven. I don't even know why he is still here. I told Pudge to get rid of him, but . . ."

Mara did not hear the rest of his warning. It took her a moment to get over the initial fear of the dog, to really look at his eyes in the lamplight, but she soon recognized that familiar grizzled head. It was Toirneach, the pup she'd been forced to leave behind when she'd fled Kulhaven. She figured him dead or running wild in the woodland. She'd never thought he would still be alive and living at the castle.

She set the saddle slowly to the ground. The dog growled low and deep. Refusing to show any sign of fear, Mara carefully extended her hand.

"No, Arabella."

"Shh," she whispered, trying to keep the dog's attention focused on her while assuring St. Aubyn she knew what she was about. "Hello, you great beast. What a pretty creature you are. I will not hurt you. Come, see that I mean you no harm."

She took an advancing step. The dog lifted its nose in the direction of her hand. Never for a moment did she believe he'd actually take hold, but she knew St. Aubyn believed he would. "Shh," she continued in a soft voice. "It's all right, boy. Come, now. Come to me."

The dog began to ease at the sound of her voice. He cocked his head slightly to the side. Yes, she thought, that's it. It is me. You still do recognize me, don't you? Keeping her hand palm upward, she allowed the dog to come forward and nuzzle her glove.

A firm believer in the intelligence of animals, she knew when she saw the spark of recognition in his eyes. He raised his head and began wagging his great tail, whining softly as he licked her wrist where it wasn't covered by her glove.

"That's it, boy. There's a good beast." Mara patted his head, rubbing him gently behind his ears.

Hadrian remained standing several feet away. "I do not believe it. My leg still bears the marks where he took hold of me."

Mara smiled. "I've always had a special way with animals, a sort of connection. Some have called me strange for it, but I seem to be able to somehow show animals I mean them no harm. He didn't really wish to hurt me. I was just a stranger to him, a temporary threat to his home. Once he saw that I did not mean to harm him, he let down his defenses. I am certain that was the way of it the day he took a bite of you. Come closer, my lord, you will see he really is quite gentle."

Hadrian stepped forward. The dog glared at him from the corner of his eye and emitted a low rumble.

"He obviously recalls your last meeting. We must show him you are not the beast you seem either."

Hadrian shot her a look at that remark.

Mara smiled. "Now, extend your hand, palm upward as I did so as to show him you do not mean to strike him."

Hadrian did as she asked and the animal took a sniff, then obligingly allowed Hadrian to stroke him on the head.

"See. You really should reconsider your wish to have him removed from Kulhaven. A dog with such loyalty to protect his home would surely be good for Kulhaven to have."

Hadrian did not respond. He just watched as Arabella knelt before the dog, this beast who moments before had been baring his teeth to her, and allowed him to lick her chin.

Every time, it seemed, he thought he'd come up with an explanation for her actions, she brought him up short again. He'd discounted the kiss they'd shared moments before, pushing aside the feelings it had brought, the muted memories of their night together.

He'd just been telling himself, convincing himself that the reason she'd been so readily accepting of the people of the village earlier that day had been because she needed to show a good face, to make him believe she'd be on his side.

Long ago Hadrian had convinced himself that the true reason for Cromwell's agreement to the match he'd proposed with Arabella had been to install someone at Kulhaven who could keep watch and report on Hadrian's movements. Cromwell was well known for his distrust of the closest of his circle of advisors. He'd even been known to install children as pages to his highest officers for the sole purpose of reporting on their daily workings.

Because of this, Hadrian could not allow himself to trust Arabella, no matter how much she seemed to contradict everything he believed she would be.

He really didn't know what it was he had expected of her, perhaps daintiness and frailty, her thoughts occupied with embroidery patterns and recipes.

The one thing he did know was that he could never have expected this.

This fearless woman who'd embraced her new life wholeheartedly, refusing to be daunted by the seeming rejection of her people, or even a vicious mongrel dog. Her tenacity was truly astounding. Though seeming fragile on the outside she definitely was not made of the softer stuff most members of her gender were made of.

He watched her then as she moved from the stables and on into the courtyard. The dog followed at her skirts, leaping like a puppy when she tossed a stick for him to fetch. No, he'd never expected this in his wife.

But, even more, he'd never expected the pang of sheer panic that had run through the length of his body when he'd seen her cornered by the dog, his only thought having been that of protecting her from the certain harm before her.

Chapter Thirteen

Mara entered her bedchamber and peeled off her gloves, tossing them with her riding crop atop the bed as she crossed the room to the looking glass. She took one look at her reflection and groaned out loud.

She looked like a bedlamite, an absolute fright. Her hair was dyed black as coal and trailing in a tousled braid over one shoulder, wisps of it hanging wild about her face. The plume on her hat was broken and hanging at an odd angle. And her lace collar was turned crookedly over one shoulder.

It was no wonder St. Aubyn had stopped kissing her the way he had to walk into the stables.

But somehow Mara was reluctant to believe that was the sole reason for his pulling away from her. No, it was something else, what she did not know, but she knew for the barest of moments, he had wanted to kiss her, indeed, had done so quite boldly, before he had pulled away. It was almost as if he was afraid of something, oddly, as if, in some way, he was afraid of her.

But that was ridiculous. St. Aubyn, that great and massive man, afraid of her? And then it hit her, making her feel the fool for not realizing it sooner. It was the promise he'd made the morning he'd woken to find Arabella in his bed. He believed he had ravished her unwillingly. That he'd taken her virginity in the most brutal of ways. And he had promised never to do so again. That must be the reason for his having walked away in the courtyard after he'd kissed her. It must also be the reason for his reluctance to be within three yards of her at any given time. Every time he came near her, looked at her, spoke to her, it must remind him of what he did, rather what he thought he did that night.

If there was one thing Mara had learned in the time since her arrival at Kulhaven, it was that despite being English and a supporter of Cromwell, St. Aubyn was no blackguard. He was the type of man who lived by a certain code, priding himself on propriety and a sense of honor, ever the gentleman, never going beyond the accepted.

Except, for that one night.

In his mind, on that night, St. Aubyn had broken every rule he'd ever lived by. How his conscience must be wearing on him. This realization, while an explanation of his odd behavior, only caused Mara's compunction at fooling St. Aubyn to double. She had never thought of the consequences when she'd embarked on this plan to regain Kulhaven. She had been so bent on revenge and on regaining Kulhaven that she had never considered how she'd feel when she actually got what she wanted.

She suddenly wished events had never transpired the way they had. But she'd had no choice. She had promised her mother to let nothing deter her from getting back their home. And, why should she feel guilty at taking back what was rightfully hers? If only there had been some other way of handling things. If only she could have avoided ruining Hadrian's self-respect. If only . . .

But it was too late for second thoughts. She'd already duped him into marrying her, or who he thought was Arabella, by making him question his honor, and there was naught she could do to change that. What she could do, though, would be to somehow make St. Aubyn see he was not the cad he believed himself to be. She had to show him that he did not frighten her, that she held no deep emotional scars from the events which supposedly had transpired that night to bring them together. She had to show him he was the honorable gentleman he had always set his standards by.

But how?

The villagers. At one fell swoop, Mara realized, she could restore St. Aubyn's self-respect and bring the villagers out of their plight. She would suggest that he help the villagers, somehow make him believe it was his idea. He had to see the way in which they lived. No honorable man such as St. Aubyn could stand by and let them wither away and die. For as surely as the sun set on the western Booley Hills, they would starve if they were forced to go on as they had any longer.

Settled in her decision, Mara loosened the tapes of her riding skirt and released her hair from its braid, running a gilt brush through the ebony dyed tresses till it fell in loose waves down her back. Nearly an hour later, freshly gowned in amber yellow silk, her hair twisted back beneath the white linen cap, she was ready to embark on her newfound mission.

A knock came on her chamber door and she grabbed

Arabella's spectacles and perched them on her nose. As had become the custom, the staid footman stood waiting for her in the corridor to take her down to supper. With each step she took as he led her down the hall, her confidence soared. She convinced herself that St. Aubyn would never be able to refuse. How could he? He would see what a brilliant idea it was to help the villagers, and he would agree to it, restoring his honor at the same time. He had to.

Mara wanted to start right into the speech she'd prepared the moment she stepped into the dining room, but realized she had to temper her tongue until the appropriate moment.

St. Aubyn nodded to her as she was seated opposite to him. With as much grace and ease as she could muster, Mara took her napkin and unfolded it across her lap. Then, raising her eyes to meet his, she said, as if it were any other evening, "Good evening, my lord."

St. Aubyn nodded. "Good evening, Arabella. Might I say you are looking rather fetching this evening."

She smiled, pleased at how easily this was going. "Do you like the gown? I had hoped it would meet with your approval."

"The gown is nice, though that is not the sole reason for my compliment. You do not give yourself due credit. You are quite lovely."

Mara smiled at his compliment. The meal, which consisted of roast mutton, new potatoes, and a delicate rice pudding with raisins, passed quickly and easily, with light conversation between them. All through the meal, Mara could feel St. Aubyn's eyes upon her, watching her as she took a sip of her wine or lifted her napkin to her lips.

Afterward, he asked if she'd like to join him in the parlor for a cordial and a game or two of piquet.

"You play quite well," he said as he took up the cards. "I've not seen another play with quite your imaginative strategy."

"Thank you, my lord. My father taught me during one particularly long winter when we were housebound for weeks. He used to say he taught me too well."

St. Aubyn nodded. "I can see why. You seem to have a system for counting the cards as the game progresses."

"It's not really a system, my lord. It is more a talent I have had since I was a child. You see, I have a good memory, especially for inconsequential things. Anything I read or hear seems to stay with me. I need only to see something once and it is locked away in my mind for good."

St. Aubyn smiled. "That is interesting. I wonder if I might test this odd ability of yours?"

"Certainly. But how?"

He stood and walked over to the shelves of books set in the wall. He scanned the titles, then pulled one from high above his head. He flipped through the pages then set the book before her, smiling. "Read the passage on that page, then repeat it to me."

She stared at him. He did not believe she could do it. Mara looked down at the page, ready to accept the challenge. It was a fifteenth century recipe for beef tea, a rather crudely written version of it, as well. Mara quickly scanned each line, then closed the book and repeated it to him, word for word, mispronunciations and all, ending it with, ". . . seethe it in a pot with water in a cauldron but top it well that no air goes out."

Hadrian's confident smile faded. "I shall remember to take you as a partner instead of an opponent in cards should the occasion arise." He stood, taking the cookbook in one hand and offered her his other, walking with her to a pair of armchairs beside the hearth. "I find I have married myself to a complex wife. Every time I turn around I find something else I hadn't expected in you."

"Is that good, or bad, my lord?"

"I would say it is good. So far you have done nothing to displease me, except, perhaps, your tricking me into taking you out riding with me today." He paused a moment. "But you were right. You are lady of this estate now, and well suited to it, I might add. I had meant to tell you earlier, Arabella, that I was most proud of you today. I do not know of many women who would have been willing to face the villagers as you did today."

"Thank you, my lord, though I do not know if I would call it courageous. I just did what I thought my duty as your wife."

"Again, you give yourself too little credit. The villagers do not welcome the English easily. They have only begun to accept me as the new landholder here. I was not certain it would be wise to present you to them so soon."

"Their scorn is understandable. Just as many of the English see all Irish as the enemy, I am certain many of the Irish feel the same about us. Trying to hide the fact that your wife is English would only serve to widen the vast gap that stands between us. These people are no more responsible for the crimes committed by the Irish than are you or I for those of the English. They are merely innocent victims of the consequences of war."

St. Aubyn did not say anything and Mara suddenly wondered if she had said too much. "Is something wrong?"

"No, Arabella. I had just thought that there were not many people left on this earth who could surprise me."

Uncertain as to whether she should take that as a compliment or a criticism, Mara decided not to pursue it further. Instead, she took the opportunity to broach the subject of the villagers and their living conditions. "I was thinking, my lord, is there not some way we could help the villagers? I was noticing that their cottages are in sad need of repair, the stock is vastly depleted, and their clothing looks as if—"

"I do not think that is necessary, Arabella."

His easy dismissal gave Mara a momentary pause. "Yes, but perhaps if you could relieve them of their rents for a short time."

"That is not feasible."

"But surely you can see that by helping them you would be helping Kulhaven to be profitable as well. With adequate clothing and stock, they could plant more crops and produce more—"

"I said no, Arabella!"

Mara silenced at the raising of St. Aubyn's voice, quite stunned and staring at him.

"These are difficult times everywhere, Arabella, not just at Kulhaven. At least the villagers have homes. Many of the Irish do not. Many were left to die in ditches at the estates that were destroyed. Others were herded off their lands with the previous landowners to eke out a living on the vast reaches of Connaught. At least they still have their families and their homes."

"But they are starving, my lord. Surely you can see that. You say that you want their acceptance. Would not giving them back a semblance of the life they once had aid you in that pursuit?"

St. Aubyn stared at her in silence and for a moment Mara thought she had gotten through. But, then he stubbornly shook his head and turned away. "There is nothing I can do about that. Your own godfather has forbidden it. The villagers will just have to find their way. Your concern for the people of Kulhaven is commendable and speaks well of your character, but I believe this subject has been exhausted. It has been a long day and I am tired. Good night, Arabella."

He turned and left the room.

Mara watched him go, drawing an angry breath at his indifference. How could he be so cold, so cruel, as to watch the hungry children while he sat here living like a fat king? She wanted to scream at him, to make him see how wrong he was in his thinking, but knew she could not. Even while she watched his retreating back as he left the room, Mara knew Arabella would never have spoken thusly to him.

She had started out trying to give him back a sense of honor, a sense of the honor that she believed she had destroyed. Now it seemed that honor never truly existed.

She wondered if she had gone too far and hoped she hadn't given him cause to suspect, but she hadn't expected his outright refusal. She'd thought him a gentleman, in fact, had been berating herself for deceiving such an honest and just man. Perhaps she had been wrong in that assumption.

Hadrian closed the door to his chamber and ran a hand through his hair in frustration. He knew everything Arabella had said was true, but he was trapped by the threat of exposure to the Protectorate. If there was some way of convincing Cromwell of the benefits of helping the people, he would do it. Arabella was right. Surely her godfather had to realize that by helping the people, he would be in turn helping the English landowners to make their estates more profitable.

What Arabella did not realize, but of what Hadrian was all to aware, was that Cromwell's objective was not to have the Irish, peasant or not, responsible for the resurrection of the land. His goal was to annihilate the entire Irish race and replace them with English settlers to work the land. But rather than lining them against the wall and ending their miserable lives all at once, he chose to have them die off slowly so as not to have the stain of their blood on his hands.

Cromwell was a coward, but a crafty coward, and would kill the first Englishman who dared not adhere to his beliefs. This thought alone brought Hadrian's blood to boiling. The people were starving, forced to live like the lowest form of life while the marauding Roundheads got rich off their labors. If there were some way he could help the villagers without arousing suspicion from outside, he would do so, in a second, if only he could be sure that by doing so he wouldn't be falling into a trap. He couldn't.

Always a man who believed he had control over his life, Hadrian hated the fact that his hands were ineffably tied. Any sympathy, even in its smallest form, shown toward the Irish was cause for concern with Cromwell. One of his finest captains had been stripped of his rank and thrown in Newgate for disciplining an overzealous Cromwellian soldier who'd beaten an elderly Irish woman. Cromwell had made it treasonous for any Englishman to marry an Irish woman, punishable by hanging, whipping, and disembowelment.

He trusted none and suspected all, and would believe one guilty before innocent. So until Cromwell's greed for power came to an end, Hadrian was helpless to give the people of Kulhaven, his people, any assistance.

Still, he hadn't meant to shout at Arabella as he had. It was his powerlessness he was angry at, not her. She was just as innocent as the people she had so valiantly defended. He realized now he'd been treating her rather coldly, somehow blaming her for her godfather's evil. But hearing her plead on behalf of the villagers, knowing that her concern was genuine, he realized that she was no more to blame than he.

On the morrow he would make up for his ill behavior. He would take her out on a picnic and show her the lands surrounding the castle. She had assumed her role as his wife quite well, despite everything that had happened, taking an interest in every aspect of Kulhaven. In fact, had he not known better, he'd almost be willing to believe Arabella in Irish sympathizer.

Hadrian laughed to himself, then shook his head at the absurdity of that thought.

Mara was more than a bit surprised the following morning when a footman came to her chamber door requesting her presence on behalf of the master for a ride about the estate and picnic that day.

She wondered if his sudden attentiveness might be an effort of conciliation for their disagreement the previous night. She herself had spent the evening hours tossing about on the huge poster bed, frustrated at St. Aubyn's stubborn refusal and worried that she'd gone too far in her pursuit on the behalf of the villagers.

Now, receiving St. Aubyn's invitation, she saw that all her worrying was for naught. She cheerfully accepted his offer, telling the footman to relay to his lordship that she would be down within the half hour and turned to get ready for the outing.

While she dressed in a riding habit of fawn-colored silk, Mara decided to set her efforts for the villagers to the side for the time being. While she would never abandon them or their plight, she realized she had put herself in a perilous position. Gainsaying her husband as she had was not what Arabella would have done. A proper wife, the sort that Arabella would have been raised to be, would never have spoken out as she had. She would accept her husband's word as law, never opposing, never contesting it as being wrong.

Mara knew her feelings had ruled her hasty words, but she would have to put those feelings aside until she could act on them without the threat of revealing her true identity.

With her dark hair coiled back and pinned beneath a high-crowned plumed hat, Arabella's spectacles perched on her nose, she fastened the top button on her riding doublet and made her way down to meet her husband. He was waiting for her at the bottom of the stairs, dressed in a fine coat of slate gray with black close-fitting breeches.

He smiled when he noticed her coming down to meet him and extended a gloved hand when she reached the bottom stair.

"Thank you for agreeing to accompany me today, Arabella. You look quite lovely this morning."

"And thank you for the invitation, my lord. I am certain you have more important things to occupy your time than to take me out riding and picnicking."

St. Aubyn helped her up onto her mount. "I find that I have been neglectful of you and for that I must apologize. Sometimes I find myself so immersed in running Kulhaven that I forget there are other things that more immediately require my attention. Such as my new wife. I have been remiss, leaving you alone in a strange house in a strange country, and for that I am truly sorry."

Mara smiled and waited while St. Aubyn mounted his own horse. His sudden change in personality was quite curious to her. "Your apology is accepted, my lord."

"You've just reminded me of another thing I wished to speak with you about, Arabella."

"What is it, my lord?"

St. Aubyn stared at her. "Exactly that. We are husband and wife now. I think it would be quite proper for you to address me by my given name. In fact, I would prefer it."

Mara felt a flush rise to her cheeks and didn't know why. Perhaps it was the intimacy of using his given name. By addressing him as "my lord" or "St. Aubyn," it seemed to keep a cool politeness between them, almost as if they weren't truly married. But, his request was a reasonable one. Married people did address each other thusly.

He was staring at her, awaiting a response and making her uncomfortable. Mara looked down at the reins in her hands and said, "As you wish, Hadrian."

"Yes, that is much better, don't you think?"

Mara nodded silently. She was grateful when a moment later he wheeled his horse about and started trotting down the pathway leading toward the northern fringes of the estate. She clucked to her horse and started after him.

They rode alongside each other for quite a distance and with each field they passed through, Mara found herself easing. She tried to put the previous evening behind her, although for the life of her, she could not fathom the cause of Hadrian's refusal. Surely he had to see that the benefits of helping the people far outweighed the risks. His consideration in taking her about today only caused her more confusion. How could a man who seemed so just and honorable refuse to help those who depended on him for their very livelihood? It just didn't make any sense.

After what seemed a long time, Hadrian stopped at the edge of the wood and dismounted.

"I know of a quiet place where we can picnic just beyond here," he said as he helped her down. "We'll tether the horses and walk from here."

Taking her skirts in hand, Mara followed him into the dense woodland. They had walked only a short distance before they reached the edge of the lough where she'd gone swimming her first day at Kulhaven.

The same place Hadrian had first seen her.

Instantly, Mara raised her guard, wondering why he'd chosen this as their picnic place.

"This is such a lovely place. However did you find it?"

Hadrian set down the basket he'd brought and spread out a woolen blanket. "I stumbled upon it once when I was tracking some poachers."

Mara tried to ease her nervousness. His bringing her there was purely coincidence. How could he ever know it had been her in the lough that day? "Did you find anyone?"

"No, it was quite a wasted effort. But, I did find this pleasant spot. I thought you might enjoy it."

While they sat and ate their dinner of cheese and cold roast chicken, Mara filled the time with conversation of inconsequential things such as what fruits they would be preserving for winter, and other household matters, certain that Hadrian must be bored to his teeth. That was, after all, what she was supposed to concern herself with. But while she spoke, she noticed that Hadrian watched her closely, listening to even the most minute of details. She tossed a stone into the water, hoping to divert his attention away from her. She didn't like his direct scrutiny, found it quite unnerving, and wished he'd find something else to hold his interest.

"Tell me about your childhood, Arabella."

His question brought Mara more on edge. She knew next to nothing of Arabella's upbringing, only what she had gleaned from her letters to Hadrian. "There really isn't much to tell."

"What about your home? Do you miss it very much?"

"I suppose, at times, I do, but Kulhaven reminds me

of it a great deal. We had a small lake much like this one there. I used to play there as a child. I read a book once by Sir Thomas Mallory about King Arthur and his knights. Have you read it?" she said, trying to change the subject.

Hadrian was smiling now, his eyes lit. "Yes, I believe I have."

"I used to pretend I was the Lady of the Lake bringing King Arthur his sword Excalibur, which really was an old tree branch I'd found." She paused, the lies flowing freely now. "My maid used to box my ears for dirtying the hemline of my dress. My mother said I'd never catch a husband if I continued with such unladylike pursuits."

Hadrian smiled, glancing up at the sky above them. "It appears as if we might be in for some rain. Perhaps we should start back for Kulhaven. I'm sorry we will have to cut our picnic short."

Mara didn't mind; she was, in fact, grateful for the interruption.

Together they gathered the remnants of their meal and returned to the horses. Hadrian helped Mara onto her horse before starting for Hugin. As she arranged the train of her skirts around her, the sky overhead seemed to split and a late summer shower began to fall.

"Seems we had our picnic just in time," Hadrian said as he began to fasten the basket to the back of Hugin's saddle. "I'll be finished in a moment and then we can start back. You can go on ahead if you'd like."

"It is all right. I do not mind. I have always loved the rain."

While Hadrian secured the basket, Mara looked

down at a button that had come undone on her riding doublet. She was about to fasten it when she noticed several dark spots on her coat. Had she gotten some mud on it in the brush? Just then another spot appeared, then another, and another. A drop of rain trickled down her cheek. She reached up to wipe it away and froze when she brought her hand back and noticed a black drop of liquid staining her fingers.

Chapter Fourteen

The dye.

Mara looked to where Hadrian stood beside his horse. He was still occupied with securing the basket to the saddle, oblivious of her and the rain and the droplets of black dye quickly spreading their way over her fawn-colored silk riding doublet. Her heart began to hammer, knowing that her stylish plumed hat would do nothing to stop the dye from running.

She glanced around for some place, anyplace to take cover from the rain, which was falling faster with each passing second. There were the trees, but Hadrian would surely join her there, and then he would see the black dye running down from her hair.

The rain began to fall even harder now, pouring down, the wind whipping it about in thick, wet sheets. Another droplet trickled from the tip of her nose to her sleeve, dotting black on the white starched cuff. She had to do something—quickly.

Without wasting another second, Mara set her boot-heels against the horse's sides, sweeping her riding crop against his flank with one swift slap. Startled at his rider's sudden onslaught, the horse reared and bolted instantly for home, throwing up clumps of moist earth in his wake. Mara cried out then looked back, noticing that Hadrian had turned and was now attempting to mount his horse to come after her. Knowing she could not allow him to see her this way, with the dye running down her face, she urged the horse on faster. Even tearing breakneck through the countryside, she realized his stallion would overtake them far before they ever reached Kulhaven.

The only possible way to avoid him would be to try to lose him in the woodland.

Mara waited until the last possible second before pulling her horse as hard as she could to the right. The horse tossed his head and snorted in protest of his mistress's rough handling, then veered right through a slight break in the tree line. She could hear Hadrian shouting her name behind them but dared not turn back to look. Her hat tumbled to the ground and she lowered her head against the horse's neck to keep from being toppled by any low-hanging tree limbs.

Carefully she directed the running horse through the labyrinth of trees, weaving in and out of them without breaking stride. In moments they had broken through the wood to the clearing on the other side. Chancing a glance behind her, Mara was relieved to see that Hadrian was nowhere in sight. She said a silent prayer, hoping that just this once, he'd fall from his saddle and land on a soft, muddy plod of earth.

When she reached the Kulhaven stables soon after, her heart pounding, her body trembling, hair now hanging like seaweed in black, dripping strands, she was grateful that Davey had found other things to occupy his attention and was nowhere to be seen. The rain was fair pouring from the sky now, the dye running in thick lines down the sides of her face. She pulled her horse to a halt on the cobbled courtyard and leapt to the ground, leaving the horse with its sides heaving from their run and the reins trailing conspicuously at his hooves.

Mara dashed through the servant's entrance, startling Mrs. Philpot and the kitchen maids, and ran up the back stairs to her chamber on the second floor. Once inside, she bolted the door firmly behind her and stood leaning against the heavy wood, trying desperately to catch her panicked breath.

It was thus that Cyma found her seconds later.

"What the devil?"

She had come in from the withdrawing room, carrying a stack of bed linens, and stopped dead at the sight of her dye-stained mistress.

"You were right, Cyma," Mara managed between breaths. She motioned to her soiled riding habit. "The dye did run black as the waters of the Liffey."

Cyma just stared at her, mouth gaping open. After a moment, she shook her head. "Get yourself out of those clothes before someone sees you and we both end up gallows' bait. Sit by the fire so we can dry that hair before it turns your entire face black. I'll fetch some vinegar from my room to wash the color from your skin."

Mara hurried across the room, flinging her doublet to the floor as she tugged off her riding boots. The dye had soaked through the doublet to the white cambric shirt underneath. Frantic, she discarded her riding shirt, dropping her skirts to the floor as she rushed to the washbasin. She splashed some cold water over her face and neck and began wiping the dye off as best she could. Not five seconds later, heavy bootsteps were rushing down the corridor outside her chamber.

"Arabella!"

It was Hadrian, of course, his voice sounding panicked. He stopped at her chamber and pounded his fist upon the door. "Arabella, are you there?"

Standing barefoot in her shift, Mara looked to Cyma as if to ask if she should answer.

Cyma put a finger to her lips then motioned for her to move behind the dressing screen across the room. She handed her a small bowl that was filled with vinegar and a clean cloth to wash with. After she was hidden, Cyma unbolted the door.

"Where is she? Stand aside, woman. I am looking for your mistress. Is she here?"

Behind the screen, Mara began furiously wiping the dye from her face, trying to ignore the overpowering smell of the vinegar.

"Aye, she is here, my lord. She is changing right now."

"Well, move aside so I can see her."

"You should not be here. It is not fitting. My lady is not decent, my lord."

There was no mirror on the dressing table. Mara cursed inwardly, trying in vain to see her reflection in the bottom of a tarnished silver trinket box. All she could see was a blurry, distorted image.

"Arabella is my wife. It is perfectly acceptable for me to be in her bedchamber and to see her however and whenever I want. Now, move aside."

Mara could hear him advancing into the room.

"No, my lord, you must not!"

Mara froze at the raising of her maid's voice. No one,

not even Cyma, would be permitted to speak to his lordship thusly. Silence fell on the other side of the screen. She would have to do something. Immediately.

"It is all right, my lord, uh, Hadrian," she called from behind the screen. "I am really quite fine."

Hadrian was silent a moment. "Arabella, please come out here so I can see you."

"I am not dressed right now. Perhaps—"

"Arabella, if you will not come out here, I will be forced to come there. I must be assured you are unharmed."

Of course she was unharmed. She was speaking to him, wasn't she? "I am perfectly fine, my lord, I . . ."

"I said I would like to see for myself, Arabella."

Mara heard the finality in his voice and knew he would not leave until he saw her. Why did he have to be so blasted stubborn? "All right, but allow me a moment to cover myself, please."

Mara soaked the vinegar cloth with water and gave her face one final swipe before grabbing the dressing robe hanging on the side of the screen. She pulled it around herself and combed her fingers through her hair, giving a sigh of relief when her hand came back clean and only slightly damp. With a last fruitless glance at the bottom of the trinket box, she prayed she'd gotten all the dye off her face. She took a steadying breath and slowly emerged from behind the dressing screen.

Hadrian was standing in her room, his large body framed inside the doorway. His shirt was mud-splattered and he still held his riding crop in his hand. His face was a mask of worry and concern.

"You see, Hadrian, as I said, I am perfectly all right.

Not a scratch upon me. I must confess I am more embarrassed than anything else. You must not think very much of my skills as a horsewoman after today."

He started to speak, then stopped, a confused expression crossing his face. "What is that smell?"

"Oh," Mara smiled, "that is vinegar. I use an herbal vinegar wash as a rinse for my face. I find it keeps the skin clean and soft."

His expression eased a bit, but maintained its concern. "Well, I most definitely am going to see about getting a more suitable mount for you. That horse is obviously still green."

Mara stepped forward and took his arm. At that moment she didn't care if the horse had two heads, she just wanted Hadrian to go. And quickly. She started to lead him toward the door. "If you must, but really, it was more my fault than the horse's. A bee flew by my head and I swiped at it. I startled him and he bolted. He may have even been stung. He is not a temperamental mount. Just a bit skittish."

Hadrian did not appear convinced. "You are certain you are unharmed?"

Mara nodded, stopping at the door. "Yes, yes. I am fine. And please forgive my maid for speaking to you as she did. She was just concerned for my modesty. She did not mean any offense, I am certain."

Hadrian glanced to where Cyma still stood silently by the bed, watching the exchange. He did not say a word.

"Now, if you do not mind, I should like to make myself more presentable before dinner. I look a fright and do not much like being before you this way."

Hadrian looked down at her and his eyes softened.

"You look charming. But I am afraid I will not be joining you for dinner this evening, Arabella. There is a matter which requires my attention on a neighboring estate and I will be gone until quite late."

Again, he would be gone all night. "You must go this evening?"

"I am afraid so. In fact, I will be leaving Kulhaven immediately. I apologize for barging into your chamber like this. I just wanted to be assured you were unharmed. When I saw the horse standing riderless in the courtyard, I assumed the worst. I am relieved to see that you are all right."

Hadrian smiled then and reached out to run a gloved finger along her chin. Mara raised her face, readying herself for his kiss, which she felt certain was coming, but he pulled his hand away a moment later. He looked down at the gloved tip of his finger.

"Perhaps you should use some extra vinegar on your face. You've some sort of strange black dirt on your chin."

Mara nearly dropped to the carpet as he closed the door behind him.

Mara stepped from the bathwater, which was scented with a mixture of balm oil and rosemary and was now murky and gray from the dye left remaining in her hair. She pulled her wrap around herself, rubbing her hair vigorously with a drying cloth. St. Aubyn was gone and her door was locked, so she decided to let her hair dry before reapplying the dye. She stepped from behind the privacy screen and sat before her dressing table, peering at her reflection in the glass.

In just a few short days, she had become accustomed to seeing the persona of Arabella staring back at her each time. It seemed as if she had forgotten what her true reflection looked like, it had been so long since she'd last seen it. She ran her fingertips back through her hair, her *red* hair, allowing the damp, springy ringlets to fall into place. It was then that she caught sight of the folded parchment note sitting atop the pillow on her bed.

She stared at it a moment in the reflection of the glass, wondering how it had gotten there. No one had come into the room while she was bathing, except the maid to bring her supper to her and she'd left immediately after. Still, Mara had not seen her, for she'd been hidden behind the screen.

Mara slowly rose from her seat and walked over to the bed. The note was addressed to Lady St. Aubyn. She wondered why it had been placed on her pillow and not on the silver salver in the entrance hall with all the other Kulhaven correspondence. The red wax seal was not imprinted with any insignia and the handwriting on it was scratchy and rather difficult to read. She opened it quickly, scanning its few short sentences.

Clever little scheme you play.
If you wish to keep your true
identity secret, meet with me
at the top of the Bloody Tower
at midnight. Come alone and
tell no one of this.

It was not signed. The tiny hairs at the back of her neck stood on end as a heavy sense of dread came over her. She read the note again. Who? Who could have found her out and so quickly?

She realized then it could be a number of people, from Old Sadbh to any one of the villagers, but somehow she did not think any of them would have written the note. She wished Cyma were there to ask who she thought it might be, but she had gone to visit Sadbh in the village, leaving a fresh mixture of the dye for Mara to apply herself. She would not return until very late. But, perhaps that was for the best. She would split a seam if she knew of this.

For the next several hours the note was all Mara could think about. Each time she heard a creak on the stair or a servant passing by, she tensed, waiting for Hadrian to present himself at the door and announce that he knew her true identity. But he did not come and with each passing hour, her fear began to ebb and she thought instead of the impending meeting with her unknown incriminator.

Midnight took forever in coming. Mara decided she must do something to disguise herself so that some servant wouldn't recognize Arabella as slipping about the house at such a late hour, bringing questions as to why. And what better disguise than her own identity? She'd nothing to hide from the person she was meeting. They already knew who she was. She would dress in the blue servant's frock Cyma had found for her to wear the day she'd gone swimming in the lough and no one would know the better.

At precisely a quarter hour before midnight, Mara wrapped a cloak about her shoulders and started for the tower. She encountered no one as she made her way through the dark and silent hallways leading to the older part of Kulhaven. When she emerged from the stairwell out onto the tower, a quick study revealed that no one was about.

High above, the moon was full and bright, illuminating the whole of the bailey below. The wind was blowing through the trees, ruffling the edge of her hem around her ankles. She lifted her chin to the night sky and allowed the brisk breeze to blow over her face.

Oddly, Mara felt quite calm as she strolled about the circular walkway that surrounded the tower, watching the shadows for sign of any movement. She should be shaking with fear at being found out, but somehow she maintained her composure. She would find some way to avoid Hadrian's learning the truth, once she knew who it was who had discovered her identity. She stopped walking when she reached the part of the tower that faced out to the front of the castle. The brick beneath her feet was still discolored in places, even after all the years.

It was here that her mother had stood denying Cromwell's soldiers entrance to Kulhaven. It was here on the crooked stone floor where she had fallen. Time had not erased the blood that had flowed from her. It had merely faded it.

"I see you received my note."

Mara spun about at the sound of the unfamiliar voice behind her. She could see nothing save the darkness and its obscuring shadows. "Who is there?" she called.

"I am wounded, Mara. You do not recognize my voice? You once could hear it from three stories up and would come running. It hasn't been that long, has it?"

Mara narrowed her eyes, trying to make out the stranger's shape in the darkness. She took in a startled breath as a large form advanced from the shadows before her.

"Owen."

"Yes, dear sister, it is me, your beloved brother. Why do you not come and give me a welcoming embrace? Did you think me dead, hanging as raven bait along some country road?" He paused. "Yes, that is what most everyone believes, but you see, I planned it that way. With a dead body sworn to be mine, the posters offering the reward for my head quickly came down."

Mara still could not believe he was standing there before her.

"You can close your mouth now, Mara. I assure you I am not an apparition."

Mara was so stunned by his appearance she could not speak. It was her brother, Owen. He had given her the information necessary to make her return to Kulhaven a success. And then he'd vanished without a trace.

He look harsher, his chin now covered by a short beard. His face was dark and toughened from the sun, and his hair, a dark reddish brown, hung long around his shoulders. His eyes, narrowed and so very cold, stared back at her.

Owen chuckled and continued forward, stopping just in front of her. He reached out with a gloved hand and touched her softly on the chin. His touch gave her an unpleasant shudder.

"And I return after all these years to find a filthy Englishman living in my home with my sister for his whore."

"I am not his whore. I'm his wi—" She stopped herself, not wanting to reveal anything to him.

Owen smiled. "His wife? Yes, I already knew that. That was the plan, wasn't it? I never for one moment doubted you could pull it off. But I don't see how that makes you any better than his whore. Especially when he thinks he is married to someone else entirely."

Mara narrowed her eyes. "Why have you come here now? There is nothing for you here. Mother is dead. Father is dead. As are Colin and Niall. Kulhaven was confiscated just like every other Irish estate and given over to the English. Trying to get it back would be fruitless."

"Ah, but you are here. Apparently you do not believe Kulhaven completely lost. You obviously believe that by selling yourself to an English pig you can regain Kulhaven somehow, despite the fact that you were already promised to another. What would your betrothed say if he were here to see this? It would surely kill him. Thankfully he has been spared that disgrace. He is already dead."

Mara felt a chill run over her at the mention of the man she once thought to marry. "Liam is dead?"

"Yes, killed by an Englishman, just like the one you married. I was there when he died, gasping your name like some sort of lovesick gallant. If only he knew that his beloved betrothed would become a whore to one of those who had killed him and before he'd even grown cold in the grave."

"I am not St. Aubyn's whore. I am his wife and we haven't even consumm—"

Mara covered her mouth with her hand to stop her hasty words, wishing she could learn to temper her tongue.

"Ah, so the happy groom has yet to visit his new

bride's bed. Seems your idiotic little scheme was for nothing. How unfortunate for you."

Mara narrowed her eyes. "What I am doing here is none of your concern."

"Oh, but it is just that fact that has brought me here to see you, dear sister." He paused. "You see, I did not return to claim this place. I couldn't have cared less if it had been burned to the ground. I came because you are going to help me."

"I will do no such thing."

"Oh, but I believe you will for if you do not, I will see that your bridegroom somehow discovers the truth of who he is really married to."

"You wouldn't."

Owen crossed his arms over his chest and leaned back against the wall behind him. "Wouldn't I? You seem to forget, Mara, I am not Colin or Niall. Nor am I Liam Shaughnessy, who used to turn to milk the moment you flashed your faithless green eyes at him. The fact that we share blood means little to me. Why do you think I arranged it so you would learn about St. Aubyn's engagement to Arabella? Why do you think I had their letters intercepted and sent to you? Why do you think I arranged for you to be able to pull this little scheme off, knowing you would play right into my hands? Your success has hinged entirely on my actions, not through any cleverness you believe you have. And, now I am here to collect my due. Oh, yes, you will help me sister, or it is you, and not I who will end up as raven bait."

Hadrian allowed his horse to walk at its leisure up the rise toward Kulhaven, taking the time to attempt to cool his raging anger. He'd been led for a second time on a fool's errand through the countryside by his Irish contact. Damnation! He did not take kindly to being thought a fool. But, he had little choice in the matter. Had he been able, he'd have turned the Irish patriot in and taken his chances with another. But he needed the information he'd been promised and he knew he would have no other choice but to dangle like a puppet at the end of the string, performing at will until he got it.

As he rounded the bend in the curve leading up the front drive of Kulhaven, he caught sight of something high on the old Kulhaven Tower. He gathered the slack in the reins and pulled Hugin to a stop, squinting up at the object above in the darkness.

He could not believe his eyes.

He could not see her face for the distance between them, but her red hair glimmered in the moonlight, blowing about in the breeze like a cape of burning fire. It was her, the Flaming Lady, standing on the battlements as so many had reputed, the spirit woman who had pushed his Uncle James to his death.

Touching his heels lightly to Hugin's sides, he started for the tower.

Chapter Fifteen

Owen flicked a bothersome clump of mud and grass from the top of his jackboot, saying to her quite smugly, "Now that you have agreed to help me, dear sister, you can rest easily knowing your secret is once again secure."

Yes, but for how long, Mara thought, looking at him and wishing he would just disappear. "I have not agreed to help you by any means, Owen. I am being forced by your means of blackmail."

"Forced. Agreed. Call it what you wish." Owen moved to the edge of the battlement and stared out at the moon beyond. For a brief moment, Mara felt the urge to push him over and let him fall to the rocks below, to become the next gruesome statistic of the Bloody Tower, brother or not, for as evil as he had become. But then there would be questions as to who he was and why he'd fallen from the Kulhaven tower. Someone might have seen her going there. Or someone might discover Owen's identity.

Instead, she was left to staring at his back, wishing every sort of misfortune upon him while he bribed her into stealing information from Hadrian for his own purposes.

"What is it you want me to get from St. Aubyn?" she asked, hoping to end this bitter reunion.

Owen turned, smiling. "I will notify you as to what I need when the time is right. Until then, perhaps you should relax and take this time to concentrate your efforts more on bedding your husband instead." He chuckled. "Before he begins to question if he's wed himself to a nun."

Mara itched to slap him, but knew she could not. She turned and moved to the edge of the tower, clenching her hand into a fist atop the rough stone. Down below, the moon lit up the whole of the bailey, casting shadows on the statues of the lions that guarded the front stairs.

She took in a sharp breath when she saw Hadrian's horse tethered to a tree there.

She spun about. "Hadrian has returned. His horse is just below. I must get back to my chamber before he notices I am missing." She started for the stairs, but Owen grabbed her by the arm.

"Take the hidden stairs, Mara."

She had nearly forgotten about the secret staircase built into the tower. It had saved her life the night the castle had been stormed. And it would save her skin now.

Mara stared at her brother a moment, wondering at his sudden show of solicitude.

"Go, Mara. Now."

"But, what about you?"

"Do not worry over me. I managed to get here without your seeing. I will manage to leave the same way. Now go."

Rushing to the opposite side of the tower, Mara pulled her hood over her head and pushed at the hidden mechanism in the wall there. A portion of the brick moved away, allowing just enough space for her to squeeze through. Inside, she turned the mechanism back and the wall closed behind her, swallowing her into the blackness inside.

Hadrian took the stairs to the top of the tower two at a time, yanking the door open when he reached the last step. A gust of the night wind blew across his face as he stared at the empty space before him.

She was gone. The Flaming Lady had vanished.

Damnation! Was he going daft? He refused to believe that some ethereal spirit woman resided in this tower, his tower. It just didn't sit with him. Yet, still, he'd seen her. He was certain of it, for there was no mistaking that fiery hair. Where had the woman, whoever she was, gone to? She couldn't have vanished into the night. He tried to tell himself she must be a servant, or someone from the village he'd yet to meet, for he certainly would recall it had he seen her before she'd risen from the waters of the lough in all her naked splendor.

But there was only one way down from the tower, the stairs, and he'd taken them, encountering no one along the way.

Hadrian raked a hand through his hair in utter frustration. What in perdition was going on here? There had to be an explanation, albeit a strange one, for he was certain he'd seen her standing atop the tower. Perhaps she'd sprouted wings and had flown off into the night like some sort of mythological harpy. Or perhaps Rolfe had been right. Perhaps he had been too long without a woman in his bed and was suffering from the effects of his celibacy.

Yes, that must be it. He was randy as a goat and just the sight of this red-haired delusion caused his sex to grow hard and his mind to go soft. Once he took a woman, a real woman, with soft skin and sweet-smelling hair to his bed, this preoccupation he had with the thought of this Flaming Lady, this ridiculous obsession, would be gone and banished to oblivion.

He was married now. And Arabella was a lovely girl, vinegar-washed skin and all. He'd every right to bed his wife—in fact, should have done so long ago and would have, except for that night he'd ravished her, of which he had no memory.

This time would be different, he told himself. He would go to her and he would be gentle, for after that first night, she'd surely be frightened. He'd give her pleasure and listen to her soft-spoken cries as she experienced the wonder of release for the first time. And he'd bury himself within her, then and every night until she carried his child. A child. He wanted a son to teach and to carry on, and a child would keep Arabella occupied and away from his other business.

Yes, it was the perfect remedy for his present afflictions. He didn't know why he had not thought of it sooner. Even now, his body was growing taut just thinking about it. There was no point in delaying it any longer. Tonight was as good a night as any other. In fact, the sooner he was free from this idiotic daydreaming, the better it would be.

Turning toward the door that led to the narrow spiral staircase, Hadrian made his way for Arabella's chamber.

Mara was breathless both with fear and from running by the time she reached the safety of her bedchamber. She closed the door tightly, turning the key in its lock before depositing it atop her dressing table. She said a silent thank-you to the knight Rupert de Kaleven for having the foresight to install the hidden staircase in the tower. Built directly beneath the other stairs, it led to a secret passage beneath the castle. It had been built as a means of protection for the Kulhaven people. Twice she'd used it to escape from danger.

She wondered if she'd be so lucky a third time.

Had she not seen Hugin standing below, she had no doubt she'd be on her way to a prison cell in Dublin this moment. All her planning, all the careful and meticulous attention to detail. It would have fallen to naught had Hadrian found her on the tower with Owen. This thought made her realize that though meant as a gibe, Owen was right. She had to find a way for Hadrian to bed her, immediately, and get her with child. It was the only way she could secure her place at Kulhaven, for time was indeed running out for her.

A soft knock on the door that adjoined her chamber to Hadrian's startled her from her thoughts. Her heart began to pound anew. It was him. Hadrian. What if he had seen her and was coming now to confront her? But surely he wouldn't be knocking so softly had he learned of her deception. She did not answer, could not answer for her hair was still quite red. She prayed to St. Ida he'd think her asleep and would leave.

But, this time her prayers were not heeded.

"Arabella?" she heard him say softly. He knocked again, this time more insistently. He tried the door, but it was locked. He jiggled the handle.

"Arabella, are you all right?"

Panic began to fill her. If she continued not to answer, he might believe something wrong and break the door down. But if she answered, he would surely question why Arabella suddenly had sprouted red hair. She looked around the room, trying to find something, anything to rescue her. Or give her time. The pot of dye Cyma had left for her sat on the dressing table like a pot of gold at the end of the rainbow. But she did not have the time to apply it now.

Hadrian knocked again, persistent, calling louder this time. She spotted one of Cyma's nightcaps sitting on an armchair. She grabbed it and furiously began stuffing her hair beneath it until not a single strand of red hair showed. If this worked, she thought to herself, she would surely die of disbelief.

"Arabella, I can see the light from your candle so I know you are awake. Please open the door. I wish to speak with you."

And then she heard it. The sound of a key, his key, being pushed into the lock.

In the flash of a moment, Mara doused the candle and raced beneath the bedclothes, pulling them over her head. She heard the sound of the door opening. She tried to control her frantic breathing as Hadrian stepped into the room.

"Arabella, are you there?"

Her response was muffled by the heavy bedclothes. "Yes, my lord."

"Is everything all right? Why did you not answer my call? Is something wrong?"

"I am not feeling well. I was indisposed when you called. I am sorry, my lord."

Hadrian advanced to the bed. Mara nearly jumped out of her skin when she felt him sit beside her, his hand resting lightly on her bottom. "Come, let me see what is wrong. Perhaps I can help."

"No."

Hadrian started to pull on the bedclothes. "It is all right, Arabella. I am your husband now. If you are ill, I wish to help you."

Mara clutched the covers over her head. "No, my lord, please, I do not wish for you to see me like this. I have been physically ill and I am not presentable. Please do not embarrass me further. I assure you I will be fine. It is most probably just something I ate with dinner. Perhaps the dessert torte was too rich for my stomach. I have sent my maid to fetch some tea. She will be back soon to attend to me."

Hadrian was silent a moment. Mara begged every saint above to make him leave. She remained still, and a moment later she felt him rise from the bed. Relief flooded through her every bone.

"All right, Arabella, you win. Although it goes against my better judgment, I would never wish to cause you such distress. I will leave you to the able hands of your maid. Sleep well and I hope you are feeling better come morning."

"Thank you, my lord," she called from beneath the bedclothes, afraid to move so much as a muscle.

"Would you like me to stay until your maid returns?"

Would he never leave? "No, that is not necessary. She will be back only momentarily, I am certain."

"Good night then, Arabella."

"Good night, Hadrian."

Mara did not move for several minutes after she heard the door close behind him. As soon as she was certain he'd gone, she threw back the covers and ran to the dressing table to begin applying the dye to her hair.

It was thus that Cyma found her not too long after, her hands covered with a liberal amount of the blackened muck, trying desperately to cover every strand of red hair.

"What are you doing?"

Mara turned to look at her, a blob of black matter staining her cheek. "What does it look like I'm doing? I'm trying to get this dung into my hair!"

Cyma set her cloak on the chair, shaking her head. "There's no need to be nasty, missy. I only asked a question." She crossed the room to her and took over the task of spreading the dye through Mara's hair. "Wash that dye from your hands before you turn them black, too. Devil take me if I know why I came back early from my visit with Sadbh just to have cross words flung at me like rocks."

"I am sorry, Cyma. You've just no idea what I've been through this night."

Cyma looked at her in the reflection of the looking glass. "Saw Owen, did you?"

Mara stared at her, surprised. "You knew Owen was here?"

Cyma's lips tightened to a thin line as she nodded. "Just learned of it tonight. Old Sadbh saw him in a dream. Said your *bráthair* was coming back to Kulhaven, but that he was not the same boy from before. Said he would bring much trouble with him."

"That he did. He is threatening to expose me if I do not steal secret information from St. Aubyn for him."

"What sort of information?"

"I don't know, military strategies and the like, no

doubt. He said he would tell me when the time was right."

"And did you agree to it?"

"Do I have any choice in the matter? I cannot risk his seeing his threat through, and St. Aubyn finding out the truth. What else can I do?"

Finished with the dyeing, Cyma twisted Mara's hair atop her head and secured it with pins before wrapping it in a drying cloth. "You can do nothing. You must do everything within your power to keep Owen from revealing who you are to St. Aubyn. Sadbh believes the only way you will ever restore Kulhaven is to continue with this disguise. She has convinced me that this scheme of yours can succeed, but only if you are very careful. If not, it will end in disaster. For you, and for all of Kulhaven."

They were coming!

She could see them, at least a hundred of them, seeping through every opening at Kulhaven. Their guns were raised, the smoke from their torches burned at the back of her throat as she tried to escape before they noticed her. Around every corner, it seemed, they were there, laughing as they tossed a frightened maidservant among them, groping at her breasts as she screamed in terror. She was running, her chest tight with pain as she fought for every breath, but still she could hear them coming closer and closer behind until she could feel their hands upon her, grasping at her arms and she was being dragged down and . . .

"Missy, wake up now."

Mara startled awake at the touch of someone's hands

on her. She opened her eyes. Cyma's concerned face stared back at her.

"You were having a dream, tossing about and crying out loud."

Mara put her hand against her chest. Her heart was still pounding. "What time is it?"

"Just after dawn. Do you want to tell me about it?"

"About what?"

"The dream. Was it the same one you used to have? The one with the soldiers?"

Mara nodded. "I thought I was over that. I haven't had the dream in over a year. Why would I have it now?"

Cyma frowned. "It must be that Owen's return has upset you and brought it back." She sat on the bed, running her fingers gently against Mara's sweat-dampened brow. "Now, you just put the dream out of your mind. There are no soldiers coming to get you anymore. That's all in the past."

"But they could be coming to take me, if St. Aubyn ever learns who I truly am."

Cyma patted her hand, smiling her calming smile. "How could he ever learn who you are? Sadbh is the only one who knows the truth and you know she would never tell a soul. I certainly would never betray you."

"Yes, but Owen would."

"And what good would that do him? He'd have no one to get his precious information for him. Your brother will only do something for his own benefit. There is no benefit to him if you are found out. He'll not be saying anything of the like whilst he still needs you here at Kulhaven. You just need to make certain he continues to need you here."

Mara sat up on the bed. "You are right, Cyma. Without me, Owen has no way of getting the information he needs. As long as I am willing to give him what he wants, he would never reveal who I am to St. Aubyn. I'll just have to make certain I never give him everything he wants. I'll give him just enough to satisfy him that I am doing as he asks, but not enough so that he wouldn't still need me."

Mara's spirits had lifted decidedly as she made her way down to the dining room for breakfast two hours later. She hummed a little tune, knowing she had nothing to fear from Owen. He needed her there at Kulhaven. Without her, he would have no chance at getting the information he sought. As he had said, he was the one responsible for orchestrating her successful return to Kulhaven. But now, if anything, she was the one in control, the one who could give him what he wanted, only at her doing.

Still she could not allow this position to go to her head. She would have to give him something, for if she played him for the fool, she had no doubt, he'd betray her eventually.

Mara was surprised to see Hadrian sitting at the table when she entered the dining room, for he was usually gone by this hour. "Oh, good morning, Hadrian."

"Good morning, Arabella. I trust you are feeling better today?"

"Oh, yes, much better. My maid's tea was just what I needed. She makes a special blend with the leaves of the lime tree that is quite calming for the stomach. This morning found me feeling fit as a pudding, or something like that, Mrs. Danbury always says. I am sorry for my behavior last night."

"There is no need for apologies. I am just pleased you are feeling better today." He rose from his seat. "I've some business to attend to this morning at a neighboring estate. I will most probably be gone most of the day. Do not wait for me for dinner as it will most likely be after dark when I return."

He stopped before her then, his eyes taking on an odd expression. "But I will see you when I return this evening. There is a matter of some import I must discuss with you when I return. I will try to get back as soon as I can."

Before Mara could respond, Hadrian gathered her into his arms and brought his mouth down to hers. He kissed her fully, taking her breath away so that she swayed when he finally did release her.

Her heart was pounding as she watched him walk away without another word.

Chapter Sixteen

Once again, the clock was ticking as Mara waited for her husband to return. She was sitting on a softly cushioned settee in the parlor, the door to the entrance hall open and wide so she would know the moment Hadrian returned. The hearth fire crackled warmly beside her, and she was trying to read what would normally be a rather fascinating text on the circulation of blood and how it was moved through the body by the heart written by a man named William Harvey. But the words printed on the page were nothing but a blur, for her thoughts were filled with Hadrian and his announcement to her earlier that morning.

What was the matter of import he wished to speak with her about? And why the devil hadn't he discussed it with her during breakfast? Instead, he was making her wait all day, sitting on pins and needles, and watching the clock for his return as she wondered what it possibly could be.

She was so involved with these mental questions she did not hear him enter the parlor behind her.

"I'm pleased you waited up for me, Arabella."

"Oh, Hadrian, I did not hear you come in." Mara

rose from her chair, dropping the treatise she was reading and crossing the room to meet him. "What did you wish to speak with me about? You said it was a matter of great import."

"Yes, yes I did." He crossed the room to the sideboard. "Sherry?"

Why the devil was he drawing this out? "Yes, thank you. Now, what did you wish to discuss?"

Hadrian was smiling when he turned to offer her the glass. "Please, let us take a seat here by the fire."

It seemed an interminably long period of time before he was settled in his chair and had taken two sips of his brandy before he began speaking.

"Arabella, do you like children?"

This? This was what he'd kept her waiting all day for? To hear Arabella's opinion on children? Why was that so important? "Yes, yes, of course. I love children. Before I came to Kulhaven, I had taken to teaching ciphers to several of the village children. I quite enjoyed it."

There. That seemed a plausible response, a thoroughly "Arabellian" response. What next? Arabella's favorite color? Judging from the clothing she'd found in her trunks, she would have to guess it was some shade of gray.

"That's nice, but what I meant was children of your own. Do you wish to have a child of your own someday?"

What was he getting at? "Yes, of course I do. Doesn't every woman?"

"Not necessarily. Some women do choose not to give birth for whatever reason."

"I would not know of such a reason. What reason could you be speaking of, Hadrian?"

Hadrian exhaled loudly in frustration. He was obviously not getting his point across at all as he had planned. "Arabella, what I would like to know, and what I am not doing a very good job of asking, is would you want to have a child of your own—with me?"

Mara was stunned by his question. Of all the possible matters he could have chosen to discuss with her, she had never expected to hear those words from him. Before she could frame any sort of a response, Hadrian went on.

"I realize this marriage started with less than a favorable beginning. I would hope that we could put that incident behind us now and move on. I know I have been neglectful of you and sometimes downright rude. For that I am truly sorry. I told you I valued trust and honesty between a man and wife above all else. And I know I damaged that trust and honesty between us, but I want to try and earn that back. What I am saying, Arabella, is I would like to make a clean start of it with you. This time, I would not hurt you. I want you to be my wife, Arabella. Not just in name or for appearance's sake. I want you to be my wife in every sense of the word."

Mara just stared at him, not knowing how to respond. Here he was offering her everything she wanted, nay, needed to truly complete her plans and she didn't know how to answer. All the time she had been trying to find a way for Hadrian to bed her, she'd never really thought of what she'd do when actually faced with it. All her attentions up till then had been focused on getting to that point. Now that it was here, right in front of her, she wasn't sure she was ready for it.

But she could not refuse him now. "Yes, Hadrian, I would like that as well."

Hadrian rose from his chair and took her hand, pulling her up to face him. Slowly, gently, he took her face in his hands and lowered his mouth to hers. His kiss was soft, tender, and she dropped her head back and brought her hands to his shoulders, allowing every part of her to respond to him.

When he pulled away moments later, they both were breathless.

Hadrian began walking her toward the stairs. "I will join you in your chamber shortly in order to give you time to ready yourself for me."

Mara's head was still spinning from all that had occurred in this short period of time. "Yes."

She did not truly hear his words until she was nearly at her chamber door. He would come to her chamber. To her bed. Her heart began to beat faster at the thought of what those words meant.

She quickly lit a branch of candles and started across the room to the withdrawing chamber. "Cyma, you must wake up. St. Aubyn is coming to my chamber tonight. You cannot remain here."

The maid rubbed her sleepy eyes, pushing her linen nightcap back over her forehead. "How on earth did you manage to get him to agree to that?"

"I do not know. I did nothing. It was by his suggestion. We certainly did not take that into account, did we? He said he wanted Arabella to be his wife in every sense of the word. He said he wants a child. Come, unfasten these hooks on my gown. I must ready myself for him." She opened the doors to the wardrobe, looking through the items folded there. "Would any of Arabella's night rails be appropriate for this sort of thing?"

She quickly dropped her gown to her ankles and removed her stockings as Cyma unlaced her stays. She pulled her shift over her head and froze when she caught sight of her reflection in the looking glass.

"Cyma, there's something else we did not take into account when we began with this plan. We may have been able to disguise the color of my hair, but how will we disguise the rest of me?"

She motioned to her naked reflection and the more than obvious thatch of red curls at the joining of her thighs. Her voice took on an edge of panic. "What am I to do? He's coming here now!"

Cyma threw a white linen night rail at her from the trunk across the room. "Calm down, missy. Put this on and get yourself under the bedclothes. We haven't the time to worry over this now. Douse those glaring candles and keep them out while he's here. Make him believe that you are a frightened virgin. Although you're not supposed to be a virgin any longer, are you? Tell him that you are embarrassed to have any light in the room."

"But he thinks he's already taken me!"

Cyma took her by the shoulders. "All right, listen to me very carefully. When he comes inside of you there will be pain when he breaks through your maidenhead. You must not show him that pain. Grit your teeth or bite the back of your hand if you must, but if he thinks there's pain, he'll know he did not take you that first night. And he'll surely wonder why."

She opened a drawer in the wardrobe and removed a small vial. "Before you take him to your bed, you must make certain he swallows three drops of this. Any less will not be enough, any more may be too much. Be very careful with the potion. I've no wish of trying to explain why we cannot rouse his lordship from your bed."

Mara shook her head. "No, Cyma. This will never work. I must tell him he cannot come to my bed tonight. We need more time to prepare."

A knock sounded on her door. It was too late.

"It's him," Mara said in a frantic whisper. "What will we do now?"

"Not we. You. It is all up to you now." Cyma pressed the vial into her hand. "Three drops, missy, and no more. I brought a bottle of mead from the pantry to have a glass before I retired. Put the potion in the glass and get him to drink it. I don't care how, but do it. There is no other way."

Cyma disappeared through the door leading to the hallway just as Hadrian turned the handle on the door adjoining his chamber to hers and came in.

"I see you are ready for me."

Mara forced a smile and turned about. "Yes, Hadrian. I am ready for you."

He was dressed in the royal blue dressing gown she'd put on the night she'd gone to his chamber to wait for him. His legs were bare beneath it, showing well-muscled calves which were covered with dark hair. He came to stand before her and he lowered his mouth to kiss her again. She stepped into his arms and met his kiss, but as she felt his hand slide down over her shoulder, pulling the fabric of her wrap aside, she pulled away.

"Just a moment, Hadrian. Please. I'm sorry. I must be a little nervous. I'm not quite used to this sort of thing." She turned. "Perhaps something to drink would help. Would you have a glass of mead with me to help calm my nerves?" She motioned toward the bottle on her bedside table.

"But there is only one glass."

"We shall share it."

Mara lifted the bottle and filled the glass halfway. Hadrian started to reach for it, but she quickly lifted it to her lips, hoping he wouldn't notice the shaking of her hands, and downed the sweet liquid in one full swallow. "Now, I will pour yours. While I get it for you, will you please stoke the fire? It seems a bit chill in here of a sudden."

As he turned to do as she asked, Mara pulled the vial from her robe pocket and tilted it over the glass, tilting it till a drop formed at its top. Her fingers trembled anxiously as she watched three drops fall into the bottom of the glass. She hoped she had added the right amount. She couldn't have him falling asleep this time. She quickly pocketed the vial and poured the mead into the glass.

"Here you are, Hadrian."

Hadrian's eyes were intent on her as he took the glass and tilted his head back to drink. Mara watched as he downed its contents and set the glass on the table. She released a steady breath.

He reached for her then and his hands came to rest on the buttons that lined the front of her night rail. "Now, is there anything else, madam wife?"

In that short span of time, he'd already managed to unfasten two of the buttons. Mara pulled away, clutching the top of her night rail closed. "Yes, there is one more thing. Please douse the candles."

Hadrian took in along breath. "Arabella, there is nothing to be ashamed of. You are my wife now and we will be spending the rest of our lives together. Surely you realize at some time you must become accustomed to my seeing you unclothed."

Mara was biting her lip. "Yes, but I am still uneasy. It will take a little time for me to adjust to the way of married life. I am nervous enough as it is. The darkness would serve to help me relax. Please, Hadrian, douse the candles."

Hadrian hesitated a moment, then turned, shaking his head, and extinguished each candle on the silver branch. The room was dark, except for the faint glow of the fire in the hearth. Mara sat hesitantly upon the bed.

"Would you please also draw the curtain around the bed?"

"But, it will be black as pitch."

"Please, Hadrian?"

He frowned. "All right. But let me say that in the future I would prefer to see just who it is I am sharing my bed with."

Mara settled back on the pillows as he pulled the velvet drapery closed around them, throwing them into total darkness. She looked around. No light could pervade the heavy fabric. She could see nothing. All she could hear was Hadrian's heavy breathing as he settled himself beside her. She lay very still, trying to relax.

She could hear Hadrian leaning toward her and a

moment later he was pulling her into his arms to kiss her. His mouth met the tip of her nose rather than her lips.

"Damnation, it's so dark in here I can't even see what I'm kissing!"

Mara put her hands around Hadrian's neck and brought her lips to his, silencing any further complaint. Her heart was pounding and every muscle was taut with tension. She could feel his hands rubbing down over her shoulders, lower still to cup her breast. Memories of their first night together came flooding back, the feelings he'd evoked in her, the way she'd responded. Once again, she began to lose herself in the newness of it all.

With each kiss of his mouth on her body, down her neck, across her throat, her edginess began to ebb. In the darkness, it was easy to forget it was the enemy she was about to couple with. She tried to picture Liam, her once betrothed, but she could not so much as summon his image in her mind. Time had served to erase even that memory from her life. No matter how she tried, the only image that came to mind was Hadrian's face, his golden brown eyes, his tousled hair. Unwittingly her hands moved there and began stroking through the dark locks as she felt his mouth move downward to her breast.

Cloaked in the darkness and unable to see what he was doing to her brought a strange, thrilling excitement to their lovemaking. She did not even realize he'd already unfastened the buttons on her night rail and she gasped aloud when she felt his mouth close over the tip of one breast. Shock waves jolted through her as he ran his tongue over her nipple, teasing it to hardness, until she was trembling from the sensations running through her, unable to stand anymore, yet still wanting him to continue.

She felt his hands move up along her legs, raising her night rail to pool it at her hips. She raised her arms and in one swift motion, he pulled it over her head and tossed it to the foot of the bed.

She was then totally and utterly naked, completely exposed to him. Mara was suddenly grateful for the darkness. She felt him move from her and heard the whisper of silk as he removed his dressing robe. When he returned to her a heartbeat later, the touch of his skin on hers was hot and oddly exciting. Flesh on flesh, he lowered himself between her legs and began kissing a line down her chest to her belly, his teeth nipping lightly at the sensitive skin of her hip. She felt his hands slide down her thighs, parting them, then cupping her buttocks. And then she felt something hot and soft on her most private place and nearly screamed aloud when she realized it was his mouth.

God, the feeling was unlike anything she'd ever felt before. She could feel his tongue entering her, probing inside, flicking back and forth across her tingling flesh. His hands were kneading her buttocks, lifting her hips higher and closer against his mouth. She could feel the blood rushing through every inch of her body, pounding through every vein, as his mouth continued its sweet assault. Every sense was alive and tingling in her, every nerve ending screaming as waves of intense heat thrashed through her body.

She began to work for every breath as the feelings increased, growing stronger still, her hands clenching in his hair, her muscles tightening as she sought release from his relentless mouth until she did not think she could stand it any longer.

And suddenly, it felt as if the entire world around her had exploded into a shower of white hot intensity, and she was finally released from the torturous prison, soaring higher than the heavens on the wave of release. She cried out his name at the feelings that rocked through her, and fell back on the bed, exhausted and unaware of anything except the wonder of what had just happened between them.

She was vaguely aware of Hadrian moving over her, but was unprepared when he thrust into her suddenly, burying himself inside of her. She cried out at the shock of the sudden pain as he rent through her maidenhead, then realized what she'd done and froze.

Above her, Hadrian froze as well. He was sheathed within her. He could feel her body tightening instinctively around him, so tight it nearly pained him, but his mind was suddenly muddled. Had he not known better, he would have sworn he'd just taken a virgin.

He had entered her too quickly and too hard to know if he had encountered her maidenhead. Why, then, had she cried out as she had? Arabella could not be a virgin any longer, for he'd broken her maidenhead that first night. Hadn't he? There had been blood. He'd seen it himself. And, she had told him herself that he had ravished her.

"Are you all right, Arabella?"

Mara clenched her fists into the sheets to keep from showing the pain that was now burning and throbbing inside of her. "Yes, I'm sorry. I did not realize what you were doing. I was not ready."

Again he could feel her tighten her inner muscles

around him. God, she was so tight. He pulled back then and found himself driving forward into her softness once again. He suddenly forgot all about her crying out as she had as he continued to thrust into her. Again and again. Harder and faster. He grabbed at her shoulders, wanting only to find his climax and empty his seed that was now screaming for release.

God, it had been so long for him. He wanted to savor the pleasure of it, but knew he would not be able to hold back much longer. He tried to move slowly, to bring her to pleasure again, but each time he thrust, she felt tighter around him until he was pounding against her without restraint.

He finally reached his climax and yelled out loud with his release, continuing to thrust deeper and deeper as he emptied his seed inside her. When he was finally spent and his chest was heaving for breath, he collapsed against her breast, mumbling something inaudible in her ear.

In seconds he was deep in sleep.

The potion Cyma had given her had been his final undoing.

At least this time, she thought to herself as she lay there in the darkness, he had been able to finish before he'd fallen under the effects of the decoction. Mara was afraid to move but knew she had to get him off her. She lay still for several minutes, remembering what had just happened between them. It had all gone so quickly, leaving her to wishing she could just curl up into a ball and cry.

She didn't know what she had expected to feel when she finally lost her innocence. All through her life, she'd known when the time came, it would be with someone she loved more than any other, someone with whom she would spend her life. She'd been told the actual mechanics of it by her mother when she'd turned fifteen. Edana had been a firm believer in preparing her daughter for every aspect of her eventual role as a wife, and was not at all embarrassed to discuss even the most intimate of details.

But her mother had not prepared her for the feelings she would have when the day finally came for her to become a woman. She'd not told her of the wondrous feelings she would feel, how her body would rise out of itself and float higher than the heavens. And she'd not told her how absolutely intimate it would be, how by taking a man inside of her, she would become as one with him, forever bound together by the experience.

She had heard of the women who earned their livelihood by doing this very thing. She had seen them strolling about the dock area in Dublin, wearing their garish gowns that barely covered their breasts and calling out boldly to the sailors. They were called *striapachs* by the local fishwives and were treated with the highest disdain. Having experienced this thing, this age-old act between men and women now firsthand, Mara could only pity those women who out of necessity would do such a private and personal thing with any number of men, never to see them again.

Hadrian was growing quite heavy atop her now and she managed to push him to the side enough for her to slide from underneath him. He did not move even a muscle and for a moment, Mara wondered if she'd accidentally given him one too many drops of the potion. She pressed her ear against his chest and listened. His breathing was slow and even. How long would he remain drugged if she had?

She slipped her night rail back over her head and hurried to fetch her maid. Cyma was already waiting for her in the hallway.

"It is done?" she asked.

Mara nodded.

"And you are all right? He did not harm you?"

"No. There was pain but only when he broke through my maidenhead. I do not think he realized I was still a virgin."

Cyma stared at her a moment, causing Mara to lower her eyes. Had she heard her cry out Hadrian's name when he'd given her such pleasure as she had never felt before? She was supposed to have forced herself to bed with him. Out of duty to her cause. She was not supposed to have felt anything except revulsion and disgust.

"Come," Cyma said, "we've work to do."

She entered the room and started to light the candle at the bedside table.

"No, Cyma. It might wake him."

"No. There is no chance of that. The wild prickly lettuce I received from Sadbh will keep him sleeping soundly as a babe until morning."

"Wild prickly lettuce? But isn't that . . . ?"

"Poisonous? Yes, if taken in a large dose, it can prove quite fatal. That is why I told you to be sure to use only three drops of the potion."

"Cyma! I could have killed him."

Cyma struck a match and touched it to the wick of the candle. "Yes, I know."

Mara could have sworn she saw the ghoulish flicker

of a smile on her maid's face, but put it off as the play of the candlelight. "Had I known that, I never would have agreed to give him the potion at all."

Cyma pulled back the drapery on the bed. Hadrian lay naked and sleeping, snoring, in fact, oblivious of their presence above him. There was a small amount of her virgin's blood still on his member.

"I would that I had a hatchet to chop that rod from him for what he did to you tonight," Cyma said lowly.

Mara was beginning to worry about her maid's ill-concealed feelings for St. Aubyn. "It is all right, Cyma. He did not hurt me all that much."

The next two hours were spent removing any evidence of the taking of Mara's virginity. The bedclothes were pulled off and replaced with new, a monumental task which involved both women attempting to move Hadrian's drugged and sleeping body from one side of the bed to the other while they spread the sheet across the feather mattress. At one point, his head got knocked against the bedpost. Both women froze when Hadrian stirred, moaning something in his sleep, then they carefully finished rolling him back when they were certain he was still asleep.

Taking a cloth and a bowl of warm water, Mara carefully washed the blood from Hadrian, her virgin's blood, before cleaning the blood and his seed from herself as well.

When everything was done and the bloodstained sheets had been thrown in the hearth fire, Mara climbed back into bed and settled herself against him to wait until morning.

Chapter Seventeen

Mara awoke the instant she heard Hadrian begin to stir beside her. She was in her bed, lying with her back to him, staring straight ahead and waiting. She did not move. After a minute or two had passed, she heard him roll toward her and she could feel his eyes staring at her back. He remained silent for several moments before he finally spoke.

"Arabella, are you awake?"

His voice was soft so as not to waken her if she truly was still asleep.

For a brief moment she thought to feign that she was sleeping, to avoid facing him after what had happened between them the previous night, but she decided against it in the end. She would have to face him sooner or later and better to have it sooner and done with.

"Yes, Hadrian. I am awake."

He reached out and touched her shoulder, pulling her around gently to face him. He smiled. "Good morning, madam wife."

Mara found it difficult to look into his eyes after the previous night. "Good morning."

"You do not have to lie there waiting for me to wake,

Arabella. You could have called me when you first awoke."

Mara returned a hesitant smile. "I was uncertain as to the way of it with husbands and wives. My parents slept in separate beds in separate chambers. When you started our marriage doing the same, I thought that was the way for all married couples."

"Well, I was wrong to have done that. I prefer to share my wife's bed, be it in my chamber or hers. In fact, I haven't slept as soundly as I did last night for quite some time."

Mara instantly thought of the potion with the wild prickly lettuce.

Hadrian sat up. "I imagine it will be quite a many years before we would tire of each other such that we would seek out separate rooms. At least I hope it would be. Now, would you like to join me in the dining room for breakfast, or would you prefer that we take tea and sweet cakes here?"

Mara shook her head. "We need not have our breakfast here. I will join you in the dining room after I have washed and dressed."

Hadrian started to rise from the bed, then stopped, rubbing his temple. Mara watched him warily.

"Is something wrong, Hadrian?"

"I do not know for certain, but there's a lump the size of a walnut on my head and I don't remember at all hitting it."

"Oh," Mara quickly broke in, remembering how they had struck his head on the bedpost when they had been changing the bedding the previous night. "You must have hit it on the headboard while you were sleeping last night. My bed is much smaller than yours and so you are not used to it."

Hadrian nodded, accepting her explanation. "Next time, then, we will have to sleep in my bed. It is much larger and will not be the cause of any injury. I will leave you now to wash and dress."

He stood, fully naked, and waited for her at the side of the bed. He did not move to cover himself, completely at ease with his nudity. Mara stood on the other side of the bed and turned as if to dismiss him. She saw him glance to the bed sheets and wondered if he was looking for signs of her virgin blood. Did he somehow realize that she had been a virgin and he had not taken her on that first night? What would he say?

"Is there something else, Hadrian?"

"No." He was still staring at the sheets when he retrieved his dressing robe from the foot of the bed. He did not move to pull it on. "I will see you downstairs shortly."

With that he turned and started for his chamber. Mara watched him go, her eyes straying to his gloriously muscled buttocks as he moved away, closing the door behind him.

It was later that same day, while she was sitting in her bedchamber trying to find her pomander with the sprig of yarrow Sadbh had given her that Mara received her first instruction from Owen.

It came in the form of a note tied to her underthings which had just come from the laundry, hidden beneath her black silk stockings. She opened it quickly and read the words written inside.

In his study,
behind the desk,
you will find a hidden door.
Inside is a map
showing the troop locations
along the eastern coastline.
Memorize it and come to the
tower at midnight.

He had not signed it. Mara touched one corner of the note to the lighted candle on her dressing table and dropped it in a small porcelain bowl, watching as the flame quickly consumed it. She was frowning when she dumped the charred remains in the corner chamberpot and turned to leave the room.

Hadrian had left to survey the harvesting in a field on the southern edges of the estate near the village. He would be gone for hours, long enough for her to find the map and get the information Owen sought.

She made her way quietly to the study door. A quick study showed that no one was about. She slipped inside and after making certain she was indeed alone, she closed the door behind her.

She found the secret door, just as Owen had said, set in the oak paneling behind the desk. It was cleverly hidden behind three very tall and fat tomes, thoroughly dull reading about the weather patterns in the region since the beginning of the century, sure to keep the door hidden from disuse for years. She turned the small latch on the equally small wooden door. It was locked.

She searched through Hadrian's desk, finding no key. How was she to get the blasted door open?

She was ready to write a note back telling Owen the

next time he wanted her to steal information, he could at least get her a key, when she remembered reading a novel once that told how to spring a lock.

The story had been about a beautiful princess who had been locked away in a tall tower by an evil villain when she refused his offer of marriage. He had kidnapped her from her family, promising to keep her locked away until she agreed to wed him. The princess, who was really quite clever, had escaped by using her hairpin to open the lock.

Mara removed a pin from the rigid bun in her hair and fashioned it into the shape of the letter L. She pushed it carefully into the lock and twisted it around inside. It took her several attempts, but she finally managed to spring the catch free, much to her surprise.

She opened the door and found a small compartment inside that contained a stack of papers, the top of which was the map Owen was looking for.

Mara quickly surveyed the map. It was a rather crude drawing, in fact it was barely legible, but after a moment of looking closely at it, she recognized several distinct landmarks and was able to locate the eastern coastline. It appeared as if the English had camps at each major point along the coast, completely cutting off any route from England below Dublin and the Pale.

County Wicklow was occupied at three separate points, Wexford at four. The only penetrable point along the entire coast was at a small inlet on the southern shore of Wexford near a narrow peninsula, but Mara remembered once reading—she could not recall where—that the winds in Wexford, the "westerlies" they had been called, could come up without warning at any given time.

Many ships had been downed on the sharp reefs after being caught in the winds while trying to navigate a course around that area. Of course the people who lived in that area knew well how to avoid the westerlies. But did Owen's contacts know as well?

Suddenly a voice sounded from the hall outside. "Shipley, I've some paperwork to look over in the study. If you would, please ask Mrs. Danbury to bring tea. That blend she makes with the elderberry leaves. I've a slight headache and that tea always seems to help."

"Yes, my lord. Right away."

Hadrian!

Mara looked to the door. It was still closed. She quickly folded the map and replaced it in the compartment where she had found it. Her fingers were shaking as she placed the books that masked its place back on the shelf and turned toward the door to leave.

"Hello, Arabella. I wasn't expecting to find you here. Was there something you needed from me?"

How the devil did he move so quickly and so silently? She hadn't even heard him come in. Mara smiled, wondering how long he'd been standing there, and hoped the look of guilt was not obvious on her face. "No, Hadrian. I was just looking for something to read, but nothing seemed to spark my interest. I think I'll take a brief respite before dinner instead. Sorry to have disturbed you. I'll leave you to your work now."

As she started past him, Hadrian snaked out a hand and grabbed her by the arm. "Just a moment."

Mara froze. Fear claimed her like a dark shadow. He knew what she had been doing. He had seen her putting the papers back in the hidden compartment and now was going to question her about it. She took a deep breath as Hadrian came around to face her. She stared up at him, unable to think of what to say. She didn't have to. Hadrian lowered his head and touched his lips softly to hers.

"Perhaps my paperwork can wait until later. I think I'd prefer to join you instead."

Mara smiled nervously at his unexpected outburst. "Now? You want to join me in my bed? In the middle of the day? But that would not be proper, Hadrian."

"Anything is proper between a man and his wife. But, you are right. There are a few matters to which I must attend, which is why I returned from the harvesting early. Though I must say the prospect of bedding you is a definite temptation." He kissed the top of her hand. "Go now before I throw all thought of duty to the wind and take you now on the floor of this room."

Mara could but stare at his bold words. This certainly was a change from the man she'd known days before. She didn't how how to respond to this new Hadrian.

Rather than attempt to speak, she smiled and turned to leave, rather hurriedly, so that he didn't have the time to change his mind.

Hadrian watched Arabella leave. When she had closed the door behind her, his smile quickly faded to a frown. It was no use. No matter how he tried, he could not banish the image of that red-haired witch from his mind. Bedding Arabella certainly had not helped as he had thought it would. In fact, her insistence on having the room in total darkness had only served to make it easier for him to picture himself making love to her, the Flaming Lady, and not Arabella.

First he'd seen her floating in the lough, then she had appeared in the tower. Now, she was invading his mind, his very thoughts, as well. Was he losing his mind?

No, he told himself stubbornly. It was impossible. He did not believe this fable, this delusion of a witch who haunted Kulhaven. If it took bedding Arabella every night for a year to banish her from his mind, then he would do so.

All he had to do was insist on having a candle burning at the bedside so he would not be able to forget who it was he was bedding. Although, the thought of looking down into a bespectacled face with her hair pulled back beneath that wretched white linen cap made the prospect even less desirable.

"You have done well, sister. This information should prove most beneficial to our cause. Now, the next thing I want you to do is find the list of Cromwell's top advisors. St. Aubyn has it in his desk drawer, beneath his writing parchment."

"What? You did not say I would have to continue to get information for you."

Owen smiled. "Nor did I say I would only ask it of you once."

Mara crossed her arms. "Well, I will not pry into Hadrian's private papers for you anymore. I could have taken it when I went for the map earlier today. Why don't you get this list yourself? You seem to know where he keeps everything hidden."

Owen grinned. "Acquiring a soft spot for the Englishman, are you?"

Mara frowned. "No, it is just too risky. He very

nearly caught me this time. How am I to explain my constant presence in his study? He's bound to wonder why I'm continually going in search of books to read. He's sure to get suspicious."

"You were always very clever. You've managed to keep him ignorant of your wiles this far. I'm certain you will think of something. Just get the list, Mara, or else your new husband will learn he's not wed to the godchild of Cromwell as he thinks. I believe you'd rather explain being in his study looking for a book than who you really are and why you are impersonating his wife."

Mara was trapped. She knew it and she hated the fact that she could do nothing about it. Now she was glad she'd neglected to tell Owen about the fourth camp in County Wexford on the map. She hoped it caused him a great deal of trouble, hoped it ruined his plans, whatever they might be.

She didn't know what he was up to, why he needed this information so badly, but she was certain if he was involved, it could be nothing good. She'd tried to pry in a roundabout way into what he was doing with the information, but he refused to tell her anything.

"I cannot continue to sneak away in the middle of the night like this either. How shall I get you a copy of this list you want?"

"No copies. I want no evidence that could incriminate me. Just use that wonderful memory of yours and meet me tomorrow at midday along the eastern edge of the estate. Surely the lady of the house, the Countess of St. Aubyn, is allowed to ride about the estate. There is an abandoned cottage there that was partially burned when Cromwell came through Kilkenny. Come alone and make certain no one follows you." He looked at the moon above. "Now, it is getting late and I'm sure you are anxious to return to the loving arms of your husband. Tell me, how is it you are able to couple with a man you claim to despise?"

Did he know everything? "I don't know what you are talking about."

Owen chuckled. "Come now, Mara. You needn't try to deny it. You know you finally managed to lure him between your legs. The entire household knows, although looking like that, it is a wonder you managed to pull it off."

Mara opened her mouth to say something utterly unladylike, but Owen cut her off.

"You will be happy to hear the servants are much relieved that the lord and lady have finally consummated their marriage. They were beginning to worry about the future of the St. Aubyn line. Now, the question is will you be able to keep him there? Obviously he did not have too much of a sport in your bed, else you'd not have made our meeting tonight. You'll have to be more inventive, sister, to keep a man like St. Aubyn satisfied in your bed."

He was gone in an instant, which was fortunate for him, for had he stayed a second longer, Mara would have surely pushed him over the edge of the tower herself. He was a wretched, vile creature who she found it increasingly difficult to believe she could possibly share a drop of blood with.

What had happened to change Owen this way? Where had her teasing, overprotective brother gone to? Cromwell had stolen that part of her life, it seemed, as well. Oh, how she longed for it to be ten years earlier again when everything in her world had been right.

As she slipped back into her chamber not a quarter hour later, she didn't notice the door that adjoined her room to Hadrian's standing ajar. Nor did she noticed him standing at the threshold, wearing his dressing robe, and waiting for her in the darkness.

"Arabella. I was beginning to worry. Where have you been all this time?"

Mara nearly jumped out of her skin at the sound of his voice coming from the shadows. "Oh, Hadrian, I did not see you there. I'm sorry if I caused you to worry. I . . ." Her mind suddenly went blank and she didn't know what to say. "I was restless and I couldn't sleep, so I took a walk to settle me."

What a stupid excuse. Why, when she needed her wits about her the most, did they always seem to desert her?

"A walk? Where did you go?"

He didn't believe her, it was obvious. "Oh, just about. I wandered through the western wing, and well"—she lowered her eyes, feigning embarrassment—"I became lost. I feel like such a dolt. I continue to do such silly things. First I am unable to control my horse, then I get sick, and now I get lost in my own home. What next? Will I forget my own name?"

A distinct possibility, she thought to herself, given the fact that living this double identity life was getting increasingly confusing.

Hadrian stepped into the room. "Do not be so hard on yourself, Arabella. You've had a big change in your life in just a short amount of time. You've traveled to a different country, a hostile one at that, married a man you'd never set eyes upon, and moved into a house you've never seen before where you know no one except your maid. I'd say you're doing pretty well considering the circumstances."

He came to stand before her, taking her hand in his. "I think you are trying to do too much at one time, worrying over doing the slightest something wrong. You are exhausting yourself is all. Look at you. You're so worried about being a perfect wife, you cannot even sleep. Why don't you lie down and try get some rest? I've some work to do in my study. If you'd like I'll have some tea with chamomile brought up for you."

Mara shook her head.

"All right. You go on to bed then. We can talk more in the morning."

He kissed her forehead softly, turned, and left the room.

Mara sank into the soft cushions of the armchair that sat before the hearth. How was she ever going to continue with this charade? Owen had her running about like a dog gone mad. Everywhere she went she had to try to remember which persona she was supposed to be portraying. And on top of all that, it seemed her husband's experience with her in bed had been so unenjoyable that he preferred to pore over paperwork in his study than repeat it again.

All in all, she wouldn't be surprised if Cromwell himself showed up at the doorstep the following morning for cakes and tea.

Life certainly was getting complicated.

Mara had just finished relating the names that had been printed on the list in Hadrian's desk to Owen.

"Very good. I must say, you are more suited to these

covert little missions than I thought you would be. You surprise me, Mara."

She was not flattered by his compliment by any means. "I have brought you what you wanted. I will be leaving now."

"Just a moment." Owen pulled something from his jacket. "I will need something more of you this next time. Three nights from tonight you will come back to this cottage. You will bring with you a pardon signed by your husband releasing one John MacDugan from Dublin Prison."

"What?"

"You will stamp it with his signet ring which bears the image of a lion, and then you will bring the signed and sealed pardon to me."

"You are completely daft. How am I supposed to get Hadrian to sign such a document?"

"Oh, he won't sign the pardon. You will, after you've had three days to practice his signature. Here is a sample." He handed her a folded piece of foolscap.

"I thought you wanted no evidence," she said with barely concealed sarcasm.

"You are correct. I do not want any evidence that could be found on me. How you keep it from being discovered on you is your business. Why don't you tuck it inside your underclothes? The only one going there these days is you."

Mara glared at him.

"After you have mastered St. Aubyn's signature, destroy that document. Bring the pardon to me at our next meeting. This will be the last mission I require of you. If you are successful, I will never trouble you again."

"And you will promise never to reveal who I am?"

"Yes. You will be free to pursue your own interests again. And," he added, "if you are successful with the pardon, I will reward you most generously."

"Reward me?" Mara looked at him narrowly. "How could you possibly reward me?"

Unless, of course, you happened to vanish from the face of the earth, which indeed would be most rewarding.

"You are seeking a certain object that was left by our mother at Kulhaven when it was stormed, are you not?"

The Tapestry. Owen had it. He was the one who had taken it from the secret vault. "You have the Kulhaven Tapestry?"

Owen smiled. "It is perfectly safe and hidden away in a location known only to me. Once you have done what I ask of you, I will return it to you. I have no use for dust-ridden relics. It was merely a bargaining tool in case you proved stubborn and refused to do as I asked."

He stopped then as if he'd heard something. He moved to the window and pushed the tattered curtain aside to peer outside. "My other contact is coming now. It is best you go. I wouldn't want anyone to recognize the wife of the Earl of St. Aubyn coming from a furtive meeting with another man. Even if the other man is her brother. Lord knows you are having trouble enough getting your husband into your bed. I wouldn't wish to be the cause of any more difficulty for you."

Mara wanted to slap him, but turned to leave before this other person arrived.

"I will see you three nights hence, and Mara," he called as she hurried toward the door, "if you think not to come, I will promise you this. You will regret it for the rest of your life."

Mara knew that he meant every word of his threat. She turned without responding.

Outside she quickly mounted her horse and started for the cover of the woods.

She looked back just in time to see Hadrian's horse thundering up the rise toward the cottage.

Chapter Eighteen

The realization did not strike Mara until she had already returned to the stables at Kulhaven and she suddenly remembered Owen's words at her leaving.

His other contact.

Hadrian?

It was not possible. For if the rider coming to meet Owen had been Hadrian riding Hugin, then that would mean that Hadrian was a spy, and that was simply a ludicrous notion.

But she was certain the horse carrying the rider to the cottage had been his black stallion Hugin.

To assure herself she was indeed mistaken, Mara marched into the house and directly to Hadrian's study. She was a little surprised to find it empty. When she had told Hadrian earlier that morning that she was going out for a ride, he had told her to enjoy herself, that he was planning to stay holed up in his study all day working on estate business. So, where had he gone?

She searched out and found the steward, Peter Shipley, standing in Mrs. Philpot's warm cozy kitchen, discussing a matter with Horace Crow, the castle's man of ledgers, over a mug of ale.

"Yes, my lady?" Shipley said as he instantly detached himself from his conversation.

"Mr. Shipley, do you know where Lord St. Aubyn has gone?"

"Yes, my lady. He is out on an errand. He said he had much work to do and would return shortly."

Mara stared at him. She could not believe it, but it seemed to be true. Hadrian, a spy? It just did not seem possible.

"Thank you, Mr. Shipley," she said absently and turned to go to her chamber.

"Oh, my lady," Shipley called to her before she reached the stairs, "Mrs. Danbury informs me that his lordship and Pudge took the coach and team to Kilkenny to see about purchasing a new mount for your ladyship. He said to tell you he would be back by supper."

If Hadrian had taken the coach on his errand, then who had been riding Hugin? Perhaps it had not been Hugin, but a horse similar in size and color. Yes, that must be it.

In fact, she told herself, she would wager were she to look right now, she'd find Hugin in his stall happily munching a mouthful of sweet oats. And, to prove it to herself, she headed next for the stables.

Before she reached the back entrance through the kitchens, she met Mrs. Danbury, who had come running up behind her.

"Oh, my lady, I am so glad I caught up with you. I'm afraid there is a matter which requires your immediate attention in the dining room."

"Can it not wait, Mrs. Danbury? There is something I need to do at the moment."

Mrs. Danbury was insistent. "I'm afraid it cannot wait, my lady. Lord St. Aubyn is having guests for supper this evening, Lord and Lady Lakewood from across the River Nore, and there is some question as to which service to use. I suggested the bone china, which is more suited to the occasion of guests, but, well, that mule Mr. Shipley insists on the pewter. Since we could not come to an agreement amongst ourselves, we decided to leave it up to your ladyship to decide."

Mrs. Danbury stared at her, awaiting an answer. "My lady?"

Mara was still preoccupied with the whereabouts of Hadrian's horse earlier that day. "Hmm?"

"Which service would you prefer we use for supper, my lady, the china or the pewter?"

"What? Oh, whatever you think is best, Mrs. Danbury." She started for the door. "I have the utmost confidence in your good judgment in these matters."

Mrs. Danbury's face broke into a wide smile. "Why thank you, my lady. I'll see to it right away." She turned. "Oh, Mr. Shipley . . ."

Mara closed the door behind her and started across the courtyard. She had no time for petty differences between the members of the staff right now. There was something else she just had to see, to prove to herself she had been mistaken about Hadrian's horse.

She was nearly at the stable door when she collided with Davey, who had been carrying an armful of logs. The logs and Davey went flying to the ground. She hadn't even seen him coming.

"Oh, Davey, I am so sorry. I did not see you."

Davey rose quickly to his feet and retrieved his hat from where it had fallen, dusting it off. "No trouble, my lady. I should have been watching where I was walking." He started picking up the fallen logs.

"Here, let me help you." Mara bent to join him in retrieving the logs.

"Oh, no, that's not necessary, my lady. I can manage it myself."

"Nonsense, Davey. I can—" Mara stopped in midsentence when she saw Rolfe leaving the stables then. He wore a wide-brimmed hat and looked to see who was about, walking quickly to the gateway leading out of the bailey to the front of the castle. Mara was certain it had been him.

When she turned, Davey was standing, arms full of the logs except for the one she held. She placed it atop the pile he held.

"Here you are, Davey."

"Thank you, my lady. Is there something I can do for you? Would you like a horse saddled for a ride?"

"No. I must have left my gloves in the tack after I went riding this morning. I was just going to see if they were there. Sorry again for causing you to drop the logs."

Once inside the stable, Mara headed directly for Hugin's stall. The great black beast was standing there, just as she had thought he would be, munching on his oat dinner. She started to turn, satisfied that she had been mistaken when she'd seen the horse approaching the cottage earlier that day. Suddenly she stopped short.

Hugin's sides were slick, his coat marked and wet from the saddle. She opened the stall gate and ran her hand gently down his flank. His skin was hot to the touch. He'd just been ridden, and ridden hard, and whomever had ridden him had not taken the time to walk him cool or curry him.

Patting him softly on the muzzle, Mara turned to leave.

"Davey," she said once outside the stable again, "has his lordship returned from his errand yet?"

"No, my lady. But I expect them back soon. My ma's waiting on Pa, too, because she asked him to pick up some fabric in town for a dress she's makin'. Did you want me to tell his lordship you're looking for him when he gets back?"

"No, that is not necessary. I was just wondering because it looks as if Hugin was ridden not too long ago."

Davey nodded his head. "Yes, my lady, he was. Lord Blackwell took him out just before midday. He said something about having to meet someone and he was running a bit late so he needed a fast mount."

"Oh, Hadrian, she is just beautiful."

And indeed she was, a spry bay mare with four white socks and a star on her face that was centered perfectly between her lovely dark eyes. Mara ran her hand softly over the horse's velvety muzzle, scratching her behind the ears as she munched on the sweet carrot she offered her.

"And what will you call her?"

Mara thought for a moment. "I believe I shall call her Munin."

Hadrian smiled, but said nothing.

"You find that name amusing, my lord?"

"No, I find it amazing that a young English miss such as yourself would know of the Norse legends. I did not think Norse mythology was a general subject taught to young ladies."

"You are correct in saying it is not a subject of study usual for the female gender. In fact, my mother would lecture me thoroughly if she knew I had just told you that. The only reason I know about the legends is because I once read a book about Norse mythology. I recall reading that the chief Norse god, Odin, had two ravens who supplied him with all of his knowledge. One was Hugin, or Thought, for whom your steed is named. The other was Munin, or Memory."

"The story must have made quite an impression on you for you to have remembered it all this time."

She shrugged. "No, not really. As I told you before, I just seem to have an ability for remembering things, no matter how inconsequential they might be, once I read them or hear them."

Hadrian grinned. "Well, then, your horse has been very aptly named. Tell me, though, I am curious—why would your mother lecture you for knowing something so inconsequential as a Norse legend?"

Mara lowered her eyes as she thought Arabella should do. "My mother once told me that men did not like educated women. In fact, she was against my reading anything but recipes and embroidery patterns. My father finally convinced her to allow me to read, but only on the condition that I never reveal to anyone anything I learned other than the usual subjects taught to women."

Mara knew what she said was not entirely true for although her mother had told her that men did not like educated women, both she and her father had been of the opinion that a woman needed an education just as much as a man. And, with her brothers' ages being so widespread, she had had the benefit of their tutors through most of the years of her childhood.

"So, why have you revealed the fact that you are educated to me now?"

Mara gave a small smile. "Well, you have already wedded me, so it is too late. You are trapped into a marriage to a learned woman. Does that displease you, my lord?"

Hadrian chuckled. "No, not at all. In fact, on the contrary, it pleases me to no end, for you see, I know nothing of embroidery patterns so without your rather unconventional education, conversation between us would surely be limited. I enjoy conversation in the evenings, meaningful conversation, so do not feel as if you must hide your knowledge any longer. I have always been of the opinion that a woman's mind is in no way inferior to a man's." He added under his breath, "Sometimes too much so."

"What was that, my lord?"

"Nothing. Now, since you have christened this lovely little mare with what I feel is a very appropriate name, shall we get on to seeing if her previous owner was truthful in saying she was a well-mannered and sweet-natured mount? I will have Davey saddle Hugin. He is bound to be anxious to get out of his stall for a little exercise."

Mara seized the opportunity to broach the subject of Rolfe's ride earlier that day. "Oh, but he has already been exercised. Lord Blackwell took him out for a ride earlier today."

Hadrian hesitated only a moment and if Mara hadn't been looking for a reaction, she most probably never would have noticed it. "No, Arabella, you must be mistaken. Rolfe was nowhere near Kulhaven today. He is in Dublin, two days' ride from here, on his way there to catch a ship bound for England."

Before she could argue further, he turned and started for the stable to saddle Hugin, leaving Mara to stare in confusion at his retreating back.

She didn't for a moment believe that Rolfe was in Dublin. She had seen him, plain as the nose on her face, leaving the stables earlier that day. And she'd seen Hugin riding up the rise toward the cottage where Owen awaited. The question was did Hadrian truly not know of his friend's whereabouts, or was he just trying to hide the fact that he did?

Hadrian was one of Cromwell's most trusted advisors. Surely he could not know of Rolfe's meeting with Owen. No, it must be that Rolfe was using his relationship with Hadrian to gain information to give to Owen. He was acting as a spy, and using Hadrian's position.

She recalled the night she'd first met Rolfe when he'd come to have supper with them soon after her arrival at Kulhaven. He'd questioned her about her "godfather" Cromwell's plans. She remembered Hadrian telling him she would not know of such things. She hadn't thought much about it at the time, but now she found it odd that he'd ask a woman for such information.

What Mara found even more curious was that she should be displeased with Rolfe's activities. Though she really didn't give her allegiance to either side in the war—all she really wished for was peace—it bothered her that this man who professed to be Hadrian's closest friend would use his relationship so.

But why should it trouble her at all? She was no better, she told herself. She was using Hadrian as a means to gain her own ends, duping Hadrian into thinking she was Arabella, but knowing that Hadrian thought of Rolfe as a lifelong friend, and that Rolfe was using that relationship as he was, made Mara want to expose him for the fiend he truly was.

But, of course, she knew she could never do that, for by doing so, she would be revealing her own treachery as well.

The Right Honorable Hadrian Augustus Ross, the Earl of St. Aubyn.

Later that night, Mara sat alone in her bedchamber, a single candle sitting beside her on the rosewood marquetry writing desk as she began the task of duplicating Hadrian's signature. With each stroke of the quill, she began to dislike herself more and more for what she was doing, for what Owen was forcing her to do. She wished she could just go to Hadrian and tell him the truth, but knew that thought was ludicrous. He would immediately have her arrested and thrown into prison and any chance she had at regaining Kulhaven would be completely and utterly lost.

Still she kept the wish in her heart that things could be different. She wondered, if circumstances weren't what they were, if there had never been a war or had Cromwell never existed, what would have happened, what turn her life would be taking right now.

She was so deep in her thoughts and so intent on the signature she was writing that she did not hear the door open behind her. She saw something move out of the corner of her eye and nearly jumped out of her skin when she noticed Hadrian coming across the room.

"Hadrian!" She grasped the parchment and pulled it toward her to keep him from seeing what was written on it. The open bottle of ink that had been sitting atop it toppled from the reckless motion, spilling the black liquid across the top of the desk and everything lying there, including the parchment. "Oh, dear . . ."

Mara grabbed another piece of parchment and in the guise of trying to sop up the mess, succeeded in covering every stroke of the quill showing her copy of Hadrian's signature. By the time she was finished, the desk and her fingers were completely covered with the ink, but not one incriminating quill stroke remained.

When she looked at him again, her fingers dripping with ink, she thought to herself that Hadrian must truly think himself married to an idiot, so clumsy had she become around him.

"Let me help you," Hadrian said, reaching for the mess she held.

"No, Hadrian, there is no sense two of us walking through life with blackened fingers. If you would, please just call for my maid for assistance."

Hadrian crossed the room and knocked on the small door that led to Cyma's room. Moments later, Cyma, her head covered with her sleeping cap, shot her mistress a curious glance as she bustled in to come to the rescue. Hadrian stood to the side as the two women started cleaning the desk. Nearly a half hour later, the mess from the ink was finally cleaned and the only evidence remaining of the debacle were Mara's very black fingertips and the dark stain atop the writing desk.

"I hope that what you were writing wasn't anything

too important," Hadrian said as Cyma closed her door behind her.

Mara looked up. "Excuse me?"

"Whatever it was you were writing. I said I hoped it wasn't anything important."

"Oh, no, it was just a letter to my mother. Nothing I cannot do another time. I am sorry for the mess I made of the desk. Perhaps it can be stained again to hide the ink."

Hadrian shook his head. "Nothing to worry over. I am sorry for startling you. I should have knocked before entering your chamber. I was just coming to say good night to you."

It was then that Mara noticed he was dressed to go out. "You are going somewhere?"

"Aye. I am afraid I must go to Dublin."

"Dublin? But that is two days' ride from here. How long will you be gone?"

"If everything goes well, I should be back by week's end. If you need anything, all you need do is ask. Peter Shipley and Mrs. Danbury will be at your disposal. I am sorry I could not give you prior notice, but I only just received word that my presence was needed."

"You must leave in the middle of the night? Is that not dangerous? Wouldn't it be better to leave first thing in the morning when it is light out?"

Hadrian shook his head. "Actually, it is safer for me to ride at night than during the day when the Irish patriots are watching the roads. I will be back as soon as I can. You will be in no danger, just stay close to the castle and take Davey with you when you go riding. Is there anything you would like me to get for you in the city? If you'd like, I could wait until you finish your letter to your mother and take it with me to post it from there."

Mara shook her head. "No, that is not necessary. I was getting tired anyway and really had nothing to write about. It can wait. I do not need anything from town, but thank you for asking. Just hurry home."

Hadrian smiled. "I will." He came forward and drew her into his arms. "And when I do, I hope we can continue our pursuit of attempting to have a child. I did enjoy our first effort."

Mara felt her face redden. She lowered her eyes. "That would be a nice idea."

"Arabella, I know you have been taught that such things were not to be discussed so openly and you are embarrassed by my directness. There is nothing to be ashamed of when it comes to what happens between a man and his wife. It is not wrong for you to show that you enjoyed sharing your bed with me, in fact, I would prefer it if you would. It also is not necessary to have total darkness when we do make love as if to somehow hide what we are doing. You need not be embarrassed in front of me."

"I'm sorry, Hadrian. I was just raised to believe that the relations between a man and wife were something to be kept in the closet, so to speak. Not to be discussed so openly."

"Arabella, if men and women did not share this act, there would be no continuity of the human race. Life as we know it would cease to exist. I will never understand why mothers insist on instilling it into the heads of their daughters that coupling with their husbands is their duty or something unpleasant that they must endure. Did you really find it that unpleasant?"

Mara lowered her head to hide the flush that rose to her cheeks. "No."

"Good. Then, from now on, there will be no hiding behind neck-high nightgowns or darkness. When I return, we will commence with the task of exorcising everything you were ever told about bedding with your husband, beginning with the theory of total darkness. I want to see, as well as hear, that you are enjoying what I am doing to you. Sometimes it will even make it more pleasurable for you. We will make love in the morning, at noon, and by the edge of the lough at sunset."

"Hadrian!"

"There is nothing to be ashamed of. Trust in me. I will show you how wrong your mother was. You have five days to ready yourself for my return. When I come back, I want every one of those girlish nightgowns burned. I will bring back new ones made of silk and lace. And I want candles blazing so I can see what you look like. Five days, Arabella."

With that, Hadrian took her mouth with his in a demanding and passionate kiss that left her senses reeling. She didn't have the opportunity to disagree for he was gone as soon as his lips left hers, closing the door behind him.

Chapter Nineteen

The next morning, Mara woke just as the sun was rising over the heather-carpeted Slieverdagh Hills, casting a lovely pink-orange glow through her chamber window. After recovering from the shock of Hadrian's bold words and worrying through most of the night just what she was going to do about his plans of bedding her in daylight upon his return, she realized, in the early hours of morning, that his leaving had also presented her with a great opportunity.

With Hadrian away and unable to refuse her, she could do something about helping the villagers. She believed in her heart that he truly wanted to help them. Perhaps he just didn't know how to go about it. And she knew he had the funds to give them assistance. The first thing she planned to do was to see just how much she would have to work with.

Mara didn't even pause for breakfast but dressed quickly in a plain gray woolen gown with a white apron to match her white linen cap and made her way directly to the chamber where Horace Crow, the castle's man of ledgers, worked each day. She knocked softly at the closed door. When there was no answering call from the other side, she knocked more insistently, then finally tried the door handle.

Inside, the room was empty.

It was a small chamber that looked as if it had once been used as a storage closet of sorts, for there were a number of shelves built into the stone walls as well as several tenter hooks for hanging food stores. The room was lit by a tall and narrow window set high in the wall near the ceiling which faced to the east so it would be afforded the best morning light. A small brazier sat beside the desk that would be filled with hot coals from the parlor hearth fire to warm Mr. Crow's feet in the winter.

Below the window, a cluttered desk took up most of the room's space, its top littered with papers and an inkwell sporting several goose quills. The shelf behind the desk held volumes of ledgers listing the castle's income and expenditures over the past several years as well as a couple of books about the weather patterns in the region since the beginning of the century.

Mara took a seat on the wooden chair that sat behind the desk and opened the ledger lying before her. She wanted to see just how much help they'd be able to give the villagers. She scanned the columns quickly, easily learning Horace Crow's system of recording. She noted a couple of small errors in his figuring, but knew that was to be expected. It was not until she noticed a four that had been deliberately written over and changed to a nine that she really began to scrutinize the numbers listed in the neat and orderly columns.

When she began to find a number of errors, Mara took a blank piece of foolscap from the top desk drawer and began tallying the figures for herself. By the time she reached the bottom of the first page, she realized a difference of a substantial amount. She flipped back through the ledger several pages, finding that each one had several small discrepancies that at first didn't appear to amount to much, but when totaled came to a rather large sum.

And, they were always in the debiting column.

Curious now, Mara began digging through the piles of due notes spread across the desktop from merchants as far away as London. She compared their figures with the ones written in the book, and noticed that the errors continued. She called to Mrs. Danbury, who happened to be passing by the open door, and asked that a pot of tea be brought in. Three and a half hours later, she had finished every drop of tea in the pot and she closed the ledger book on its last page.

Mara looked at the total written before her. It was more than most families earned in a lifetime. Each month, Horace was effectively robbing Kulhaven and Hadrian for amounts larger than he could hope to make in a year's income. With this amount at her disposal, Mara could do more than just help the villagers along. She could save their very lives.

Mara stood and rubbed the small of her back, which ached from sitting in that very uncomfortable chair for so many hours. She was at once elated that she could give the villagers the assistance they needed and furious at the outright thievery of Horace Crow. She closed the ledger and put everything back in the place it had been before she'd come, then left holding the paper that showed the total amount of the discrepancy.

She headed directly for Hadrian's study. She called for Mrs. Danbury and requested another pot of tea and some of the fresh sweet nutty buns she could smell being baked in Mrs. Philpot's kitchen. She then called for Peter Shipley and requested an audience with Horace Crow when he arrived at his office to begin his day's work.

While she waited for Horace Crow to appear, she began making a list of things the villagers would need, starting with provisions and food. She had nearly filled the entire page when Horace Crow finally showed his face at the door.

"You wished to see me, my lady?"

Mara glanced at the tall case clock and noticed that an hour had passed since she'd first told Peter Shipley to find him. She wondered if he often started his workday at noon, then thought the reason for his tardiness must be because of Hadrian's absence. She removed her spectacles and set them on Hadrian's desk before turning to regard the cheating accountant.

"Yes, thank you for coming so quickly, Mr. Crow. Please do sit down." She motioned toward the chair she'd set directly before the desk. It was a small and uncomfortable-looking chair much like the one in his office. She didn't want him sitting on fine, soft cushions when she confronted him about his criminal behavior.

Horace took the seat offered. He had thin black hair that bore the telltale shine of being greasy to the touch, his nose long and pointed over a thin and pinched mouth. His eyes were colorless and seemed to be constantly darting about as if seeing everything in the room all at one time. All and all, Mara thought to herself as she finished her inspection, she'd never seen a more aptly named man as he.

"Would you care for tea, Mr. Crow?" Mara asked and began pouring herself a cup.

"Yes, thank you, my lady. That would be nice."

When Mara leaned forward to set his cup in front of him, she detected the distinct odor of brandy on his breath. No wonder he hadn't come to work until now. He'd been too busy partaking of the fine brandy he'd bought with the stolen funds. Mara sat back down.

"How long have you been in his lordship's employ?" she asked without a hint of the suspicion that was running through her.

"Since before the new Lord St. Aubyn came to Kulhaven. His uncle, James, brought me on when he took over the estate in '54."

Mara nodded. "Do you like your position here, Mr. Crow?"

Horace had taken a sip of tea and his eyes narrowed slightly as he set the cup back in its saucer. "Yes, I do. Is there something amiss, my lady?"

"No, no. I am new to Kulhaven and I am just trying to acquaint myself with everyone here. I plan to interview everyone employed in the castle as well. I was wondering, Mr. Crow, since I noticed that you have not had an increase in your income since you were first hired, if you were happy working here at Kulhaven."

"Well, it takes time for an estate to start making enough to show a sizable profit. I'm sure once his lordship has had the time to make this a producing estate, he'll be able to give us more. I'm willing to wait."

Mara nodded, thinking if he had his way and continued stealing from the Kulhaven accounts, it would be quite some time before they realized their true profit. "Your loyalty is commendable, Mr. Crow."

Horace puffed up his chest, not noticing the sarcasm in her voice. "I've always been a believer in doing my share and taking the good with the bad. Work is scarce enough these days what with the war and all. I know I am fortunate to have a position at all."

"Yes, you most definitely are."

His eyes shot up at the now unmistakable sarcasm in her voice.

Mara went on. "I see you brought your ledger with you."

"Yes," Horace said, pulling it from beneath his chair. "I wasn't sure why you were calling for me or if the ledger would be needed."

"Well, I hadn't planned on reviewing the accounts, but since you did bring it with you, I suppose it wouldn't do any harm for me to just take a quick look at it."

Horace's face turned a slight bit red. "Well, it may be hard for you to tell what it all means, being a woman and all."

He instantly realized what he'd said and looked up at her quickly. "No offense meant, my lady."

Mara smiled sweetly. "None taken, Mr. Crow."

"It's just that I know most women don't know much about ciphering and all."

Mara reached for the book, taking up Arabella's spectacles. "Well, I did have a little schooling so the numbers won't be completely foreign to me. I just want to see what it is you do in your job, you know, acquaint myself with every aspect of the estate."

She opened it to the first page and pretended to read it. "Your columns are very orderly and your penmanship is quite nice."

"Thank you, my lady."

Mara hesitated a moment on one of the more obvious mistakes. "Uh, Mr. Crow, it seems as if there has been an error made here in the total of the column." She pointed toward it. "Although, being a woman of limited education in ciphering, I cannot be certain. Would you please recheck the figures for me?"

Mr. Crow swallowed as he peered down at the figure she was pointing to. She could read his thoughts quite clearly. He was trying to decide whether to admit to the mistake, or risk telling her she was wrong in her tallying. Finally, after a silent moment, he sat back.

"Yes, my lady, you are correct. It seems I transposed the six into a nine there. I can adjust the figures and give you a correct total." He smiled sheepishly. "I apologize for the error, my lady. I try to do my best."

"That is all we can ask of you, Mr. Crow," Mara said, taking the book back. She flipped through several pages. "I am certain your next employer will appreciate your efforts."

"My next employer?"

Mara looked at him over the lenses of her spectacles. "Yes. You see, we will no longer be needing your services. You may vacate your quarters by supper, Mr. Crow, having a care to take only what you came here with. I do not expect you to still have every pence you've stolen from this estate, but you will return what you have left to me before leaving."

Before he could respond, she rang the small silver bell sitting on the desk. Peter Shipley appeared at the door directly. "Mr. Shipley, it seems Mr. Crow will be leaving his position at Kulhaven today. Please see to it that Pudge drives him to the nearest town and deposits him there. I would that you would have Crumb, the blacksmith, escort Mr. Crow to his quarters to see that he only takes that which he owns."

"Yes, my lady."

"And"—she turned back to Horace Crow—"if you do not return every pence remaining, you can be sure I will have you brought up on charges of thievery before the magistrate. They do hang thieves, Mr. Crow, so be certain to think on that while you are packing your belongings."

Horace opened his mouth to argue, stopped himself short of it, then closed it again. He glanced down at his feet. "Yes, my lady."

"I know precisely how much has been taken, for you see, although being a woman, contrary to your beliefs, my education in ciphering was quite extensive, so do not think to leave with any of it. I'm sure, once you've thought it through you will see that this is more than a fair settlement."

Peter Shipley and the blacksmith, Crumb, a giant of over six feet with arms the size of tree trunks, stood waiting at the door. "I am sorry to say I will be unable to furnish you with a reference for a future employer, but under the circumstances, I am sure you understand. Good day, Mr. Crow."

Mara stood and circled the desk, watching as Horace Crow turned and walked to where Crumb awaited. The giant smith grabbed the accountant by the shoulder and nudged him along ahead of him down the hallway. When they were gone, Peter Shipley came in and stood beside her, handing her a fresh cup of tea.

"Good riddance to that one," he said. "I never trusted him from the moment I first saw him. You did very well, my lady, very well, indeed. I am certain his lordship will be very pleased that you have rid Kulhaven of that rabble."

Mara smiled. "I hope so."

"You said you had something else to discuss with me, my lady?"

"Yes." Mara returned to the desk and picked up the list she had been writing there. "I have written the names of each of the villagers here. Beside each name is an amount. When we have received the stolen money back from Mr. Crow, I would like each villager to be given the amount written by their name."

"But, my lady . . ."

"Then," she went on, retrieving another list from the desk, "his lordship gave me his permission to do whatever I saw fit to redecorate the castle. I have listed the villagers again and beside their names this time is listed their trade. I want to employ them to help refurbish the castle."

"But, my lady, whatever goods you need can be purchased in Dublin."

"Yes, Mr. Shipley, I am aware of that. But, tell me, why should we have the added expense of paying for something in Dublin that we can obtain here at half the cost? It helps in two ways, you see. First, it saves us the money of hiring someone to come the two days' ride from Dublin, and it also helps the villagers by putting them to work. I will never understand why we would waste the time and money to travel to Dublin for something as simple as"—she scanned the list for an example—"candles when they can be made in the village just as easily, and probably will be of much better quality. Does that make any sense to you, Mr. Shipley?"

The butler appeared dumbfounded. "No, but, my lady, his lordship has always sent to Dublin for whatever was needed. I believe there is some restriction about hiring the Irish."

"Nonsense. And, won't his lordship be surprised when he returns to see what we have accomplished? We haven't much time, Mr. Shipley. His lordship will be back in four days. We must be able to show him how much better it is to do things this way. Are you willing to help me, Mr. Shipley?"

"Yes, yes, of course, my lady. I am at your complete disposal."

"Good." Mara handed him the lists and started for the door. "Ask Mrs. Danbury to help you with the lists. In the meantime, I will be going to the village to speak with the people. Ask Davey to accompany me since Pudge will be occupied with driving Mr. Crow from Kulhaven. I will be down in a quarter hour to leave. Thank you again, Mr. Shipley."

She flew through the door like the whirlwind that came from the mountains sometimes without warning, stirring up everything in its path.

Peter Shipley could but stand back and watch as she disappeared up the stairs, astounded at the tempest that had just blown by him.

"Thank you, Seamus Chandler, I hope you will be able to dip this many candles for us by week's end without too much difficulty."

"Yes, my lady, I can." The grizzled-haired man bobbed his head graciously, wiping his hands on his work apron. "'Tis no trouble at all."

Mara smiled, pulling on her riding gloves. "Good.

And be sure that you continue making the candles from now on. It takes a vast quantity of candles to light a place as large as Kulhaven. We will be in constant need of a steady supply from you."

"You can be sure I will, my lady. Thought I'd never be using these wicks again. I've a special recipe that was handed down to me by my father's father. I make it with the lavender flower. Burns longer and smells sweeter than all the flowers in the field. Used to make it for the old lord of Kulhaven, before that bloody Cromwell came . . ."

Seamus stopped short and his eyes grew wide as he realized he'd just cursed the supposed godfather of the person standing before him. "Please, my lady, I meant no offense."

Mara smiled. "It is all right, Seamus, war is a terrible and destructive thing. Just be sure to make that special recipe for me. I am quite partial to lavender. I shall send one of the castle's footmen at week's end to collect the candles and pay you for your good work. Good day to you, Mr. Chandler."

Seamus wiped the tear from his eye as he watched the new lady of Kulhaven whisk through his shop door on her way to the next villager.

By the time she returned to the castle at dusk later that day, Mara had employed every able-bodied villager in performing his trade, work they'd long since abandoned since the coming of Cromwell and the war. She'd received even more of the stolen money back from Horace Crow than she had expected, which allowed her to return it to the Kulhaven coffers, where it belonged. That would serve to make Hadrian even more pleased.

Back at Kulhaven, the castle was fairly bristling with energy. Each family in the village had been given a ham from the smokehouse for supper that night and now, standing before the open window of Hadrian's study and staring out at the night sky, Mara felt that she had truly accomplished something.

She hoped Hadrian would be pleased with what she had done. How could he not when it hadn't cost him a single pence more than he'd thought he had? And, what better to do with the extra funds that had been lining Horace Crow's pockets these past years than to give the villagers the help they so desperately needed? The villagers would no longer be hungry and without work to do, and Kulhaven would flourish as a result of it.

How could he possibly disagree with that?

Mara turned from the window and from the corner of her eye, she spied the blank parchment lying on Hadrian's desk. All day she knew she should be practicing his signature, for she only had two nights left before she had to meet with Owen and give him the forged pardon, but somehow she just could not bring herself to do it.

She wished she could think of something, some way to avoid giving Owen the forged pardon, but she knew if she refused, all would be lost. He would expose her and everything she'd done. He would never tell her where she could find the Kulhaven Tapestry. And everything she still hoped to accomplish for the villagers and Kulhaven would be lost with her.

She tried to tell herself she shouldn't feel so guilty. Hadrian was the enemy, after all, and his kind had taken her family and home from her. But that argument was growing more tiresome and implausible with each passing day.

Hadrian had shown himself to be a true and honorable gentleman, not the bloodthirsty fiend she'd conjured up in her mind when she'd first embarked on this scheme. He'd been showering her with attention of late, always concerned about her health and comfort. But it was not her he was doting on, she reminded herself. It was Arabella, or who he thought was Arabella, the young English girl he'd written all those letters to, the girl he believed he had wed.

Still, though she pretended to be another, she could not in all honesty pretend the feelings she had didn't exist. Their time together was forever burned in her memory. She could still feel his lips on hers, the way she'd felt when he'd been filling her completely, joining them as one. She'd not been prepared for the feelings their night of lovemaking had brought to her, for even now, just remembering it made her hands grow damp in the palms.

She hesitated to admit it, but she liked the way it felt to be held in his arms as if nothing in the world could harm her. How she wished that were really true. She wished somehow Hadrian could make the world outside the walls of Kulhaven go away and they could go on living as they were, but for one difference.

The one thing she wished above all else was that she could tell him who she really was. She was tired of playing at being someone she was not, tired and frustrated at having to hide her true identity.

But she knew that was one wish that would never come true.

Hadrian had taken the Parliamentarian side in the war. He'd taken a stand against the Irish, against her. If Hadrian ever learned the truth of who she was, if he somehow found out she was not Arabella Wentworth, godchild of Oliver Cromwell, but was really the daughter of the man whose castle he'd taken, wife or not, he'd see her hanged.

Still, Mara knew her time posing as Arabella was limited. Sooner or later, he would learn that Arabella had not come to Kulhaven. And she could not continue to insist that he douse every candle and draw the curtains each time he came to her bed. Her only hope was to get with child and as soon as possible. Were she pregnant, she could plead her belly and could evade the hangman's noose. At least for a while.

Though she had originally planned to use a child against Hadrian, to make him face the choice of making his own child a bastard as his father had tried to do to him, she now knew she could not do that to him. Enemy or not he did not deserve to be put through the pain of his childhood again.

But if she were to carry his child, she somehow knew he'd never allow harm to come to her, for how could he explain to his child that he'd been responsible for the death of its mother?

Mary closed her eyes and said a silent prayer that at that moment, a tiny life was nestled deep in her womb, though she knew, having only lain with Hadrian once, the chances of it were few. But there was still hope. Time. Time was all she needed. And once she had the threat of Owen out of her life, she would have all the time she needed to accomplish her goal.

She just needed to be rid of Owen and life could go on from there.

Mara eyed the blank parchment lying on the desk. She took a seat and picked up the quill lying there, studying Hadrian's signature before she began practicing once again.

The Right Honorable Hadrian Augustus Ross, the Earl of St. Aubyn.

Chapter Twenty

Two nights and a full quire of foolscap later, Mara had finally perfected the forgery of Hadrian's signature.

She set the goose feather quill in its brass holder and sat back in her writing chair to inspect her creation, the pardon she'd finished crafting just moments before. She compared the St. Aubyn signature she'd just signed to the bottom of the thick sheet of official-looking vellum to the signature Owen had given her to use as an example. No one would think to question the pardon's authenticity, for the signatures looked to have been penned from the same hand, identical right down to the slight curl Hadrian made at the top of the letter "E" in the word "Earl."

Satisfied that the forgery would pass muster and checking to make certain the ink had dried, Mara carefully folded the pardon in thirds and stashed it in the pocket of her black woolen cloak before starting for the door. She'd left her hair red and trailing in curls down the back of her black riding habit, thinking that should someone happen to see her riding about, it would be far easier for them to believe that they'd been granted a peek at the elusive Flaming Lady, than to wonder why the lady of the house was out at such an hour.

Once inside the stables, she had to feel her way around inside the dark tack room for Munin's saddle. It took her quite some time, but when she had finally secured the girth around her belly, she took the four empty grain sacks she'd found in the storeroom and placed them over Munin's hooves, tying them off with a bit of twine. With this little improvisational slipper, no one would hear her leaving on the graveled drive and come to question who might be out riding at such a late hour.

Mara slowly led the slippered Munin from her stall, her hooves making a soft thudding noise on the courtyard outside. Once beyond earshot of the bailey's stone walls, she removed the grain sacks and with the aid of a small tree stump, climbed onto the saddle and started for the cottage—and her meeting with Owen.

The moon was full and bright, hanging low in the night sky and lighting her way well through the open grassy fields. In the distance she could hear the faint triple hoot of a long-eared owl as it searched in the night for a wood mouse for supper. She listened keenly as they moved slowly along the path at the edge of the woodland, watching Munin's alert ears for any indication that she was not the only rider out tonight.

It was not long before she spotted the cottage up the rise not far away. The soft glow of candlelight shone through the small window. As she drew nearer, she noticed three horses in the shadows tethered to the crude wooden hitching post outside. Mara dismounted and tied Munin to a tree just inside the cover of the trees, then started quietly toward the cottage.

She stopped where the horses were tied and ran her hand along the flank of one, a well-muscled gray who nudged her playfully with his muzzle. His coat was damp and hot to the touch, indicating that he had been ridden hard and had only recently arrived at the cottage. Inside she could hear the sound of muffled voices coming from an open window. She could not make out the exact words, but it sounded as if something of great import was being discussed.

Leading into the small cottage was an old-style Irish half-door, its top swung open enough to afford her a view inside. Three men stood around a crude wooden table, studying a large map of some sort. One of the men was Owen, who was pointing to some locale on the chart and the second who stood beside him was a very large, gruff-looking man with dirty blond hair and a scruffy beard that nearly covered his entire face. She could not readily see the third man, for he had his back to her and he was partially hidden in the shadows.

Mara stepped before the doorway, causing Owen to look up from the motion.

"Ah, here she is now. I was beginning to think you were not coming. But, you would never disappoint me, now would you? Did you bring what I asked of you?"

Mara began to remove the forged pardon from her cloak pocket. "Did you bring what you promised me?"

"Just a moment," Owen said, shooting a sidewise glance at his companions. "I will discuss that matter with you in private. Gentlemen, if you will excuse us?"

The third man turned then, and Mara froze. His face was entirely covered by a dark mask with only two openings for his eyes. He said nothing, but he stared at her quite intently, which instantly set her ill at ease. Who was this man? Perhaps one of the men from the village? Or maybe Rolfe, the spy acting as Hadrian's friend? She was not near enough to read any expression in his eyes, nor did she get the opportunity to make a closer study, for Owen grabbed her by the elbow and pulled her quickly out of sight.

Mara didn't know why, but something about the way the man had stared at her gave her a frightening chill.

"You may hand the pardon over now, sister," Owen said when they were away from the others.

Mara started to remove the pardon from her cloak to hand it to him. She pulled the folded parchment back just as he reached to grasp it from her. "What about the item you promised me? What about the tapestry?"

"Don't play with me now, Mara. I would see the pardon first. Do you think me a fool? If it is not satisfactory enough to pass as authentic, you will not get the tapestry."

Mara didn't trust him, but she had no other choice. Reluctantly she handed him the forgery.

"Very good, sister," Owen said, scanning her handiwork. "You are wasting your talents on that heap of rocks called a castle. You should be working with us. But there is one small problem."

"What?" The pardon was flawless. If he thought to play some game and refuse her the tapestry now, after she'd written the damnable pardon, she would surely strangle him with her bare hands.

"You forgot the seal. St. Aubyn's seal must be affixed to the bottom of this pardon. Without it, it will never pass as legitimate."

"What about the tapestry, Owen? I would that you would show it to me so I at least know you are telling me the truth about having it."

Owen smiled at her, the moonlight giving him a

more sinister appearance. "What? You do not trust your own brother? I have the tapestry, but it is not with me at the moment."

"You promised you would bring it."

Owen's eyes grew dark. "Well, you were supposed to get St. Aubyn's seal."

"I will get it."

"And, when you do, you will be given the tapestry. Not a moment before. Since St. Aubyn is gone from Kulhaven, this will be an easy task for you to accomplish. Affix the seal to this pardon and bring it back here tomorrow at midnight. I will have the tapestry with me and we shall exchange them then."

Mara leveled her eyes on him. "This will be the last thing I do for you, Owen."

He chuckled. "Of course. After that, you can forget you ever knew I existed. You can welcome your husband home without any fear of being exposed any longer. And you will have your priceless Kulhaven Tapestry. Just get the seal and I will see you on the morrow."

By the time Mara made it back to her chamber it was past three in the morning. She reluctantly wakened Cyma to help dye her hair for the morning, then lay awake in her own bed, staring at the delicately stitched canopy and contemplating the evening's events.

She could not sleep. She wondered if Owen's hold over her would ever truly end. Each time she performed one of his dangerous assignments, he promised it would be the last, yet each time he requested something more of her. She felt like the trained bear she'd once seen on Gathering Day at the Puck Fair when she was a child. The bear had been chained to a tree and had been forced to dance at will each and every time he was called to, or suffer the blunt end of his trainer's blackthorn stick. But she knew she had no other choice. Somehow she had to find a way to release Owen's hold over her without the risk of his exposing her to Hadrian, or losing her chance at retrieving the Kulhaven Tapestry.

But, short of pushing him to his death from the tower right after she had gotten the tapestry from him, how was she to do it?

If only the solution would come knocking on her door.

Mara finally gave up trying to sleep at dawn and rose from the soft feathered mattress. Her mood was ill as a result of the lack of sleep and the constant cloud of Owen hanging over her head. At Cyma's suggestion, she decided to take a ride to the village after breakfast to see how things were progressing there. Seeing the improvements would cheer her, so she asked Davey to saddle Munin and took a seat at the dining table for her morning tea and sweetened rolls.

No sooner had she taken her first sip of the sweet blackberry tea than Peter Shipley presented himself at the door.

"My lady, I am so sorry to disturb you while you are at breakfast, but there is a group of soldiers at the door asking to see his lordship. When I informed them he was not in residence, they asked to see you instead."

Soldiers? Mara's heart began to beat faster. "Very well, Mr. Shipley. Please show them into the parlor. I will joint them directly."

"There are a quite a number of them, my lady. Would you wish that I have them all come in?"

"No, just ask whomever is in charge to come in. I will be right there."

When the steward had gone, Mara stood and moved quickly to the glass hanging between the tall windows. She glanced at her reflection, patted back a wisp of black hair from her temple, and adjusted her spectacles on her nose. As she turned to make her way to the parlor, she noticed the group of mounted soldiers waiting on the drive outside. Their armored helmets shone in the early morning sunlight, just as they had in the light of the moon the night they came to kill her mother.

Their faces had been hidden that night beneath the sinister visor of the helmet which had given them their name of Roundhead, and they'd come armed with their flashing swords and murderous muskets. They brought with them an orgy of pillaging and death and she could still hear their laughter ringing out as they stormed through the great hall like flies to the feast.

"My lady?"

"Hmm?"

The steward's voice broke the spell which had wound its way into her thoughts. "Yes, Mr. Shipley?"

"They are awaiting you in the parlor as you directed."

"Thank you." Mara took a deep breath, knowing she would have to hide her disgust for them when she faced their leader. She smoothed down the skirts of her navy blue riding habit and started for the parlor.

"You wished to see me?" she said as she entered the room.

There were two men waiting for her, one standing by

the hearth, one sitting and sipping a cup of tea obviously offered by Peter Shipley.

"You are Lady St. Aubyn?"

"Yes. I am Arabella Ross, the Countess of St. Aubyn. My husband is Hadrian Ross, the earl."

The man, who looked to be nearing fifty, narrowed his eyes in speculation. "Excuse me, my lady, did you say Arabella Ross?"

"Yes. Is there something wrong, sir?"

"Are you Arabella Wentworth, the godchild of our Lord Protector Cromwell?"

Mara began to taste the beginnings of panic. She swallowed it back. "Yes, I am. Why do you ask?"

"I was told your marriage to St. Aubyn had never taken place. Something about smallpox . . ."

"Well, unfortunately you have been given false information. As you can see I am here and we are now wed. I am afraid Lord St. Aubyn is not here to speak with you. He was called to Dublin for a short visit, Mr. . . ."

"Oh, excuse me, my lady." He removed his helmet and bowed before her. "I am Sergeant Major John Weeks. And this is my second in command, Sergeant Elias Haygood."

He motioned toward the man who was still sitting and sipping tea. The man made half of an attempt at standing, nodded his head, then returned to his teacup, obviously more interested in partaking of the fine tea than in social niceties.

"A pleasure to make your acquaintance, gentlemen. Now what did you wish to see me about?"

"Well," Weeks began, "we've received word that there are several Irish outlaws with some hefty rewards on their heads in this area. We have come to ask whether you might have seen any suspicious characters in the vicinity of your estate of late."

Mara started to answer negatively, but then hesitated, thinking of her troubles with Owen. Hadn't she just been wishing for a way to get him out of her life? This could most definitely solve that problem. She wondered what the sergeant major would say if she told them that one of the most wanted Irish outlaws who they believed was dead was actually alive and living in a cottage on this very estate.

She could tell them that he would be at the cottage at midnight that night, and she would never have to give Owen the forged pardon, or see his face again.

But then, she thought further, if she did that, she would be assured of never seeing the Kulhaven Tapestry again either.

"I am sorry, Sergeant Major Weeks, but I am afraid I cannot be of any help to you. We have seen nothing out of the ordinary here that would give cause for suspicion. Sorry to have wasted your time."

The sergeant major smiled, bowing over her hand. "Oh, I would never think of any time spent in the company of such a lovely lady as yourself as wasted, Lady St. Aubyn. Lord St. Aubyn is a lucky man. Please, give him my regards when he returns from Dublin."

He turned and had nearly made it through the door to leave when Mara called him back. "You know my husband, Sergeant Major?"

"Aye. We were stationed together in Dublin before he resigned his commission and came to take over this estate at the death of his uncle."

They had been stationed in Dublin together? Mara smiled prettily, looking at him from beneath her thick lashes. "You know, that part of my husband's life is still unknown to me. I mean, I am curious as to why he chose to leave the service. Why did he resign his commission, Sergeant Major?"

The sergeant major was instantly bewitched. "Well, there was an unfortunate incident. You see . . ."

"Sergeant Major Weeks"—one of the soldiers from outside was standing at the door—"a messenger's just come from the campsite. One of those Tories was spotted not ten miles up the road. If we hurry, we might catch him."

Weeks set his helmet on his head. "Sorry I cannot stay and chat, Lady St. Aubyn, but duty calls. Come on, Haygood."

She had been so close! Mara gnashed her teeth in frustration as the two men turned and left the room.

Although the sergeant major had been called away before he could finish telling her about Hadrian's time in Dublin, she now knew that her initial suspicions had been right. Something had happened to Hadrian while he'd been posted in Dublin, something bad enough to cause him to resign his commission as a soldier and hie off to Kulhaven. But what had it been? Every time she tried to question him about it, he would fall silent, changing the subject as deftly as he could. Why was he so secretive about it? What was he trying to hide?

"Lady St. Aubyn?"

Mara turned, finding Davey standing at the door, holding his dusty brown hat in hand. "Yes, Davey, what is it?"

"I saddled Munin for you. She's fair chomping at the bit to get out today. I've got her waiting for you on the drive out front whenever you are ready to go."

Mara smiled. A ride would do her good to help clear her head. She would go to the village to see how things were progressing there. That would certainly bring some levity to her mood. "Thank you, Davey. Let me get my gloves and hat and I'll be right out."

Davey rode alongside her to the village, filling her ears with ceaseless conversation along the way, which although quite tedious, also served to make the ride pass quickly. "And, when I turn seventeen in two springs, I'm going to join up with your godfather's forces in the army."

"What does your mother have to say about your plans?"

Davey's wide smile faded. "She thinks it a foolish idea and says I should stay here at Kulhaven and take over for my father when the time comes."

"I would tend to agree with your mother, Davey. Remaining on here at Kulhaven would certainly be a much safer avenue to pursue. Surely some pretty girl in the village has caught your eye."

Davey's freckled cheeks blushed furiously and he stammered. "Well . . ."

Mara thought she saw something move in the trees to the right of them and pulled Munin up. "Davey, did you see that? It looked like there was someone, or something standing just inside the woods there."

Davey shaded his eyes against the sunlight. "I don't see nothing now, my lady. It was most probably a deer or something like that. You've nothing to worry about. I've my pa's pistol with me in case we run into any trouble."

Mara nodded, nudging Munin on, her eyes straying to the trees again, certain someone had been there.

The rest of the way to the village, Mara continued to feel as if someone was watching her. Every time she heard a twig snap, she looked back. And, each time, there was no one there. When they came into the village, stopping at the well, the sight of the people coming forward to greet them with smiles made her forget all about her odd feelings.

"Good day, Lady St. Aubyn," said John, the man with whom Hadrian had spoken the first time they'd come.

"Good day, John. I've just come to visit and see how things are progressing here."

Mara spent the remainder of the day touring the homes of the village and visiting with the people. Later, she chatted with Sadbh, who had taken a nasty spill on a patch of mud, causing her to twist her ankle. She sat with the women of the village, drinking their raspberry tea around the turf fire and watching as they wove the fragrant rush baskets she had ordered for Mrs. Philpot's kitchen. All the while, she wished Hadrian could be there to see what had transpired in the short time since his departure for Dublin.

Finally, when the sun had started to set and she had seen everything she possibly could, Mara mounted Munin and, with Davey in tow, started back for Kulhaven

After leaving Munin with Davey at the stables, she entered the house through the kitchens, asking Mrs. Philpot to boil some bathwater and have a light supper sent to her bedchamber. She then headed for Hadrian's study to affix his seal to the pardon in order to give it over to Owen later that night.

Mara removed her riding gloves and pulled at the top drawer to Hadrian's desk. It was locked. Being a man of meticulous habit, he would always be certain to secure his desk. She remembered once seeing Hadrian with a key. There must be one hidden in the room somewhere. But where?

She glanced about the room, trying to think where he would put it. She looked beneath the desk and under the Aubusson carpet. Nothing. And then she spied a small vase without any flowers sitting atop the bookcase. Odd place for a vase to be, she thought, pushing Hadrian's chair underneath it. She climbed up and reached for the vase, jiggling it softly. The sound of something small and metal chinked about inside of it. She smiled.

The key fit the lock to Hadrian's desk perfectly. She sifted through the papers jammed inside in search of his signet ring. Mara found it stashed far in the back of the drawer. Removing the forgery from her gown pocket, she took the red candle she'd lit from its holder and tipped it so that several drops of the wax fell in a small puddle on the bottom of the page. Waiting a moment, she pressed the flat of the seal on the ring into the quickly cooling wax.

When she was finished, she stuffed all the papers back into Hadrian's desk drawer, locked it again, and returned the key to its place. As she started from the room, she stopped just before she reached the door. In the hearth, jammed between two logs and sticking out just a bit, was something small and white. As she moved closer, she saw that it was a piece of paper. Since no fire had been lit in the hearth with Hadrian's absence, it had not been burned as was obviously its intention. Mara removed the paper and read it.

A List of Those Persons to be Dispossessed
Lord William Mulcaney, of Castle Craigh
Aged Fifty, No legitimate issue
Removal and Transportation to Connaught

Lady Cavendish, of Ballygrand Castle
Aged Forty-Two, widowed
Removal and Transportation to Barbados to be Indentured

Lord and Lady Connelly, of Castle Connelly
Aged Thirty-Eight and Twenty-Four
Dispossess and Destroy
No Survivors

At the bottom of the page were instructions to burn any evidence of the list after reading. It was signed by "O. Cromwell."

Mara felt a lump form in her throat as she read the third entry on the list again. She knew the family well, for the Connellys had lived on the estate just north of Kulhaven for years. She read the last words of the entry again.

Destroy.

No Survivors.

Visions of what the soldiers had done at Kulhaven came instantly to her mind. She had to warn the Connellys. Somehow she had to tell them that they were going to be attacked. But how?

Owen. She could tell Owen and he would warn them. He'd come of age with one of the Connelly children. Surely he would save them. When she went to bring the forged pardon to Owen, she would give him the list.

She tucked the paper into her skirt pocket and started for her chamber. She would eat quickly and bathe to wash the dye from her hair, then she would go to the cottage to meet Owen.

The bath she'd requested was already waiting for her before a roaring fire when she opened the door to her chamber. She tossed her gloves and hat on the bench at the foot of her bed and started to unfasten the buttons on her doublet.

Suddenly, she heard something moving beside her near the bed. She turned.

"Hello, Arabella."

Chapter Twenty-one

Mara nearly fell to the thick pile of the Flanders carpet. "Hadrian!"

It was him. He was there, in her chamber, lying atop the thick feather-filled mattress on her bed, four plump pillows stacked behind his head, his booted feet crossed leisurely at the ankle and stretching just over the side of the embroidered coverlet. He was not in Dublin as he was supposed to be. He was there, gloriously handsome before her. His hair was windblown, as if he'd just ridden hard and long to return, and his boots were spotted with mud. He'd removed his neck cloth and navy riding jacket, taking the time to fold them neatly and hang them over the back of her chair, and had unfastened the top two buttons of his shirt. He'd even rolled the sleeves back at equal lengths over his forearms.

As she looked at him now, unable to believe he was lying there on her bed, he was smiling at her as if he was pleased to see her, but something in his eyes, a strange and dangerous glint, gave her definite pause.

She didn't know how she'd taken in all this detail in just a few short seconds. "You returned early from Dublin," she managed to blurt out, thinking her statement quite obvious the moment it left her lips.

"Yes, I have. Are you surprised, Arabella? I had hoped you would be pleased to see me. I decided to quit Dublin sooner than I had originally planned, for you see, I had grown tired of meetings about troop locations and military strategy given by long-winded, thoroughly boring men. I found myself longing for my wife's company." He stood, his golden-brown eyes sparking in the firelight. "Especially at night."

Mara remained standing at the door, gripping the edge. There was something very different about the way he spoke to her, something that was beginning to frighten her. But why should she be frightened, she told herself? He was her husband, and he had just told her he had missed her. The sentiment should make her happy.

"That is very sweet of you to say, Hadrian. There is so much I wish to tell you, so many things that have happened in your absence. I, too, have missed your company."

"Have you now?" He stood and advanced toward her, his eyes still holding that odd glint. "Well, then, we shall have to see what we can do to remedy the situation."

He reached for her then to take her into his arms, but Mara skittered away and crossed the room, putting some distance between them. "My lord, should we not wait till we retire for the evening?"

"Whatever for? We are both here, admitting that we missed each other's company. Why should we delay it any longer? I have waited long enough. I want you, Arabella. Now."

"But do you not wish to hear what has been happening at Kulhaven in your absence? There is much to tell."

Hadrian stepped before her. "Later. Now I only wish to see how much my wife missed me."

Mara looked around in a panic, trying to find something, anything to avert his attention. She spotted the tub set before the fire, the water steaming invitingly. "I was just going to have my bath. I have been riding all day and would like to have myself smelling clean and fresh for you when we—"

"A good idea. I think I shall join you for I, too, have been riding all day. A bath would prove most invigorating."

Hadrian started to unfasten his breeches.

"No!"

He stopped in midmotion and looked over at her, one brow raised in question. His eyes still held that odd, unknown spark.

Mara smiled timidly. "The tub is too small for two people to fit."

"Then, we shall sit you on my lap. Why should we put Mrs. Philpot through the trouble of warming enough water to fill another tub when this will do perfectly well?"

Mara turned about. "Perhaps the bath can wait. The water looks a little steamy. It would be best to allow it to cool some." She walked over to the tapestry bellpull that hung on the wall, grabbing at it as if it were a lifeline. "Would you like tea while we wait? I can ring for some."

"Nay. The bathwater will grow cold and I prefer my bathing water hot. Come, Arabella, there's no need to be modest. Let us take our bath together. The tea can wait for later."

He came up beside her and unhinged her fingers from the bellpull. He began unfastening the buttons that lined the front of her doublet. His fingers caressed her shoulders, her cheek, her bottom lip, and she closed her eyes, losing herself to his touch. She opened her eyes again a moment later, saw him standing there, and instantly backed away.

"No, Hadrian, we cannot do this."

He grinned. "Why not?"

"It is unseemly. What will the servants think? Surely they will realize . . ."

"To perdition with what the servants think. They will simply say the lord and lady missed each other. We are newly wed, Arabella. It is time we began acting as we should. I am beginning to think you do not wish to be in my company."

"Don't be silly, of course I want to be with you."

"Good. Now I am of a mind to take a bath with my lovely wife and once my mind is made up, I will settle for nothing less. You may undress yourself, or I will do it for you."

"But, really, Hadrian, the tub is too small. We will never both fit . . ."

"Or, since the thought of being naked in front of your husband distresses you so, we can simply forgo the removal of your clothing and bathe just as we are."

Before Mara could utter a response, Hadrian scooped her up into his great arms and tossed her over his shoulder.

"Hadrian!"

Ignoring her cries, he crossed the room in three

quick strides and deposited her unceremoniously into the tub, gown and all. The water sloshed heavily over the sides of the tub, soaking the carpet underneath it, spilling across the floor and under the high tester bed. Mara screeched and floundered about, trying in desperation to get out of the tub before the water wet her dyed hair.

Hadrian stood back and watched her. "I had a cat once who reacted much the same way when I tried to give her a bath. But she got used to it after a spell."

Mara gripped the sides of the tub, trying to stand. Hadrian held her down. He then picked up a sponge and squeezed the water from it directly over her head.

Oh, dear God, no. Mara tried to scream, but her mouth filled with water and she began coughing and sputtering like a drowned wharf rat.

"Faith, lass, you weren't jesting about needing a bath. The water's turning blacker than stagnant bog water. Here, let us take the sponge and wash some of that dirt from you."

At those words, Mara began to kick and scream even harder, but to no avail. Hadrian was holding her arm firmly to keep her from slipping away and squeezing water from the sponge over her head with his other hand. Finally, after what seemed an interminably long period of time, he abruptly released her and stood, stepping back to watch as she struggled to get out of the tub.

Mara somehow got to her feet, the wet velvet of her gown weighing her down and making it difficult to stand. Her hair hung in wet and drooping strands about her shoulders and she could feel the water still running down her face. She knew without looking that the dye was washing away with it. She wished she could sink into the floor and disappear. She tried to think of something to say, some semblance of an explanation as to why her hair was changing colors, and looked up to see Hadrian standing three feet away, his arms crossed on his chest, his eyes dark with anger.

She suddenly knew the day she'd dreaded since coming to Kulhaven had arrived.

"Now," he said, his voice filled with a deadly calm, "you may begin by telling me just who in the hell you are and what you have done with my real wife."

Mara swallowed back her fear. "I am your wife, my lord."

"That is a lie. It took me a little while, but I finally figured it out. I don't know who in Hades you are, but you are not Arabella. The question is, where is the real Arabella? Do you know what they do to murderesses here?"

Murderess? She may be a liar, she may have disguised herself as someone else, but she could never take another person's life. "I am not a murderess."

"Then, what have you done with Arabella? I mean you could very well be an Arabella, but not Arabella Wentworth, the Arabella Wentworth I thought I had married."

Mara simply stared at him.

"I will only ask it of you once more. Where is Arabella?"

Hadrian's voice had dropped dangerously low. He looked fit to kill her if she didn't answer him. There would be no lying her way out of this one. The only possible explanation would be the truth, only that would most definitely sound too bizarre to be believed.

"Arabella is well and unharmed and back in England where she belongs."

"Is that so? And who in the hell are you to say just who belongs where?"

Mara raised her chin and stepped from the tub with as much grace and ceremony as she could possibly muster. "My name is Mara. Mara Catherine Despenscer of Castle Kulhaven."

If Hadrian was at all surprised by her admission, he did not readily show it. He simply nodded his head as if to say her statement had been perfectly expected, and said quite blandly, "You have five minutes to tell me what in the hell you are doing disguising yourself as my wife and living in my home."

"Your home? On the contrary, my lord, this was my home long before you ever stole it from my family."

"You expect me to believe you are the daughter of Charles Despencer, the former lord of Kulhaven? The entire family was killed. There were no survivors."

"Yes, my family was killed by you and others like you. You are one to talk, you know, my lord, accusing me of being a murderess. If not for you and your kind, every member of my family would not be lying in unmarked graves all across Irish soil. But, back to your question, if you will recall, no one ever knew what became of the Despencer daughter. When your murdering soldiers came, they did not quite finish the job. I managed to escape."

Hadrian frowned. "Those were not my soldiers. I never ordered them to do what they did."

"No, but your leader, Oliver Cromwell, the lord Protector, did. Such a God-loving man, so pious, so just. He wanted to make certain there would be no survivors, no one to come back and claim their land, land that was rightfully theirs." She pulled the list she'd found stashed in the hearth in his study wet and dripping from her skirt pocket and shoved it under his nose. "Tell me, my good Lord St. Aubyn, was the notation on the list under my family's name the same as this one? Destroy. No Survivors."

Hadrian reached for the list, but Mara pulled it back. "Where did you get that?"

"That is of no matter. Why do you not tell me—how does it feel to sleep under the roof of the man you are responsible for murdering?"

Hadrian stepped forward and grabbed her by the shoulders, shaking her. "I did not have anything to do with what happened to your family. If I could have, I would have prevented it. Your parents refused to give over land that had been confiscated by the Protectorate. They would be alive today had they simply surrendered Kulhaven in the beginning."

"Bah!" She spat in his face. "Alive and living in exile like all the other landowners who did give over in the far reaches of Connaught? Are you telling me it is wrong to fight for what is yours? Or, is it more just to kill to steal land that you have no right to and do so in the name of God? Your Lord Protector saw the Irish as a thing, not a people. Something to be captured and destroyed. All the Irish people did was fight for what was rightfully theirs. And, you are no different. You have been doing that all your life, haven't you? Fighting for what you believe is your due."

"What do you know about my life?"

"I know enough to know your own father refused to acknowledge you and even tried to label you a bastard because he believed your mother had cuckolded him with his own brother. But he failed and you became the next earl even though your father would rather have allowed the family title to fall to extinction than give it to you. I also know that your uncle, James, the man with whom your mother had this illicit affair, gave you this estate, my family's property, as some sort of compensation for your father's actions. But you did not care that he had given you stolen land. All that mattered to you was that it would give you added wealth and with it added *legitimacy*. What other way for a bastard earl to make his fortune?"

Mara instantly realized she had gone too far. She felt Hadrian's grip on her shoulders tighten and closed her eyes, waiting for the blow that she felt sure was coming. But it did not come. When she opened her eyes, he was staring at her, his mouth turned down in a frown, an odd sort of expression in his eyes.

"You have waited all this time, five years, to reclaim your family's estate?"

For a moment, Mara thought to keep silent. What would it matter to him, her reasons for doing what she had done? But then she decided she wanted to tell him, needed to tell him her reasons for coming there. And she would tell him everything. "In the beginning, after the soldiers had come and taken Kulhaven, I waited for an end to the madness, thinking it could never be allowed to continue. But, I was wrong. It did continue and it grew worse as more and more innocent people were killed. I hoped for the return of the heir, Charles II, to the throne, thinking he would restore the land that had been confiscated back to the rightful owners and bring peace. But it does not seem as if that is ever to happen. Not as long as Cromwell is alive.

"When I learned of your arranged marriage to Arabella, I saw a way to take back what was mine. You had never met her, so how would you know if it was really Arabella, or me posing as her?"

Hadrian released her and sat down and was actually listening to her speak. "I wouldn't have known because, as you stated, our marriage had been arranged. We had never met. But tell me, did you plan to live as Arabella for the rest of your life? Surely you did not think I would never find out?"

"No, I knew you would find out, in fact, I planned to be the one to tell you, but only after I had taken my revenge on you." Mara hesitated, wondering if she should continue. "You see, I knew about your past, about what your father had done to you, even before you told it to me. I figured I would wed you, have your child, then tell you who I truly was. I did not believe you would banish me and annul the marriage if there was a child involved. For if you did that, you would be doing that which you despised your father for. You would be making your own child a bastard, an outcast, just as your father had tried to do to you."

"And is there to be a child?" His voice had dropped as if he feared the answer.

"I do not know."

Hadrian did not speak for several moments. She saw several emotions, pain, anger, even regret pass in his eyes and knew she had put every one of them there. "You certainly did think your plan out well."

"Down to the last detail. Except I was wrong about one thing."

"What was that?"

"I thought I could punish you without feeling any guilt. I believed I could take my revenge on you and feel nothing but satisfaction. I despised you for everything that happened to my family because you had a face, a name. The soldiers who came here that night, even the one who pulled the hammer on the musket that killed my mother, none of them are known to me. But, you were. You were someone I could lay all the blame on. I did not believe I could ever come to feel anything for you but hatred." She paused a moment, adding, "But I was wrong."

She looked into his eyes. "I was wrong, Hadrian, because I did not know that while doing what I was doing, lying to you and betraying you as I was, I would begin to feel guilt, even hate myself for doing it. I did not know I would be torn as I was, wanting to come to you and tell you the truth, but knowing if I did, everything would be lost. I did not know, never would have thought, I would come to love you."

Hadrian searched her eyes for some sign of insincerity. In them he found nothing but truth. She had every reason to lie to him, to tell him anything that would keep him from seeing her hanged. But somehow, someway, he knew she was telling him the truth. She'd lain herself completely open to him, revealing everything about herself to him. She'd even told him that she'd fallen in love with him, a man she considered her worst enemy.

What he hadn't expected was his reaction to her words. She was right in saying that all his life he'd been an outcast. Despite the King's refusal to label him a bastard, no woman of quality would ever accept him.

The titled looked on him with scorn, as if he'd been the cause of his mother's betrayal and his father's subsequent death, not the end result. Yet, here this woman was, the one person who had reason to hate him above all else, the one person who'd been wronged more than he, and she was telling him that she loved him.

Once the initial shock of what she had done and who she truly was had subsided, Hadrian knew he could not condemn her. She'd fought for what was hers, just as he had been doing all his life. He admired her for her courage in doing what she had done, coming to Kulhaven disguised as another. He knew men, soldiers, who would not have attempted what she had. And, she had succeeded.

Until now.

Hadrian was surprised at the way he felt, for with this woman, everything he had worked toward the past years could come crashing down around him. But, it didn't seem to matter. He was her enemy. He was the man who'd taken what her family had died defending. And, still she accepted him and more, had opened her heart to him, knowing she had nothing to gain by it.

Even his own mother had not done that. The question was what was he going to do now?

"Come with me."

Hadrian took Mara by the hand and started for the door.

Chapter Twenty-two

Hadrian very nearly dragged Mara along behind him down the corridor leading to the stairs. Her gown was still soaked and left a narrow trail of water on the thick carpet as she walked along behind him. Even though she knew this would be the result if he ever learned the truth, even though she'd gone into the plan knowing this could happen, Mara still could not believe Hadrian was going to go through with it.

He was going to turn her over to the authorities and see her hanged for what she'd done.

Mara berated herself for her utter stupidity. How could she have thought that by opening herself up and revealing everything to him, he'd have done anything different? Even the possibility of a child mattered naught to him. He was an Englishman, a man without remorse, and he'd been fooled by a mere slip of a woman. It was surely a trouncing blow to his pride.

Still, she would not beg him to release her. She would stand before him like a true Kulhaven lady and face the consequences of her deeds without a hint of fear or trace of cowardice.

As they started down the stairs, on their way to, most probably, the buttery, where he would lock her until the soldiers came to take her, they encountered Cyma, who was just coming toward them from the bottom of the flight. She stood back to let them pass and knew the instant she saw her mistress, the dye washed from her hair, her expression downcast, that their plan had been discovered.

And she knew exactly what she would do.

Hadrian did not say a word, simply passed the maid and continued onward into his study. By now, every servant in the main hall had come from their chambers to see what all the shouting was about. They could but stare as the lord led what appeared to be his lady into his study without a word and closed the door behind them.

Hadrian released Mara at the center of the room and continued over to his desk. "Sit down."

She remained standing, crossing her arms stubbornly over her chest, and waited for him to speak. Above his head she could see her mother's portrait. Somehow it gave her the strength she needed to face him.

"Do you know what I am doing, Miss Despencer?"

Mara raised her chin, refusing to show the edge of fear that was causing her to shiver inside. "I have a good idea."

"Do you now? And what would that be?"

"You are going to send off for a troop of soldiers. You will lock me away in the buttery until they arrive, when you will remand me to their custody. I will then be taken in chains to Dublin, where I will be thrown into prison to await the eventual day of my hanging."

Hadrian stared at her. A slight grin came to his mouth. Was he truly so heartless as to grin at knowing he was about to send her off to her death?

"Well, I am sorry to disappoint you, but you are wrong, very wrong, in that assumption."

Mara blinked. "Excuse me?"

"I am not going to have you taken away in chains, nor will I see you hanged. You claim to know me so well, Miss Despencer. Do you really believe me to be that kind of man?"

"I had hoped not."

Hadrian took a seat behind his desk, sitting back in the chair. "Now, will you please sit down? I give you my word, as a gentleman, that I have no plans of locking you away in any buttery. There are some things I wish to tell you, and it may take a while, so you may as well be comfortable, as comfortable as you can be wearing clothes that are sopping wet, as you listen."

Mara lowered herself into the softly cushioned chair before him.

"Thank you. Miss Despencer, do you recall the day when you said you saw Lord Blackwell riding my stallion?"

Why was he bringing that subject about now? "Yes."

"Well, you were correct. Rolfe was riding Hugin that day, but only in an effort to act as a decoy for me."

Mara did not understand at all what he was talking about. "A decoy?"

"Yes. I believe you were told I was going to town that day, to purchase you a horse, wasn't that it?"

"Yes."

Hadrian nodded. "Well, I had recently discovered that I was being watched, secretly, by a soldier in Cromwell's army, a man who was supposed to report on all of my activities. Rolfe did take Hugin out that day, and he did return with him later. But, during the time in between, it was I who had been riding Hugin, not him."

Mara thought for a moment. "Are you saying that you were the one who went to the cottage to meet with Owen?"

Now it was Hadrian's turn to look confused. "How did you know about the meeting at the cottage?"

"I had gone there to see Owen as well. I slipped out when we heard you coming up the hill. I recognized Hugin and when I saw Lord Blackwell coming from the stables later that day, I assumed he had been the one who had gone to see Owen."

"How is it you know the Irish Tory's name?"

"I ought to know his name. He is my brother."

Hadrian came forward in his chair. "So, you are the one who has been giving him all his information. I could not for the life of me deduce how he had gotten his hands on the locations of the posts along the eastern coastline. I even checked to see if he had somehow stolen my map, but it was still hidden where I had left it."

"In the wall behind the books on the weather patterns in the region."

Hadrian looked at her, surprised. "That map was hidden away and locked."

"The lock was easily opened."

Hadrian crossed his arms, grinning. "So, I have married a liar, an impostor, and now a lockpick. Are these subjects generally taught to young Irish girls by their governesses?"

Mara frowned. "I did not give Owen all the locations. I purposely omitted one of the posts in Wexford. And I did not give him anything willingly. Just after my arrival at Kulhaven, Owen contacted me. He told me if I did not give him the information he wanted, information vital to his cause, he would tell you who I really was. I had to give him what he wanted. I had no other choice. He promised me that when I had given him what he wanted, he would leave. But, every time I gave him something, he asked for something more."

"What more have you given him?"

"He also wanted the list of Cromwell's top advisors you kept in your desk drawer. And, then, this last time, he wanted me to forge a pardon for someone being held in prison in Dublin, signing your name and affixing your seal to the bottom."

Hadrian's grin faded. "Who was the pardon for?"

"I do not know the man. His name is John MacDugan."

"I might have known." Hadrian rubbed his eyes as if he was very, very tired. He exhaled loudly. "And did you give your brother this pardon?"

"No. Not yet anyway. I was supposed to meet him tonight at the cottage to give it to him. I had just finished affixing your seal to it when I found that list in the hearth indicating who was next to be dispossessed of their estates." She suddenly remembered the notation beside the Connellys' name. "Oh, Hadrian, I know this will be of no matter to you, but one of the families written on that list is well known to me. If I do not warn them, they will be attacked and killed just like my family was."

"I am sorry, Miss Despencer, but I cannot allow you to warn them."

Mara moved to the desk, placing her hands upon it. "But you said you did not condone what the Roundheads did to my family. You said you would have prevented it had you been able. You have the means before you now to prevent this from happening again to another family. How can you simply stand by and allow them to be killed?"

"I have no choice in the matter. You see, I am the only one who has knowledge of that list. If the Connellys are forewarned about the attack, the Proctectorate will know that the warning somehow came from me. I cannot take that risk."

"But they will be killed!"

Mara's eyes were filling with tears and she was staring at him, unable to understand his refusal. Hadrian hesitated, trying to come to a decision before he offered her an explanation. If he told her the truth, the real reasons for his wanting to marry Arabella, everything he had worked for the past seven years could come to ruin. Still, as he looked over at her, her cheeks stained where the black dye had run in rivers down her face, he wondered if he could trust her. She was a stranger to him and someone who could very well buy her freedom with what he was about to tell her.

But even after he had found her out and she believed he would turn her over to the Roundheads, she had still told him everything.

And now the time had come for him to do the same.

"Sit back down, Miss Despencer. There is something I must say to you."

Mara's first inclination was to refuse, but something in his voice told her it would be better to do as he asked. Silently she returned to her chair.

"I told you when I had been stationed in Dublin, I had never been involved in the actual fighting of the war.

But what I did not tell you was that before I was sent to Dublin, I was a foot soldier in England. I was involved in only one battle before I came to Ireland. It was the Battle of Worcester."

Mara looked at him. "Worcester? Is that not the same battle where the heir, Charles II, escaped to France?"

"Aye. We were canvasing a thick wooded area near an estate called Boscobel. My troop decided it would be better for us all to split up and search on our own through the wood. Divide and conquer, or so they say.

"We were not having very much luck in finding anything but hedgehogs and wood owls in the darkness that night. Not that I was trying that hard to succeed. I was tired, we had been going nonstop since the previous day, so I sat down to rest a spell beneath the thick branches of a rather large oak tree. It did not take me long to realize there was someone else resting nearby. In fact, directly above me in the tree."

Understanding dawned on Mara's face. "Charles II. You were sitting beneath the Royal Oak."

"Yes. He looked right at me. Scared me more than I did him."

Mara smiled at him. "You helped him to escape, didn't you? You saved the life of the heir to the throne."

"Not as far as the history books will be concerned, but, yes, I did. I had to. You see, I joined the side of the Parliamentarians not long after Cromwell had been successful in seeing the King, Charles I, beheaded. I did not join to aid them in their cause, I joined to circumvent it."

"I do not understand."

"I could not abide a man who had become so filled

with the greed for power that he would justify regicide by quoting from the Bible while committing it. I knew Cromwell had to be stopped."

"So you are a spy."

Hadrian simply looked at her. "I would have to deny it were I accused of it. I was too young at the time that the Civil War began to understand the reasons for it. My uncle, James, who was more a father to me than an uncle, had been there and had been discontented with Charles I's visions of an absolute monarchy that ruled without the balance of Parliament. He used a goodly portion of his fortune to help fund Cromwell's rise to power. But he never had expected regicide. When he was given Kulhaven as a reward for his financial support, he almost did not take it. But he hated what England had become, hated himself for helping to make her that way, and since he believed your family dead, he decided to come over and escape from being involved in the Parliamentarian side of it any longer. Had he not taken possession of Kulhaven, Miss Despencer, someone else would have."

Mara was silent for quite some time. She stared at the pattern woven through the thick carpet, digesting everything Hadrian had just told her. Hadrian was a spy. She almost couldn't believe it. All the while since she had returned to Kulhaven, she had been living a double life, trying desperately to keep him from finding her out. And, all that time, he had been doing the same. She looked up to him.

"I thank you for being so honest with me. This war has done so much to so many people. And it is precisely for that reason that I cannot stand by and allow another family to die."

"I'm sorry, but as I said before, I cannot allow you to warn the Connellys. We are too close to getting Charles II restored to the throne. I cannot take the risk."

Mara started to stand. "I am going, Hadrian, with or without your permission."

"Well, then you leave me no choice." Hadrian stood from his chair and came forward, grabbing her by the hand.

"What are you doing?"

"It seems I am being forced into locking you up in the buttery after all so you cannot warn the Connellys."

Mara tried to pull her arm free, but Hadrian just tightened his grip. "No, Hadrian. You cannot lock me up. Please, let me free." She started pummeling him with her fists. "I will take responsibility for warning them. You can turn me over to the soldiers after I return. I do not care. I just cannot sit by and watch another family die."

Hadrian grabbed her by the wrists and yanked her forward, shaking her. "No. It will do you no good to fight me. You cannot overpower me."

"Let my lady go!"

Hadrian didn't stand a chance. He turned just as Cyma came running across the room, a thick and heavy candlestick raised above her head, screaming like a woman gone mad. She swung the candlestick at him like a warrior wielding a battle-ax and struck him directly on his temple.

Hadrian's hold on Mara instantly slackened and he crumbled to the floor.

* * *

At first when Hadrian opened his eyes he thought he'd gone blind from the force of the maid's blow. He could see nothing but the blackest darkness around him. His head throbbed and even the slightest of movements caused a stabbing pain to go right through his brain.

He managed to sit up with some effort and felt around in the darkness for something, anything but the nothingness that surrounded him. He realized then that he was lying on a bed and the bed drapery had been drawn so tightly around him that no light could break through to the inside.

He pushed the heavy velvet to the side. The drafty air outside rose up against him, chilling him in places he'd never been chilled before. It was then he realized he wasn't wearing any breeches.

She had bested him with a candlestick to the head and then she'd stripped him bare. Actually he wasn't totally bare, for she'd had the distinct courtesy of leaving him wearing one of his long nightshirts, the ones he only wore in winter. It was made of soft cambric and reached to his knees and as he stood from the bed, he wondered for a brief moment why she had bothered to put it on him. But then he realized it was just one of her tactics of keeping him from going too far should he happen to wake from his state of unconsciousness and find himself lying in God knows whose bed.

And just whose bed was he in, he asked himself even as he knew, somehow, he wasn't sure how, that he was in Arabella's chamber.

But it wasn't Arabella's chamber, was it?

No, it was the bedchamber of his wife, his true wife, Mara Despencer.

There was no light in the room, no fire in the hearth, and the curtains had been drawn on the windows so tightly that no moonlight could filter inside. He made for the door, cursed aloud when he tripped over something that sent him sprawling on the floor, then stood and finally managed to reach it without further injury to his person.

He tried the door handle, but even before he felt it resist he knew it was locked. She would never have gone through the trouble of dragging him all the way up the stairs, depositing him on her bed, and drawing the bed drapery so tightly if she had planned to leave the door unlocked.

She was no fool, he'd give her that. For a moment he wondered how she and that candlestick-wielding crone of a maid of hers had managed to get him to the second floor. But then he realized a woman who could accomplish what she had thus far, disguising herself each day and managing to keep him from learning her true identity would have no trouble getting him up a flight of stairs and locked away.

The question was, how was he going to get out of her little prison cell so he could wring her beautiful neck?

First thing would be some light so he could at least see what he was doing. He'd not spent a great deal of time in her chamber, only one night if memory served, so he was not certain of where things might be. He believed he could recall a writing desk somewhere in the vicinity of the hearth. Keeping one hand on the wall as a sort of anchor, he started moving about the room, trying to find a candle, anything to give him back his sight.

He managed to locate the writing desk and the candle that had been left atop it. Grasping the candle in one hand, he felt his way along the wall to the hearth and knelt before it. A few barely glowing embers remained from the fire that had burned there earlier that night. Fanning it softly, he touched the wick to the coals to light the candle.

With his sight restored, he began to search for a way out of his makeshift prison. She had managed to do a very thorough job of keeping him detained, the minx. She'd removed any object that might have been fashioned into a lockpick. No sewing needles, not even a single hairpin had been left behind. Seeing the thoroughness with which she had canvased the room, he wondered just how long he'd been knocked out cold.

Hadrian began to pace. He had no idea of the time, but knew she must have gone to warn the Connelly family despite his efforts to convince her otherwise. And she must have left hours ago, as dark as the night sky was outside. Didn't the little fool realize she could get herself killed? And if she didn't, if she somehow managed to warn the Connellys and return without being noticed by the soldiers who were camping in the woodland nearby, he would be more than happy to kill her himself when she did return.

If she returned.

Now that her little scheme had been uncovered, now that he knew who she truly was, what would she do? She could very well disappear without another trace to avoid hanging, leaving him locked away in this room till all eternity. This thought bothered Hadrian more than he cared to admit. He didn't want her to disappear, never to return again. He wanted her back so he could wring her little neck himself. He hesitated to admit it, but he wanted her back because the thought of spending the rest of his days without her left him feeling oddly empty inside.

He heard a sound in the hall outside and made for the door. Footsteps and they were coming closer. He waited until the footsteps had drawn nearer, then pounded on the door.

"Who is there? This is Lord St. Aubyn. Can you hear me?"

The footsteps halted just outside the door. "Yes, my lord?"

It was his wonderful and loyal steward, Peter Shipley. Hadrian smiled, realizing his luck. "Shipley, open the door. I seem to have somehow gotten myself locked inside her ladyship's bedchamber. I cannot find the key to get out."

"Yes, I am aware of that, my lord."

Hadrian narrowed his eyes at the door. "What do you mean you are aware of it? Just open the door, man."

"I am afraid I cannot do that, my lord."

"Why the hell not?"

"Well, her ladyship left strict instructions, my lord."

Hadrian felt his temper begin to rise. "Oh, she did, did she? And who is the one in charge of this household, Mr. Shipley? Who has been the one in charge of the house long before her ladyship ever came to Kulhaven? Who is it that pays your wages, Mr. Shipley?"

The steward cleared his throat. "I know you do not mean that, my lord. Her ladyship said you would probably resort to saying such things in order to get us to release you, but, believe me, my lord, it is for your own good."

Hadrian stared at the door in disbelief. "For my own

good? How the devil can being locked in a room be for my own good?"

"Until the disease has passed the contagious stages, it is better for you to remain sequestered. You wouldn't want an epidemic, would you? I do apologize, my lord, but I couldn't release you even if I wanted to. Her ladyship suspected you might be able to coerce one of the more vulnerable housemaids to open the door for you, so she took all the keys with her. Why do you not try to lie down and get some rest? It shouldn't be too much longer, though. Her ladyship should be back with the physician soon and then he will know for certain if it is the smallpox or not."

Hadrian was so stunned by what he'd just heard that he didn't realize when Peter Shipley had left from the other side of the door.

Smallpox?

Oh, she was a clever one.

Chapter Twenty-three

Mara turned the key slowly in the lock, and trying to keep its creaking at a minimum, opened the door to her bedchamber.

She stepped inside, having a care to do so quietly, and allowed Toirneach to follow before closing the door behind her. It was late, quite late, and the sun would soon be rising across the lavender-peaked eastern hills of Kilkenny to dawn on another brilliant Irish day. She hoped she would find Hadrian still sleeping on the bed, hidden behind the bed drapery, his senses yet dulled from the blow Cyma had delivered him. She certainly hoped she did not find him waiting to pounce on her like a crab spider lurking beneath the pretty yellow blooms of the moneywort the moment she entered the room.

"So, there is some truth to the legend after all. The Flaming Lady doth exist."

He had awakened, and from the sounds of it was not at all in a very good humor. In fact, he sounded quite fit to kill her. Well, at least he was speaking to her. That was a favorable sign. "I am greatly relieved the blow Cyma delivered to your head did not have any ill effects, my lord, for you obviously are still possessed of your cutting turn of speech."

"Do you know I used to think I was losing my mind because of you? I had seen you swimming in the lough and standing at the tower battlements, but whenever I tried to get close enough to confront you, you somehow magically vanished. I could find no logical explanation for the odd visions I kept having of a red-haired witch. I became obsessed with it, looking for you to be floating around every darkened corner, afraid you were going to come and murder me in my bed or push me from the top of the tower like my Uncle James."

Mara started removing her gloves. "I cannot see you being afraid of anything, human or spectral, and I did not kill your uncle, Hadrian. I was in Dublin at the time, trying to make enough money to eat. If you would like, I would be happy to furnish you with witnesses."

She was too tired for another round of verbal fencing with him. She'd just ridden for her life, and the knowledge of it still brought her to trembling each time she thought of it.

She removed her black high-crowned riding hat, setting it negligently on the chair of her dressing table, and ruffled out her red curls which had been twisted beneath it. She stepped from the shadows near the door and into the small dull-glowing circle of light given off by the fire in the hearth. "I see you found a way to light a fire."

"Yes, I did, madam. Thank you. It took a little time, but I did eventually manage. It was most remiss of you to leave a few coals in the hearth. I am surprised you did not take the time to remove them. Tell me, for I am mad with curiosity, how did you manage to get me up here? Surely you and that misfit maid of yours did not drag me up the stairs yourselves."

"No, we did not. Shipley helped us, and Crumb, the blacksmith."

"Why did you not invite all the villagers as well? You could have made a party of it."

His voice dripped with sarcasm. He was seated in an armchair before the fire, his bare feet crossed before him, wearing the nightshirt she had left him in and nothing else. He had been waiting for her to return with what appeared to be the bottom ruffle to one of her chemises tied about his forehead. A small stain of blood had come through the white fabric where the makeshift bandage was knotted at his temple.

Mara dropped the jacket she had been wearing, his jacket, and crossed the room to him. "Oh, Hadrian, I did not realize Cyma had hit you so hard. I am sure she didn't mean to."

"We will discuss what your soon-to-find-herself-unemployed maid did or did not mean to do at a later time. I am afraid I must admit, though, that this lovely little bump on my head is not a result of her handiwork, but rather an injury I received while trying to find my way across this room without benefit of any light. It matches the one on the other side of my head which was indeed caused by your raving mad maid. I'm sorry to say your tea table did not fare nearly as well."

He motioned to the pile of splintered wood that had once been her carved and inlaid rosewood tea table. "It was a well-crafted piece and it made for fine kindling since you did not have the foresight to leave any wood for the hearth." One eyebrow shot up as he suddenly noticed her attire. "I was wondering what you had done with my clothing."

Mara looked down at the breeches, shirt, and boots she wore. "I needed something to wear that wouldn't hinder me with layers of fabric on horseback. Since I also needed to ensure that you did not try to leave, I figured I could borrow your breeches while I was gone. The drapery cord did well to hold the breeches up."

"Tell me, since you took all but my smallclothes and didn't leave me with any wood for the fire, was it your plan to allow me to freeze to death, or were you hoping that I'd break my neck after tripping over that damned tea table?"

Mara frowned at him. "I did not intend for you to fall over the tea table at all, I was quite fond of that table actually, nor did I plan to leave you here long enough for you to freeze. If you will recall I left you lying on a very thick and very soft coverlet on the bed. If you weren't so pigheaded, you could have it wrapped about your shoulders right now. Now, stop being petulant and let me take a look at your forehead. I need to make certain you are not suffering from vertigo or some other such affliction."

She walked to him and reached for the makeshift bandage. He lifted his hands to block her from proceeding.

"That is not necessary, madam. I am fine. I have the fortunate good luck of being possessed of a rather hard head."

Oh, if that wasn't putting it mildly. "You mean a thick skull, don't you, my lord? Enough of this nonsense, Hadrian. You could very well have caused yourself more injury than what is showing on the outside." She probed gently at the lump which had formed on his forehead. "Does this hurt at all?"

He looked at her with an expression of impatience and said dryly, "Yes, terribly."

Mara ignored him and continued with her inspection of his wound, pushing aside a lock of hair to get a better look. "Well, it's a nasty gash, I'll grant you that, but I do not think it will require stitching." She stepped back. "How many fingers am I holding up?"

"Seventeen."

"There is no reason to be nasty. I was just trying to help."

"Oh, was I being rude? How very ungentlemanly of me. I apologize, madam, if petulance doesn't become me. The smallpox does tend to make one grouchy."

Mara hesitated. "You heard?"

"Aye. I must say that you certainly did well with that inventive tale. Mr. Shipley wouldn't budge an inch. Fine steward he is. He can join your maid in her new unemployed status when I get around to dismissing him. Tell me, did you manage to win all the other servants over to your side while I was away those few days in Dublin?"

Mara shrugged. "As for Mr. Shipley, he did nothing wrong. I am sorry that it was necessary to tell the servants you had contracted the smallpox, but I had to find a way to explain why you were passed out cold on the study floor, your eyes rolled back in your head, and why you could not be allowed out of my chambers until I had returned. That was, of course after I told them you had been taken over by an uncontrollable fit and had dumped an inkwell over my head, thus explaining the dye on my face. None of this would have happened, you know, if you would have just agreed to let me warn the Connellys. But you refused to listen to reason. I could not simply stand by and watch while another family was destroyed. I had to do something to help them."

"And, did you?"

Mara nodded, reaching to scratch Toirneach behind the ears. "The Connellys are now on their way to England to live with relatives until this madness ends. We got them out safely just as the troops were coming up the rise leading to their home."

"You're lucky you weren't seen."

A look came over Mara's face that instantly told Hadrian she was holding something back.

"What else happened out there while you were on your mission of mercy, Miss Despencer?"

"Wouldn't it be proper for you to call me by my given name?"

"I wouldn't know which name to use. You've acquired quite a substantial list of addresses, many of which were given to you recently by me and are not to be spoken of in polite society. Now, tell me what the devil happened out there."

Mara bent to place another piece of wood on the fire, the delicately spiral-carved leg of the destroyed rosewood tea table, it appeared, and affording Hadrian a new view of her breeches-clad bottom. She turned, noting the direction of his bold stare, and moved to the side of the fire, opening her hands outward to warm them. "It really is nothing to get so worked up about. While we were taking the Connellys to safety, a small troop came upon us in the wood. We split up, thinking to elude them, but I think Owen might have been captured. He did not return to the cottage as we had arranged to do afterward."

"Damnation, woman!" He came forward and grabbed her by the arms, shaking her.

Just then, Toirneach launched at him out of the shadows, baring his teeth and barking loudly at him. Mara looked at Hadrian, speaking in a voice quite calm.

"You need to release me and step back very slowly. Do not move quickly or speak loudly." She turned to the dog then. "It is all right, boy, you can go back to lie by the fire again. He is not going to harm me, are you, my lord?"

Hadrian removed his hands from her, saying in a voice that was deadly calm, "Not at the moment, although I will not make any promises for later."

Toirneach, sensing that his mistress was no longer in any danger, turned reluctantly and moved to the hearth. He lowered his huge grizzled body to the carpet, but his ever-watchful eyes stayed on the two of them, ready to return if need be.

"I should have done away with that mongrel when I first came to Kulhaven," Hadrian said under his breath.

Toirneach let out a grumble at his words.

Hadrian turned to Mara then, keeping his voice at a pleasant level. "Do you at all realize the danger you have placed us in? Your brother is an outlaw, one of the most wanted men in Ireland. Do you know what he has been doing? Why he needed the information you were giving him?"

Mara frowned, quite disliking the way he was speaking to her as if she were a naughty child. "Owen would never tell me why he needed the information."

"Your brother is trying to raise an army of his own, an army made up of the most hardened, unconscionable felons in Ireland. These are not just men who were taken as prisoners of war. These are men who would sift through the bodies of dead soldiers, English and Irish alike, removing anything of value they could find. John MacDugan, the one whose pardon you forged, do you want to know the sort of man he is?"

Mara just stared at him. She didn't respond.

"He cut off the finger of a dead Irish woman when he couldn't remove her wedding ring."

A shudder of revulsion swept through Mara and she had to swallow several times to keep her stomach from retching.

"Your brother planned to take over first Ireland, then England. He planned to become the Irish Cromwell, to go through England desecrating and killing. He doesn't want peace. He thrives on the fighting, the killing and maiming of innocent people. And now he could very well turn us both in to the Protectorate and we'll be hanged right along with him."

"Owen wouldn't do that."

"He wouldn't, would he? Need I remind you that he was ready to expose you if you did not do what he wanted before? He will be desperate now and will use any means he can to escape execution. What is there to stop him?"

Mara knew that what Hadrian was saying was true, but she still clung to the foolish belief that her brother wouldn't betray her like that. "Perhaps it will not matter at all. Owen told me he heard a rumor in Dublin that Cromwell is near death. He could very well have passed on by now."

If Hadrian had also heard the rumor, he did not readily show it. He sat in his chair. "I do not believe many will mourn the passing of that man. In the beginning, he brought hope and promise of a better England. I think most everyone realizes now that the England he is leaving behind is far worse than what it had been before. At least now he will be forced to face the responsibility of his actions."

Mara took a seat in the chair beside him and rested her head in her hands. "Yes, so now there should be no reason why the heir, Charles II, could not return to claim his crown."

"Except there are still those who have tasted power and, quite frankly, have grown to like it. They will not be so eager to relinquish that which they have attained. There is still much work to do."

Hadrian was staring into the fire, thoughtful now. "And, then there is my other problem."

"Your other problem?"

"Yes." He looked at her levelly. "You."

Mara did not know what to say.

"Yes, my dear bride in disguise, I must now decide what to do about our less than honest union. As you so aptly put it to me earlier, you could very well be carrying my child. Given my past, you were correct in your assumption that I would be less than willing to name my son a bastard. So, I have two choices standing before me."

He stood and began circling the room. Mara found she liked the way he looked wearing naught but his nightshirt, his hairy legs sticking out from underneath, as he paced the thick carpet barefoot. "I can wait a month to see if you have your flux. If you do bleed, then I need not worry over it any longer. I can dissolve this marriage and try to begin my life anew."

Mara felt a strange chill at his words. "I must tell you that I will continue to fight for Kulhaven. This is my family's land and—"

"Or," he went on, touching his finger to her lips to quiet her words, "I can keep you as my wife, child or no child. At least that way I would be able to keep an eye on you. And then there's always the Curse of Kulhaven. The only way to lift the curse is for a Despencer to return as heir to Kulhaven. For posterity's sake, I wouldn't want to upset the spirits into cursing this castle for all eternity. Although deemed legitimate, living my life being known as the Bastard Earl of St. Aubyn is enough notoriety for one man to bear."

Mara stood. "You are not a bastard."

She lifted her lips to his then and kissed him before he could open his mouth to argue.

She could feel his resistance at first, but he soon began to respond and drew her forward into his arms. Mara literally melted against him. She had longed for this day for so long now, to love him not as Arabella, but as who she really was, that she wanted to prolong it so it would forever be burned in her memory. She did not know what Hadrian's plans were for her, if he would turn her over to the soldiers and let her be hanged. Or, if he would keep her. Nor did she particularly care at that moment. She would deal with that possibility if and when the time arose. Right now, all she wanted was to be his, she wanted him to be hers, and the rest of the world be damned.

They did not even make it across the room to the bed. They tore at each other's clothing, which, in

Hadrian's case, was not all that difficult, being that he wore a shirt that fell to his knees and nothing more. And when they were naked and standing before each other, the light of the fire playing across her fair skin, Hadrian stepped back to look down the length of her.

He'd never seen a more lovely sight in all his life. Her hair fell in shimmering ringlets like a shower of copper fire down to her narrow waist. Her eyes were alive and watching him behind her lashes without her usual cover of the spectacles and he found he couldn't resist the urge to kiss each lid.

"I have been dreaming of making love to you since the day I first saw you swimming in the lough," he said, his voice thick with need.

She smiled at him then, her eyes the color of smoky emeralds, sparking in the firelight. "Then what's stopping you?"

Hadrian pulled her against him and covered her lips with his, plunging his tongue into her mouth to taste of its sweet nectar. His hand slid down over one smooth shoulder and cupped the weight of her breast in his palm. He wanted this to last forever, but at the same time he was desperate to have her. He rubbed his thumb over her rosy nipple, teasing it to pebble hardness, then lowered his mouth gently over it, rolling his tongue around it until he could hear her gasping for breath.

He pulled her down with him, his mouth never leaving hers, and he made love to her there on the thick pile of the carpet, bellowing out his release just as the sun began to rise over the horizon. And when he raised his head from her shoulder to look down at her in the light of morning, he smiled, pleased to see it was still her, and not Arabella lying beneath him.

"I was not dreaming. You did not disappear with the night."

"Not this time, I'm afraid."

Hadrian lay back and pulled her over him so that she was resting her chin on her hands atop his chest. She was looking up at him, a stray curl hanging over one eye, and he gave in to the urge to smile.

"What is it that has you smiling so."

"I was just remembering a book I read once about Irish mythology. I was reminded of a goddess called the Mórrígan who would often disguise herself in the form of a raven."

"Or perhaps in the form of another woman with raven-colored hair?"

"As I remember it, she was quite prone to inciting war and trouble. I find it interesting, the similarities between this goddess and you."

"And will you, like the great warrior, Cúchulainn, discount my aid and assistance and reject my offer of love and land?"

Hadrian smiled. "As I recall, Cúchulainn died because he rejected the Mórrígan. I would certainly hate to make the same mistake as he."

"What is it you are saying, Hadrian?"

"What am I saying, dear wife," he said, rolling her beneath him, "is that I think I would be better served to have you remain here as my wife so I can keep my eye on you at all times. I wouldn't want to be the one responsible for unleashing the wrath of another war goddess on Ireland."

"Are you saying you will accept my love and return it?"

Hadrian lowered his head and kissed her then, feeling the renewal of his desire stirring once again, and giving her all the answer she needed.

Chapter Twenty-four

When Hadrian awoke four hours later, feeling alive and refreshed despite the throbbing of the tender lumps on both sides of his head, he was greeted by the sight of his wife sitting before her dressing table, her hand immersed in a pot of blackened gunk, ready to spread it on her glorious red hair.

"What in perdition do you think you are doing?"

She looked at him in the reflection of the looking glass with an expression that told him she found his question quite stupid. "What does it look like I am doing? I am dying my hair, of course, as I have every day since I arrived inside these walls. I cannot very well appear at breakfast this morning, asking for tea and rolls as has become the lady of the house's custom, and looking like this. I do believe the servants would notice a slight difference in my appearance, don't you, Hadrian?"

He left the bed in two strides and pulled the pot of gunk from her hand. He lifted the pot to his nose, wincing when he caught a whiff of it. "This is going right where it belongs, which is down the privy hole and quickly, before it stinks up the entire western wing. This stuff could melt the rust from the latch on the gate leading out to the eastern pasture. I cannot believe you would put this in your hair. You're lucky it didn't all fall out and leave you bald. And, as for what the servants will think, I do not particularly care. To perdition with what the servants think. If they value their positions at this estate, they will refrain from making any comment at all."

He hunkered down beside her, lifting one of the burnished corkscrew curls from her shoulder. He twisted it around his finger. "I much prefer your hair this color, especially when it is hanging loose and wild about your shoulders while you are screaming with pleasure."

Mara looked at him from the corner of the eye as she began twisting a white ribbon through her hair. "I do not scream."

"Is that so? I think the servants whom you are so worried would notice the change in your hair color would beg to differ with you on that point, madam." He stood and picked up her gown from where she'd laid it on the bench at the foot of the bed. "And please, kindly dispose of these dreadful mourning clothes. They do not at all go well with your lovely hair. Green the color of emeralds and brilliant blue, those shades would serve to compliment you better, I think. And yellow. A gown made of fabric the color of sunflowers. Yes, that is it. I shall see about having a dressmaker come from Dublin for you immediately."

"Yellow makes me look sallow."

He kissed her playfully on the top of her fiery head. "You, my dear wife, could never look sallow."

Mara could but stare at the man standing before her, this man who still was her husband, and who was so very different from the other Hadrian she'd come to know. This Hadrian laughed and smiled at her. He gave her fashion advice, for God's sake. He certainly didn't avoid his wife at every turn.

It seemed she wasn't the only one who had been hiding behind a disguise all this time.

"All right, Hadrian. You win. You have my word that I will not dye my hair any longer. And I will instruct one of the footmen to deliver the dye in this pot immediately to the privy hole, although he'll probably question as to why he is being punished with such a distasteful task. Now go to your own chamber and get yourself dressed before you give the maids a shock standing all hairy and naked as you are in the light of day."

Hadrian grinned. "I will be waiting for you in the hallway to walk with you down to breakfast."

"Dressed, I should hope."

Hadrian turned then and started from the room. Before he made it to the door, he stopped, eyeing something atop the mahogany inlaid chest of drawers that stood against the far wall. Mara watched on as, without saying a word, he picked up the small white linen cap she'd always worn when she'd been in the guise of Arabella, walked over to the hearth, and with great ceremony, deposited it in the fire.

Mara smiled and turned to continue with her morning ablutions, eyeing the black silk gown she'd planned to wear that day. Hmm, she thought to herself industriously, perhaps with a few small alterations, it could be made more to her husband's liking.

She stood and walked to Cyma's chamber in search of her sewing basket.

A half hour later, she opened the door leading out

into the hallway. Hadrian was lounging a few paces down from her, staring at a portrait hanging on the wall.

"You know, I believe I will commission an artist to come and paint you. I think you—"

Hadrian never finished his sentence. He had turned to look at her and was now standing as if his feet were fixed to the floor. The expression on his face was one of acute shock and it looked so genuine it momentarily gave Mara cause for concern.

"What? Is something wrong? Are my skirts askew? You do not like the gown?"

"No. You are stunning. I never realized how very soft and white your skin could look. And your hair—it looks like it is on fire. Do I like the gown? I love the gown. I never knew one could look so very strikingly alive in the color most associated with death. You may add black to the list of acceptable shades for your gowns."

Mara beamed, taking her skirts in hand and sweeping him a ceremonious curtsy. She had slashed the full puffed sleeves so that the white of her chemise showed from underneath, discarding the starched white wrist-length cuffs as well.

"I am so very glad you approve, my lord. Being that I was more interested in running about with my brothers than in spending time with Mrs. Peebles, my governess, I was never known for my skill with needle and thread. In fact, if I recall, Mrs. Peebles had declared my sewing abilities as 'deplorable,' Cyma would most probably scold me for uneven stitches, but I managed to make it serviceable. Now then, shall we go down to breakfast, my lord? I find, for some unknown reason, my appetite is quite demanding this morning."

As they walked down the hallway to the stairs, Hadrian could not seem to take his eyes from her. If he'd ever been taken under the spell of the Flaming Lady before, he was now utterly and irreversibly bewitched. She'd discarded the white laced falling band that usually fastened under her chin, exposing the pale and temptingly soft skin of her shoulders and her frighteningly seductive neck. The neckline on the gown was rounded and deeply plunging, showing the firm swells of her soft white breasts.

And, that hair. That brilliant and beautiful red hair. She wore it loose and hanging down her back in a spill of radiant curls. He wanted to twist his fingers through it, longed to bury his face in its softness and inhale its flowery scent. He was growing hard just looking at her.

He took a deep and steadying breath and tore his gaze away, knowing if he didn't stop assessing every one of her lovely attributes, he'd most likely be dragging her into one of the bedchambers and throwing her skirts to her chin so he could bury himself within her again.

Mara hesitated when they reached the top of the stairs, pulling him back. "Hadrian, are you certain you do not wish to at least speak to the servants first? What will they think when they see me looking like this?"

"We'll never know if we continue to stand here atop the stairs speculating about it. Where is that lovely sense of adventure that brought you crashing into my life? Come, let us go down and see if any one of them takes notice."

He set her hand in the crook of his arm and started down the stairs. Mara gripped his jacket sleeve. The first person they encountered was Peter Shipley, who awaited them at the bottom floor.

"Good morning, my lord. So pleased to see it was not the smallpox after all." He looked at Mara. In perfectly Shipley-like manner and without batting an eye, he added, "You are looking quite fetching this morning, if I may say so, my lady."

Mara smiled as they continued on past.

Standing before the dining room door, two serving maids whispered to each other excitedly. Peter Shipley delivered them a quelling look as the lord and lady moved on.

Hadrian seated Mara at her usual place beside him, his hand lingering on her shoulder after he gently pushed her chair in behind her. True to his word, he acted as if this were any other day, that she had not suddenly sprouted hellish red hair, and much to her surprise the servants did likewise, after, perhaps, a moment or two of initial eye-popping.

When the meal was nearly finished, Mr. Shipley presented himself at the door.

"My lord, there is a Mr. John O'Hanlon here to see you. He wishes to speak with you, something about some furniture that he was making."

"Show him in, please, Mr. Shipley."

Oh, dear, Mara thought. In all the confusion and chaos since Hadrian's return, she'd not had the opportunity to tell him what she'd done. He had no idea she had dismissed the thieving Horace Crow and had used the money he'd returned to help the villagers. "Hadrian, I wish to speak with you."

"Later, my dear. I must see what John O'Hanlon is here about."

"But, Hadrian, I know what he is here about. He is—"

She could not finish her sentence. Shipley had entered and was at that very moment announcing their caller.

"My lord, thank you for seeing me. I know I didn't have an appointment. I . . ."

John O'Hanlon froze, his body going rigid, his eyes saucer wide and staring directly at Mara. "Sweet Lord in heaven above, it's the Flaming Lady!"

He wavered ever slightly and Mara stood in an effort to calm him.

"No, Mr. O'Hanlon, I'm not the Flam—"

Her next words were cut off by the loud thud of John O'Hanlon's body hitting the polished wooden floorboards. Hadrian sprang from his chair and rushed over to his side.

"Hadrian, is he all right?"

Hadrian felt his neck for a pulse. "Yes. Not to worry, dear. You didn't kill him. I do believe he has, quite simply, fainted."

He turned to the assembly of servants who'd gathered in the doorway. "Mrs. Danbury, would you happen to have any smelling salts?"

"Yes, my lord. In the kitchen. I'll get them directly."

She returned in minutes, pushing through the others in haste. Hadrian took the small glass vial and waved it slowly beneath John O'Hanlon's nostrils. The man moaned and turned his head to the side, and after a moment, his eyelids fluttered slowly open. He coughed and sputtered. "Oh, Lord St. Aubyn, I saw her. The Flaming Lady. She was standing right there in your dining room."

"It is all right, John. Let's get you up and on your feet now and we'll talk about it."

Mara came forward. "Here, let me help."

John O'Hanlon scrambled backward across the floor, screaming as if in fear for his life. "Aiee! It's her again. She's come back to take me to my grave!"

Hadrian turned toward Mara. "My dear, I think it would be best if you step away for a moment."

Mara nodded and returned to her seat.

"John," he said, shaking the babbling man by the shoulders, "it is all right, man. She is not a ghost. It's just my wife, Lady St. Aubyn."

"But, I see her right there, my lord. It's her with her red hair and she's dressed in the color of death. It's the Flaming Lady come to punish us all."

It took nearly half an hour to calm John O'Hanlon enough to explain who Mara really was. Even after he'd downed three glasses of Hadrian's finest brandy, his hands still had a slight shaking to them, and he sat staring at Mara while clinging to the edge of his seat, ready to run should the need arise.

"Now, what did you wish to speak with me about, John?"

Reluctantly he looked at Hadrian. "I was just going to tell you I've finished the new walnut candle stand you ordered and I'll be starting on the bed early tomorrow. I should be able to get it done by Michaelmas."

Mara cringed.

"Bed? What bed are you speaking of, John? I do not recall requesting that you craft me any furniture, although, I must admit, my wife is in need of a new tea table."

"Your lady commissioned me to make her a candle stand and bed for you." He looked to Mara, still trying to see past her red hair. "I hope I didn't ruin a surprise, my lady."

"No, it is all right, John. I was just about to tell his lordship about the stand and bed. Thank you for coming to tell me of your progress. I'll see that you receive your payment directly."

She stood and started walking him to the door, noticing the look of suspicion on Hadrian's face.

"My wife and the others have been working night and day on the new bed coverings, too, my lady. And, with the materials you supplied, we should be able to thatch over all the roofs in the village before winter comes."

"Thank you, John. And please, thank your wife for me, as well."

When Mara returned to the dining room, she took care to close the door behind her. She certainly had no need of the servants watching as Hadrian bellowed at her for what she'd done. Hadrian did not say a word, but sat staring at her as she returned to her chair, waiting for an explanation from her.

"I'm sure you are wondering what that was all about."

His eyes did not waver. "The thought did cross my mind."

"I had every intention of telling you about it all last night, but, well, things became complicated and it slipped my mind."

"Yes."

"Well, let me begin by saying none of the money used was taken from the castle coffers."

Hadrian's raised a brow. "Is that so? Did you find a hidden money chest left behind by some eccentric old noble who'd buried it and had forgotten where it was?"

Mara took a sip of tea. "In a matter of speaking, yes. It is a little complicated. I'll start at the beginning. You see, I dismissed Horace Crow."

"You what? Horace Crow has been with me since I came to Kulhaven. He was with my Uncle James before."

"Yes, and he has been systematically stealing from you for quite some time. Have you had the occasion recently to review the ledgers?"

"Well, it has been some time. I have been occupied of late."

"Yes, and most probably did not thoroughly check the figures the last time you did review them. That is probably when the good Mr. Crow realized he could take advantage of your negligence. He did not even attempt much of a denial when I confronted him with his thievery and he returned most of the money he had stolen before he was escorted from here. I used that money, the money he returned, to help the villagers. Not a single pence came from the castle's accounts that had not already been taken from it." She grinned, pleased with the manner in which she'd explained it so well. "Now we can help the villagers and it will not cost Kulhaven a pence."

Hadrian shook his head. "It was not the cost that prevented me from helping the villagers in the first place. Mara, don't you understand? Helping the villagers like that will draw suspicion from the Protectorate. Cromwell issued strict orders that no English landholder should use Irish services or purchase Irish goods. And no landholder should give assistance in any manner to the Irish tenants."

"But, that is ridiculous. By doing so, you are helping Kulhaven as well."

"I know that, but it doesn't matter to Cromwell. He believes any sympathy shown to the Irish shows weakness. he doesn't want his *new* English to become friendly with the Irish as did the *old* English landowners who came over in the Elizabethan settlement."

"Don't attempt to disguise his true intention, Hadrian. What he wants is a total annihilation of the Irish race."

Hadrian did not respond. He didn't have to. What she said was the truth.

Finally Hadrian stood and set his hand on her shoulder. "Which is why I took the cause I did in trying to return Charles II to the throne. Cromwell has become intoxicated with power. He's addicted to it like a drug. He uses God and his religion to justify his actions."

"How many more must die before he is stopped?"

Hadrian shook his head, circling the room. "At first we thought the people of England would see what he had become. We believed he would eventually be taken from power. But too many have lost their lives now, English and Irish alike, and he only grows more maniacal the longer we allow him to remain. Which is why we have even now started the beginning of his end."

He had stopped at the windows and was looking out at the front of the castle with his back to her so she could not see his grave expression. "The news of his impending death does not surprise me, Mara. It only tells me that our people have succeeded in their mission."

"Do you mean assassination?"

Hadrian did not confirm or deny, but Mara knew the answer.

"What will happen when he is gone?"

"It will take time, but if all goes as planned, Charles II will return from French shores to claim his rightful crown. It is not the solution I had hoped for, but it seems the only avenue left to us."

"Now," he said, turning and rubbing his hands together, "much as I love that gown on you, why don't you go up to your bedchamber and change into your riding habit while I have Davey saddle the horses, so you can show me just what it is you've done in the village?"

Chapter Twenty-five

Mara fidgeted in the saddle all during the ride to the village, nervous as a child sitting before an angry parent and about to be punished for a misdeed. It was a lovely day, much like the last, with the sun shining down from a blue and cloudless sky, birds singing happily in the thick-leaved oak trees, while woodland creatures frolicked in the tall, reedy grass.

Not that she noticed.

All along the way, she kept looking at Hadrian from the corner of her eye, secretly trying to see if she could tell what he was thinking. She wasn't at all sure what she might expect Hadrian's reaction to be when he finally saw the improvements she'd funded in the village.

Hadrian kept his expression impassive, sitting back in the saddle as if it were any other day. After a while, she didn't even try to hide her furtive sidelong glances, but stared rather openly and directly at him. But damn the insufferable mule, he would not give her even the barest of trappings. Not a smile. Not a frown. Not even a crease between his thick, dark brows. Nothing.

Their journey seemed to last a lifetime, and by the time they reached the wildflower-covered hill that stood above the cozy village, Mara felt certain someone had somehow lengthened the distance between the castle and its namesake village. Even after they arrived at the communal well and were surrounded by the grateful and adoring faces of the villagers, Hadrian still would not crack that oblique exterior he'd erected to mask his emotions.

If he was at all angered by what he saw, he certainly did not show it, which gave Mara the smallest inkling of hope. He walked along beside her, tucking her hand gently at his elbow and listened, nodding only occasionally as John O'Hanlon explained every improvement along their tour.

If she hadn't been so worried about what Hadrian would think, Mara would have been pleased to notice the remarkable transformation in the village. Several of the narrow cottages had been freshly lime-washed, the hipped roofs newly thatched with fresh-cut oat straw gleaming golden in the sunlight. The women were humming as they sat at their wheels spinning wool into coarse yarn for clothing which would then be dyed red with the rootstock of the madder. Others were busy weaving their fragrant rush mats and *súgán* baskets while the laughter of their children at play filled the air around them.

All along the way, the excited murmur of the villagers could be heard at every turn behind them as they exclaimed over the change in the former lady of Kulhaven to that of the famed Flaming Lady. The people saw it as a miracle, an omen, and a sign of the better days to come. Dear, sweet Sadbh, who had portended the return of the Kulhaven guardian spirit just smiled a toothless grin, scolding those who had scoffed at her prophecy which had once again come true.

When they finally finished their tour at midday, John O'Hanlon walked with them back to the center of the village where several tables had been laid out beneath the wide-spreading boughs of the trees.

"We know it isn't the custom for the lord and lady to sit down to dinner with their tenants, but the women-folk have been busy baking since dawn and we hoped you would join us for a spell."

By their offer of food, the villagers were saying that they now accepted Hadrian as their new lord. Mara wondered if Hadrian realized the symbolism, for if he condescended to dine with them, Hadrian would be telling them he did not disdain them like so many of the other English landholders. The people around them waited in silence for his reply. Even Mara held her breath.

Finally Hadrian clapped John on the back, grinning. "We would be most honored to sit down to dinner with you."

As they ate the simple meal, which consisted of the traditional *drisheen* served with buttered farls of hard oaten bread, boiled periwinkles, and pie made with whortleberries, each family gathered round to present them with the gifts they had made to show them their thanks for what had been done in the village. A set of newly sharpened goose feather writing quills were presented to Hadrian, and a heather-and-lime-blossom-scented pomander for Mara to hang in her wardrobe and give her garments a sweet smell.

For Mara, their simple homemade gifts were more precious than the finest gold and jewels. These fair tokens had been crafted by the hands of the villagers to show their newly found esteem for the lord and lady of

Kulhaven. Even so, Mara was still not quite sure how Hadrian felt about the changes. He did not speak much, except to ask what was planned for this cottage or that field, and he never looked at her to allow her some insight into his thoughts.

When they were finished eating, the women of the village came forward to show the progress being made on the new embroidered linens for their lady's bedchamber. Fine and careful stitches depicting a myriad of flowers and birds covered the fine Irish linen underneath. The coverlet had been stuffed with the softest goose down and then sprinkled with a potpourri of fragrant herbs and flowers.

By the time they returned to the horses, ready to start back to the castle, the sun was beginning its descent over the famed Kilkenny mountains. Hadrian slipped his hands around Mara's waist and lifted her onto Munin's back. Then, after bidding good day to John and the other villagers, they started back for Kulhaven.

The fact that Hadrian still had not spoken was driving Mara nearly mad with anxiety. They were skirting the woodland along an overgrown path when Hadrian suddenly drew his mount to a halt. Without saying a word, he dismounted and started toward her, and when she could not stand the silence any longer, she blurted out just as he reached for Munin's reins, "Are you going to tell me what you think, Hadrian?"

Hadrian looked up at her as if he'd no idea what she was speaking of. "What did I think of what, my dear?"

His eyes had a strange look about them as he reached up and clasped her tightly about the waist.

With little effort his great hands lifted her down and set her gently before him.

"What did you think of the village, of the improvements there?"

He smiled, taking her hand and kissing it lightly. "I think you are a remarkable woman. I think the people of Kulhaven are vastly fortunate to have you as their lady."

"You are not angry?"

"No. I am not angry. You did what I should have done long ago, the Protectorate and Cromwell's laws be damned. Now, I think I would like you to quiet your tongue and come with me before I drag you by your glorious red hair through the trees."

He took her hand then and started for the wood.

"Hadrian, where are we going? I should like to discuss this now. Hadrian . . ."

But he was in no frame of mind to discuss anything. When they reached the edge of the lough where he had first seen her swimming, he released her hand and turned her about to face him. Mara's heart started pounding when she noticed his eyes dark with desire and she stood very still as he cupped her face in his hands and lowered his mouth to hers.

Mara let her head fall back, her stylishly plumed riding hat falling to the forest floor, and took his kiss fully, wrapping her arms about his neck and moving closer into the haven of his arms. Never had she felt so needed. She felt him lift her upward and when he set her down moments later and released her, she watched with half-open eyes as he began to remove his boots, then unfasten his breeches.

She did not have to ask what his intentions were, for she knew, and indeed relished the thought of it.

"I want to see you naked and beautiful as the first time I ever saw you swimming in this lough. I want to feel you against me in the water and taste of your sweetness. I want to make love to you right here on the forest floor so I can yell aloud when I empty my seed into you."

Mara trembled inside from the fierceness she heard resounding in his voice. "Aye, my lord."

"I am burning with need for you, Mara. I want you naked and beneath me now or I will surely die."

He was completely unclothed now and standing before her looking like a magnificent statue. He slowly unhooked the fastening of her gray woolen cloak around her neck, dropping it heedlessly to the ground, then started pulling at the buttons that lined her moss green velvet riding jacket. When he could not get them unfastened quickly enough, he simply yanked the fabric apart, then pulled her riding shirt over her head, releasing the tapes that held her skirt in place until she was standing before him in only her stockings and boots.

He removed these last two items with deliberate slowness, untying the satin garters that held her stockings in place above her knees and running his hands slowly down the length of each leg. Mara shivered, though not from the cold. She felt afire with her need for him and even the chill in the air could not cool it.

He lifted her up against him then, locking his mouth with hers, and carried her slowly into the water. The cold water against her skin created a sensation that only heightened her arousal and she threw back her head as he lowered his lips over one rose-peaked nipple. The shock of his hot mouth on her chilled skin was nearly enough to send her over the edge. She had heard once that cold water would soften a man's desire, but it seemed only to increase Hadrian's need for her more.

He set her down gently to stand then, the water covering her legs to midthigh and stared down at her, giving her feather-light kisses on her eyelids and face, nibbling deliciously on the lobe of one ear. His mouth was hot against her skin and she could feel the hard swelling of his sex against her belly, pressing against her. Unable to resist the temptation, she moved her hand to cover him.

Hadrian's entire body went still beneath her touch and she found that she liked the sense of power she had over him. His sex was hot and hard and at the same time silky to the touch and she could feel his rapid pulsebeat there as she tightened her fingers around his length.

Hadrian jerked, groaning against her mouth. "Though I would like nothing more than for you to explore my body at will, if you persist with that manner of exploration, my lady, you will soon cause me to embarrass myself."

He took her hand then, clasping his fingers in hers, and led her back to the soft moss-covered bank to lay her down on a carpet of fragrant fen violet and tormentil blossoms. He moved beside her with deliberate slowness, raining soft, sweet kisses along the flatness of her belly, nipping lightly at the sensitive skin at the curve of her hip, and running his tongue over her breast.

"Close your eyes, Mara, let yourself be released to the feelings."

She did as he bid, waiting, somehow knowing he was about to do something exquisite to her. And then she felt it, something with a touch like the softness of a feather trailing down over her shoulder to the curve of her breast. She released a trembling breath as she felt the softness of it tickling her belly, and opened her eyes slightly to see. He was holding one of the soft, reed-like leaves of the white willow, rubbing its silky-haired length lightly over her skin. He circled it softly around her nipple, teasing it to erectness, and sending delicious tinglings radiating through her body. She closed her eyes again, taking in a deep breath, and never wanted him to stop.

Suddenly the wet heat of his mouth had replaced the softness of the willow leaf as he clamped his lips over her breast. He suckled at her nipple, pulling at it with his lips till she was clenching her fingers in his hair and crying out from the sweet torment running through her. She could feel his fingers moving downward then, parting her woman's flesh and probing at the wet slickness of the tiny bud, rubbing over it until she was writhing and gasping for breath. She didn't want it to end. His fingers seemed to know exactly what movement would bring her the most pleasure and they moved relentlessly, bringing her to the near brink of her release, her hips rising up against him, wanting more.

"Please, Hadrian, don't stop. Please let me—"

She never finished her words. He had given her that last needed touch that suddenly sent her soaring over the edge of her release and beyond, waves of desire crashing through her until she was breathless and trembling and weak with it.

"Look at me, Mara," he said, his voice seeming to come from afar somewhere above her.

She opened her eyes ever slightly, unable to speak, staring up at him in wonderment, still lost to the far reaches of her climax.

"I want you to watch me as I fill you with my body," he said, his voice thick as he rose above her and guided himself gently into her tight sheath. She could feel herself stretching to accommodate him, taking in the length of him, and let out a soft sigh when she felt him filling her completely.

He began to move then, in the age-old fashion, drawing back from her slowly, then filling her again. The sensations that had only begun to subside reconverged then, taking her back toward the heights of sweetness. She watched him above her, his eyes closed and his face a study of rigid concentration, and he began moving faster now, his body thrusting against her. Mara's hands gripped at his arms, her legs wrapped around him, wanting to draw him even closer inside, needing to feel him against her very soul. It was as if time had become suspended and it was only the two of them on the earth just then, with the sunlight shining down on their intertwined bodies and the gentle breeze blowing through the trees around them.

And then Hadrian let out a yell that echoed through the treetops, plunging himself into her one last time. His body convulsed above her as Mara felt him empty his seed inside her, his breathing ragged, his eyes squeezed shut through the intensity of his release. He gathered her up against him then, his sex still filling her completely as he wrapped her in the safe haven of his arms. He was kissing her ears, her neck, her face, his arms trembling as they held her so close, and Mara never wanted him to stop.

A short time later, he reluctantly released her from his embrace. "It is getting dark quickly. We should be returning to Kulhaven."

Mara let out a sigh of disappointment when she felt his arms loosen from around her, bringing her back to reality.

"I wish we could stay here forever," she said, watching as Hadrian stood and began pulling on his breeches.

"I'm sure they would begin to worry and come looking for us. Mrs. Danbury would turn three shades of red if she were to find us as we are."

Mara pulled her riding shirt over her head, laughing. "Yes, but not Mr. Shipley. He would simply glance at us with that bland expression of his, acting as if it were any other day, and ask us politely if we wished wine or mead with our supper."

When they had both finished dressing, Hadrian pulled Mara into his arms one last time, kissing her with a tenderness that left her eyes tear-filled.

With the last rays of sunlight peaking over the horizon, they rode back to Kulhaven astride Hugin, with Munin trailing slowly behind. Mara sat before Hadrian, her legs dangling over the side of the saddle, her head resting contentedly on his broad shoulder.

The feel of Hadrian's strong arms around her made her feel more safe, more secure, than she'd ever felt before. She wished every day could be like this one, filled with ease and contentment, for she did not think she'd ever truly been more happy than she was now. She hoped after they returned to Kulhaven things could continue on as they were, without any worries from the world outside to come and shatter their newly found peace.

But perhaps she should have kept that wish buried inside.

As they rounded the turn in the drive leading to the front stairs, Mara saw two horses tethered at the hitching post there. Before they reached the stairs to dismount, Davey came running toward them.

"My lord, there's two rough-looking men here to see you. Mr. Shipley, he told them we didn't know when you'd return, but they said they wanted to wait. They're in the parlor waiting for you now."

Hadrian tossed Hugin's reins to Davey then dismounted. "I'll go and see what they are here about."

He helped Mara down and she followed him as he made his way to the parlor.

Seated inside, just as Davey had indicated, were two very large, very dangerous-looking men. Mara recognized one of them as Owen's colleague from the cottage the night she'd gone to meet him there. The other was large as a bear, with the expression of one as well, his dark hair wild about his rugged face.

"We've a message for you from Owen."

Hadrian remained standing at the door. "Which is?"

"He's in the prison at Dublin Castle. He wants you to come there."

"And, if I don't?"

"He says he's got information that could put you in the cell beside him. If you don't come, he'll make sure you fill the vacancy there."

The muscle in Hadrian's jaw tensed. "Tell him I will be there."

The two men stood, their boots thudding on the floor. "And bring the wench with you. He wants to see her, too."

Hadrian's voice dropped an octave. "The *wench* happens to be my wife, a countess and no less, and as such you will address her either directly or indirectly with respect."

The man grunted and turned, motioning for his silent companion to follow.

After they had gone and the sound of their horses had faded into the night, Hadrian turned toward her. "Pack your things for a trip to Dublin, Mara. We're going to see your brother."

Chapter Twenty-six

The ride to Dublin took a full day longer than it should have due to the fact that it rained in full and heavy sheets till they reached the two towers of Newgate along St. Thomas Street leading into the city.

Part of the delay was due to the carriage getting stuck in a muddy ditch beside the narrow road near Kildare when Pudge misjudged a blind turn. The rest of the delay was caused by the necessity of stopping each time they encountered a troop of Parliamentarian soldiers to inquire about the status of the Protector, Oliver Cromwell.

The last troop they had stopped was a band of foot soldiers who looked road-weary and hungry, their uniforms soaked from the rain. They were headed by a man named Colonel Fretteridge, who looked like a wharf rat with his pointed nose and beady eyes. He informed them that Cromwell was fair dancing at death's door, but seemed not to care, and added that none of the physicians in London could attribute his sudden failing to any known illness.

At this news, Hadrian had drawn even more into himself, if that was possible, for up to that point he'd been barely conversant. It seemed, Mara thought, remembering what Hadrian had told her, that the assassination attempt was to be a success. Mara couldn't readily tell if Hadrian was pleased or not at this bit of news. He'd barely spoken above five words through the course of their journey to that point, and after hearing the news of the Protector's failing condition, he barely spoke above two.

His silence, though, gave Mara the opportunity to reflect on what might lay ahead when she went to see her brother in prison. Hadrian had told her they would certainly hang Owen, for he was one of the most wanted Irish Tories, with a reward exceeding fifty pounds on his head, a fat purse, no doubt, the soldier who'd captured him was enjoying right now.

Night had barely fallen when they rolled through the torch-lit gate and turned down the now-deserted High Street. In the daytime, the street would be a mass of color and activity, with the women hanging their laundry out to dry over every windowsill and the street merchants setting up their displays of fish, fruits, and every sort of bread imaginable on the steps of the Christ Church.

Pudge pulled the coach to a stop at a dark corner, and the candles burning through the windows in the house beside them gave off enough light for her to read the street sign above. Skinner's Row. They were near Christ Church, not far from where she had lived with Cyma in the back room of the dressmaker's shop where she'd worked, sewing, despite her lack of talent, until her fingers were numb and her eyesight was blurred from the poor light.

Mr. Cheapside had been the proprietor, a name that fitted him completely, for he paid her poorly and worked her hard until the day she'd walloped him over the head with the tiny and uncomfortable wooden stool she'd been given to sit on, when he'd tried one too many times to put his hand down the front of her dress.

She'd been dismissed that day and after collecting the wages due her, all of three shillings, and her meager belongings from the cramped attic where they'd slept, she and Cyma had gone to the home of Captain Greene, one of the English officers posted in Dublin. There they'd worked in the kitchen, helping to prepare the meals and serve at the endless row of parties Mrs. Greene had hosted. This, the second of many positions they had held until the day Cyma, after Mrs. Greene had slapped her for dropping a napkin on the floor, had added one of her secret concoctions to the boiled mutton stew, which caused everyone who'd eaten it to break out in a nasty, itchy rash.

It was while she was working at the house of the Greenes that Owen had come to her first, telling her of Hadrian, the Earl of St. Aubyn, and new owner of Kulhaven Castle. It was there that she learned of Arabella, and the plans for her to wed Hadrian. And it was there that she'd first begun to form her plan to return.

Hadrian took her hand. "Mara, put your hood over your head. We are staying at the home of one of my colleagues and neither one of us can afford to be recognized."

Mara obeyed without question and followed him as he stepped down and through a door at the side of the house they'd stopped at. The room they entered was dark, but she relied on Hadrian to lead her. He must have stayed there many times, for he seemed to know the layout of the rooms very well. They walked through two more doors and up a small flight of stairs until they came to a halt. Mara could see nothing and she was gripping the edge of Hadrian's coat, knowing if he left her, she'd never be able to find her way out.

She heard the sound of wood scraping on wood and suddenly, Hadrian was gone. Her heart was pounding, but she dared not call out to him for fear of discovery. And then she felt his great hands clasping her about the waist, felt herself being lifted upward, and Hadrian whispered to her from somewhere below.

"Grab the edges and pull yourself up."

Mara splayed her fingers outward and found the sides of what seemed to be a small opening above her head. She grabbed the edge and with Hadrian pushing her up from beneath, she managed to wriggle her way through enough to sit at the edge of the opening.

"Move back a bit so I can climb up behind you."

Mara pushed back, wondering how Hadrian would fit his large frame through so tiny an opening, stopping when her back hit something hard and cold. It was dark and she remained as still as stone while she listened to Hadrian climbing up behind her. He managed to get through, with the silence of a well-trained soldier. She heard a loud thud and Hadrian's florid curse soon after, then came the sound of a drawer opening and closing again.

A moment later, he had lit a candle, giving the room the barest of light.

"There. Now I know it isn't as cozy as Brooke's Inn down the street, but the bed will not be lousy, the sheets will smell clean, and you'll not need to worry about any drunken sot crashing through your door to ravish you in the middle of the night."

Mara nodded, smiling.

They were in the attic of the small house and the ceiling was so low Hadrian had to duck his head, which, Mara surmised as she watched him rub his temple, was the reason for his cursing earlier. There was a small bed and a dresser beside it atop which was the candle and a washbowl and pitcher. Hadrian was standing at the dresser and poured some water into the bowl.

"Would you like to wash up after our long coach ride?"

Mara nodded and walked to the bowl to splash some of the water over her face. It was ice cold, but it felt good and it washed away the grime from the carriage trip.

"Now, I have to leave for a short time," Hadrian said. "You will stay here. I will close off the opening behind me, then I want you to move that dresser there over top of it so no one can come up. It looks heavy, but deceptively so, so you should be able to push it."

"But, wouldn't it be better for me to go with you?"

"No. I need to go several places, a couple of which are not fit for a lady. I didn't want to tell you this earlier because I knew you would try to prevent me from coming, but this summons from your brother could very well be a trap set to capture me. If Owen has already told the authorities about my role as a spy these past years, this may just be an easy and convenient way for them to take me without having to come to Kulhaven. I will not know until I go to the prison tomorrow."

"I don't want you to go there, Hadrian."

He smiled, tipping her chin with his finger. "I must go. Your brother has given me little choice. He could very well ruin our chances of getting the heir restored to the throne." He turned, motioning across the room. "There is some kindling in a basket by the side of the hearth there. Light a small fire and climb into bed. The nights can get quite chilly up here. I'll be back as soon as I can."

Mara watched him go, not wanting him to leave, but knowing he would never listen to her pleas. After he had vanished through the attic opening and had moved the board back into place, she pushed the dresser across the floor over it as he had asked.

She turned and looked about the stark room, and felt a cold draft of air blow over her. She decided to take Hadrian's advice and light a fire. Once she had managed to get a small blaze going, she started to pace about the room, then decided that perhaps she shouldn't in case someone below might hear her walking. She sat on the bed, staring at the flickering orange flames in the hearth, and her eyes soon began to grow heavy. The coach ride had been long and bumpy, giving her little opportunity to sleep the past few days. Not knowing when Hadrian might return, she decided to give in to her fatigue and she lay back on the bed to wait for him.

She didn't know how much time had passed when she heard the soft knocking that woke her sometime later. When she opened her eyes, the fire had nearly gone out and it took her a moment to remember where she was. She rose from the bed and moved toward the trap in the floor.

Another soft knock. "Mara, are you awake? Move the dresser back so I can come up."

She pushed the dresser back away from the trap.

"I brought some food. It's not much, but it will do till morning." He handed her a small sack. "There's wine and I even managed to find a sweet cake for you." He looked at her then and must have seen the fear that was running through the entire length of her body for he touched his gloved finger to her chin and said, "Don't worry, love. Everything will be all right."

Mara nodded, wishing she could believe him, and opened the sack to remove the things from inside.

After they'd eaten the soft crusty bread and sharp cheese wedges he'd brought, washing it down with a goodly amount of tart wine, Hadrian pulled her down beside him on the narrow bed. He wrapped her in his arms, against the length of his body, instantly warming her against the night's chill.

If only she could believe everything would be all right. But if it was, if the threat of danger was really that remote, then why was Hadrian taking such precautions?

She wasn't some ignorant fool to be put off with false words. She knew it was dangerous for Hadrian to be in Dublin. She knew he worried his activities had been discovered. And it was all because of her. She had placed him in this position by refusing to listen to him when he'd told her not to warn the Connellys. Everything she had done since the very day she'd met him had put him at risk. She'd allowed her desire for Kulhaven to rule her every thought and action, and now she had placed the man she loved in grave danger.

If anything happened to him, she knew she'd never be able to forgive herself.

Had he given her over when he learned who she truly was, he would not be facing the trouble he was now. She remembered, not all that long ago, thinking nothing on this earth could be more important to her than regaining Kulhaven. Now she realized that there were things far more important than having her revenge. And the most important one of all was lying beside her.

She said a silent prayer, offering to give up Kulhaven and everything else for Hadrian's safety.

The following morning, Hadrian rose before dawn, rousing her in his efforts to climb over her and off the small bed.

"Damnation," he muttered when he saw she was awake, "I didn't wish to wake you. This bloody bed isn't fit to sleep a dwarf, let alone two grown people."

Mara blinked the sleep away from her eyes and yawned. "It is all right, Hadrian. I wanted to get up with you anyway."

Hadrian took his turn at the washbowl, taking in a sharp breath when the force of the water hit his face. "God's blood, if that couldn't wake a dead man, I don't know what would." He turned, his magnificent well-muscled chest open to her view. She wanted to bury her face in the warmth of his skin and stay there all day and all night, but knew she couldn't. Instead, she, too, doused her face with the water and patted it dry with a towel.

When she turned back around, it was to see Hadrian fully dressed and pulling on his boots.

"I am going to see Owen this morning."

Mara nodded, already knowing that had been his plan. "Give me a moment to dress and I'll join you."

"No."

Mara turned and looked over to him.

"I am going alone, Mara."

"But Owen said he wanted to see me as well."

"You will be given the opportunity to go once I am certain there is no danger for you. It would do no good to have us both captured and clapped in irons."

But if you are taken, I want to be taken with you, she thought. "How will I know if it is safe to go?"

"I will come back for you. If I do not return by noon, you must assume I have been taken into custody." He pulled a piece of parchment from his inside coat pocket. "Here. Take this letter. This will ensure that you are given passage by a ship called the *Wayfarer* to England."

"That was the ship Arabella came over on."

"Yes. Her captain is one of my colleagues. His name is William MacDuff and upon receiving this letter from your fair hand, he will sail you to a town called Weymouth in Dorset. From there, you must find a man called Chancery. He is large and gruff-looking, but completely harmless to ladies, and is most often found seated at a small table in a tavern called The Silken Sow. He will take you out of the city near a small village called Chatley to my family's ancestral seat, Rossingham. I have not written any of this down since, with your remarkable memory, I know you will remember each word.

"You would have made a wonderful spy, Mara, but I digress. My mother's sister, Hesteria—you may call her

Tantie like everyone else—will be at Rossingham. She will see to your safekeeping. You are the Countess of St. Aubyn legally and rightfully, and since there are no other living relatives to claim the title, will most probably be the last Countess of St. Aubyn. It was a doomed line from the start. Never very productive of heirs. I had hoped to be the one to change that, to bring about some semblance of respectability, but as it is, that may not be. So, the line will fall to extinction with me, the only legitimate bastard as the last."

Tears were running down Mara's cheeks when he finally reached the end of his bitter diatribe. Even after all she had done to him, all the danger she had brought upon him, he had still seen to her safety and future.

And without knowing whether or not she carried his child.

"You are not a bastard," she said, thinking she could never deserve him.

He cupped her face in his hands then, giving her a small smile. "Do not cry, my love. I will tolerate no regrets from you. I admire you more than I admire most men, for I have never met a more courageous and resourceful woman in my life. If it is deemed so, then I will die a happy man knowing that I loved the most beautiful red-haired wood nymph in all Ireland."

With that he kissed her, long and full, leaving her breathless when he finally stepped away.

"I must go now. And, remember, at twelve bells, you are to go directly to the *Wayfarer* and Captain MacDuff, and start out for the shores of England."

He was through the trap and gone in seconds, leaving Mara to choke on the sob that rose in her throat as she watched him go.

Chapter Twenty-seven

Hadrian kept his eyes staring straight ahead, his face devoid of expression, so as not to give cause for suspicion. The guard posted at the gate which led to the prison area at Dublin Castle scanned his papers of passage. He knew in an instant that the rather overfed man did not realize the papers he held were forgeries, for it was obvious he hadn't understood a single word printed on the page before him. He'd read it too quickly and his eyes had not run along the length of each line, but rather had dropped to the bottom of the page in one fell swoop before returning the papers to Hadrian.

Printed on the highest quality of vellum, the pages looked official enough, bearing the seal of the Lord Protector Cromwell himself, or rather the seal that had been forged by his colleagues, enough for the guard to allow this man entrance to the prisoners.

"Them papers din't say which of the prisoners you were wantin'. Who you be 'ere to see?"

"I am here to see the Irish patriot they call Owen Despencer."

"That one's set to 'ang first thing tomorrow morn. Been posting notices advertising it all over town. 'Ad a price on 'is 'ead of fifty pounds, 'e did. Seems a shame to waste all that coin on a dead man, but they wants to set an example on 'im, get a big crowd to come watch 'im dangle in the wind, they are."

The guard had a string of mucus dripping from his nose then that he wiped on the filthy cuff of his sleeve, sniffing loudly. "Bloody cold down 'ere in the belly of the castle. Me nose is running like the bleedin' River Thames back 'ome in Lunnon."

He led Hadrian down a narrow and damp set of steps, passing cells that were closed on other prisoners, and continued to the end of a dark and low corridor before stopping at a small wooden door. Hadrian thought to himself that he was glad he had refused Mara's request to come to such a filth-ridden place, watching as a yellow-eyed rat walked the length of the wall above him. The guard's ring of keys jangled as he took them from his pocket and began fishing for the one that would open Owen's cell.

"Just call me when you're wantin' to leave and I'll come open the door for ye. If'n he causes you any trouble, club 'im over the head with this." He handed Hadrian a rough-hewn wooden club, the end of which was stained dark with old blood and was stuck with a few hairs from the last unfortunate it had come in contact with. The guard turned then, leaving his lantern swinging from the door handle. "I'll be just up the stairs there."

The door closed behind him and Hadrian watched through the tiny barred window as the guard started back, wiping his nose on his sleeve once again, and swallowing from the hidden flask he'd just pulled from inside his coat.

Hadrian turned then toward the center of the cell, trying to find Owen in the darkness.

"Well, I see you received my message," he heard a hoarse voice say from the shadows to his right.

Hadrian lifted the lantern from the door handle and moved toward the source of the voice. Owen was sitting on the stone floor atop a small pile of straw that reeked with the smell of urine. He had a dark bruise on one cheek and a patch of dried blood at the corner of his mouth where his lower lip had become swollen from a blow. He licked at that lip now, his saliva glistening in the lantern light. Hadrian remained standing where he was.

"Yes, obviously I did receive your summons. Why else would I be here in this stinking hellhole?"

Owen stood and the sour odor of urine seemed to double. "Oh, I think you already know the answer to that."

"I cannot get you released from the prison, Owen. I have no authority here any longer."

"Well, I believe you can get me released, and you will, unless you wish to face some rather incriminating accusations."

Hadrian slanted a brow. "Haven't you heard? Cromwell is dead. Word hasn't yet reached Irish soil, but it is only a matter of time. So, anything you wish to report about my activities is moot at this point."

Owen's smile widened. "Who said anything about my making accusations to Cromwell? I am not stupid, St. Aubyn. No one would believe the word of an Irish patriot set to hang over that of one of the Protectorate's most trusted men. I was speaking of someone else entirely."

Hadrian did not change his expression. "Who?"

"How is my sister these days?"

"What does Mara have to do with this? She is not involved with your capture in any way."

Owen picked at his tooth with a dirty fingernail. "She is involved, but not in the manner you would think. You see, before our family was dispossessed of Kulhaven, back when life was grand and carefree, Mara was betrothed to a young man from a neighboring estate."

"Why should that matter to me now? She is married to me and seems quite happy with it, I might add."

"The name of the man to whom she was promised was Liam Shaughnessy."

Hadrian's entire body grew rigid.

Owen grinned. "I see I have gotten your full attention now. You remember Liam Shaughnessy, don't you, St. Aubyn? He shared a cell with me when I was in this hellhole before. He was killed here, too, his life ended by an overzealous English soldier who found him wrapped in the arms of a no-account English whore." He paused. "I wonder what dear Mara would think if she knew the man she was married to now had been responsible for the death of the man she was supposed to have married?"

Mara started counting the toll of the bells echoing out across the rooftops from the spire at Christ Church as she had each hour since Hadrian's departure that morning. Only this time she stopped, refusing to continue when the bells rang out their deadly twelfth toll.

He had said if he hadn't returned by midday, she was to take the coach to Ringsend to where the ship *Way-*

farer was docked and she was to set out for England. Immediately.

Hadrian couldn't have been taken. She refused to believe it. Instead, she decided to wait a little while longer to give him a chance to come back for her.

After the bells had tolled again, signaling the passing of yet another hour, Mara still refused to consider that Hadrian might have been taken. She couldn't believe that Owen had been so lowly as to expose him. No, it was just taking a little longer than he had expected. She would wait another hour. Just one more, and then she would follow his instruction. Surely he'd come knocking on that trap door any minute and would tell her all was right and well.

She looked to the trap door. She wanted to go down and look out a window, to see what was going on outside these four walls. She could hear the sounds of the city and it was driving her nearly to madness, this waiting, this not knowing what was happening to Hadrian at the prison.

Nothing was happening, she told herself. He was too smart, too cautious and thoughtful to allow himself to be caught in a trap, a trap that might have been set by her brother. Owen was most probably trying to convince Hadrian to help gain his release, as if that was possible.

And then she heard something, a sound coming from below. At once she stopped pacing the floor as she had these past hours, and listened. A light knocking sounded on the trap door.

"Mara, it is all right. You can open the door now."

Mara nearly leapt with delight at the sound of Hadrian's voice coming from below. She dashed across the attic room and pushed the dresser aside, heedless of the noise it might make, pulling the board from the opening to allow him up to her.

"Oh, Hadrian," she said, burying her face in his jacket minutes later, "I knew if I waited just a little longer, you would come. I knew you would be all right."

"Yes, but we've got to leave this house and right away. Gather your things and we'll be out of the city by nightfall."

"But what about Owen? I thought he wanted to see me as well."

Hadrian started stuffing any evidence of their being there into the sack. Mara noticed he avoided her eyes. "I am afraid you will be unable to see Owen, Mara."

"What is it, Hadrian? Is something wrong?"

He turned then, his eyes dark in the candlelight. "I'm sorry, Mara. There is nothing I can do. Owen is scheduled to hang tomorrow morning."

Mara gasped. She knew her brother had committed countless crimes, and he had blackmailed her into stealing information from Hadrian. She knew he was not the sort of brother who professed a tie of love to her, fighting for her honor, but still, he was her brother.

"Is there nothing you can do for him?"

"I'm afraid not. Cromwell is dead and everything is up in arms. The rumors of assassination have gained credence since the true cause of his death is unknown, so the government is seeking to make an example of those who were working against the Protectorate, those like your brother. They do not care whom they lay responsibility on, as long as they are known enemies of the Protectorate. Your brother has become one of the scapegoats. It is just a matter of his being in the wrong place at the wrong time."

"What did he want to see you about?"

Hadrian looked away from her. "He wanted to try to bribe me into gaining his release, even though I'm sure he knew it was futile. He was not aware of Cromwell's death. Most of the public is not. Those left behind are scrambling now to find a new leader and a plausible cause of death before making a public announcement. Owen realizes now there is nothing I can do for him."

Tears were forming in Mara's eyes as she remembered the Owen she had grown up with, the Owen he had been before the war had come to Ireland. "I cannot even tell him good-bye."

Hadrian took her into his arms then and stroked his hand over her hair. "I'm sorry, love. I know that despite what he has done, you still carry an affection for him. He is family to you, the only family you have left. I wish there were more I could do, but believe me when I say I am powerless. Now, we must return posthaste to Kulhaven to pack. With the leadership of England in such chaos, I need to travel to London as soon as possible to bring about the return of the heir to the throne. With the confusion now muddling everyone's minds there, this may be our best chance at bringing Charles II back to English soil. I cannot say how long I will be gone. It may be awhile, months perhaps."

However long it took him to get rid of the guilt he was feeling over knowing he had killed her betrothed, and knowing he was purposefully keeping it from her. If he ever could.

Mara stepped back from his embrace. "Hadrian, I want to go with you."

"That's not a wise decision, Mara. I think it best you remain at Kulhaven. That is your home. It has always been your home. It is rightfully and now legally yours. You have gotten it back just as you wanted."

"But I do not want it without you."

Hadrian refused to be swayed. "This is the only way, Mara. You will see, once you entrench yourself in the running of the estate, you will be too busy to notice that I'm not there. I know you can make Kulhaven the great estate it once was. In fact, I'm counting on you to. Now let's get these things into the coach and be on our way."

Why did he sound so decided, so final? He had turned and was starting down the trap, leaving Mara to watch him go. There was something else, she realized, something he was not telling her.

There was something in his voice that told Mara once he was gone, he wouldn't be coming back.

Chapter Twenty-eight

The law-abiding citizens of Dublin were literally stunned the following day when, during the much publicized hanging of an Irish Confederate, the condemned managed to escape when a riot broke out in the crowd while he was being brought through on his way to the gallows.

The countryside around the city was thoroughly canvased, houses were searched, and every carriage and cart leaving through the city's six gates was stopped for questioning.

These efforts, however, were wasted, for three days later, the authorities found abandoned on the sandy banks near Ringsend at a place called Salmon Poole downstream on the River Liffey the small skiff that had taken him to safety.

By the time they arrived back at Kulhaven two nights later, with the moon full and white in the starless sky Mara was certain that Hadrian was keeping something from her. She'd had a niggling sense of it in Dublin after he'd returned from his visit with Owen at the prison, but now, after spending the past silent hours with him in the confines of the closed carriage, she was absolutely sure of it.

It was nearly midnight when the coach pulled up the main road and rolled to a stop on the semicircular graveled drive in front of the castle, but the house was put into instant action by the ever-diligent Shipley, who had been watching for their return.

"My lord," Shipley said, bearing a dully glowing lantern to light their way up the perilously dark front steps, "we are most pleased to see you have returned. We had heard from a passing tinker the rumors of the death of the Protector. Is it true, my lord? Is Cromwell really dead?"

"Yes, it is true, Shipley. And because of it I will be leaving for London in the morning. Her ladyship will not be traveling with me. If there is any business which requires my direct attention, bring it to me now, else Lady St. Aubyn will have to handle it in my absence. I am placing her in complete control while I am gone."

He turned in the entrance hall and headed for the door to his study. "I've some papers to attend to before my departure. There will be no need for you to wait up for me."

Mara wasn't sure if he'd directed that last statement to her or to the general assembly standing there to greet them in the hall, and she wasn't given the chance to ask, for he had disappeared into his study and had already closed the door firmly behind him.

During the next hours, Hadrian attempted to put the Kulhaven accounts into some semblance of order. The ledgers were an abominable mess as he saw firsthand the depths of Horace Crow's thievery. He wrote out a directive giving Mara full right of action on his behalf, and he left instructions as to how she could reach him through his aunt at his family's ancestral seat, Rossingham.

And then he sat down to write the letter he'd been composing in his mind through their interminably long trip back from Dublin.

He'd decided not long after leaving Owen in his lice-ridden cell in the very belly of the dungeon below the ancient walls of Dublin Castle that he would tell Mara the truth, that he had been the one responsible for killing her betrothed, Liam Shaughnessy, when he had been posted in Dublin all those years ago. It wasn't that he feared Owen telling her himself. How could he when he was now hanging from the gibbet that stood outside the city walls for all the good people of Dublin to see.

He had to tell her because he could not, in all good conscience, keep that sort of thing from her. He owed it to her, and would not leave her, knowing he would never be coming back, without giving her that truth.

Moreover, he had to tell her because he loved her.

Hadrian didn't think he could bear the pain of seeing the look on her face when he told her, the hurt at finding out he had been her lover's murderer.

He'd thought to leave her a letter to find after he'd gone to London, explaining the whole debacle in detail so she could read of his regret at what he'd done and so he wouldn't have to face seeing the hatred she would then feel for him burning clearly in her beautiful gray-green eyes.

But a blank page stared back at him half an hour later.

A soft knocking on his door pulled him from his

troubled thoughts. He looked up at the carved case clock that stood against the wall. It was three o'clock in the morning.

"Yes?"

The door opened slowly and Mara came in then, her hair down and flowing about her shoulders in soft red ringlets, wearing a silky-looking white night rail with lace at the collar, and looking so damned virginal, so damned beautiful.

And so damned vulnerable.

She stopped just before his desk, her bare toes curling in the thick carpet. "Hadrian, have I done something to displease you?"

"Good God, no, Mara. Why would you think that?"

She looked to her feet. "I could think of no other reason for your leaving for England without me. You tell me you will only be gone a short time, but I sense, no, I know you are not being truthful. I know that you will stay away a long time, that is if you ever come back at all, but what I don't understand is why. There must be some reason why you do not wish to be with me. I thought perhaps it was because I had tricked you into believing I was Arabella, but then I thought you had forgiven me for that. What is it, Hadrian? Is it because I fired Horace Crow? Is it because I used the money he returned to help the villagers? Or is it because I helped the Connellys escape despite your orders not to? Please tell me the truth because I cannot bear not knowing why it is you wish to leave me."

Hadrian stood and circled the desk. He pulled her against him, wrapping her tightly in his arms, and tucked her head beneath his chin. He found he'd come to like her thusly, her cheek resting against his chest, her flower-scented, brilliant red hair, filling his senses.

And then he knew he had to tell her, right then and there in his study while she stood before him wearing her virgin's nightgown, looking like a child, but with the body of a woman. Mara deserved to know what he'd done. And she deserved to hear it from him in person.

Hadrian reluctantly released her, setting her back from him. "Mara, please sit down."

Mara did as he asked without questioning why, just took a seat in one of the cushioned armchairs that stood before the hearth fire, folding her hands neatly in her lap and watching him, waiting for him to begin. He sat opposite her and rested his elbows on his thighs, staring at the floor, unable to look into her eyes, knowing that he was going to hurt her, and trying to find the words to begin.

The words that would break her heart.

"Mara, do you remember when you first came to Kulhaven?"

She shifted slightly forward, leaning her chin on her hand. "As Arabella, you mean?"

"Yes, that first night when we met in this very room."

"Yes."

Hadrian looked up at her then. "You asked me about my time in Dublin when I was a soldier there, and I gave you some passing answer and quickly changed the subject." He paused, drawing a steadying breath. "I did that because I had hoped to forget that time in my life. I had wanted to erase it from my memory. You see, it was a very dark time."

Mara nodded, watching him raptly but remaining silent.

"When I was in Dublin, I was posted at the Dublin Castle prison. I was in charge of guarding the prisoners there."

"You mean where Owen was when you went to see him the other day?"

"Yes. But, Mara, that was not the first time Owen had been incarcerated there. He had been there before. I met Owen and began my connection with him when I was posted at the prison. While I was there, I also met a girl whom at the time I believed to be a very innocent, very guileless young woman. I even fancied myself in love with her." He paused, searching for the words to explain what he had to say. "She was the daughter of the colonel in charge of the prison. She lived at Dublin Castle, one of very few women there. She drew a lot of male attention because she was very beautiful, and I started courting her.

"She came to me one day and told me one of the prisoners had made unwanted advances toward her when she had been out walking. She made me believe she was frightened of this man. One night, when I went to check on the prisoners, I found her in his cell, and"—he looked at her levelly—"in his bed. I became enraged. I never even stopped to consider why she was in this man's cell or how she had gotten there. I acted without thought, believing this prisoner had forced himself on her—she told me as much when I came upon them—and when he made a grab for my pistol, I shot him and I killed him. I found out later that this girl, this innocent I had fallen under the wiles of, had been secretly trysting with this prisoner for weeks."

Mara leaned forward and took his hand in hers. "Oh, Hadrian, I am so sorry."

"Wait. There is more. I was never punished for killing the prisoner because he had tried to disarm me. This, in addition to his being an Irish patriot, made his death justified in the eyes of the Protectorate. But it was not justified in my eyes. Never before in my life had I acted so rashly. I left my post in Dublin then, resigned my commission, and came to Kulhaven. I had already been working toward getting Charles II returned to the throne. I then began uniting myself with Cromwell, doing whatever it took to become one of his 'trusted few.' Marrying Arabella was just one of those things I did to gain his trust and approval."

"But, Hadrian, it is not your fault. You believed this prisoner had harmed the girl. You had no way of knowing otherwise. He could have taken your pistol and killed you instead. You only did what you had to do to defend yourself."

"Thank you for being so understanding. I have tried to put that incident behind me ever since, but your brother has brought it all back now. You see, the reason he summoned us to Dublin was so that he could attempt to bribe me into getting him released. He threatened to expose what I had done, how I had killed this prisoner."

"But you were cleared of any wrongdoing at the time. Who could he possibly expose you to now?"

Hadrian looked into her eyes. "He could expose me to you."

Mara shook her head in confusion. "Me? Why would he think his telling me about this prisoner would matter?"

"Because, Mara, the name of the prisoner I killed was Liam Shaughnessy."

Mara became very still, the shock at hearing his confession registering on her face. She said nothing, just continued staring at him, her hands folded neatly in her lap. The silence was too much for Hadrian to bear.

"And, had I been able to somehow get Owen released from prison, I probably would have, —anything possible to keep you from possibly finding out that I had been responsible for the death of your betrothed. But there was nothing I could do to help your brother. He'd already escaped once from that same prison, so they were doubly cautious with him this time. You see, Owen orchestrated this whole debacle from the very beginning. He told me that he knew my uncle had left Kulhaven to me, and he somehow arranged for you to return as Arabella. He used both of us to gain what information he wanted. Then, when he was captured, he decided to play his final trump and threaten to tell you I had killed Liam. I cannot deny it. It happened and were I able to change it, I would. I understand that you will detest the sight of me now, so that is why I am leaving for England. We are still married, so you may live out your life at Kulhaven without me."

He handed her a folded and sealed piece of parchment then. "This letter gives you full ownership of Kulhaven. Call it a wedding gift. In the event of my death, it will be yours and yours alone. No distant unknown relative who might somehow inherit the earldom can lay claim to it because it is not entailed. It was given to me by my uncle and I now give it back to you. You are the rightful owner. You risked your life posing as Arabella in an attempt to get it back. Now it is yours."

He held the document out to her.

Mara looked into his eyes. She did not reach for the parchment. "I will not take it, Hadrian. I do not want it. Not without you." Instead she took his hand. "Yes, when I came back to Kulhaven it was to get it back and to have my revenge on you for taking it from my family. I watched my mother die trying to defend this castle and I wanted to punish those who had taken it. I believed you were one of them. But I know now that you were not. You were no more guilty of the murder of my mother than you are for the death of Liam Shaughnessy."

Hadrian could not believe the words he was hearing. He could but stare dumbfounded as she went on.

"I thank you for being so honest with me, Hadrian, especially when you really did not have to be. Now it is my turn to be honest with you. Liam and I were to marry, yes, but it was a match that had been arranged when I was barely twelve years old. I fancied myself in love with him much like a girl who had read too many fairy tales while growing up and who had spent her days dreaming about a knight in shining armor coming to her rescue."

She paused, smiling slightly. "I guess there is something to be said for restricting the materials read by young girls. I know now that I was never in love with Liam. What I felt for him was more a sisterly affection, for it pales in comparison to what I feel for you."

"So, what is it you are saying, Mara?"

Mara stood up from her chair, glaring down at him with mock fury in her voice. "What I am saying, you stubborn English brute, is that if you still plan on leaving for London in the morning, be prepared to take along some extra baggage, for I am going with you, with or without your permission. You cannot escape me for I will follow you to the ends of the earth. I will haunt you every day of your life, for do not forget, I am the Flaming Lady, and a curse on the man who dares think to deny me."

Chapter Twenty-nine

Mara opened her eyes and stared silently at the window across from the bed where she was lying. She'd been sleeping quite contentedly, relaxed and drowsy from their tender lovemaking, until, for some reason, she'd woken.

She wondered what had woken her, for it was now peacefully silent. Outside it was still mostly dark, for the sun was just beginning to rise, peeking out from behind the thick clouds from the recent rain. The fire in the hearth had long since died out, but she could feel the warmth of Hadrian's body beside her, his arm flung carelessly over her belly.

Not two seconds later, she heard the sound again, the sound that had obviously woken her from her peaceful slumber.

It sounded as if there was something scraping at the wall somewhere below them, not too loudly, in fact barely detected, then a pause before the scraping started again. She lay still in the darkness, waiting and listening for a short while, and each time she heard it, she grew more and more curious as to what could be causing the sound.

And then she felt Hadrian stirring beside her in

sleep and took hold of his arm, squeezing it gently to wake him and pressing her finger against his mouth when he opened his eyes to indicate he should keep silent.

"Listen," she whispered.

The sound came again, this time a little louder. It seemed to be coming from under the floor below the bed. And then she heard the distinct shattering sound of glass being broken.

"What the hell was that?" Hadrian said, flipping the coverlet back, ready to spring from the bed.

"What room is beneath your chamber, Hadrian?" she asked quietly.

"My study."

Without making a sound, Hadrian rose from the bed and slipped on his dressing robe, knotting it with a yank at his waist as he started for the door.

Mara followed not two steps behind.

"Stay here," he said when he noticed her behind him in the corridor. "It could be a thief and I wouldn't want you to come to harm."

"No, Hadrian. I want to go with you. I would be far safer with you there for protection than alone in the bedchamber."

Hadrian frowned at her in the hazy morning light. "All right, you may come, but stay quiet and keep behind me at all times. I do not want you getting yourself hurt."

Mara nodded.

The sound had stopped by the time they reached the top of the stairs leading down to the bottom floor. In the growing sunlight pouring in through the tall windows that faced to the east, they could see that the door to Hadrian's study was open slightly, which was odd since, being a man of meticulous habit, he was always certain to keep it closed whenever he was not inside.

Hadrian motioned to her silently and they walked down the staircase. Mara stayed close to the wall as they edged their way toward the study. Using his foot, Hadrian pushed the door open wider. Mara peered around his shoulder, trying to see inside.

It was dark, only faint portions of sunlight spilling in through the windows across the pattern of the carpet, which was also odd, since as well as keeping the door closed in his absence, Hadrian was in the habit of keeping the drapery drawn when he wasn't inside.

Hadrian stepped inside the doorway and Mara followed, peering around his arm at the interior of the room. Nothing seemed out of place, the furniture was positioned as it should be, and his desk seemed to be well in order. She looked at the bookshelves, noting that they seemed undisturbed, even the three tall tomes that disguised the opening to the hidden vault. Her eyes followed every tier, tracing each section until they came to rest on her mother's portrait hanging above the hearth.

Her survey of the room halted there. She squinted, trying better to see. The painting had been cut along two sides, leaving it hanging like a loosened flap in the wind, the glass vase that normally stood beneath it laying shattered and in pieces on the floor.

"Hadrian, my mother's painting."

Just then something darted at them from out of the darkness, impelling itself like a cannon into Hadrian's chest and knocking him back hard, which, in turn, knocked Mara back against the wall. Mara grunted, her head knocking sharply on the paneling before she dropped to the floor, landing squarely on her bottom.

"Who is there?" she heard Hadrian yell.

There were bootsteps running out in the hall and then the sound of a door scraping along the floor.

"Are you all right, Mara?" Hadrian was at her side in seconds, fingers gently pushing back her hair, his eyes searching hers for some sign of recognition.

"Yes," she said, taking his offered hand. "Just startled a bit." She shook her head to clear it. "Who was that? Why was he trying to steal my mother's portrait?"

"I don't know, but I have a pretty good idea where he is going to."

Mara followed Hadrian as he rushed from the room and down the hallway leading to the older part of Kulhaven. The great oaken door with its nicks and scars that led to the former keep stood ajar and Hadrian went on through, walking directly to the stairs leading to the Bloody Tower. Not far above them Mara could hear the sound of someone running up the narrow spiral stairs to the top, each footstep echoing down through the emptiness.

Hadrian and Mara started after him. When they had reached the top of the stairwell, and the door leading outside was open and wide. The landing was empty in the morning sunlight.

"Where did he go, Hadrian? I cannot see—"

Mara screamed as a hand suddenly grabbed her by the arm, the other hand covering her mouth and pulling her roughly backward. She swallowed as she felt something sharp and cold and metal being held to the skin of her throat.

"Stop right there, St. Aubyn, or she goes over the edge."

Owen! Mara tried to turn about, but he held her tightly against him.

Hadrian had stopped dead in his tracks, his eyes dark and dangerous.

"You would kill your own sister, Owen?"

"She is an Englishman's whore now, just like her mother before her. No true Irish woman would ever lower herself to warm an Englishman's bed. Besides, she is of no matter to me now. She has outlived any use I ever had for her."

Hadrian took a step forward, testing Owen's threat.

Owen pulled her back, pushing the blade closer against her throat. "I said come no nearer. Would you have me draw blood to prove it?"

Hadrian didn't answer. "I will not ask how you managed to escape the hangman's noose, for you have proven yourself very adept at escaping from English prisons, but what I am wondering now is why you would come back to Kulhaven. Surely it wasn't to bid your sister farewell, not when you have a sharp blade pressed dangerously close to her throat. You must have had good reason. You know the authorities must be close behind and the first place they would look for you would be the place where you were captured."

Owen smiled. "I do not plan to be here when they do come for me. I plan to be here only long enough to retrieve something that was too valuable to leave behind."

"I cannot believe it was for a portrait of your mother, Owen, whom you have just termed an Englishman's whore."

Mara tried to turn to face him, completely forgetting that he held a sharp blade at her neck. "It's the tapestry. You came back for the Kulhaven Tapestry, didn't you?"

Owen smiled, his face taking on an image of pure evil in the hazy sunlight. "How very clever you are, *siúr*. But, you were not clever enough. You never knew that while you were running about like a headless chicken, ready to do anything I asked to get that worthless piece of Kulhaven history, it was here, right here, under your very nose the entire time."

"You had hidden it behind Mother's portrait. I asked Hadrian if he had ever seen it, but he said it was not among the things left after the castle had been stormed."

"It was here, but only I knew where, for you see I cleverly tucked it away inside the frame so no one looking could possibly detect it. I put it there for safekeeping after I retrieved it from the vault in her bedchamber."

"How did you know where it was? I was the only one Mother told about the secret vault."

"Yes, you, her dear daughter, the next Kulhaven lady to carry on the legacy. I had been listening outside the door the day she showed you her special hiding place. And when I came back to Kulhaven, I decided to see if it was still there. I told you it would be better to sell that thing, but you wouldn't listen to me. Well, now it is going to get me far, far away from here. It should fetch quite a fortune; in fact, I already have a buyer for it, some crusty old noble interested in medieval artwork."

"But you can't sell the tapestry, Owen. It has been in

our family for generations, since the days of Rupert de Kaleven."

"Bah! You seem to forget, there is no family anymore. Your husband and men like him destroyed our family and took everything we owned, all except the two of us. And now you, my blood, my only living relation, are going to help me get away from here. There is a rope hanging just over the side of the battlement there, Mara. Take hold of it. Now."

He pressed the blade closer against her chin. Mara looked to Hadrian, unsure of what to do. He nodded to her.

Mara grasped the rope, her fingers trembling as she handed it to her brother. Owen had to loosen his hold on her for a moment to position himself behind her and grab the rope. Just as he did, a fierce, driving wind came from out of the very air around them, blowing up from the bottom and from the top of the tower all at once, causing the leaves and debris that had collected in the corners over the years to fly about.

Owen had to release Mara to cover his eyes from the swirling dust and sand. Taking advantage of the diversion, Hadrian grabbed Mara by the hand and pulled her safely from her brother's reach.

"Come back here!"

Owen came after Hadrian, the knife pointed straight at his chest. Hadrian grabbed his arm and held it away, the blade dangerously close to his heart. Mara could only watch as the two wrestled for control. The knife was knocked from Owen's grasp and went skittering along the flagstones, landing in a dark corner. Mara went after it and when she turned back, Owen had somehow positioned Hadrian with his back to the edge of the tower and was now fighting to push him over.

"No!" Mara raised the knife above her head like a war lance and ran at Owen full-tilt. He turned at the sound of her outcry and just before she reached him to plunge the blade into his heart, he bowed down, driving his shoulder into her stomach. The knife went flying, the breath was knocked from her, and Mara fell to the ground, clutching her stomach and gasping for air.

Hadrian's voice boomed out over the blowing winds. "Mara!"

She looked up, unable to speak the words to warn Hadrian. She watched on helplessly as Owen went running, yelling like a crazed madman, toward Hadrian to push him over the edge.

Just as he came tearing toward him, Hadrian managed to move out of his path and Owen went tumbling over the edge of the battlement, his scream of anguish ending abruptly when he hit the rocks below.

Hadrian was at Mara's side in seconds. "Are you all right? Did he hurt you?"

"I am fine. He just took me by surprise is all. I can't seem to catch my breath."

"Take in deep breaths until the tightness passes. That is it." He grinned down at her. "If ever I believed you the war goddess *Mórrígan* it was just now when you came tearing at your brother with that knife raised, screaming and ready to save my life."

"He was no longer my brother, at least not the brother I had always known. The war had changed him, made him into someone else, someone I did not like. He frightened me."

Mara had managed to steady her breath enough to

rise to her feet. Hadrian helped her stand. "It is over now, Mara. Except . . ." He bent down then to retrieve a small satchel that she hadn't noticed lying there. "I believe what is inside here belongs to you."

Mara took the satchel and opened its buckled flap. She removed the folded cloth that was tucked carefully inside. Threads of silver and gold shimmered from the picture woven there in the morning sunlight as she unfolded it carefully to their view. It was the red-haired maiden Gráinne and her warrior lover, riding atop a fierce and mighty destrier, and the sun behind them was ablaze with shimmering threads of color. It was magnificent. It was the Kulhaven Tapestry. And it was hers.

Just then, the winds that had been blowing so fiercely around them stopped, leaving in their place a peaceful calm. The leaves that had been swirling around them grew still once again.

"Yes," Hadrian said, placing his arm around her shoulder and leading her toward the tower door, "I do believe the Kulhaven Tapestry is right back where it belongs."

Epilogue

Castle Kulhaven
August, 1662

"There is a rider coming up the carriage drive, my lady, and he's wearing the King's colors!"

Mara shaded her eyes against the late summer sunlight that had just begun its nocturnal descent behind the Kilkenny mountains, and watched as Davey came running toward her, leaping over the row of fragrant hawthorn hedges that grew along the graveled walkway. She stuck her small iron hand spade into the black dirt where she had been digging and wiped her soiled hands on the front of her apron before pushing herself up from the ground. It took her some time, as she was in the final stages of pregnancy, but she finally managed to stand with the aid of the low branches that poked out from the great oak beside her.

The cabbage roses she'd been tending were bursting with brilliant colors, reds, pinks, yellows, and whites, set off by the quaint little row of purple sweet violet blossoms she'd just finished weeding in her mother's garden. The shiny brass sundial Hadrian had brought for her from Dublin stood on its veined marble stand in the center. She looked over to the dial and saw that it was nearly time for supper.

"I'll be right there, Davey. Have you told his lordship yet?"

The lad, who was now really more of a man, stopped directly before her and took in great gulps of air to catch his breath, panting between each word. "No—I have not—I'll go and find him—right now."

Gone was the sweet boy's face full of freckles, for Davey had somehow sprouted to a height of well over six feet during these past years. He was as thin as the bean pole that Hadrian had recently titled him, with all the arms and legs and energy of a nineteen-year-old young man soon to be twenty. And, just recently, she'd heard from his dear, sweet mama, Davey had found himself heedlessly and hopelessly in love with one of the young girls from the village, a lovely young thing with sunny-colored hair named Anna.

"His lordship is down with your father by the stables. They were to be discussing the plans for the new paddock and measuring to see how much wood they would need. They hoped to have it built by the time Munin goes into foal. Run and tell him we have a visitor from England. And, on your way back to the house, please ask Mrs. Philpot to set another place for our guest for supper."

"Aye, my lady."

While Davey ran to fetch Hadrian, Mara bent to pick up their son, Robert, who was playing with his wooden soldier, his gift from his father's recent trip to Dublin, beneath the shady boughs of the great oak beside her.

"Hello, sweet boy," she said, kissing the top of his

head when he wrapped his arms tightly around her neck.

Robert was the very image of his father, with his dark brown hair, mischievous golden brown eyes, and the dimple set directly in the center of his proud chin. Setting him on his still slightly unsteady feet, Mara took his small hand in hers and walked with him toward the front of the castle to meet their newly arrived guest.

"Ah, I see my two favorite people are waddling up the walkway to meet our mysterious guest."

Mara turned halfway about and shot her husband a dangerous glare. "I'd like to see how steady you would walk had you a ten-pound pumpkin strapped to your belly."

Hadrian set his arm about her burgeoning waist, which seemed to grow more so with each passing second, kissing her lovingly on the forehead. "Would it make you any happier if I told you that you were the most beautiful waddler in all Ireland?"

"Why don't you go on ahead," she said, pinching his arm. "I wouldn't want to keep you from greeting your guest, with my 'waddling.' "

"And have my wife miss finding out what the King's messenger has come all this way about? Never."

Hadrian scooped up Robert in his great arms and placed him, amid a rain of high-pitched squeals and giggles, on his shoulder as they continued up the drive together.

Mara smiled. She loved watching the two of them together, the way Robert would furrow his tiny brow when he was concentrating very hard on what Hadrian was showing him, as if it were the most insurmountable of problems to be tackled. Just like his father.

She placed her hand on the swell of her belly when she felt the new life stirring within her womb. This child would be a girl, with her green eyes and the fiery red hair to carry on the legacy of the Kulhaven women. Sadbh had predicted it even before Mara had known she carried this babe, so she had no doubt it would be true.

She would name her Edana, after her dear mother, and she knew her mother approved of that, for she'd felt it clearly when she'd gone to place a fresh bunch of sweet-smelling rose blossoms at her grave the other day. And when this daughter reached the age of ten, Mara would take her and show her the magical Kulhaven Tapestry, and she would give her the treasure box that was to be handed down to her from her namesake.

Toirneach was standing atop the front steps and barking like the thunder for which he was named at their newly arrived visitor, when Mara and Hadrian rounded the curve in the drive minutes later. Mrs. Danbury came charging from inside the house and chased the gentle beast away with a snap from her dusting cloth, locking him behind the wine cellar door with a muttered curse under her breath about the dog being naught but a nuisance.

"Be you Hadrian Augustus Ross, Earl of St. Aubyn?" the rider said, dismounting and stepping forward. He was dressed in a messenger's uniform made of regal purple-and-gold satin, the colors of the new King of England, Charles II.

Hadrian set Robert to sit on the step beside one of the stone lion statues. "Aye, I am Lord St. Aubyn of Kulhaven Castle. Is there something I can do for you?"

"I am Tobias Jamison, messenger for His Royal Highness, Charles II, King of England. I have come to deliver this missive to you. It comes directly from His Majesty. He said it required a response and wishes me to wait for your reply."

Hadrian took the letter which bore the King's seal. "Well, then, Jamison, you'd best come into the house and rest your saddle-sore bones while I see what His Majesty wants of me."

Inside the hall the news of the arrival of the King's messenger had spread like fire through a hay field on a hot and dry summer's day. The servants had gathered at every window facing the carriage drive, their curious faces pressed against the glass, eager to see what the messenger had come all the way from London about.

As Hadrian and Mara led the messenger Jamison inside, Peter Shipley cast the now-chattering servants a quelling look that told them to return to their business. They scattered in every direction when they saw the lord and lady coming, all whispers and searching glances as they hurried to their respective stations.

Hadrian threw open the door to his study, striding inside. "Care for a refreshment after your long ride, Jamison?" he said, setting Robert in the chair behind his cluttered desk. "Lady St. Aubyn makes a tasty cherry and currant cordial that will ease your aching muscles for certain."

Jamison bowed his head after removing his plumed hat. "Thank you, Lord St. Aubyn."

Mara walked to the walnut sideboard by the window and poured Jamison a goodly amount of the cordial. She handed him the glass, returning his friendly smile, just as Hadrian began opening the letter. The room was utterly silent while he read the contents.

When he was finished reading, Hadrian set the letter down on the desktop. His face gave no indication as to what it contained. "I will respond to His Majesty after we have had our supper, Jamison. I believe Mrs. Philpot is making her specialty, roast mutton with peas and carrots. Do you like mutton, Jamison?"

The young man nodded, the fact that he'd not eaten since early that morning showing on his face. "Yes, my lord, very much so."

"Good. Then you will join us for supper since I'm sure my wife has already had your place set. While we are supping, I will have one of the guest chambers prepared for you and you can leave with the first light of morning."

"Oh, no, Lord St. Aubyn. I couldn't. I'm supposed to leave as soon as you give me your response."

Hadrian grinned, clapping Jamison on the back. "Well, it seems my response is going to require a fair amount of time. I most probably will be up all through the night and into the early hours of the morning composing it."

He drew the young man away from Mara, lowering his voice as if trying to keep her from hearing. "There's an old Irish saying that warns one should never turn out a stranger until after he's had a warm meal in his belly and a soft pillow beneath his head. My wife will be terribly put out with me if you do not consent to stay." He motioned toward her. "Believe me, Jamison, she may look all sweetness and innocence right now, being with child and all, but you've never been on the blind end of her temper. I have and I can tell you, it's not a pretty place."

The young man smiled, unable to refuse his host. "Thank you, Lord St. Aubyn. I am much obliged for your hospitality."

Hadrian moved away then, smiling broadly. "Good. Shall we adjourn to the dining room then?" He motioned to the door where his ever-dependable steward stood waiting for his instruction. "Mr. Shipley, if you would please show Mr. Jamison to the dining room. Lady St. Aubyn and I will join you shortly. I've a feeling my wife is fair bursting with curiosity as to what His Majesty has written about, as is, I'm sure, most everyone else. But, I must give my wife precedence and discuss the matter with her first, for she would not look too kindly on me if I didn't. And I wouldn't want to be the one responsible for sending her into an early labor."

Mara remained standing as Jamison was ushered through. She waited, chewing her lip in frustration until Hadrian had closed the door behind them and had turned before she opened her mouth to speak.

"Well?" Mara said, crossing her arms atop her large belly. "What does His Majesty write?"

"It seems, my dear, I am being summoned to London."

"London? But you cannot leave now. As far as Cyma can tell the babe is due near the end of the month. You cannot leave me here alone. I will not allow it."

"But His Majesty has requested it, madam."

Mara's voice rose. "I do not care. Let him wait. Haven't you done enough for him already? You fought for him, spied for him, risking life and limb for him, and then you saw him restored to the throne. Now he thinks to call on you again? You are married. You can no longer be at his beck and call. It is my turn now, Hadrian. I need you more."

Hadrian was laughing at her, *laughing*, his face turning red and his eyes watering and she wanted to smash him over the head with her new rosewood tea table for it.

"What is it you find so funny? I do not see anything at all amusing about this, Hadrian. If I have to bear this child alone, I will make certain she grows up to marry the son of a poor Gypsy tinker."

"And then I will be forced to lock her away until she reaches the ripe old age of thirty." He took her hand. "Breeding does have a way of bringing your temper up, my love. But don't get yourself in a dither. I will send off my reply and inform His Majesty, King Charles II, that we will not be able to come to London until after the first of the year. Then we—all of us, Robert and the babe included—will travel to London together as a family. It isn't just me the King wishes to see, madam. He has requested the presence of all of us. In fact, I believe his words stated that he 'could not wait to meet the woman who dared disguise herself as Cromwell's goddaughter just to marry a sot like me.' "

Mara narrowed her eyes suspiciously. "Why would he want to see all of us?"

"I shall let you read that for yourself." Hadrian strode over to the desk and picked up the letter lying there. Robert, his tiny body still seated in his father's huge chair, was slumped over to the side with his chubby cherub's cheeks resting on the velvet-covered armrest, taking his afternoon nap.

Mara took the letter and scanned it quickly, her eyes

slowing when they reached the part about their summons to London.

"... and by your request, as of the first of January, Sixteen Hundred and Sixty-three, all lands and rights to the estate known as Kulhaven in the County of Kilkenny, in the Kingdom of Ireland, will be returned to the ownership of Mara Despencer Ross, rightful heir to Charles Despencer . . ."

Mara stopped reading, her heart instantly beating faster as she looked up at her smiling husband. "You did this?"

"Yes, I'm afraid I did. And I will brook no arguments from you. I know you have told me hundreds of times that it does not matter to you anymore. What's mine is yours, and what's yours is mine, good or bad, and all that nonsense. But this does matter to me, Mara. Kulhaven is yours, by right and by law of the land. And when we've both gone on to our final resting places, I want it to be known through history that way."

Mara smiled, tears forming in her eyes at this generous and wonderful gift. She let the letter fall to the Turkish carpet, and lifted her arms around his neck, kissing him soundly.

"There is more to the letter, Mara," Hadrian said, pulling away a moment later. He bent down and retrieved the letter, giving it back to her. "There is another reason for His Majesty's summons to London."

Mara took the letter and read on.

"... and on this day as well, the title of Marquess and Marchioness of Kulhaven will be bestowed upon the present Earl and Countess of St. Aubyn, in thanks for their heroic efforts in aiding Us in the regaining of Our Father's royal crown."

Mara looked to Hadrian and for the first time in his married life, he actually saw his wife speechless.

"Well, future Lady Kulhaven of Castle Kulhaven in the County of Kilkenny, what say you now?"

Mara smiled, taking his arm. "I think that the future Lord Kulhaven should take his lady's arm and lead her into supper directly, for their babe is growing mighty hungry."